Praise for Eric Jerome Dickey

Between Lovers

"Another winner . . . from an author who only seems to be getting better. Dickey shows a skillful hand once again with sensational relationships and heady sensuality. . . .another spicy slice of African-American dramatic fiction."
—*Publishers Weekly*

"A hip, funny, and realistically bittersweet love story of our times."
—*Washington Sun*

"Provocative and complex."
—*Ebony*

"*Between Lovers* will hook audiences and draw them into a world where characters are multilayered, language is street-smart, and emotions are intense. But most important, Dickey's latest novel reminds us that no matter how far into someone else's world we get, there is always part of the story that we never quite understand—that part is what goes on between lovers."
—*Style Magazine*

"A refreshing voice in contemporary literature."
—*The Macon Telegraph & News*

"Another gold star for Dickey."
—*The Detroit News and Free Press*

"If two's company and three's a crowd, it's about to get a little crowded as Eric Jerome serves up an all-new sexy, unique tale of a love triangle."
—*Urban Spectator*

"Emotion-packed and filled with love-laced excitement."
—*The Michigan Citizen*

"Hot stuff. There's a lot of searching, soul and otherwise, as the bestselling Dickey tells a good story and adds his special brand of wisdom."
—*BookPage*

continued . . .

Liar's Game

"Steamy romance, betrayal, and redemption. Dickey at his best."
—*USA Today*

"Dickey hits the mark with *Liar's Game*."
—*The Detroit News and Free Press*

"Fast-paced . . . sexy, sassy . . . a high-spirited roller-coaster ride of a novel."
—*Florida Star* (Jacksonville)

"It's almost scary how well Eric Jerome Dickey knows women."
—*The Cincinnati Enquirer*

"Witty and engrossing."
—*Booklist*

"*Liar's Game* is a sassy story."
—*Chicago Defender*

"Masterful . . . humorous and convincing . . . avoids all the usual clichés."
—*BookPage*

"Dickey hits his stride . . . with wit, energy, and deft sensitivity."
—*Heart & Soul*

"Seductive."
—*Publishers Weekly*

"[*Liar's Game*] really has the power."
—*Kirkus Reviews*

"Skillful . . . scandalous . . . a rich gumbo of narrative twists."
—*Minneapolis Star Tribune*

"Brimming with steamy romances, stinging betrayal, sweet redemption, and well-placed humor."
—*Miami Times*

Cheaters

"A deftly crafted tale about the games people play and the lies they tell on their search for love." —*Ebony*

"Wonderfully written . . . smooth, unique, and genuine." —*The Washington Post Book World*

"Raw, street-savvy humor." —*Publishers Weekly*

"You can't read *Cheaters* without becoming an active participant." —*Los Angeles Times*

"What gives the book a compelling edge is the characters' self-discovery. . . . Thankfully, Dickey often goes beyond the 'men are dogs and women are victims' stereotype." —*USA Today*

"Hot, sexy, and funny." —*Library Journal*

Friends and Lovers

"Crackles with wit and all the rhythm of an intoxicatingly funky rap. A fun read." —*The Cincinnati Enquirer*

"The language sings . . . fluid as a rap song. Dickey can stand alone among modern novelists in capturing the flavor, rhythm, and pace of African-American speak." —*Ford Lauderdale Sun-Sentinel*

"[A] sexy, sophisticated portrayal of hip black L.A. . . . engaging, dynamic." —*Publishers Weekly*

"Dickey uses humor, poignancy, and a fresh, creative writing style." —*USA Today*

"A colorful, sexy tale." —*Marie Claire*

"Written with wit and sarcasm . . . produces both laughter and tears." —*The Cleveland Plain Dealer*

"Remarkable . . . not only perceptive but also witty and moving." —*Booklist*

continued . . .

Milk in My Coffee

"Rich *Coffee* steams away clichés of interracial romance. . . .
Dickey fills his novel with twists and turns that keep the
reader guessing as he describes a true-to-life, complex story
of relationships. Along the way he smashes one stereotype
after another."
—*USA Today*

"A fresh romance . . . heartwarming and hilarious."
—*The Cincinnati Enquirer*

"Frothy and fun. . . . Dickey scores with characters who
come to feel like old friends . . . smart and believable. After
the last page is turned you'll still have plenty to savor."
—*Essence*

"Dickey is just as adept at giving voice to female characters
as he is to males." —*New York Daily News*

"Dickey demonstrates once again . . . his cheerful, wittily
acerbic eye for the troubles that plague lovers."
—*Publishers Weekly*

"Controversial and sensitive." —*Today's Black Woman*

"Entertaining . . . humorous." —*Boston Herald*

"Juicy . . . a carefully woven tapestry of vibrant characters
and turbulent situations that will have you hooked."
—*Advocate* (Orlando, FL)

"Engrossing, entertaining . . . the surprising twists and
turns bring a good novel to a very satisfying conclusion."
—*Booklist*

Sister, Sister

"Dickey imagines [his characters] with affection and sympathy. . . . His novel achieves genuine emotional depth."

—*The Boston Globe*

"Vibrant . . . marks the debut of a true talent."
—*The Atlanta Journal-Constitution*

"A hip, sexy, wisecracking tale." —*New York Beacon*

"Bold and sassy . . . brims with humor, outrageousness, and the generosity of affection." —*Publishers Weekly*

"Dickey is able both to create believable female characters and to explore the 'sister-sister' relationship with genuine insight." —*Booklist*

"A good summer read you won't be able to put down . . . depicts a hard-edged reality in which women sometimes have their dreams shattered, yet never stop embracing tomorrow." —*St. Louis Post-Dispatch*

"Will captivate your fancy . . . an engaging read."
—*Cincinnati Herald*

"One of the most intuitive and hilarious voices in African-American fiction." —*St. Louis American*

"There's a little sumthin', sumthin' in this book we can all relate to. Buy the novel, read it. Relate. Relax. Release."
—*Crusader Urban News*

Other Books by Eric Jerome Dickey

Liar's Game
Cheaters
Milk in My Coffee
Friends and Lovers
Sister, Sister

Anthologies

Got to Be Real
Mothers and Sons

ERIC JEROME DICKEY

BETWEEN
LOVERS

A SIGNET BOOK

SIGNET
Published by New American Library, a division of
Penguin Putnam Inc., 375 Hudson Street,
New York, New York 10014, U.S.A.
Penguin Books Ltd, 80 Strand, London WC2R 0RL, England
Penguin Books Australia Ltd, Ringwood,
Victoria, Australia
Penguin Books Canada Ltd, 10 Alcorn Avenue,
Toronto, Ontario, Canada M4V 3B2
Penguin Books (N.Z.) Ltd, 182-190 Wairau Road,
Auckland 10, New Zealand

Penguin Books Ltd, Registered Offices:
Harmondsworth, Middlesex, England

Published by Signet, an imprint of New American Library,
a division of Penguin Putnam Inc. Previously published in a Dutton edition.

First Signet Printing, May 2002
10 9 8 7 6 5 4 3 2 1

PUBLISHER'S NOTE
This is a work of fiction. Names, characters, places, and incidents either are
the product of the author's imagination or are used fictitiously, and any
resemblance to actual persons, living or dead, business establishments,
events, or locales is entirely coincidental.

For Virginia Jerry
Miss ya

PART ONE

When a Man Loves a Woman

1

I'm naked.

Across the room, in my rented bed, Nicole is naked too. Her honey-blond locks shadow her face.

Next to my open laptop is the novel *Lolita*. And next to that novel are a few pictures, some pretty beat up. Memories stained by time, coffee, and tears.

A lot of these photos were taken an hour before me and Nicole stood in front of one God and two families. I pulled them out a while ago, propped them up on top of my cassette recorder, and sat here with my feet bouncing in another chair, my testicles and penis at ease, cold, but ready for play.

I'd been reading *Lolita*. An obsessed man who modified the truth to fit his own needs.

Jack London Square is yawning in the fog. Underneath my fifth-floor window, men unload a truck on the cobblestone walkway between Jack's Grill and TGIF. Then somebody drops something heavy and it crashes to the cement, loud enough to make me jump.

Nicole's bracelets jingle an easy song when she jerks a bit. Those eight pieces of Mexican silver are something else new, another change that defines her new self.

I lean back and stare at her bare breasts, watch her through the white plantation shutters that separate the living and dining area from the bedroom, horizontal prison bars made of wood, watch her and clear my throat, cough a bit. Her dreadlocks are getting longer; what started out as little black twisties now hang below her shoulders when she's on her feet. Her red scarf has slipped away from her head so her locks are free, covering most of her face. She wipes them away and grumbles like an angry kitten. Not a morning person. Not at all.

At first I smile, then wonder if she remembers where she is, if she remembers meeting me at the airport with a red rose in her hand yesterday morning, if she remembers saying fuck the negotiations with South Africa, ditching work, then taking me down on Broadway to *Head to Toes* and letting Ana redo my twisties. If she remembers that she was hand-in-hand and cheek-to-cheek with me last night, that we spent the evening at Yoshi's, first eating dinner, then watching Joshua Redman before flirting our way over to the Urban Blend Café for late-night poetry and java, ending the night with haikus that were as potent and smooth as the lattes.

Those silver bracelets on her arm jingle again. Nicole coughs. A very rough cough.

I ask, "You okay over there?"

"Dreaming." She coughs again. "Dreaming I was at the Mid-South Coliseum with my daddy, watching wrestling. Tojo Yamamoto and Jackie Fargo were beating up Jerry Lawler."

Those things, those dreams are about good old Memphis. That's where Nicole was born. Where part of her heart still lives. While I grew up dealing with the Watts riot, smog alerts, and earthquakes, in a liberal Babylonia where you can get a haircut on Crenshaw all day on both Easter and Christmas while NWA raps "Fuck the Police" in the background, the land of sunshine where people dance half-naked on Venice Beach on Sundays, Nicole grew up down in the Bible Belt in the shadows of Elvis Presley, STAX records, and Rick Dees singing "Disco Duck." Rufus Thomas doing the "Funky Chicken." Where Al Green was the uncrowned king on the black side of town. Garbage strikes and Black Mondays after the assassination of Martin Luther King Jr. Where she told me she would see old black people addressing snotty-nosed white kids who were young enough to be their grandchildren "yes, sir" and "no, ma'am" while those same snotty-nosed rug rats called black people old enough to be their grandparents by their first names. The land of don't pop your fingers on Sunday, don't play blues on Sunday, don't curse on Sunday, don't point at a graveyard or your fingers will fall off, can't buy liquor after midnight on Saturday until after the noon hour on Sunday.

Three times she yawns, each sounding like a soft orgasm, the kind you have when your parents are in the next room. Each time her mouth opens in the most sensuous way, each time it excites me.

I yawn too. Yawns are contagious. Yawn and inhale. The room has hints of frankincense and patchouli, scents Nicole traded in her Chanel No. 5 for, earthy and spiritual aromas that remind people of a period of Black Panthers and revolution, also of women's rights and free love.

She covers her mouth and yawns again. Then she says, "Don't believe you're up already."

And just like that she mumbles her way back to sleep. Starts to snore. A light, intense snore.

I play with one of my twisties; pull my hair straight until it sticks out around two, close to three inches. Soon my hair will be like Nicole's, in dreadlocks. That sign of resistance that originated in the motherland. I hold my hair and look at those old photos again. Pictures of me and my groomsmen decked out in black tuxedos. Nicole and her bridesmaids. Most of those girls are judgmental women who no longer talk to her. Not even a card at Christmas.

Nicole groans, sits up, stretches until her joints pop, moves her tongue around the inside of her mouth, like she's fighting off the last weight of an opium-induced sleep.

She clears her throat and lays back down. "Writing?"

"Some." I drop the photos back in my messenger bag. "Freaking laptop tripping again."

"Told you not to buy a Compaq. Told you, but did you listen? What's wrong this time?"

"A-drive won't recognize my disk."

"Won't recognize your dick?"

"D-i-s-k."

"Oh."

"I see where your mind is at."

She puts her hand over her eyes and giggles, sets free a very sensual, very vulnerable laugh. I wonder if she shoves her corporate image aside and acts this sweet and kind with her other lover.

She asks, "Cycle power?"

"Four times. It still can't find the d-i-s-k."

"Oh, you got jokes."

"I got jokes. Clock runs slow. Crashes whenever I'm on-line. What you think?"

"Device manager might have a conflict"—she stretches again, covers her mouth, sets free another orgasmic moan—"or too much junk is running in the background. I'll look at it later, sweetie."

She's a smart woman. I love that. Intelligence is a wonderful and powerful aphrodisiac. To me, it enhances beauty, makes an ordinary woman look like a movie star.

She smiles. "Had so much fun yesterday. You make me feel so young, you know that?"

"You are young."

"You are too good for my ego."

We're not old, but we're not young. Way beyond high school, far enough beyond college where our colorful and idealistic dreams of the way life should be have been painted over by the realities of this world. We're not quite at the point where gray hairs are popping up in ungodly places, although we do have a few. I'm six years older than she, but not close to the point where I need to get my prostate checked every hour on the hour. But with the way time flies, not that far away either. In some ways, Nicole seems older. In this world, women mature faster and age faster than men.

Nicole is staring at that borderline age where a woman needs to make those maternal decisions, before the egg-dropping bartender in her womb dims the lights and starts screaming last call.

I'm at that age where, if it doesn't happen in the next few years, I'll never be a young man with a child. If it happens, I might end up being an old man with a hyperactive rug rat that I can't keep up with for more than a minute. Or if too much time slips by, I'll be an old man sitting on a park bench, eating a cold tofu sandwich, and watching other people have fun with their kids.

She says, "You really should move to Oakland. We could kick it strong, like we did in L.A."

She's been telling me that since she moved here.

I say, "Tell me this: if I did buy a crib up here, how would that work out?"

"What do you mean?"

"Don't go stupid on me."

"Not playing dumb, sweetie."

"Which one of us would you kick it with on the regular?"

The radio kicks on, setting free voices on 98.1. The news says that the temperature is around forty-six going up to fifty-eight and cloudy, maybe rain in a day or so. Nicole stretches, takes her time about turning the volume down, attempts to use the distraction to save her from answering my question.

I put the pressure on: "Which one? A queen can have only one castle."

She runs her tongue over her teeth and stares at the ceiling, says, "Love you."

"Why do you always change the subject when you get uncomfortable?"

Her eyes go to the clock, then to the phone. She wants to check in; I know she does. Last night, while we were together, her pager started blowing up. Each time she looked at the number on the display. Each time she sighed. Then came her cellular. Five times in five minutes, she looked at the caller ID on her c-phone and didn't answer. She was restless, waited for a good moment to excuse herself and sneak out of the restaurant with her itty-bitty cell phone in the palm of her small hand, coming back sounding a little strained, as if she were being pulled in two directions, being torn in half.

Just when I think she's about to reach for the receiver, she relaxes back into the softness and warmth of the bed. Kicks the covers away, lies there naked, skin still moist from the massage oil, her right arm over her face. Her small, wondrous breasts reaching for the ceiling. Her golden-brown skin glowing.

I stare at her innocence, at the softness of an oval face that possesses the quality of a woman-girl-child, and my penis throbs. I touch myself as I watch her in her most vulnerable state, then I'm seeping. I want to get duct tape, tie her up, put her on the Amtrak, steal her from Oakland, take her back to L.A., to where we were when we were engaged, before that trip to Paris, before this indefinite state of disrepair.

I've been with her for seven years; we were engaged four years ago, and for the last year, she's been living here in Oaktown. Came up after the wedding. Alone. Needed space to think. And now that hiatus has changed into a long, frustrating year of uncertainty that has dragged by, and my feelings haven't changed. Sometimes I know that I'm going insane, especially when I don't hear from her for days, maybe a week, if I don't get an e-mail, if she doesn't return my e-mail. Firecrackers pop inside my head, and I go crazy when I imagine that her love is moving away from me, racing in a new direction, while mine remains in place, like a stone that is forever a part of the Roman Colosseum.

Nicole asks, "Sweetie? Be my coffee and wake me up."

I know what she's asking, can tell by the wanting sound in her voice.

I go toward the bed, step over my stone-washed dungarees, her velvety thong underwear, Lycra top, stylish high-heeled boots with an animal print, shoes she no doubt paid too much for, other things taken off in a heated moment. I move her empty wine glass away from the edge of the pine nightstand, crawl under the blue and beige covers, move my cool body against her warm flesh, my soul asking hers to desire me in the same way I hunger for her.

The pinkness of her tongue reaches for the pinkness of mine. My morning breath mixes with the tart taste on her tongue. Her hand comes to my face, rubs my flesh up to my short twisted mane. Hair in a style similar to hers. My attempt to become like the creature I see as so perfect. When she changes, I try and change along with her.

She kisses me and I forget the rest of the world. Her lips touch mine and all that matters is Nicole.

My wide hands touch her small breasts. I lick her nipples. Nicole shivers, moves her backside against my groin. So electric. So intense. My finger goes under the cover, eases inside her wetness, curls in a come-here motion, and when she's ready, it vibrates against her nerves in the sweetest rhythm, like David Benoit playing "Linus and Lucy" on his baby grand piano, her moans the song I love to hear.

My rhythm is corrupted when I wonder how she responds when her other lover touches her. If that same crooked smile covers her lips as she coos, if that devious expression comes across her face then.

In a lousy French accent she begs me, "*Mange moi.*"

"Nope."

"*Mange moi, mange moi, mange moi.* She misses your face."

Love it when she wants me like that. Love her to beg. Her begging pumps my ego up ten notches.

I put my hand before her open legs, light-brown legs that open like a book she wants me to read. I take the long route: kiss her feet, savor each toe and feel the arch rise in her back, enjoy her calves, her thighs, get close to where her legs meet, to where her sun shines so warm it can tan my face. My skin grazing her flesh, my tongue lapping those thighs in a catlike rhythm, and she shudders. She glows. That makes me smile so wide it hurts.

My tongue snakes down her skin, glides over the silver ring in her navel. She opens her legs, spreads her wings, and her eight silver bracelets jingle as she pushes the top of my head down. I push her knees toward her shoulders, widen her, lick across her slivers of hair, taste that meaty part of her, write a soft message of always and forever on her fleshy folds, show her how much I love her nectar.

She woos, "I love, love, love the texture of your tongue, that makes me, that feels sooooo—"

She spasms, eyes open wide then tighten and remain closed. Her hips move with fire.

Her hand palms and rubs the top of my head; she pushes her hips toward me, plays in my hair.

She catches her breath, swallows. "I should call her Bermuda."

"Why?"

"Because you stay down in the triangle so long, sometimes I think you're lost."

We laugh some more and then she hums with the radio as I play in her love.

"What . . . *ooooo* . . . in the hell. . . . *damn, sweetie* . . . are you doing down there?"

"Working on a sequel to *War and Peace*. Want me to stop?"

"Do and I'll hurt you. You . . . misspelled two words. Erase 'em . . . write 'em again."

"What words were those?"

"Antidisestablishmentarianism and psychoalpha-discobetabioaquadoloop."

My flesh touches a special spot and she curses, coos, jumps with pleasure.

Her eyes are on fire when she pushes herself up on the palms of her hands. Watches me and chews her bottom lip, lets out low, intense growls: "That's my spot damn that's my spot my spot my spot."

I know she lets somebody else do the same thing. Another mouth, another tongue, another set of teeth. She's never said, but I know. So many nights I've imagined them together. I'll make her forget that motherfucker. I'll get her back to me, one way or another. She belongs with me. I work harder at loving her, work longer, and want to be better, always have to be better, want to make her forget any other tongue but the one she's feeling now.

She pulls me up, kisses me over and over. "Let me please you, sweetie."

Her mouth warms me in places that years ago was illegal, might still be forbidden in some backward towns that have refused to change, does things that should get her sentenced to a lifetime with me. The look in her eyes saying that my pleasure is her pleasure, that my wicked sounds and reaction excites her beyond reason.

"Lay back, sweetie. Relax."

On top of me, she's big in voice, small in frame, soft where a woman should be soft, but still so toned and strong. She giggles, puts her fingers in my mouth, watches me savor them, pulls them in and out, switches fingers, does that again and again. She giggles her way into a decent laugh.

I grin. "What's funny?"

"I'm sorry. I have no idea why, but that serious look on your face made me think about the first time we made love—*oooo, that feels good, just like that*—the night you seduced me inside your Jeep."

"Seduced? You're tripping. You wanted me as much as I wanted you."

"Slow, slow, yeah, slow. Don't go Mt. St. Helen's too quick."

"Okay."

"God, you have me so spoiled." She moves with me, glows, hums out "Talk to me."

"Thinking about the Jeep. That was a great night."

"Get real. Any time a man scores it's a great night."

"True."

"No one had ever sucked my toes before. No one had ever gone down on me before."

"Nobody?"

"Shit, not like that. Greedy bastard. Thought you had found some collard greens, black-eyed peas, and corn bread down there or something."

We laugh.

"Anybody else acted like they were afraid Bermuda might bite." She moans over and over, each time her vagina muscles tighten around me. I'm moaning just as much, just as loud.

Nicole groans: "We're so symmetrical it's frightening. Can't control myself, want to make love to you every second I see you."

"That's dangerous."

"You've turned me into a nymph."

"I'm your nymph too, baby."

"Yeah, in your Jeep we did it hard." She chuckles and that makes her muscles squeeze me, an oyster clamped around a pearl. She says it feels so damn good, then with the sweetest, softest voice, she goes back to her story. "We did it . . . from the front seat . . . to the back seat . . . then you had me on the hood . . . heat felt so good . . . under my ass . . . hold my ass . . . hold my ass."

With each word, the talk excites her. Makes me harder than times in '29. It's as if we're reliving then and loving now, all at the same time. I look up at her boldness and admit that she's changed so much. That perm is long gone, the dirty brown hair has been dyed too many colors to remember, braces have corrected her teeth, silver fillings replaced with white so you can't see any defects when she throws her head back and laughs out loud. The knee-length skirts have vanished, the five-and-dime underwear with the days of the week embroidered into the white cotton has been traded in for colorful and lacy Cosabella. All of that gone, as if they never existed, gone, vanished, just like her inhibitions.

Moving with ease, her stomach rolls down into the starving motion of her hips, her arms keep her hovering over me, moving up then down then up then down, gets to feeling good and that makes us both so aggressive, taking just enough of me to make me go insane, nerves exploding in waves, so many pornographic noises escape her mouth, blending with the sounds that hum in my throat.

"Fuck me baby fuck me damn you're fucking me."

I want to know where she met her friend, what

words were shared, how the fuck she ended up liking somebody else besides me, where did that magic come from, what laughs were served back and forth, how they ended up fucking the first time, if something was done that I wasn't doing, or can't do, or won't do, what obscene sounds Nicole makes, if she makes the ugly face and trembles like she does when she's with me, what she feels when she's fucking the other. If she thinks about me.

Over and over I slap her backside, some slaps in love, some in frustration, all making her sting. Envy becomes the match that falls on my liquid lust.

I pull Nicole's face to mine, when I turn her over—

"Damn, you're rough this morning. Damn, I like that."

—and get on top over her damp body, and wonder whose leftover flavor I'm kissing.

If my love were water, it would fill this room and drown both of us.

My frustration would do the same, but not as fast as my jealousy.

"Fucking me, baby. Damn you're f-f-fucking me." Her mutterings are vulnerable, sometimes incoherent, sometimes the sweet rambles of a naughty child. She holds the sheets with one hand, wiggles in pleasure, her hips moving her love up toward my body. I pull her legs up, rest her ankles on my shoulders, all she can do is grab the sheets and enjoy. That's how I make her my prisoner.

"Tell me you love me."

"Damn, you're fucking me. That's it, that's it, f-f-fuck me like you think I should be fucked."

Her crude words attempt to disconnect the emotion, but they can't dilute how I feel.

With my thrusts I say, "Tell. Me. You. Love. Me."

"I love you, I l-l-love you, and you know, oh God—"

"Whose pussy is it?"

"Yours. It's. Yours. It's. All. Yours. I. Love. You. This. Pussy. It's. Yours."

"Say my name. I want to make sure you're here with me."

I refuse to be reduced to my lowest common denominator, refuse to be seen as a single body part, refuse to become just a dick putting out the fire in her hole.

2

Nicole says, "I still want you to meet her."

I don't respond to that.

I lay there in the bed with my eyes closed. Nicole is on top of me, her hands tracing over my body, wide awake like she's been IV'ed to a double latte mocha cappuccino espresso.

Another commuter train rumbles by out on Embarcadero.

She kisses my lips before she heads for the bathroom. Nicole walks in a way that lets you know she used to do ballet many moons ago, as a child, that she does yoga as an adult, using the core of her body to move herself, her abs and inner thighs tight from doing most of the work.

Nicole leaves the bathroom door wide open. She sings a Pru song, the one about the candles. She sings that all the time. Her singing is terrible, but it has raw passion. The toilet flushes.

The sandman sprinkles sleep dust all over me. Try to shake it off. Body heavy.

Water runs in the sink. She's washing up. Her bracelets jingle with her scrubbing.

I feel warm. At peace. Then I'm gone to dreamland.

Just that quick I'm in Paris. At a strip club. A slim European woman with freckles coming toward me and Nicole. The woman is naked in high heels. The dancer performs, sings, her voice so clear. She sounds as smooth and hypnotic as that wonderful vocalist Ondine Darcyl, croons "Black Orpheus" in perfect French, moves her body with a Brazilian feel.

Sudden heat on my groin frightens me, makes me yell back to consciousness.

Nicole laughs. "You jumped up like Al Green getting splattered with hot grits."

"Scared the shit out of me."

Nicole whispers, "Relax."

She has two towels, one hot, wet, and soapy, the other just hot and wet. She wipes me down, removes all the leftover love with the soapy towel, then wipes away the soap with the other. She does that with a smile. So nurturing and compassionate. When she's done, she kisses the tip of my penis.

She asks, "Did you hear me when I said that I want you two to meet?"

I sit up. We stare. I tell her, "I'm not deaf."

"Last month, when I asked, you said that you'd think about it."

"Help me out here. Why would you want us to meet?"

"Then I won't feel guilty. Like I'm cheating."

"Are you?"

She pauses. "Then you won't act like she doesn't exist. I love you. I love her."

"You don't love her."

"How do you know?"

I say, "Adam and Eve. Adam and Eve."

We stare at each other, restless, indeterminate gazes that reach deep.

She says, "I'm a divided soul, sweetie. And I can't go on like this. Not much longer."

"Then choose."

This is a discussion we've had countless times since the wedding. Each time it becomes harder.

She tells me, "I have a solution. If you're still open to new things, it can work."

She wants me to ask, but I don't.

With a wounded smile, she hand-combs her locks, untangles that hairstyle that started off as a sign of resistance, and still is, and she takes my running shoes from the closet, tosses them at my feet.

She gently says, "Get dressed."

Fog walks the streets. Dark skies give Oaktown that Seattle appeal.

I have on black running tights, white T-shirt, gray St. Patrick's Day 10K sweatshirt. She wears blue tights and a black hooded sweat top, a red scarf over her golden hair.

We take a slow jog out of the Waterfront, by all the gift shops, head through the light fog. Rows of warehouses that are being converted into lofts line the streets. All in the name of profit and gentrification, the reversal of the White Flight is in progress. The homeless are out peddling *Street Spirit* papers for a buck a pop. Some are sleeping on the oil-stained pavement while people pass by in super-size SUVs and foreign cars that cost more than a house in the 'burbs of Atlanta, Georgia. The dirt poor, the filthy rich, all live a paper cup away from each other in the land of perpetual oxymorons.

I say, "You want me to meet this chick—"

"Don't say *chick*. That's a misogynistic word."

"Nicer than what I usually call her."

"Which is disrespectful. Yeah, I think meeting will benefit us all."

"So, this thing with her is pretty serious?"

She smiles because I've given up the silent treatment. "It's serious. There's more to it."

Acid swirls in my belly.

Nicole goes on, "I think we can resolve this situation."

"More like what?" I ask. "What more is there?"

"We . . . just more." She has a look that tells me this is deeper than it seems, but can't tell me all, not right now. She says, "Let's talk while we run."

We take the incline up Broadway, my mind trying to react to what she just asked me about meeting her soft-legged lover, whirring and clicking and whirring as we jog by the Probation Department. We come up on a red light and stretch some more while we wait for it to change. The signal makes a *coo-coo, coo-coo, coo-coo* sound when it changes to green, that good old audio signal for the blind folks heading north and south. It chirps like a sweet bird going east and west, so we know we have the right-of-way and it's okay to get back to running north toward freedom.

Before we make a step, a Soul Train of impatient drivers almost mows us down.

We jump back. Both of us almost get hit. That lets me know that both of our minds are elsewhere.

Nicole says, "Be careful here, sweetie. This is where all the assholes rush to get on the Tube."

Someone driving a black car with a rainbow flag in its window slows and allows us to cross.

I run behind Nicole. Check out the fluid movement of her thighs. Seven years ago they weren't so firm.

Back then she had a whacked Atlantic Star hairdo that hung over one eye and she looked like Janet Jackson, not the *Velvet Rope* version, but the chubby-faced Penny on *Good Times* version. Now her belly is flat and the muscles in her calves rise and fall, lines in her hamstrings appear, her butt tightens; all of that shows how much she's been running, doing aerobics, hiking up every hill she can find.

It fucks with me. I try not to, don't want to, but it fucks with me and I can't help thinking about her being naked with another woman. Keep thinking about all the videos I've seen with women serving women satisfaction, but refuse to see Nicole in that light, in that life. I want to believe that they sit around baking cookies, knitting sweaters, and watching Lifetime Television for Women.

Those silver bracelets jingle as she gets a little ahead of me, not much. My shoes crunch potato chip bags and golden leaves. Buses spit black clouds of carbon monoxide in our faces.

The light at 13th catches Nicole. I catch up and ask, "Why does she want to meet me?"

"Because. Curious, I guess. I love you; she knows that. Sometimes she sounds intimidated."

"Because I'm a man."

"Maybe. After seven years, we have a solid history, don't you think?"

That makes me feel good. The simple, five-letter word *solid* makes me feel good.

The signal *coo-coo*s three times. We run north.

We race the incline toward Telegraph, a liquor store–lined street that leads into good old Berkeley.

At 20th, under the shadows of a sky-high Sears and World Savings building, she turns right toward Snow

Park. We avoid a million chain-smokers who are congregated out in front of Lake Merritt Plaza, the black-lunged outcasts of a politically correct world, then cross several lanes of fast-paced traffic and head toward the children's park and petting zoo called Fairy Land.

I maintain a steady pace and ask, "This hooking up, is this for her, or for you?"

"For me. Because I'm in fucking purgatory."

"Where do you think I am? I'm standing next to you."

"Feels like I'm dancing naked on the sun."

"That sounds painful."

"Wanna see my blisters?" She clears her throat, spits. "It's important for her because she needs to get comfortable with my needs, and wants, with my love for you, to be secure. And it's for you."

"How in the hell is this hooking up for me?"

"Because I see how much it hurts you. You're an open book."

"Don't go cliché on me."

"You put it in all of your books. Especially the one with the orange cover. The one where you wrote about the wedding."

"A fictional wedding."

"Save that bullshit for your fans. I read your books and I see me, hear the things I've said, see you, your words, hear your voice, feel sad and bad because I know that all the pain you write about is us."

"Maybe you should write a book. Let me know how you really feel, what's going on with you."

She goes on, "Be honest. Would you be this, I don't know, well, for lack of a better word, understanding if I were—"

"I'm not understanding; I don't understand this whole lesbian shit."

"I'm not a lesbian," she says with force. Then she backs off. "Sweetie, I'm not a lesbian."

I tell her, "Look, I'm being patient. Waiting for you to get through this . . . this . . . this phase."

"Okay, patient. Would you be acting like a stunt double for Job if I were having a relationship, okay, even living with another man?"

"Hell, no. I'd break his neck. Go Left Eye and burn down the house. Not in that order."

She says, "Going Left Eye. Now that turns me on. That evil side you try to hide."

"Try me."

"I'm serious. I want you two to meet. We have to. I want both of your spirits to be at ease. I want my spirit at ease. I want all of us to be able to lunch together from time to time, have conversations, run races together, that way I don't have to be stressed and trying to figure out who I'm going to be with. It's a lose-lose for me, and I'm trying to make it a win-win for us all."

"So, she's scared of me."

"You don't see her as a threat, not the way she sees you as a threat."

"Nothing that menstruates is a threat to me. Ain't *scared* of nothing that bleeds."

"Okay, Mister Macho."

Nicole has immeasurable passion when she talks about her soft-legged lover. I wonder if when she's talking to her friend about me, if she speaks with the same heated tongue, one that drips adjectives made of sweet mangos, verbs made of ripe kiwis, says my name as if it were a fresh strawberry.

I say, "So, this is for me, you, and her."

"At this stage in my life, I do know what I want. And I'm going after it. I'm being honest with myself and I have the courage to follow it."

"How long did you practice that *Fantasy Island*–sounding speech?"

She extends both her middle fingers my way.

I ask, "You want it to be like that?"

"Ideally, yeah. If could wake up every day knowing I was going to share my life with two people I adore, do that without any stress, yeah, my world would be perfect."

I say, "World ain't perfect."

"Our world can be perfect enough for us. We can create new boundaries, new love."

We. I notice she uses the word *we* a lot. The ultimate team player. A company woman.

"Dunno, Nicole. Dunno. Me, you, and your friend. That puts a chill in the pit of my stomach."

"That chill is your sense of adventure tapping you on your shoulder."

"You're quoting me."

"The unknown is always an added attraction."

"I told you that too."

"Yes, you did. Got me to drop my drawers when that honey-rich baritone voice of yours whispered those words in my ear. Had me doing all kinds of shit for your ass. In and out of bed. Helped you out when your money was low, was your shoulder when your daddy gave you grief. I gave all of me to you. Your turn to give a little. Push the envelope, sweetie. Live up to your own standards."

Our pace gets closer to eight-minute miles. She's a great runner. Five inches shorter than I am, and a minute faster on a hilly mile. Arms low, nice smooth kick, floating, she moves as if my orgasm has given her strength, doubled her stamina. I'm a slow starter and I use her to motivate my stride.

A few miles and a million thoughts later, Nicole leads me over to Harrison and we run past Westlake Middle School, beyond the 580 freeway, keep heading toward a rolling hill that reaches up to the sky.

"Where you taking me?"

"C'mon."

Like a used car salesman she wants to show me every feature of the city. Doesn't talk about The Village, or Sobrante Park, parts that are the Bed-Stuy of the Bay, forgets all about the Twomps or the Rollin' 20's over in East Oakland. Places that mirror how we grew up, her in Memphis and me in L.A.

Nicole sequesters me from that part of the city, keeps me away from the coal and leads me to the diamonds, takes me a few miles uphill into the area called Piedmont Hills. Tells me a half-million will buy a two-bedroom home; two million might get five thousand square feet.

Eighteen minutes later, we reach Highland, which is almost at the top of the hill, then head toward the row of mansions leading to Piedmont High School. She's sweating, face glowing with pain, back of her oversize sweatshirt damp, but not too damp because her T-shirt steals most of the moisture.

No nice way to put it, right now I'm hurting like hell and making fuck faces.

She slows a bit, says, "Think . . . about moving . . . up this way. Get some . . . investment property."

I wipe my face with the sleeve of my sweatshirt. "Sell crazy . . . somewhere else. A blacksmith in one village . . . becomes a blacksmith's apprentice in another."

"Smart ass . . . what does that . . . mean?"

"What kind of fool do I look like? Can't be your number two. Not going out like that."

"Dammit." Her breathing evens out. "There you go again. It's about love, not competition."

"Everything in this world is about competition."

"Not if we let it be about love," she says with enough force to show her inner struggle and frustration, then she softens her attitude, "Not if we let it be about love."

In a tone that doesn't hide my jealousy and frustration, doesn't mask my anger, I ask, "Hypothetically, if I moved here, where the hell would you stay?"

"You'll think about it?"

"Then what? Who gets you at sundown? Do I have to flip a coin every night, pull straws, what? Or do we go to court and get an order so I can get you every other weekend and every other holiday?"

She's offended. I want to offend her.

She takes off running, speeds up when I get too close, challenging me like I challenge her. We both move like we want to make up for lost time. But lost time is never recovered.

I run faster, zip by homes, everything from Classical Greek to Armenian Revival to French Restoration. Run faster and match her pace. Jealousy pours out of my system by the gallon.

Three more. I see three more houses with unique rainbow-hued flags, one with a multicolored cat as we run downhill and trek from Highland to Harvard back to the shops in Lake Merrit.

We find our way back over to Grand Street, run the outskirts of the lake back up 20th, then challenge each other's pace down Broadway, through the crowds, passing by women with white gauze gowns and scarves swirled around their faces, by sons whose ancestors were slaves, daughters of immigrants.

Nicole is in full stride by the time we come up on 6th, her tailwind stirring all the debris on the uneven, oil-stained boulevard, her bracelets jingling as she pumps her slim arms and races for the Tube.

Can't let her win. Ego chases ego.

She makes it out of the 980 overpass a good five seconds before me, flies across the entrance to the Tube, crosses 7th before traffic can take off. I break out of the darkness underneath the block-wide overpass and approach that good old Tube.

Death is waiting for me.

The light is green, the illuminated white man is on, those three sweet *coo-coo*s telling me I have the right-of-way. With me coming both out of darkness and from behind a huge column that supports the 980, and everybody and their momma rushing to get on the Alameda on-ramp before they lose the light, that is a deadly moment in the making. I'm sweating, legs aching, but feeling invincible, trying to catch the Road-runner, in a zone, and when I sprint off the curb, traffic doesn't give a fuck about me.

I'm facing a fast-moving death disguised as one of those ugly-ass PT Cruisers, that atrocious car that is built like a hearse for a midget, this one with windows tinted pallbearer black.

The driver of the uglymobile is on the phone. Zooming right at me. I can't move. Can't break left because it looks like that bastard wants to do the same. Can't break right because that would throw me in front of the traffic that is zipping up Broadway.

The sparkling grill on that Chrysler widens; death is smiling. The engine rumbles out a soft chuckle.

I think of *Lolita*. I think of the obsessed man who dies at the end. This is where I meet Joe Black.

The driver drops his cell phone, cringes, makes a wide-eyed, oh-shit face as he cuts left, his tires screeching a bit, then his sideview mirror slaps my arm so hard I think I'm shot.

Brotherman sends back his curses and speeds on, his radio blaring *"Shake ya' azz, watchya self."*

Nicole is still running, accelerating like a bullet, has no idea that I just cheated death.

I come alive, race through the other cars before they mow me down.

Nicole zips by the row of sushi joints and a plant store offering Psychic Reality, her heels smacking her ass with every stride. I don't give up, lengthen my stride, arms pumping, knees high like Olympic great John Carlos. I dig as deep as I can. She's doing the same.

She stops at the edge of Second Street, not once looking back. She never looks back.

Fifteen seconds later, which is a runner's lifetime, I catch up and stop next to her, my chest heaving, muscles burning, sweat coming from every pore, my face cringing with pain stacked on top of pain. There is a glimmer in her eyes, the shine she gets whenever she wins. There is competition. She's pimp-strutting like she just left Maurice Green and Michael Johnson in the dust and won a gold medal.

I check my watch. We've covered ten miles in an hour and twenty. Not bad, considering we lost a good five to ten minutes talking. She spits like a pro athlete, wipes her mouth on the sleeve of her damp sweatshirt, and then walks in circles.

I take deep breaths, in through my nose, out my mouth, and tell her, "You run like a cheetah."

Her shoulders are tense, face cringes, fights to control her breathing. "You call me a cheater? It's not cheating. If both of you know, it's not cheating. I have never lied to you. Never lied to her."

There is a pause. "I said cheetah. C-h-e-e-t-a-h. Not cheater."

"Oh."

"At least I know where your mind is."

A flash of embarrassment skates across her face.

I ask, "Are you comfortable?"

She gets animated, talks with her hands, like a teacher before a class breaking down a problem to its simplest terms. "A lot of women are attracted to women, but are scared to admit it."

I pause and we stare. "I meant are you okay. I thought you were limping."

Her mouth becomes a huge letter O.

I say, "Let's try this again. How do you feel?"

"Like screaming."

"Because of me?"

"Because of my cellulite."

I laugh. That's just like her, to jump to the trivial concerns stirring inside her head. "What cellulite?"

She groans. "Years of running and I still have big legs."

Her legs aren't big. And she hardly has enough ass to mention. There is no cellulite, not enough to worry about. She magnifies the flaws that Superman's telescopic vision can't see.

I remind her that she's the most beautiful woman in

the world, that the anorexic airbrushed images on the covers of *Cosmo* and *Body and Soul* can't touch her.

She smiles. "Another reason I'm hooked on you."

"Cold?"

"Not really. Body temp way up."

"Let's go in before we get sick."

"Wait. Air feels good." She blows; her breath comes out like steam. She's hyped. "Miss being with you all the time. Move up here. It'll be so cool if you moved up here. So many things I want to do with you, sweetie. Wanna take you to this salsa club in Emeryville. On the Black Panther Legacy Tour."

"Slow your stroll." I spit; wipe my mouth too. "You're trying to wear me out."

"Wanna share my world with you," Nicole says as she scrubs her face with a corner of her sweatshirt. "Maybe I can kick in on the down payment if that'll help convince you."

"You're talking about a grip. Maybe thirty thousand."

"If all goes well, my sloptions are going to break through the roof in the next year or two."

Sloptions is San Francisco–Silicon Valley slang for stock options. Her soon-to-be large techno Internet company offered her a chance to leave her old life and her program management position at Boeing in Anaheim to come here and be a contract renewal specialist. She left the shaky aerospace business behind and moved on to better things in dot-comville.

I ask, "What you looking at, moneywise?"

"At least a million. I wanna be a baller like you."

"Nobody balling but you. Sounds like you got all the cheddar."

"With the cost of living and property, that's chump

change up here. Hate thinking what the capital gains taxes are gonna be, but either way it'll be a nice piece of change."

"Need any help before then, let me know."

"I'm cool. Thanks for offering. That's sweet of you."

I'd give her my all, but she relies on me for nothing but love.

She doesn't have that Cinderella gene. Anything a man can do, she can do to the nth degree. She'll let the man be the head of the house, be it for his ego or the way she wants it to be, but she will not become dependent. That lets me know that the reason she's with me comes from the heart. She's better than Cinderella. She has beauty and skills. Outside of a dysfunctional family and a glass shoe, Cinderella had nothing but beauty and that fades with each tick-tock of the clock.

And at the same time, I want to be her prince. Want to ride up to her window on a black stallion, let her throw down a lock of her hair so I can climb up into her castle and snatch her ass down to my reality.

A beautiful sister walks by. Both of us stare at her, then at each other.

Nicole puts her arms around my shoulders, kisses the side of my face, tastes my drying sweat before she tongues me with a true passion, allows me to taste her salty emotions, each kiss asking me to accept her as she is, pimples on her butt, dry scalp, PMS, soft-legged lover and all.

She says, "Okay, now I'm getting cold."

As we stroll, she does a couple of gymnastic walk-overs, first forward then backward, then laughs, puts her face to mine and sucks my lips again. Even her moist skin is as sweet as a mango. With people rushing by, heading into all the seaside specialty shops, we close our eyes and kiss. Her bracelets sing and jangle as she hugs me. I pretend we're still engaged and that sound is the sound of wedding bells.

3

We head through the lobby, chitchat with the beautiful Ethiopian women who're working at the desk. One of them heard I was back, brought a book for me to sign. A girl I've seen quite a few times over the last few months. Generous smile and bright eyes. Brown flesh that looks good in her blue uniform, white blouse. Her fine and curly reddish-brown hair always pulled into a long ponytail.

I read her nametag. "Your name is Tuesday?"

"No, it's T-s-e-d-a-y."

"How do you pronounce that?"

"Sah-day."

"Pretty. And your last name?"

"A-b-e-r-r-a. Oh, but don't use my last name. Make it real informal. Write something juicy, you know, so it'll sound like I know you. Wanna make my friends jealous."

We laugh.

I stop and do that, small talk with her as I write. Nicole moves on toward the continental breakfast buffet, goes near the fireplace and the fruit.

Tseday smiles whenever our eyes meet. Speaks with an intellectual, almost British accent that is an aphrodisiac to my ears. She says, "I love your book. The mother in the book was fit for the looney bin. She was a regular Jerry Falwell."

"Thank you. That she was."

"I was telling my friends that you're much lighter in person than the picture on the back of your book."

"I could stand some sun."

"And that black-and-white picture does not show how pretty your eyes are. What color are they?"

"A shade of gray. Depends on the light, changes with my mood."

"The girls talk about your eyes every time you walk by. You should hear them."

"Sweetie?" Nicole calls me. She's listening. Her eyes turning as green. "I'm getting cold. Need to get out of these wet clothes."

I tell her to wait a second.

Tseday lowers her voice. "You better go before your friend shoots me."

"She doesn't own a gun."

"Not hard to find one in Oakland."

I finish signing the book, tell Tseday to have a peaceful day, and follow Nicole up the stairs.

Nicole says, "Why didn't she just suck your dick right there?"

"Jealous?"

"Yes."

I bump her and say, "Hypocrite."

"We're all living contradictions, trying to survive in a world filled with hypocrites."

"Whatever," I say, then let out a hard grunt. "Now you know how I feel every day."

We hold hands as we walk by the Asian maids, the people in business suits.

As soon as we get in my room, I see the message light is on. I check the message while we undress.

I tell Nicole, "André called. He's in town."

"He's doing a show?"

"He's performing in Walnut Creek tonight. Wanna hang after I leave Black Books?"

"Too much work to do, sweetie."

"You're his favorite soror," I tell her. "You have to go see your frat."

"Why don't you take the girl downstairs?"

"Don't you think that's pretty fucked up?"

"Was joking. I know she's not your type."

"Not that. You can ask me to meet your lesbian, but if I ask you to support an old friend, my frat brother, one of your frat brothers, you shake your head and say no before I get the question out."

Silence.

"What are you afraid of?" I ask. "It ain't like he don't already know."

More silence.

We put our wet gym clothes in plastic laundry bags, so I can send our gear out to get laundered later. She turns on the shower. We put on shower caps. Tension is between us, but when we touch, when my flesh feels her love, it happens again. That magic.

She says, "Damn, boo. You're hard again. Thought I killed that snake before we ran."

I laugh. Sometimes she says the most countrified things. I say, "See what you do to me?"

"How much ginseng are you taking? Geesh. You work me like a pork chop in a pit bull farm."

"Only see you once a month. Gots to get what I can while I can. Either that or me and my hand."

"Can't have you going blind. Let me please you."

"Got time for that?"

"Be quick. Don't wanna be late for that conference call with South Africa."

Inside the shower I love her from behind. Water so warm we're in a tropical storm. Our shower caps making that crinkle-crinkle noise when our heads rub. She bends over, my hands on her hips as she arches into me, receives me with eagerness, her palms against the white porcelain, pushing back against me as I ease inside her. I'm searching for a special room, a place no one has found before, a room to call my own. Our fit, so right, so tight. I want to give her pleasure in a way I know her live-in-roommate can't, the way a woman was designed to receive a man.

"God . . . you're . . . so . . . intense . . . what . . . are you trying . . . to do . . . to do . . . to do . . . to me."

She pants that heaven's coming closer. My hand slides, grips her belly, pulls her into me. I hold her, keep her from slipping, let her feel me mushrooming, the heat in me dancing with the fire inside her.

She's loud, grunting, slipping into a marvelous pain.

Her movement becomes intense, pushes back at me so hard I almost lose my balance.

She moans loud, curses even louder, and when I slow, in the sweetest tone, she calls God and Jesus.

Without warning, everything changes. Her body goes cold. Chill bumps rise all over her flesh.

I ask her if she's okay, try to find out what happened, what just went wrong.

She whispers my name a thousand times, asks me not to stop, not be gentle, begs me not to stop, please don't stop, because she needs to get back to that celestial place where this judgmental world doesn't matter. But the curses, the shivers, the begging me not to stop,

this time it has nothing to do with pleasure. She's crying. Boo-hooing like a baby. She wobbles. Breaks down
with tears.

Then she wails like someone has taken a hatchet to
the center of her soul.

Her eyes close tight, very tight, she stiffens, puts her
forehead to the wall, bumps her head two good times.
I don't know if I should run and dial 911 or hold her.
She howls. Scares the hell out of me. I hold her, telling
her that it's okay, we're okay, keeping her back against
my chest, warm water washing away the scents and
liquids from the loving we just made.

She calms down. Not all the way, just enough.

I ask, "What was that all about?"

Every part of her shivers at the same time; she's still
shaking her head, quivers away from my embrace.
Then she backs into me, reaches for my hands, puts
them around her.

We shower again, neither of us talking. She cleanses
me head to toe.

I ask, "You okay?"

"Raise your foot so I can wash the bottom." She
doesn't look up at me, but I can see that her eyes have
more color than the red sands in the Kalahari Desert.
"What time is your signing today?"

"Noon. You coming?"

"Too much work. Can't get to Vallejo and back on
lunch."

"This evening? Why can't we hook up this evening?"
She sighs. "Have dinner plans."

"With your friend?"

"Don't press it."

"Why did you say that you—?"

"I do have to work too. I'm trying to balance things

out. Work, her, you. It's hard being everything to everybody. No more pressure, please."

Silence.

She says, "I promise I'll come back tonight."

"I-page me, let me know what's up. Don't flake and leave me hanging."

She rambles, "And wear your black. You look good in your black. Wear your wool pants. You have to stop wearing jeans, sweetie. Put on your Banana Republic stuff. Women are aesthetic and will buy your books just because you look good. Wear the CK body lotion. And smile a lot. Floss and don't eat again before you go there. That way food won't fly out of your mouth. Always smile a lot. Women love pretty teeth. People with funky breath and jacked-up grills don't sell as well."

"You okay?"

"And no matter what anybody says, even if they insult you or love you, always be gracious. Remember that they are putting the meals on your table. Every time you sign a book, imagine that you're writing yourself a check, because that's what you're doing."

"Nicole, you okay?"

"And take your tape recorder. Record your discussion and the questions for me, sweetie."

"Nicole, are you okay?"

"Stop asking me that."

"Don't go bitch on me."

She twists her lips. "Sorry. I'm okay. Not trying to go bitch on you."

It's still early. We dry off. She puts on a beautiful thong and bra set; Cosabella underwear. Gets dressed in record time. With glossy eyes, she says she has to go. At that moment I'm at the dining table. She's in the bedroom, gazing my way. The plantation shutters divide us.

She says, "I'll take your laptop with me."

I back up a few files to floppy, power the system down, pack my Compaq into my brown leather shoulder bag, the one with all the pictures. She's not looking, her mind elsewhere. I dig in and take three of those pictures out. I always keep a couple of them near the left side of my chest.

I ask if she's hungry. She shakes her head and looks at her watch. No time to drive into Berkeley and grub on omelettes at Crepevine, not enough time to order a quick plate of fruit from room service. She doesn't want me to walk her downstairs to her car. She grabs her purse, straps it over her left shoulder, her weak shoulder, my laptop over her other shoulder. She needs to get away from me. I know her, see it in her eyes. Nicole gets her keys, hesitates and toys with the Siebel Systems keychain, gives me a thin kiss, hurries for the door, leaving her overnight bag and toiletries here.

At the door, Nicole stops, holds the handle, then says, "Her name is Ayanna."

I stay where I am.

I ask, "She a white girl?"

The door clicks open. Those bracelets jingle as she leaves. The door clicks when it closes.

I don't ask if she's rushing to her white-collar job in Emeryville, or running home to see her soft-legged lover. Don't ask if she's leaving dick to chase clit.

The photos I took from my messenger bag, I stare at them as I stand on the balcony in my jeans and USC sweatshirt, the cold ocean air massaging my face.

Nicole is gone, but she's still here. Her earthy fragrances and green tea body wash linger.

I gaze five floors down and wonder if I jump, if that mythical place called heaven would accept me as I am. There have been days when I didn't want to wake up. I used to think that meant I was crazy, but I'm no different from the rest of the world. Only sane people feel this way. Crazy people are the ones who think they are always sane.

Nicole leaves the hotel and checks her watch as she races up the wheelchair ramp, then balances her load as she jogs the stairs leading to the Starbucks. That coffeehouse is connected to the Barnes and Noble. Nicole never looks up. She knows where my room is. I always stay in the same room. She knows I'm watching, because she knows me, and she never looks up.

In the chilling breeze, the sun in my eyes, I wait, photos in hand, lips tight, lines blooming in my forehead, the same think lines my old man gets when he's in his philosophical mode. I'm worried about Nicole, about her tears, her anger, her pain, wondering what I can do to make a corner of it go away.

Then, with reluctance, I dial a number in Tennessee. Nicole's mother. Our southern-fried diva is happy to hear my voice, at least she tells me she is happy.

I say, "It's been a while."

"Months. Thank you for sending me your new book."

She congratulates me on my last book, which, like the others I have written, she will collect but never read because of the earthy language and the frank content. It's too real for her world.

She asks, "Are you on tour?"

I tell her that I'm always on tour, always eating hotel

food, hanging out at convention centers at somebody's expo, always keeping my mind occupied.

"I'm in Oakland. Doing a few book signings."

There is a pause.

I continue, "And I'm visiting Nicole."

The faux happiness between us vanishes like darkness devoured by light.

In a callous manner that rings of intolerance, she replies, "My daughter is dead."

"Nicole is alive."

"Chile, listen. The Nicole I gave birth to is as dead as my husband. As dead as her daddy has been for the last six years. Her eight brothers and three sisters are alive, one is in rehab, but he's stood before the church and confessed and asked for forgiveness and is coming back to the Lord, so each is doing well in their own way. My child, the one that is dead in spirit, her soul rests in an unmarked grave."

"How can you say that?"

She remains firm. "Her body is still among the living, but her soul is dead."

"I know it's hard, but it's hard on her too. Can you talk to her, maybe try to understand—"

"Not acceptable. Degenerative behavior is not acceptable. People can't just do what they want to in this world." She says things that speak of infinite disappointment, of community-wide embarrassment at the wedding, the almost wedding, an event that cost thirty thousand dollars, a wasted thirty thousand dollars, and in the end she tells me, "You know, in Pakistan, men burn their women when disgraced."

"We're not in Pakistan."

"But we have matches. We have gasoline and matches."

She hangs up.

My eyes are still on Starbucks. Nicole rushes out with a tall cup of the legal liquid drug in one hand. A second tall cup of the caffeinated upper is in her other hand. I know she always orders a tall cup, she always orders Kenyan with a shot of vanilla, either that or hazelnut, but never drinks half.

Coffee. Laptop.

She's a divided soul, trying to please two people at the same time.

She slows on the stairs, adjusts the laptop strap, the purse strap, balances the exotic coffees and still manages to check her watch. Her pace doubles and she struggles to whip out her cellular phone. She vanishes ten seconds before the jingle of her bracelets fade.

I rewind my tape recorder; play back the sounds of us making love. The recorder was on. From time to time I use it to interview, to capture reality. Sometimes I sit in a room filled with people and steal what they say, steal what they talk about, steal what they care about. I'm a writer, and whether the others admit it or not, we're all thieves. That's what we do.

This morning, I thought that Nicole and I would end up talking, hadn't planned on making love, not the way we did. Not as long as we did. We loved close to forty-five minutes. Any longer and the tape would've clicked when it shut off. Maybe that would've upset Nicole, maybe that would've excited her. I don't know. She's changing, becoming unpredictable.

I listen to our words, our sounds; sounds that tell me Nicole loves me. That this isn't in vain.

Then I erase it all.

The taste of Nicole lives in my mouth, her liberal aroma smolders from my flesh, her sex rises from my stained white sheets. I close my eyes and sleep a restless, fitful sleep. Like my head is on stone.

Life is not fair.
Life is not unfair.
Life just is.

4

Two years ago, we were living ten miles below Los Angeles, just as many above Long Beach, in one of Los Angeles County's best-kept secrets, the city of Carson. My engagement ring was on her finger and a three-bedroom house was in escrow. My plan was for us to jump that good old broom, write book after book, travel every spare moment, run races in as many cities as we could, collect those useless medals they give out, and grow old studying French and Spanish. And of course, write about it all. Vacation in Montego Bay. Stay in a beautiful villa at the Half Moon Resort. Visit Kenya, Morocco, and Egypt. In Hawaii, get our own timeshare on the big island of Kona. In Memphis we'd make love at the Peabody, then go see the ducks marching along red carpet to the Italian marble fountain. Stay at the Four Seasons in Georgetown and stroll the redbrick sidewalks in search of gifts for our friends and family. Leave the country when we became restless. Africa, Spain, Mexico, I wanted to see it all with her hand in mine. With money and health on our sides, we could move according to the season, and every night sleep in each other's arms chanting out love songs that thank the heavens.

My birthday. We broke into my piggy bank and went to Paris that June, put on our dark shades, strutted and sashayed every rue intersecting with the Champs Élysées until the sun went down at 10 p.m. Took pictures of Notre Dame, Lady Liberty, that arch of triumph Napoleon had built, made love twice every night, windows open and a cool breeze on our skin, our echoes of passion dancing out onto the avenue, then did it again every morning, ate at so many sidewalk cafés until we were about to burst. Hiked and sweated our way up the iron stairs to the observation deck of the Eiffel Tower and looked out over the city, her hand always in mine.

So many smiles were on her face. So much love in her every word.

And after all that, we'd lounge in the bed, naked in our own little Garden of Eden.

She asked me, "What are you afraid of?"

"What makes you think I'm afraid of anything?"

"Everyone's afraid of something."

"Failure."

"Why?"

"If I fail, then everyone else is right."

"About doing like your brothers and being like your daddy."

"Yep. Have to prove my point."

"Then you hate being wrong."

"That too. I guess."

"You hate to lose."

"Hate to lose. I've always hated to lose."

"You seem so together; so confident."

"Enough of analyzing me. What are you afraid of?"

"Wasn't analyzing you, sweetie. Didn't mean to make you uncomfortable."

"I'm not uncomfortable."

"You shifted. Your tone changed. Your dick went limp. You're uncomfortable."

We laughed.

I said, "You're the Sherlock of the century."

"Not being liked," she whispered.

"What?"

"I'm afraid of not being liked. Not being loved."

"You're after acceptance."

"If that's what all of that means, then yeah."

I held her a little closer.

She said, "Love your legs. They look so powerful."

"Thanks."

"Love the way it curves. It's so pretty."

"Let's do something different tonight."

That night I wanted to go to the famous strip club, Folies Bergères. Had never been to one with her. Wanted my woman to escort me into a Parisian Babylon, a place where no one we knew would be, where we'd have no accountability. Let her watch me be tantalized by another faceless woman. A creature of no real value. I wanted my woman to be uninhibited, get turned on by us doing something new together. She didn't want to go to a place like that, wanted to go eat dinner at Georges, a chic art deco restaurant on the top of the Beaubourg Museum, where we could get a table on the brushed-steel floors and see all the landmarks, spotlights on the edge of the city, watch the Eiffel Tower that was lit up like a glittering Christmas tree every night.

She sighed, sucked in her lips. It was my birthday. Every step of the way she let her protest be heard, but would do anything for me. That's how it was most of the time. Me talking her into doing something new and exciting. Her saying no, and me not accepting that as an answer.

Just like at some of the gentlemen's clubs in L.A., I saw many female customers paying female dancers for moments of enticement. Only these were African women. French women. Armenian women. That made my fiancée uncomfortable and when I heard negative words, I smiled. I nudged her, told her I wanted to watch her be entertained by another woman.

"No way."

"It's my fantasy."

"Sell crazy somewhere else. I'm all stocked up."

"Baby, we're in Paris. Not like anybody we know is gonna see."

"Don't pressure—"

"C'mon."

"—me. I hate it when you pressure—"

"It's my birthday."

She sighed, made a few faces. "Sure, if it'll make you happy. I want you happy."

Yes, it was my fantasy. My birthday hard-on. My freaky-deaky wish. I loved making her nervous. A dancer came over, a girl with dark, pretty hair, thick black eyebrows, a stranger who spoke no English, but understood how to move in a rhythm that went beyond language. Light-brown freckles on her arms and shoulders. Very attractive. So beautiful. Ten American dollars for one song. I paid, motioned at Nicole and the dancer smiled, said *oui mademoiselle* and went to her without hesitation. It was strange seeing another woman that close to Nicole. The dancer started out facing her, touching her own breasts and sides, dancing with the rhythm of a swaying palm tree. It wasn't hardcore. Not like watching a video with Heather

Hunter and Taylor Hayes. It was erotic, like watching the women make love in *Emmanuelle*.

And when it was over, Nicole was quivering like a child who had just gotten off her first roller-coaster ride. As we left that place, her sweaty palms gripped my hand like they were a steel trap.

I asked, "You okay?"

She stared off into space. "Happy birthday."

Not much was said in the taxi. Most of the time she would make comments about the narrow streets and how wild the drivers were, how they always seemed to be on the verge of an accident.

Again I asked, "You okay?"

"Happy birthday to you."

"Hungry?"

"Happy birthday to you."

"Want to go to Man Rays?"

"Happy birthday, happy birthday, happy birthday to you."

"You okay?"

Her words were distant. "Wanna stop and get some Vaseline?"

"Are you pissed off?"

"I'll let you do your thing tonight, you know. Anything for you. It's your birthday."

"You okay?"

"Stop asking me that, please."

Back at the Hotel Bedford, after a long, hot bath, we ordered room service, lit candles, put my Ondine Darcyl CD in the player, listened to her soothing rendition of "Autumn Leaves," "La Vie en Rose," and "Black Orpheus," all in French, some with a Brazilian feel, all jazzy and beautiful. Savored those sounds as we ate cod and mashed potatoes, sipped White Bordeaux, and rested underneath a golden duvet on white linen sheets that smelled like spring.

When the music stopped Nicole asked me, "Would you fuck her?"

"Who?"

"The French girl you picked to dance for me."

"Hell, no."

"Even if I wasn't here?"

"Not even if you were on the moon."

"Men don't pick women they wouldn't fuck."

We experienced a soundless moment, one great enough to be put in Holland's Museum of Silence.

Then she snapped, "I close my eyes and I can't stop seeing her . . . I smell her perfume all over my skin . . . and I can't stop tingling . . . I still feel her breasts on me."

I swallowed.

"Her breasts . . . they . . . they felt . . ."

I shifted. Hanging on her every word.

"She touched me, something happened. My nipples . . . they . . . I was so wet . . ." Her anger changed, evolved into a rambling confession spoken in shame. "Her breasts, so soft, when she rubbed them up and down my skin, oh God, when they touched my face, her nipples became erect, like little bitty penises, I wanted them in my mouth, and the way they felt on my skin . . ."

She lost her breath. My heart pounded, saliva thickened while I waited for her to come back to life.

In a whisper of amazement she said, "Never felt like this before."

"Not even with me?"

There was a pause. A pause, a trembling lower lip, heavy breathing, and no answer. Nicole pulled me on top of her. Begged me to love her hard, love her deep, love her strong, to come inside her. That was the first time she made painful sounds and cried while we made love.

I stopped, asked if she was okay.

She forced me on my back, climbed on me with impatience and a solemn face, not singing and laughing like she usually did, eyes watery, chewing her lips, chest heaving, doing all she could to hide the tears. She raised her hips and howled as the peak of me rushed into the dampness of her, spreading her open, stretching her out. Heat and softness moving against my fire and hardness.

Then she stopped. Didn't slow down, stopped. Sat there tugging at the hair on my chest, lips twisted, eyes diverted, her heat turning cool. She fell from me, collapsed with her face deep inside the pillows, hid in her own world, breathing harder than a woman in labor.

My palms were sweating. I tried to hide the trembling in my hands, wanted to erase the shakiness in my voice. I reached for her, but didn't touch her. I was too scared.

"Do you hate me?" she asked. "You brought me all the way to Paris, and I'm messing up your birthday. I bet you hate me, don't you?"

"No. Just trying to understand."

"You're going to put this in one of your books."

"Stop saying that."

"You always do. All of your books are about me."

She reached back and pulled me on top of her backside, found my half-hard penis, rammed that deflating part of me in what was left of her wetness, whispered in a frantic tone, "Love me, baby. Help me get these crazy thoughts out of my head."

And when we were done, she kept her back to me, her eyes to the wall.

I ran my fingers through the back of her hair, kissed the back of her neck before I told her, "You're so fucking beautiful."

"I'm fat. Can't lose these last ten pounds no matter how much I diet, no matter how far I run. My hair is always too dry. Dandruff the size of Corn Flakes. I have to wax my lip every other Friday. And I'm too damn old to have pimples."

"One pimple."

"The size of Mt. Fucking Rushmore."

"Give it a break. You know you're beautiful."

"I'm a cross-eyed gerbil. Anyway, beauty hides faults. People are so busy looking at the wrappings of a package that they fail to see what's inside. Or what's not inside. Half of them don't care."

The thoughts had been there before the dance. Her own fantasy rising to the top. But she had never been that close. Had never felt the warmth and softness and tenderness of a woman. Had never been teased by a woman until desire dampened her underwear.

5

"One of the big problems with sex is miscommunication," the comedian says as he sips his beer, then sets the bottle on a bar stool near the mike stand. He's tall, dark, and bald. Has on a three-piece suit, one with a long, six-button coat, looking ghetto fabulous. Well dressed in a casual world. The women send laughs and wishful smiles up his way. He's under the spotlight, so I doubt if he can see beyond the second row. He goes on with his routine. "Men and women, we speak the same language, but we don't mean the same thing. Right men? Women, y'all know what I'm talking about. Now you know André ain't gonna lie to ya, so all of this is coming from the real."

André pauses and smiles down at the crowd of about two hundred people. I'm at a comedy club out in Walnut Creek, the 'burbs that are about thirty minutes from Oakland. André's about fifteen minutes deep into a twenty-five-minute set, so the mixed crowd is already heated up. They're smiling back, at least half of them laughing already, anticipating something good.

So am I.

"Like we say we wanna make love all night. Brothas

will promise that, won't they? Look at that sista nodding her head. Brought back some memories, huh? Brotha probably said"—he grabs his crotch and switches to a Barry White voice, brings the character to life and puts some old school pimp and new jack swagger in his motions—" 'Yeah baby, I'm gonna be knocking dem boots all night.' "

A lot more laughter with me leading the pack.

"Now, all night, to a woman, that means 'until the sun comes up.' That's all night. To a man that means 'until the dick goes down.' 'Cause that's all you gonna get tonight."

The room explodes with laughter.

He keeps the crowd roaring. "Most men make love like a union worker. *Clock* in for fifteen minutes, then wanna take an eight-hour break."

Another explosion. Some choke on their brews, a few slap the tops of their round black-topped tables along with their chuckles, some clap like André's a comical genius. Women sitting in the section underneath the Laurel and Hardy mural give non-stop hello, tell it like it 'tis, raise candles, and send finger snaps.

He does more on dating, his ugly children routines, slips in a pretty creative one about Bush, calls his tax plan "reparations for the rich," and gets a huge applause, which is an easy sell in this crowd. Then moves on and ranks on local rapper E-40 and his creative English.

André gets mega-laughs all the way down the line. He has the gestures and the light-hearted tone to make even the simplest routine go over. He closes his act by doing a musical spoof of Jesse "Playa Playa" Jackson singing a whacked version of Outkast's "Ms. Jackson." Nothing like seeing Jesse apologizing for cheating and not using a condom, while first dancing the cabbage patch, then getting down and rolling his ass to the Tootsie roll.

At the end of his set, he leaves the stage to huge applause. The emcee high-fives my friend as they pass on the stairs, gets back on stage.

André left them wanting more. I slip through the darkness and catch him as soon as he breaks away from some chatty people.

"Whassup, frat?"

He turns and sees me. "Whassup, nigga!"

He gives me that frat handshake, then changes to a masculine handshake, the kind that looks more like a WWF challenge than ten years of friendship. "When you get here?"

"Rolled up in here right when you went on. Chilled out in the back."

We snake around a waitress, dodge a few people, and make our way toward the bar.

I tell him, "You were actually funny this time."

He dabs his forehead with a napkin. " 'Dem damn lights were cooking my ass. Had me sweating like a felon in a high-speed chase."

I laugh.

He goes on, "So you thank I was funny?"

"Off the heezy." I'm mocking his E-40 routine. "Did better than you did on *Comic View*."

"Niggas in Oakland recognize skills. Have to see me unedited to appreciate what I do."

"Why does everybody on *Comic View* do jokes about fucking?"

"When the people stop laughing, people will stop doing jokes about fucking."

We laugh, rag on each other for a few.

"Man, you should'a had 'em brang you up front. Would'a introduced you."

"That's why I stayed in the shadows. Had a thing at Black Books Spring over in Vallejo. That was enough attention for one day."

"We could'a done did a book thing here."

"Like these chain-smoking alcoholics read."

People come up; everyone wants to touch him. He introduces me, and the people have blank looks in their eyes. Never heard of me. Here, I'm a ghost. This is his venue. He says a few things to a few people, and we snake through the crowd and move out to the café-style lobby, a part of the club that has checkerboard floors, wooden ceiling fans, and pictures of every comedian from Charlie Chaplin to Jim Carrey on the walls. With the direct access to the bar and the kitchen, I'm inhaling everything from Bacardi to Coors, tacos to burgers. The doors are heavy enough so we can't really hear the show without being inside. It looks like this part of the club is a restaurant in the day, maybe a lunchtime spot for the people in Walnut Creek.

He asks, "Still running?"

"Always. Did the Culver City Marathon back in December."

"How far that?"

"Twenty-six miles."

"Shit. You crazy. Last time I traveled twenty-six miles I took luggage."

We laugh.

I ask him, "Still teaching chemistry?"

"Man, you crazy? Hitting this full-time. It got so bad that teachers in L.A. Unified have to walk through metal detectors and they give up combat pay for dealing with those drive-by fools."

"Combat pay? Is it that bad?"

"Like Vietnam."

"You didn't go to Vietnam."

"I saw Oliver Stone's movie. That was close enough."

We get cut off when a group of women come over to the table and talk to André. His excited fans wearing sweaters, short dresses, high boots, and plenty of perfume.

My I-pager hums on my hip. It's Nicole. Wants to know where I am.

I use one finger to type her a message, push send.

When the fan club leaves, I turned to André and say, "You serious? Combat pay?"

"Yeah. Students in L.A. Unified shoot, stab, poison, and drown teachers every day."

"Wild."

"You couldn't pay me enough to sub in L.A."

My I-pager hums. Again it's Nicole. Wants to know when I'll be back at the Waterfront.

I send her another message.

Some people measure time in minutes, some in hours. I measure time by missing Nicole. I do other things, try to maintain a full, non-reclusive life, but my time with her is all that matters.

Me and André talk some more. We haven't seen each other in a while. Both of us are out of L.A., used to do our thing at the Greek shows, used to hit all the parties at UCLA and Cal State Long Beach together. Now we pretty much live on the road, have to keep in touch the way the rest of the world does, via e-mail. Today we happen to be in the same city at the same time for a few hours.

A short woman comes over in full flirt mode. She's

very nice looking. Long hair. Mixed to the bone. The kind of girl you see on BET. The only kind of black woman you ever see in front of the camera on BET. Her eyes are almost as tight as the dress she has on. She tells him, "You were funny."

In the next few seconds she says she's up from Palm Springs, came up for a technology show in San Francisco at the convention center.

He asks, "So where your man?"

"Where's your woman?"

He smiles. She smiles too.

He says, "I'm downtown at the Hilton, if you wanna come by for the second show."

She thinks a moment. A very short moment. "What time that second show start?"

"Soon as you walk in the door."

"Does it last all night?"

"One way or the other."

"Will I be laughing?"

"Not even a chuckle."

Again she thinks a very short moment. "Write your room number down."

"You need directions?"

"I know my way around."

"What's your name?"

"Guess that would help. Toyomi Wilkins."

"Toyota? Your momma named you after a car?"

"No." She laughs so soft and sweet. "Toy-oh-me."

"Pretty name for such a beautiful woman."

She gets his info, gives him her pager number, then leaves, her hips moving in a hypnotic rhythm. We both make that *mmph* sound, the constipated noise men make when they see a beautiful woman.

I say to my friend, "Just like that?"

He nods. "Just like that. 'Dey loves to laugh. This celebrity shit ain't no joke. I used to have to buy drinks and try to mack half the night. Now all I gotta do is show up and don't say nothing stupid."

I say, "Toyomi has a nice ass."

"She got booty, not ass."

"What's the difference?"

"Twenty pounds," he answers. "Ass equals booty plus twenty, gee."

"True that to a Jenny Craig meeting."

"Was that a weave?"

"Nah. Looked real to me."

We talk about women, play catch-up for a few, and then we eventually talk about old friends down in Los Angeles. Mainly the people who were in my wedding. And Nicole.

He says, "You a better man than I am."

"What you mean?"

"Most niggas would've beat her down. Or did an OJ."

"That ain't me."

"Man, look around the room. Women outnumber us nine-to-one."

I nod, let him know that I understand what he's saying. "You should come by a book signing then. It's more like a hundred to one."

"Man, I needs to change jobs. I'd rather meet a sister with a book in her hand than one with a drank in her hand. Goddamn codependent alcoholics drive a nigga crazy."

At some point I tell him that Nicole wants me to meet her friend. Use him as my sounding board. Need to say it out loud to see how it rings. He shakes his head a thousand times.

He says, "Be careful."

"I'm not scared of no woman."

"A lot of niggas resting in the morgue used to say the same shit."

I rock a bit, run my tongue over my teeth.

He goes on, "You better wear a bulletproof vest. This is real life, not all polite like that *Chasing Amy* movie."

"What you mean?"

"Them girls be acting a fool. Some of 'em anyway. Ain't no absolutes."

"Educate me."

"Man, I was in Atlanta, went by Kaya Club and Bistro to see Pru—you heard of Pru?"

"Yeah. Nicole loves her music."

"Sister off the chains," he says, then gets back to his story. "I was on the way out of Kaya, and this sista said hi to me, fine-ass girl, looked like Halle Berry with long legs. She smiled. I smiled back. Then the sista standing next to her grabbed her hair and yanked her ass through the crowd and out on Peachtree Street, screaming 'Beeeeee-yitch! I know you ain't up in my face looking at no nigga.' "

"You're joking?"

"Am I on stage? Jokey-joke time is over. Whooped her ass like she was a two-year-old."

"What did you do?"

"Watched."

"Watched?"

"She was with a sista who looked like Emmitt Smith in drag. I ain't trying to get beat down over some coochie I ain't never got."

"Geesh. Yanked her by the hair?"

"Tore that weave out her head. She went from looking like Halle Berry to Chuck Berry."

We double over laughing.

"What did the girl do when her weave got yanked out?"

"Stuck that horse hair in her purse and followed Emmitt to the car."

We laugh so hard people passing by look at us and crack up too.

"Then"—he wheezes, coughs, wipes a tear from his eye—"then, check it out, I was up here last summer, over on Piedmont, and when we stepped out the restaurant, man, you should'a seen it, two female bus drivers were going at it in the middle of the street fighting over a sista."

"Bus drivers?"

"Left the buses in the middle of traffic, crowded buses, and went at it in the streets."

"Damn."

"Check it out, come to find out they were seeing the same woman, and both buses happened to be passing by her at the same time, when she was crossing the street."

"Double damn."

"Talk about a coinky dink, and *pah-dow*, busted in broad daylight."

"White women?"

" 'Dey was as black as my momma at midnight."

"That's pretty black 'cause your momma is blacker than a quarter past twelve on a moonless night."

"Forget you. And stop doing my act. High-yellow motherfucker's always plagiarizing the black man. Over there looking like a light bulb."

"How come you can crack on your momma but I can't?"

" 'Cause she my momma, fool. You know this country gives the dark man issues. You don't see me saying nothing about your half-white momma."

I push him; "Greasy-head bastard."

"Nappy-head fool."

"You about to get hit in the mouth."

He laughs. "Wanna brew-ski?"

"Get me a Sprite. No ice."

He motions to a waitress, gives our order. Tells her to bring two orders of hot wings too.

Somewhere between the hot wings and the soft drinks, me and my frat start to talk about our friends. Our words are somewhere between gossip and testimonial.

The minority of the people we know have a life mate, and I guess that says a lot, but the road hasn't been easy for any of them. And it hasn't been impossible either. That's why I keep trying.

I try to think of who has had the low road to success. Not one name comes to mind.

My I-pager goes off again.

He tells me, "Nicole hitting you on the hip for a booty call?"

"How you know?"

"That big-ass smile on your face. You 'bout ready to shake the spot?"

I'm about ready to go. By the way he keeps looking toward Toyomi, so is he.

We head outside. André's black limousine is waiting right outside the door.

I say, "You riding in the big dick tonight."

"Best way to travel. How you getting back to the Waterfront?"

"My rental is across the street."

"Hope you can work it out with Nicole. Y'all were

good together. The way y'all was always so touchy-feelie, kissy-kissy had everybody jealous." My frat says that with a lot of sincerity. "It ain't been easy for none of us, to tell the truth. Like Pat Benatar said, love is a battlefield."

"Who?"

"Never mind. The point is a nigga gotta stick in there. Keep dicking her down. She'll come around. Easy to quit when it gets rough. Shit, that's why I ain't got nobody."

"You ain't got nobody 'cause you keep getting busted."

"Either that or they get busted. It's rough out here, dawg. You stay on a merry-go-round long enough, you get dizzy."

"I hear ya."

"The playas are getting played. We need to come up with new game for these women."

"Then how's a loser like you going to give me advice?"

"Remember; ain't but two kinds of people in this world. You either pimping or being pimped."

"Which are you?"

"You know better. I'm a pimp's pimp."

I tell him, "A pimp without a ho' is just a nigga talking shit."

"You . . . you . . . you son of a preacher."

More laughs. We're talking smack, South Central style, something I rarely do.

"You better listen to me," he tells me. "I know thangs. I know how to make it work."

I ask, "Okay, pimp daddy. What's the secret to making it work?"

"Not giving up. Not listening to people tell you who you should be with."

I nod. We do that good old secret frat handshake once more.

I say, "You better hurry up and hook up with Toyomi."

"If she shows up, cool. If she don't, no sweat. Part of the game. She ain't my type no way."

"What's wrong with her?"

"I like 'em black as my momma."

"And that's blacker than the dark side of the moon."

"Damn right. Darker the berry, dah sweeter the juice. Once you go black, ain't nothing else to like. But girls who look like that, them high-maintenance weave-erellas, they keep coming at me like I owe them money. And I ain't turning down nothing but my collar."

My laughter meets the wind head-on as I jog away, my leather coat tight around me, blocking out that night air, trying to avoid that good old hawk that's stinging the tips of my ears.

I yell back at him, "See you on-line."

"Ah'ight, frat. I'll e-mail you. Tell Nicole I ain't mad at her. E-mail a black man."

6

Before I can get back to the hotel, Nicole I-pages me again. The message says she can't make it. Tomorrow will be better. As soon as I read that I I-page her back: *Why?*

She responds: *Drama.*

I page her back: *Details.*

I don't get a reply.

It fucks with me. Sitting in my room at the Waterfront, I'm imagining what they're doing that she can't get away from. I have her address, it's on an *I love you more every day* postcard she sent me a while back, and I can punch that info into the computerized navigator in my rental car and let that digital map take me to her front door.

I can. I can cross that moat, break into that castle, and rescue her from that wretched dungeon.

My hands open and close; make fist after fist. I can go get my woman back.

Either a pimp or being pimped.

I lower my head; pull at my twisties over and over.

It fucks with me, it fucks with me, and it fucks with me.

I grab the card, my coat, my keys, walk the cold air, make it to the rental car, punch the address in the electronic navigator and leave in a hurry.

Technology is wonderful. Anybody can find anybody in ten keystrokes or less.

Where it takes me is a strip mall up near 40th. No houses. No condos. Just grocery stores, shoe stores, a Blockbuster Video, other things like that. Inside that strip mall is a MailBoxes Etc. The address outside matches the address on the postcard. All I have for Nicole is a damn P.O. box.

Smart woman. Very smart woman.

Guess she figures if I have her home address, at some point I'll bring trouble to her front door.

She's right.

And it's a good thing. I have a family: two older brothers, one younger, both parents living, waiting for me to come back to them with my prize. I have more accountability than I care to talk about.

I need Nicole to come back to me.

So I go back to my room, strip to my boxers, do push-ups, as many as I can, then sit-ups, and with sweat on my brow, my arms, my bare legs, I write. Put all of that emotion down on paper.

At 2 a.m. there's a knock at my door. It's Nicole. She has on blue-and-gray U of M sweats under her black leather coat. Her laptop over her right shoulder, files from work in the same hand, her black-and-white overnight bag is over her left shoulder, and a cup of Starbucks is in that same hand. She looks worn. Very worn. A candle burning at two ends. She smiles. That smile is like stars on a dark night, and that optimistic power makes me smile. Makes me forget everything that's wrong.

We kiss right there, before words leave our faces. We stop when her pager goes off.

I ask, "Work?"

"Ayanna. Mind if I call her real quick?"

"I mind," I say in a no-compromise tone. "You're on my dime."

She smiles like she loves it when I demand her attention like that. Her bracelets sing a happy song as she comes into my world.

I ask, "Why don't you ever take those bracelets off?"

She pushes her lips up into a schoolgirl smile. "I just don't."

We pull the curtains back so we can see the stars through the plantation shutters that divide my room. My Queen of Clean Hygiene turns on the shower as soon as she walks in, lights candles, undresses me, and we cleanse each other. She never goes to bed without a bath. We oil each other.

She asks, "How was André's show?"

"Off the hook. He asked about you."

I tell her some of his act, the new parts. And I tell her another joke.

She frowns. "Ass equals booty plus twenty pounds?"

"That's André's equation."

"He is such a pig." Nicole pauses. "Okay, which do I have, booty or ass?"

"Don't start."

We laugh a bit.

She says, "Ayanna hates his act."

"What, she can't take the gay humor?"

"Too stereotypical for her taste."

"So, she's a critic?"

"Always a critic."

"She drive a bus?"

"No. Why you ask?"

"Just asking."

"You've never asked about her before."

Nicole pulls her locks back, puts on her small-framed glasses, sits in the living room section of the room for about an hour, spreads her papers out over the coffee table facing Jack London Square and reads over her work. She mumbles to herself while she reads. I do some journal writing in front of my laptop, the Leonardo da Vinci screen saver giving extra light.

When she takes a break, she asks, "You record your signing?"

I tell her, "The tape is next to the recorder."

She pops it in and listens. "You talk too fast at some points, slow down. Take your time."

"Okay."

"Your voice is so sexy."

I smile. Seven years and I've never grown tired of her flattery. Never been bored with loving her.

At one point she rolls her eyes. "Sisters take what you do too seriously."

"Give it a rest."

" 'Are you single?' " she mocks. "What does that have to do with the friggin' book?"

"Stop playa hatin'."

She extends her middle fingers toward me, then puts the tape in her purse. She collects those.

I ask, "Why do you want those tapes?"

"Because they're you. Because it's about you. It's moments in time that will never happen again."

After that, I put on Ondine Darcyl's CD, let that sensuality play soft and low.

Nicole looks over at me and smiles.

I ask, "What?"

"Love her voice. That music takes me back to Paris."

"Want me to turn it off?"

"No. Love it. I miss this. We used to be like this all the time. Damn near every night."

I think about Paris. Think and wish I had skipped that trip, gone to Disneyland instead.

Soon after that, we're under the covers, skin to skin. Her hand is between my legs, rubbing, massaging. The room smells like strawberries. Nicole brought oils and a burner.

I ask, "Where were you?"

"Worked late then went to dinner with Ayanna. Had a long talk with her. This running back and forth between you and her, between both of you and my job, it's hard, sweetie."

"What does she do when you're with me?"

"Don't know."

"Why not?"

"That's our rule. I can't ask."

I lean forward. "What's up with that?"

"If I'm with you, I can't ask her where she is, or what she does. Fair is fair."

"That bothers you?"

"Yes. Just like it bothers me when I wonder what you're doing when you're not with me. Sometimes I miss you so much it suffocates me. Like all my oxygen goes away."

I'm thinking about the things André told me. The fight he saw in Atlanta. What he witnessed around the corner from here in Piedmont. Wonder what Nicole had to go through to get away.

I ask Nicole, "What have you told your . . . your friend about me?"

"I talk about you so much her ears bleed. Hell, she can't get away from you. Just like I can't. Walk in a bookstore, your books are staring me in my face. Caught her on the toilet reading one last week."

I don't say anything, just wait for her to give me more words.

"If they make a movie, make sure Sanaa Lathan plays me. Sister has beautiful skin. Nice mouth. I want to be pretty like her for a change."

I nod. "It's all smoke and mirrors. You're better-looking."

"Thanks." She gives me that smile. "Me and Ayanna, we've talked about first loves. Heartbreaks. Fantasies."

"Fantasies," I repeat that because of the way Nicole says that word, as if she were cueing me, leading me to ask a certain question. "What kind of fantasies?"

"This has to do with the solution to our problem. Sure you wanna know?"

I sit up. Face her. "Tell me."

She does the same. The covers fall from her chest. "God, this is scary to say."

"Did you tell your friend?"

"She knows. She knows what I want. What I need."

I tell her, "Go ahead."

"I'm not a freak or nothing, you know," she says, then pauses. She gets up, walks to the service bar, takes out a bottle of water, drinks half of it.

She says, "You got quiet."

"You got quiet. This is where I listen."

Then she rambles, "I've had fun, but I've never slept around. I haven't had half as much sex as most of the women I know. You should sit in *Head to Toes* and listen to some of the sisters talking smack while they get they hair done. Men think they are players, but women are the real players. Sisters get over more ways than one. I have not had nearly as much sex as they have. Some of those vaginas have had more traffic than the Holland Tunnel."

"Sex or sex partners?"

"Okay, sex partners. I stand corrected. And outside of listening to women talk, I read all the magazines and watch television, so I know a lot of what I feel isn't that unusual. You should see the personal ads in the back of the *Guardian*—not that I read those skanky personals."

"Of course you don't. Go ahead. Stop tap dancing and ask."

"I don't want to offend you. I don't want you to, you know, think bad of me."

"Go ahead."

"We've done a lot of, for lack of a better phrase, carnal experimenting together. Got our freak on in parks. At the library. Did it pretty much everywhere but a Burger King bathroom. Had our little toys. Found out what worked. Gave everything at least two tries."

Again she pauses.

I say, "Right now. Now stop tap dancing and ask."

"It's a whole new level."

"Ask."

Her mouth is open, but no words appear. The clicks and whirrs are getting louder, sounding like an Amtrak rolling down the tracks of her mind. Her forehead crinkles and her thin, arched eyebrows almost touch. She gets back in the bed, holds my hands in hers, asks, "So, you're open to new things?"

"Define new."

"Multitasking lovemaking."

"Don't turn into a nerd. What does that mean?"

"Like in all those films we watched together, it

would be erotic to have both of you please me. Have me please both of you. I think I'm more interested in trying to please the both of you than the other way."

Words come, but my lips don't move. "You're talking about a ménage à trois."

I blink a few times. My hands are still in hers.

She pulls her lips in. "Well? Give me some feedback."

"Have you and your friend done that before?"

"No. It would be my first time trying something like that."

"Her first time?"

"As far as I know. But you never know what people do when you're not around."

"True. Only know what people let you see."

"Would it be yours?"

Silence is my answer. I go to the service bar, get a bottle of water.

She asks, "How do you feel right now?"

"Like I've been suckered into an Amway meeting."

I'm not really thirsty, just have to move with my thoughts. In two gulps, the bottle is empty.

With softness she asks, "Would being able to experience something that wonderful turn you off?"

"Is that what your friend wants?"

"Whatever, wherever, whenever. I never hesitated to please you, to help you get to the next level of satisfaction, because I love you. Not because I thought you wanted a slave or a serf, because of love."

"Can I ask you something?"

"Ask away."

The phone rings, slows our roll. I answer. No one is there.

My tongue traces my gum.

She repeats, "Ask away."

"You go down on her?"

"Am I a carpet-licker?"

"You eat her out or what?"

"Don't believe you asked me that."

"Believe it."

"Why ask me that of all things?"

"Because . . . that's what I see in my dreams."

She puffs air. "Pussy is scary. It looks like a monster."

"One man's god is another man's monster."

"It's still ugly. Like roast beef."

"Yours is a pretty nice cut. Grade-A all the way."

"Thanks. I think."

She never answers my question. She's tapping her fingers on her flesh, arms folded under her breasts, and I don't press the issue. I'm thinking about her pussy, about how I set it on fire. When I'm with her, she tells me that she's mine, but my heart tells me that it's the part of her beyond the pussy I can't reach.

She tells me, "It's not gonna be a nasty, free-for-all kinda thing."

"What would it be?"

"Sensual. Sharing. Erotic."

"What's in this for me?"

"It'll squash all of this tension. We'll all walk away enlightened."

"Educated."

"Yep, edified to a new level of love and appreciation."

"Edified," I repeat. I swallow to push my heart from my throat. "Is that what you and her were talking about all evening?"

"Yep."

"And she's down with your extended educational program?"

"Don't worry about Ayanna. Just tell me what you think about it."

"Sounds interesting."

"So, if it's cool with her, then you're down with it?"

She tries to hide the enthusiasm in her voice, but it's too late, it's rising like ocean waves during a full moon. I want to understand Nicole without reservation. I'm curious. Very curious, I can't deny that. Curious about who Nicole is, what mask she puts on, or what mask she takes off, when she's with the other, about what my reaction will be when I see them side by side, or in a passionate embrace. Curious about what makes her friend so damn special.

Maybe I need to see that. Maybe that will rupture me to the point of freedom.

I nod. "Let's think about it. The consequences. How would you feel, morally?"

"After all I've done with you"—she chuckles—"I know you're not preaching morals."

"Well, this is different."

"Everything I did for you was different."

I pause. "How would something like this work out?"

"I'll make the rules."

I say, "Sounds like it'll be like Simon Says."

"Yep. The adult version. With a little Twister added."

"And who gets to be Simon?"

"I do, of course. I've been reading about situations like this that worked, ones that didn't. Their boundaries weren't clear. We'll have rules. That way nothing can go wrong."

She sounds eager, has changed in ways I can't comprehend. I walk over to the window, stare out toward the bay, become as still as the hard, gray statue of Jack London that stands near the waters.

Nicole says, "Sweetie?"

"Yeah?"

"Don't stand in the window naked. They might think you're a pervert."

I come back to her. Sit on the bed.

I tell her, "You didn't answer my question. You eat her out or what?"

"Well, this way you can find out."

I say, "You used to think that was disgusting. Whenever you saw Heather Hunter munching carpet, you turned your head."

"To tell the truth, I turned my head because I didn't want you to see what it did to me."

"So now you're telling me that you didn't think it was a turn-off?"

"I used to think a lot of things were disgusting. You changed that."

"Sell that guilt trip to the airlines. The seed was already in you. I didn't plant it."

"If there was a seed inside me, it was living in a desert. Didn't grow until you watered it. With all of your erotic videos, making me watch women with women, with your fantasies, you made it grow."

"You were so . . . uh . . . well, you were—"

"An inexperienced, body-shy, and frigid country girl from Elvisland. Your exact words."

"I never said no shit like that."

"You did. No biggie because I was, was I ever, and—"

"Didn't say all that. I was trying to get you to not be inhibited."

"You did a good job. Now I'm not." Then she sings, "Seems like you are, though."

Her pager hums. We look at each other.

I say, "Turn it off. You're on my dime."

She does just that.

This is what I know about Ayanna: nothing. Never wanted to know her name, because I might hear it and go insane. Never wanted to see a picture of her, because I might hunt her down and skin her alive. Never wanted any information about the five senses of her, never wanted anything that would make her solid in my mind. Wanted her to fade into the night. Never wanted her to become real. The thought of her is as solid as smoke, and that's more than enough.

I ask Nicole, "What's the most extreme sexual thing you've done since you've been here?"

"Being with her. Never planned on being in this situation."

"Outside of that. Outside of her."

"This is Oakland and San Francisco. It's just as wild as Paris up here."

"Other women?"

"Nope. Just her."

"Other men?"

"Your penis is the penis I adore."

"That's cute, but not an answer."

She falls into silence.

I say, "Truth or truth."

"Sure you want to go there?" She sighs. "You have condoms in your travel kit. Maybe I should be asking you about other women."

"What do you expect me to do while you're living with some bitch?"

"She's not a bitch. What you said is not nice. When you insult her, it insults me."

"Pardon my insensitivity. You fucking anybody?"

"Apologize."

"You fucking anybody?"

"Apologize."

"I apologize. You fucking anybody?"

She doesn't answer.

I rephrase the question, "Are you having sex with anyone else?"

"Maybe I should be asking you what are you doing out on the road. You heard me the first time. Don't think I never notice the condoms you have in your luggage."

We've put each other in check. Serious check.

She says, "I know why you don't use a condom with me."

"Do you?"

"I'm not stupid. You want to get me pregnant."

"Dunno. Maybe I do."

"Even if you did, that won't change anything, sweetie."

The clicks and whirrs from her thoughts grow, her lips move, getting ready to articulate something that is difficult to bring to the table. Stress lines bloom in her face.

I say, "When was the last time you were tested?"

"December first. AIDS awareness day."

"Same for me. What about your friend?"

"Same day. We went together."

Silence.

I rub my palms together; massage my hand with my hand.

She asks, "What are you thinking?"

"Thinking about how when people move away from all they know, they either become something remarkable or something undesirable."

"Which do you think I am?"

I take a hard breath. "What you're asking, it's not . . . not . . ."

"Normal?" Her eyes are dry but tears dampen her voice. "Normal, normal, fucking normal."

With measured calmness I say, "I wasn't going to say that. Maybe I was."

"Who in the hell gets to define what's normal?"

"Society. The majority defines normality, you know that."

"I've been living my life according to my mother's rules—"

"How did you mother get in this?"

"She always made me go to this school, that college, this guy isn't the right complexion for you, that guy isn't good enough for you, that one isn't from the right family, do this, do that. Always feeding into their definition of who they wanted me to be because of my fear of rejection. Fear is a bitch."

She takes a breath, slows herself down.

She whispers, "I did so many things for you because I was afraid of being rejected by you, know that? If you love me, you'll suck my dick. Yep, better suck the weenie or he won't love me. If you love me, you'll let me come in your mouth. Well, better let him come in my mouth, or he won't love me. Better swallow, because his last girlfriend did, and if I don't, he won't love me. Better let him get his anal sex groove on, or he won't love me."

"Nicole. Stop."

"How many times did I have to prove how much I love you? How many ways?"

"Stop. Nicole, knock it off."

"Now I'm asking you to do for me."

I say nothing.

She goes on, "What is it about my wanting more that makes you want less? Do I intimidate you?"

I shift.

"Why does the man have to be the one who drives the sex? Why?"

I let her vent, hope the batteries run down pretty soon.

She says, "Every day I have to review my life, ask myself how I got here, what's more important, pleasing others or being true to myself. I do that every day."

"What's your point?"

"What I'm trying to say is that you should feel me on that. You broke away from what was expected of you. You had to disappoint a lot of people, but you found yourself."

"True, I write." When I say that, I feel like a nervous teenager, young and wishful, the same teenager who stood in front of his old man and told him that he wanted to take a different road. And I wonder what my old man would think if he could see me, hear me now, in this moment. My voice sounds younger, almost as if I'm talking to my daddy now when I say, "That's who I am, what I do. I write."

"And I'm proud of you. I'm your biggest fan." Nicole pauses, thinks, speaks with ease, "I don't get it. Why does everyone want me to change when I love who I am?"

"Because . . . because we're assigned roles. Men do this, women do that; normal people do this—"

"*Normal.* There's that biased, subjective, insensitive word again."

"Give me a break. Damn. You know what I mean."

"People can't heat me up, pour me into a mold and make me be whatever they want me to be. They can't make me . . . conform. I don't conform."

"Even the nonconformist conforms."

"To who?"

"To the nonconformists."

For a moment, we sit and say nothing. We're planes in a black cloud, spiraling out of control.

Nicole whispers, "I'm trying to include you in all of my life. I want you to see all of me."

Silence.

"Enough bullshit," I tell her. "If I give you this fantasy, are you gonna try to get back to where we were?"

Those bracelets sing when she raises her hand to her face. "Things have changed over the last few months."

"What things? I need you to be who you were before you moved up here. I want my inexperienced, body-shy, frigid country girl from Elvisland to come back to me."

She says, "Evolution moves forward, never backward. Butterflies never become caterpillars."

7

Some time goes by. Some talking. At some point I hold her. Touch her. And that naughty grin blooms on her face. The one that starts in the left corner of her mouth, and expands with desire. We lay back under the covers. And we explore each other. The magic is always there. The chemistry remains so strong.

I put my mouth on her breast, a hand between her legs, tell her, "You're wet."

Her bracelets jingle as she moves me up and down. "I know."

"When did you get wet?"

"When you opened the door. How many times do I have to tell you that you have this effect on me?"

"Thought you were mad."

"I might get mad, might scream and shout and hit you upside the head with a pot, but Bermuda is never, never, never mad at you, don't you know that? She always welcomes you."

I kiss her. Touch her.

She says, "Seven years and I still excite you?"

"Just like you did in the Jeep."

Her tongue traces from my chest until the heat from her mouth consumes that growing part of me. She used to be afraid to do that, now she won't stop until I beg for mercy.

She stops savoring, stares at my handle with studious eyes. "Hard to believe all of this goes in me."

We turn, and like cats, we do each other at the same time, slow and easy.

Her tongue traces up and down as she moans. "You are the pussy-eating king, you know that?"

"Why, thank you."

"You always give me honeymoon sex."

I look at Miss Bermuda. Talk to her. Touch her. Taste her. I love her aroma on my face.

Nicole shudders. "*Oooo.* You're making Bermuda quiver."

My phone rings again. We're too busy pleasing each other to stop.

She pulls her locks and squirms. "I want you on top of me."

I say, "French. Ask me in French."

"*Baise moi.* Ooo, baby. *Baise moi.*"

The phone rings again.

Nicole bucks, pulls me deeper inside her, slaps my ass in a steady rhythm, chants how much she wants me, needs me, loves me.

I wake in the middle of the night, and Nicole isn't in the bed. The curtains are open and the light from the moon and stars let me see that she's not on the other side of those plantation shutters, working. Looks like she left me in the middle of the night. Then her voice wafts to my ears from the bathroom.

"How was I supposed to know you locked yourself out of the house?" She sounds sweet, sensitive, so caring. That immeasurable passion is there, being given

to her soft-legged lover in a tone I thought reserved
only for me. So concerned. Maybe she's crying a bit.
"How did you . . . called a locksmith? Two hours? In
the cold? I'll give you the money . . . no, I'll give you .
. . please . . . Ayanna . . . don't be difficult. Okay. Okay.
Sorry, baby. I'm so sorry. No, I didn't do that on purpose. You called here? The Waterfront? He answered.
Why didn't you say something? You called back . . . we
didn't answer. We were . . . were . . . yeah . . . busy."

The taste of Nicole marinates the inside of my
mouth, and I'm drowning in jealousy.

I ease out of bed, walk to the bathroom door, and
like heading into a fire, the smoke, Ayanna's voice gets
hotter, thicker. Nicole's in the darkness, door cracked,
and I can hear Ayanna's voice. It sounds as if she were
here with us. First her name. Now this. Ayanna is in-
vading my senses one at a time.

Loud and clear I say, "Nicole?"

She jumps like a child. The rattle of those bracelets
tell me that I scared her to hell and back.

I've heard Ayanna. And now Ayanna has heard me.

Nicole swallows. Bracelets jingle again, ring in a
rhythm that lets me know she's raising her hand to
cover the phone. "Be there in a second."

"What's up?"

"Using the bathroom. Be there in a second."

"You're on my dime."

I turn and take a step toward the bed. As soon as I
do, the bathroom door pushes closed, clicks, and her
words become muffled mumbles laced with stress. I
watch the clock. Ten minutes go by before she flushes
the toilet and comes back out, slips her c-phone back
in her purse, gets back in the bed. For a while we don't
touch. First her foot rubs against my leg. Then her

hand massages my back. When I don't move it away she comes closer, cuddles up next to me and I feel her breath on my neck, gets so close I can't tell where I end and she begins.

8

We run an easy six miles at the crack of dawn. When we get back, I have a message from André. He's in town for another day. Nicole picks out my clothing before she leaves, that's about seven-thirty. Once again I stand in the window and watch her hurrying into Starbucks, then see her come out with two cups of liquid brew.

Around nine-thirty, I put on my sweats and head into Berkeley.

I cruise up College and find a metered spot near an eatery called Crepevine. Not too far from the college, an area where Jerry Garcia–looking xippies—those are Generation-X hippies—with matted dreadlocks stand on the crowded streets outside the university doing palm readings, Janis Joplin does body piercing, Jimmy Hendrix is selling incense, Joni Mitchell has a deal on crystals, and beatniks who look like Shaggy from Scooby Doo offer to write your name in a grain of rice. A liberal freak fest.

André gets to the restaurant five minutes after I do. He has on a dark sweat suit, leather coat.

He says, "This one of those healthy, tofu and wheat-grass places?"

"Yeah. Like Simply Wholesome in L.A."

"Man, I'm having withdrawals."

"Need a smoke?"

"Naw. Need me some pork. Some red meat or something. At least some catfish."

"They have pork here. That's why I told you to come this way."

The place isn't fancy, but down-to-earth like the rest of the area. We stand in line and order, then we hunt for an open spot, and dump our coats in an empty chair at our corner table.

He grabs the sports section of the *Oakland Tribune*. I have a *San Francisco Chronicle*. I flip the pages, read about local politics, about how President Bush refuses to help California with the energy crisis, and then about the rolling blackouts.

A waitress brings our food. I have a three-egg omelette with spinach, tomatoes, mushrooms, onions, and cheddar. André has a Denver omelette and a short stack of strawberry pancakes.

"You see that shit?" André says. "Cal stomped UCLA by damn near thirty."

"Yeah," I answer and put my paper down on top of our coats. "But UCLA stomped Stanford like they stole something, and Stanford is ranked numero uno."

We talk about CSUN, Webster State, Arizona, Oregon, the bulk of the PAC-10, and the conference standings while we eat.

Then he tells me, "Toyomi showed up."

I chuckle. "Damn. So, she actually came through? Just like that."

"Just like that."

"Big baller."

"Here's the trip part," André says. "She said you looked familiar too. Then after I told her who you were, she got all excited, and then that was all she talked about. 'Dem damn books of yours."

"Stop playa hating."

"At 2 a.m. when my dick is hard enough to knock out Tyson, I don't want to hear a woman say nobody's name but mine."

He tells me about the night. No hard details, just a loose man bragging about his latest conquest.

He says, "She's working on her master's degree."

"Where?"

"Some college out in Palm Springs. Says she's going for her Ph.D. right after that."

We eat, stare out at all the shops, at the flower children and revolutionaries passing by in heavy coats, some with umbrellas in hand, anticipating another winter storm.

André looks like he's in a trance.

I ask him what's on his mind.

"Man," he sighs, "I've been thinking about all the women I've been with. Was looking at Toyomi. Listening to her. That girl is fine. L.A. face and an Oakland booty all the way."

"And it sounds like she's smart."

"She's intense too. Never been with anybody that damn intense."

"Sounds like she was educating you last night."

"No doubt. I was thinking, man, I don't believe I just met her fine ass and I'm hitting this."

I tell him, "I feel ya."

"Funny how that is. You meet a sister, get all excited, then after the orgasm, you want her gone."

"You, not me."

"My bad. Me, then."

I sip my orange juice and listen. Last night I gave

him all of my burdens. Now, no matter how much I'm thinking about Nicole and her offer, no matter how irked I am about Ayanna's calling and I-paging when Nicole is living on my dime, it's his turn to talk, to unload what's on his chest.

"Yeah," he says. "Outside of my ex-wife, seems like it's always like that."

I nod. "Instant gratification. Nothing but instant gratification."

"Maybe I have a defect. You've been with Nicole for as long as I can remember, and I've been married and divorced, and I've been with so many woman I can't remember some of their names."

"Hell, if I'm sticking with the same woman, maybe I have the defect."

We laugh a little.

I nod.

He tells me, "She skis with Four Seasons West. They're going up to Mammoth pretty soon."

"I need to get some more skiing in this season too. Haven't skied since Winter Carnival."

"She asked me if you had a woman, 'cause she got a friend named Shar who digs your books too."

"Nah, but thanks. Not available." I smile. And that proverbial lightbulb clicks on in my head. "That's why you still here in the Bay. Chilling out so you can kick it with Toyomi."

"I don't have another gig for four days, and that's at Mixed Nuts in L.A., so I decided to kick it up here one mo' day. She's gonna try to leave her meeting early. We're gonna hang out."

"You check out of your room?"

"Yeah. Leaving in the morning. Wanna spend some q-time with my daughter."

"Got a place to crash?"

"Toyomi's suite."

"Just like that?"

"Just like that. Toyomi, she's different."

"Guess she's not a chain-smoking, codependent alcoholic that don't read."

I give him a bigger smile. He does the same thing.

I don't bring up Nicole. Don't tell him about her solution to this triangle we're in. I want to, but I think it's best that I don't. He's my buddy, but he doesn't need to know all of my business.

Not long after that, he leaves again.

9

By eleven-fifteen, I'm in my rental car, dressed in black wool and black leather. Wearing CK cologne. Twisties giving me that artistic appearance. The high-tech navigator is on, giving me digital directions to my next stop, and my cell-phone's earpiece is in my right ear. I'm making my way through the congestion on Broadway, creeping up the gritty streets leading through downtown.

Pops asks me, "What city are you in?"

"Oakland. Trying to get to MLK so I can get to Marcus Books."

My pop's voice is that of a raspy, southern-fried blues singer, the type that keeps his mega-church filled with spiritual women with high hemlines.

And I have another tone when I talk to my old man. Not the hip and crazy one I have when I'm talking to one of my homies. Not the intimate one I have with Nicole. Like Eve, I guess I have three faces. Most people have just as many hats, just as many versions of themselves.

An ambulance siren screams in the cold as I ease by construction near Walgreen's. A lane has been shut down and construction workers are jackhammering the asphalt to little chunks. Buses are weaving in and out, making it hard to get two feet without having their fumes for dessert.

Pops grunts, his thinking noise. "How is our girl Nikki doing?"

With him, she is always Nikki. The nickname she had as a child. I see her as Nicole, a woman.

"She's cool. We hung out. Did a jazz joint. Ran. Having fun."

"Her situation changed?"

"Still the same." Before my old man can get going in that direction, I ask, "Where's Mom?"

"Shoe shopping. Nordstrom's having a sale."

"Hide your charge card. She'll close that store down."

He presses on, "You still trying to rescue our lost sheep, son?"

He takes the conversation back to Nicole. He's good at manipulating conversations, good at persuading. He doesn't see it that way, but at times I see it that way.

"I don't agree with your wording, but yeah, I'm still trying."

"Do you think you're in denial?"

That's another thing about my old man. He's so damn direct.

"No, sir. Hope and denial are two different things."

"You have always gravitated toward the difficult."

"I take the road less traveled from time to time."

He makes a sound that makes me feel like a fool. "Well, I admire your tenacity."

"Think I got that from you."

"Mine is about justice, about righting wrongs that have been in this country since we were brought over here. That's the kind of writing you should be doing, writing about righting wrongs, son."

"You're preaching, Pops. Can we have a conversation without the sermon?"

"Why don't you allow her to live her life as she has chosen. Let her and God come to terms."

Then he quiets, inserts that pause like he does in all of his messages from the pulpit, allowing the listener to soak up the importance of what he just said, allowing them to think and feel.

The feminine voice on the navigation system tells me where to turn so I can find my way over to MLK Boulevard. Like L.A., the scenery changes from block to block, switches from blue-collar and white-collar to no-collar, very urban, very South Central–esque. Block to block, I see a few brothers wandering, looking for everything but a job. Only a few, but they stand out. There are plenty of hardworking people out here who live in the middle of a bad reputation. But they don't hang out on the curbs in the cold.

My old man talks on. "There are a lot of women out there. A lot of good women. Some very nice-looking women have joined our congregation. Quite a few come to Singles Bible Study. I'm marrying two couples that met at Bible Study in the next few months. Well, one of them for sure. The other, I suggested that they review their financial concerns and family issues before jumping over that broom."

"Just like you told me and Nicole when we told you we were ready."

"Just like I tell everybody. The checkbook has made a lot of people check out of hotel happiness and move to divorce court before the sun had a chance to rise again."

"But they still get married."

"Right before they get divorced," he says with an air

of disappointment, an air of powerlessness over all of his sheep. He's just as concerned with one as he is for the others. Just as he flies away to champion the big causes, he walks across the street to champion the smaller ones with the same passion. "They do what they want without a thought. That's because everyone is driven by—"

"Damn!" I yell that before I know it.

"Son?"

A sister breaks out between two cars, comes out of that mythical place known as nowhere, and I'm doing a good forty mph, so I have to screech my brakes to keep from running her down. The traffic behind me screeches too; a tailgater almost runs up my tailpipe.

"Son, you okay?"

"Almost had a—whoa! Looks like some drama jumping off."

The sister is as beautiful as a queen, and she's running, a natural athlete moving with the stride of Marion Jones, moving as if she's late for a million-dollar deal on Oakland's version of Wall Street.

Not running. A man is behind her, looking pissed off. She's being chased.

"What's going on?"

"Either domestic violence or this brother is about to jack a sister in broad daylight."

"Stay in your car. Don't interfere with anything domestic. Dial 9-1—"

"No, wait. Hold on, Pops."

The sister has mega skills. She does a fake move, cuts across traffic. Terrified beyond belief, her heels are in her hands, her dark slacks molding to her brickhouse shape. The material of her matching jacket flapping with the wind that she creates as she moves and grooves, her cream silk blouse opening with her frantic pace, opening and allowing her beautiful breasts to bounce in such an erotic way.

Behind her is the man chiseled in muscles, running with an angry lover's stride.

As she passes my car, she grunts, glances toward me with a cry of help in her eyes. Our eyes disconnect and her pace doubles. Muscle man isn't a sprinter, but he's not giving up. He huffs and puffs by my car, sounds like a charging bull with asthma.

"Is he assaulting—"

"Wait, Pops."

She does another move that would leave Jerry Rice in awe; fakes left and cuts to the right, moves like butter. He tumbles to the left, rolling and screaming in frustration as he hits asphalt palms first, scraping layers of skin from his flesh and ripping his OAKLAND POLICE jacket.

I tell my old man, "It's the police."

In a voice that carries fear, memories from cultural abuse gone by, he asks, "You have a camera?"

"Not with me."

"Don't leave. Make sure she's not abused. Bear witness, just in case her civil rights are violated."

"Yes sir, I know what to do. Know what to do. I'm watching, I'm watching."

"Take down any information that might be pertinent, no matter how trivial."

"I remember all you told us to do. Stay out of it until it's calm. Take names, everything."

Police cars swarm from everywhere. She's trapped at a fence that walks the perimeter of the overpass. Surrounded by anxious men. Lights on the tops of ten cars are flashing in celebration.

Pops asks, "What they doing to the girl now?"

"She's still trying to get away. Shit . . . I mean shoot, she threw a shoe at the cops."

"She knows better." His voice fills with worry.

"She threw the other one. Clocked a cop in the eye."

"Are people out?"

"Plenty. Cars are stopped. People have run out of the houses. Lots of witnesses."

"Still, say a prayer. Say a prayer."

I pray. Pray that that woman is Nicole's lover. Pray that she's Ayanna. Then all of my problems will be solved, courtesy of the taxpayers and a crowded five-by-nine at the Free Hotel.

Guns are drawn.

She lowers her head in surrender.

Then she looks to the sky before she turns, puts her hands on the fence, spreads her legs in surrender. She leans forward, the arch in her back forcing her backside to curve toward heaven, her pose reminding me of the humble way Nicole positioned herself to receive me as we showered yesterday morning. Her amorous posture as she broke down, wailed, and let her tears of confusion flow like water.

That woman is crying too. Just like Nicole did in the shower.

I tell my old man, "She's in the police car. Looks like the other cops are laughing at the one who couldn't catch her. He's gonna be the laughingstock of the PD today."

"Our sheep is okay."

"As okay as she's gonna be for a while. They didn't do anything extreme."

"Good, good. You think it was drugs?"

"Either that or RWB."

"RWB?"

"Running While Black."

I readjust my earpiece, let a few anxious drivers go by before I start driving again, those flashing lights putting nonstop rainbows in my rearview mirror, and wonder if that was a sign from above, if that was real, or if that just was me chasing Nicole. If that was a sign telling me that Nicole was about to surrender. That I just need to run after her a little longer.

His voice is shaken. "But what was I saying?"

So is mine. "You were telling about the eligible and desperate women at church."

"We have a lot of eligible women. Pretty women. Very pretty. And intelligent like you would not believe. Two doctors: one is a psychologist and the other a dentist."

"I could use both. They take coupons?"

I laugh. He doesn't.

"Son, this thing with Nikki, I admire your tenacity, but your efforts may be misplaced. Call me old-fashioned, but somewhere you're going to have to draw a line."

I'm still driving up MLK, caught at a light about ten blocks shy of the bookstore. The streets are calm. Me and my old man keep on talking. He's trying to make his point, a point of logic; I'm struggling to get him to understand where I'm coming from, the emotions that drive my actions. My obsession. But no one understands obsession, not even the obsessed.

I try to explain that I've met others, been interested in others for a limited time, but none touch me in the way Nicole touches me. True, they don't bring the drama that Nicole brings, but all bring their own brand of drama, their own issues, and when combined with mine, just don't work.

"When you make a relationship," my old man says, "you're building a house of love."

I slow when I get to the bookstore. Quite a few cars are here; the best parking on MLK is already gone. I make a U-turn and hunt for a space. I tell my Pops, "I'm at the bookstore."

"Then park and listen."

"Don't want to be late."

"Black people ain't never been on time."

"True. If we were on time then Harriet Tubman wouldn't've had to make all those trips."

Pops goes on, "All buildings need a strong foundation. First the foundation, son, then you put your walls up before you put your roof up."

"Uh huh."

"Foundation first, you hear me?"

"Uh huh."

"First the foundations. Most people don't have strong relationships because they are walking around in a house with no floor, clinging to slippery walls, waiting to see who will be the first to fall."

"I know. You said that three times."

"Only said it once."

"I heard it three times."

"A hollow head carries a echo."

"Okay."

"With Nikki, does your house have a floor? Did it ever have a floor?"

I close my eyes for a second, wishing I hadn't called. Every vein in my head pulses. I want to scream my throat raw, but nothing comes out, not a word, not even air.

Maybe one day I'll look back and see how preoccupied I was with my own life, how I didn't see the changes my old man was going through. Didn't see that he wasn't repeating things, but forgetting that he had already said something, and sometimes the engines in his mind were idling, searching for the next gear, sometimes downshifting, moving back three or four conversations, before he got back on track. It's the things that are right in front of our faces that we don't see.

Yes, I did have one singular focus. And that focus was Nicole. And when a man has tunnel vision, he can't see things that are happening in his periphery.

"Okay, Pops. What else is going on?"

"If you were around, if you were more active in our efforts, you wouldn't have to ask. You haven't been around much. Haven't seen you much since Detroit."

He's right. Time has flown. That was back in the summer when we stood out in the heat and humidity at Fairlane Town Center, news helicopters overhead, with five thousand plus people who came to protest in peace: black and white, Christian and Muslim, calling for boycott of the Lord and Taylor, pumping our fists toward heaven and chanting *No Justice No Peace, No Justice No Profits.*

He says, "Generation-X has forgotten whose shoulders they are standing on."

I look at my watch, the time on the console, say, "No doubt."

"That's why I wanted you here full-time, not just sometime, working with me and your brothers."

"I'm a writer, Pops."

"But the things you write about . . ." his voice withers to nothing. I see him shaking his head, his face still lodged in the web of his hand, a hand that can palm a basketball with no problem.

"Reality. I write about reality."

"Whose reality? We create our own realities, son. You have the power to change the world, one word at a time. Don't you think that one-hundred-fifty years from now, people will look at what you're doing and think that all we black people wanted to do was have sex?"

"No more than if they read a Sue Grafton book and think all thirty-year-old white women can solve every murder, as long as they're listed in alphabetical order."

A moment of silence lives between us.

I tell my old man, "I'm outside the bookstore. People are passing by, waving. Blanche just stuck her head out and waved. Gotta go."

My old man says, "When your mother comes back from her new shoe expedition, I'll tell her that you called. That all is well in your house. And as always, she's concerned about Nikki."

"Oh, wait," I say as I struggle to parallel park at the same time. "The reason I called."

I tell my old man that I talked to Nicole's mother yesterday morning, tell him what she said pretty much verb for verb, insults uncensored.

He reacts with immeasurable concern: "Gasoline and matches."

"Her words to the period in the sentence."

"I've prayed and prayed for that ornery woman."

I say, "She's a brick wall."

Nicole's mother is an educator on the Harlem side of Memphis. A woman who doesn't go to work to make friends with children, to counsel, but shows up every day to do her job. A hard woman.

He grunts like a boxer who has been hit below the belt.

He asks, "You mind if I give Nikki's mother a call?"

"It's your dime. Gotta go."

I tense, wait for his final words of criticism.

He says, "Kiss Little Nikki for me."

"I will."

"Love you, son."

"Love you, too."

Then he's gone. I sit and soak in what he's left behind. His wisdom. His voice. His bias.

I want him to give me his blessings, but he never does. My career is my Achilles' heel. *I'm a writer and I'm sensitive about my shit.* More sensitive with my old man than I am with the handful of anti-fans who critique my every move, the ones who make it their job to try and dismantle mine. His approval would be gold. But he always sings a song of regret. Always reminds me that I am his lost sheep, the one that he will always try to bring back to his flock.

From where I sit, I see people going into Marcus Books. That look of excitement on their faces.

Wish my old man felt the same way.

I double-time my way inside the Afrocentric bookstore, see at least sixty people are here already, hug the owner, a few other people I've seen over the last eight books, grab a cup of tea. I mill around with the beautiful women from Sistahs on the Reading Edge, the book club that is sponsoring the event.

A few people new to the scene come over, holding a book, looking at the photo on the back, then looking at me first in confusion, then realization. "Oh, my God, it is him . . . I mean you. It's you."

"He looks bigger on the picture."

Everyone seems so normal, so regular. I look in their

eyes and search for secrets, for hints of what kind of lives they have after work, but all of their bones are well-hidden.

We all laugh and talk, but my mind is not here. Not yet.

Someone interrupts. "Look, I have to pick up my baby because it's flu season, and he's sick and the sitter says he threw up twice so that means I have to leave and—"

"No problem."

People are talking, but my mind is way back to the end of my high school days, when I stood in my old man's office at church and struggled to tell him that I had other plans for my life. His rugged, powerful voice chilled me from head to toe when he looked me dead in my eye and said, *"I've spent my life preparing you to help me."*

I told him about when he took my brothers and me to Chicago in the seventies. He was on another crusade, so we spent the trip visiting my mother's mother. My grandmother took us to the south side of Chi-town to see one of her friends. A man named James Baldwin. We were at a small, black, very crowded bookstore. People were snapping photos. The people, the excitement, and the things he wrote about, I don't know, that one moment changed everything for me.

Just like that one moment in Paris changed everything for Nicole.

When I finished telling my old man what I wanted to do, he said two words: *"I'm disappointed."*

"Pops, I—"

"You can go now."

"Pops—"

"Baldwin sat in Paris while all of us were over here fighting for freedom. He showed up and thought he could get off a bus and tell everybody to behave and everything would be okay. Well, this is work. Everyday work. We lose great men every day. I lose friends every day. We lose little girls every day. And you want to be like him? A man you don't even know?"

"Not like him. That's not what I'm saying. Pops—"

"I said you can go now. Let me prepare my sermon."

I leave the past behind when another sister who has to hurry back to her daily grind comes up and extends a blue pen. "Sign it 'To my best friend, the sexiest woman in the whole wide world who helped me write this book.' "

I back off a bit and ask, "Have I met you before?"

"Of course not. And sign a sheet of paper for my momma, my aunt, my cousin—"

I laugh.

My I-pager starts blowing up.

It's Nicole. Her message reads like a pissed-off diatribe. I don't I-page her back. My cell phone goes off. Nicole's work number pops up on the ID. I don't answer, just turn the c-phone off. Another I-page comes, then another comes not too long after that, while I'm taking a few questions. That's my Nicole. She gets pissed off, she will call or page until you answer her rage. Not calling her makes her go crazy. A subtle victory in this game. Another page comes. It's a long message, but the gist of it is: *Get your ass here to Siebel as soon as you finish.*

10

Siebel Systems is in Emeryville, a one-exit town that hugs Oakland like a jealous lover. Ross, Tower Records, Old Navy, Pier 1 Imports, and other stores make up the Powell Street Plaza.

Inside the corporate building, I ease by a crop of workers who dress in blacks and grays, classic tones made to absorb heat in the winter and make them look like they're in an ad for Hennessy cognac. All of the white-collar crew is moving like they are on speed, hustling and talking at a cyberpace that's too quick for me, in a cyberlingo that baffles me to the bone. So much energy is this nine-to-whenever crew, living in a get-it-done-yesterday world.

The secretary on the seventh floor stands out from the rest. She has on black and brown mud cloth; her glass-top desk shows that her skirt is short and she has a serious run in her hose, the left leg.

She motions with her head. "Please have a seat; I'll check her availability."

My palms are sweating. I wipe my hands on my pant legs and more sweat appears.

I crash on an orange sofa, fidget for a while, then, so I don't look stupid while I wait, peep at a brochure that wants me to know that this company is the world's leading provider of e-Business application software, that it has five thousand employees in twenty-eight countries, ninety-seven offices, that Fortune ranked it among the "100 Fastest-Growing Companies" with one of the "Top 25 Executives of the Year" who has produced one of the "Ten Most Important Products" in e-Business applications.

Yada, yada, yada.

The secretary calls me back, says, "Straight through that door, turn right. Back corner."

I move like chains are on my ankles, like John Coffy taking his last stroll down the Green Mile.

The entire floor has custom-built, pastel cubicles, fluorescent lighting, ceiling-high windows, designed with a view of the outside world. The openness is a well-thought-out strategy that lowers anxiety and keeps the Ritalin-deprived from flipping out.

Nicole stands at the end of the hallway, her locks hanging below her shoulders, reading something and waiting on the mauve carpet. When she sees me, she marches toward me at an arrogant pace.

Without warning she snaps, "My baby sister called me. You know why? Because my mother called her. You know why? She told me you called my mother. And guess what? Your father called my mother not two hours ago. Guess who they were gossiping about? What was up with that?"

I match her tone. "Is that why you keep I-paging me?"

"I damn near came to the signing and went off on you. Don't *ever* call my mother again."

"Calm down."

"This is calm. When it comes to my mother, this is calm."

She marches on without me. I don't follow her. She looks back and sees that I'm not chasing her and she waits. I take my time about catching up with her. It's silly, but this is us, what we do.

I've been with her seven years. This anger is nothing new.

Then I ask, "How is your day going?"

"Outside of that, I'm surrounded by idiots. Doing these freaking quotes for customers in South Africa, not sure if the e-Biz database has been updated, trying to explain the product migration strategy and product support benefits of continuing their maintenance year after year."

"Nicole, that's way over my head."

"Working on a very complicated compromise."

"Where nobody gets what they want."

Her eyes tell me she knows what I'm saying. She responds, "But with the right compromise, right set of rules, with an openness and a willingness to trust and try, everybody wins in the long run."

Nicole puts on an all-business smile, speaks to a few people as we stroll.

Nicole's office surprises me. On her stark white walls, she has colorful, framed posters that give definition to "excellence" and "motivation" and clichéd corporate proverbs that boast her as a company woman, nothing that tells who she really is, just things that reflect the professional mask she wears when she's playing this corporate role.

I move the conversation away from our drama, say, "This place is pretty clean."

"Clean desk policy. Impresses clients."

She sets free a burst of air.

I'm watching her.

She asks, "Eat lunch? I have half a veggie sandwich and a banana."

That's her subtle way of trying to apologize for going off on me. She's still angry, just hasn't figured out what to do with that temper tantrum. She hates losing control. Always has to be in control.

"Snacked at the bookstore."

I tell her that she looks good in her black jeans and orange blouse.

She asks, "These jeans make my butt look big?"

"No, but your ass makes those jeans look small."

She extends both middle fingers my way.

On her L-shaped desk, a contemporary U-shaped thing made of heavy glass and black metal, next to her cherub are pictures of her family, photos taken in front of her parents' two-level brick home in Harbor City. Her mom and stepdad surrounded by Nicole's eight older brothers and three younger sisters, the Mississippi River and land leading to West Memphis, Arkansas, in the background. Nicole's the only one absent from that picture. Her youngest sister probably mailed it to her.

My child is dead.

Nicole says, "You hear me?"

I snap out of a trance, shake off that chill, erase the echoes of that unwanted voice. "What?"

"Finished your laptop. Deleted a lot of junk. System's running at seventy-nine percent."

"Seventy-nine percent good?"

"Decent. Should stop hanging up now. Just don't get another Compaq."

A good fifteen minutes goes by before her voice evens out. She can't stay mad at me, just like I can't stay angry with her, no matter what.

She comes closer. "Tonight. We can all hook up tonight. Have some fun."

"Why so soon?"

"Ayanna's going to Italy next week. You're only here a few days, then you're off to New York and Atlanta and wherever. And since you're gonna be on the road, I'm gonna meet her in Italy."

"Italy." I try hiding my swallow, but I can't. "Must be nice."

"Only reason I'm going is because you said you were going to be on the road."

"Haven't been there since I was a kid."

"And of course, you're dealing with two women, so you have to work with other logistics."

"Such as?"

"Sister Moon." She chuckles, sounds both nervous and anxious. "It's a good time for us, both of us, right now."

"Seems kind of rushed."

"Not soon enough. It's time for all of us to meet and move to the next level before we chicken out."

"Tonight. Your friend down for whatever?"

She nods. "She's open to new things."

"Sounds like you've been busy working this compromise."

"Well, yeah."

"Never told me why you broke down in the shower." I say that without a segue, catch her off-guard.

"Really don't want to get into that. Don't push it, either."

We're still staring, still not blinking. Her eyes beg me not to press the issue.

A series of fast taps on the door breaks the moment. A welcome break.

The corporate smile returns to Nicole's face and she tells them to come in.

It's another woman, a little older than Nicole, but her subordinate. They talk about that South African thing. Nicole dominates the woman with knowledge. Hard to believe that this intelligent creature gives me her mind, body, and soul. I'm in awe of her. Have been since I met her.

Ten minutes later, the woman leaves.

Nicole locks her door.

We stand in the window that yields a view of the Bay Bridge to the left, Treasure Island straight ahead, and Alcatraz on the right, all of that history in the shadows of the Golden Gate.

Nicole says, "I want this to go right. I want it to be the right thing to do. Don't want to come off as selfish. This can work."

We hold each other and stare out the window, watch a world moving by at a pace so fast.

I ask, "You love her?"

"Love both of you, you know that."

"You love her more than you love me?"

She pulls away. "Dammit, don't do this to me. Don't push me. You've always pushed me and I've never liked that. Have to be gentle with me. That's all I ask. Don't back me into a corner."

"Nobody's pushing you. Can't push a mountain."

Her phone rings.

She answers, then covers the receiver and whispers, "It's the legal department."

Thirty minutes pass. When Nicole is done, we kiss, touch, get lost in each other. I sit her on her desk, put my face down into the crotch of her jeans, nibble at her wishing well. I look up at her warm grin, glowing eyes.

"Such a freak." She laughs and with her soft hands she pulls my face back up to hers. "Maybe one day I'll wear a dress to work and invite you up here for lunch."

"Bet."

"Mmm," she hums, chews my lips. "Have to get back to work, sweetie."

She redoes her lipstick, fluffs her locks, then hurries me to the elevator. My laptop is back inside my brown leather messenger bag. I'm using the bag and my leather coat to cover my fading erection.

Nicole squeezes my hand and says, "I saw the wedding pictures in your bag. I cried."

I squeeze her hand and feel the dampness. Nervousness and anticipation soak her hands.

As she waves good-bye, she whispers, "Tonight."

With dank palms, I nod. Nod and hear my old man's voice, *draw the line*.

As I wait for the elevator, the secretary stares. People notice me. Not because of the books. Phone calls have been made, they have been busy shooting each other intercompany e-mail. *They know.* I see it in their eyes. Ayanna has been here before. Has been in Nicole's office. *They know.* I feel that they are waiting for me to leave so the whispering can begin.

I don't give a fuck. She's the fire in my loins. My sin in high heels.

And we're standing in a house with no floor.

PART TWO

Meeting of Cod and Quim

11

Eight p.m.

The ocean has swallowed the sun. Streetlights brighten the Square.

I'm back in Jack London Square, the capitalist area named after that socialist sailor, in a place packed with people who are living for the weekend, sitting a cappella at a red-and-white-striped table inside a loud and overcrowded TGIF, just like Magic's rambunctious TGIF down in Ladera. Everyone is sipping on alcohol, eating fried food, and thanking God it's Friday. Over and over, I keep folding and unfolding a napkin in between working on a cup of hot chocolate.

Too many conversations mix with music blasting from the back room. And that blends with an Amtrak whistle that blows a long continuous shrill. The room vibrates from a serious bass line; outside the world rumbles louder and louder as the Amtrak gets closer and closer, then passes, and the rumble dies away.

"Do you think you're in denial?"

"No, sir."

Nicole's I-page said to meet here. Her live-in companion will show up as well.

We're to meet and take it from there.

We'll all be face-to-face, eye-to-eye.

Why don't you allow her to live her life as she has chosen?

I shake those words out of my head, sip my hot chocolate, and feel every drop of blood that races through the veins in my neck. Can smell the sweat in the palms of my hands; hear the salt as it dries, then feel new sweat replacing the old.

People are heading to Scott's Seafood, valet parking on the cobblestones.

I wipe my palms over my black jeans, straighten my black sweater, toy with my twisted mane. My reflection is in the window. I can see me, and see through me. Like I'm a ghost.

I watch women wearing braids, twists, locks, wavy Afros, short natural styles. Search for one that walks like Nicole, looks like her. All are beautiful. Some have more curves than Lombard Street. A million queens I could pursue and flatter. But my heart is elsewhere. Then my mind fucks with me again. Each woman that passes, I imagine that she's the one who laughs and does things with Nicole.

I watch women as they come inside, see one woman who looks like Tupac on a bad hair day, another who looks like Bernie Mac on crack, wonder if Nicole would be attracted to either of those.

Another woman at the bar sees me. I've made eye contact with her twice. This time we both stare too long. She touches her locks, hair that is deep red, the color of hearts and passion, with hints of deep yellow, the color of the sun at high noon, earth tone colors that work on her butterscotch complexion.

We hold the eye contact for a few moments.

She fondles her remarkable locks; the thin Sister Locks style that originated in San Diego. Her astonishing mane is almost to her shoulders. Again she touches her strength in a flirty gesture, picks up her purse and heads toward my table, and moves with grace and sexiness, the stroll of the girl from Ipanema. In her left hand is a book; I would recognize the dark orange cover from a million miles away. It's one of the books I wrote, the one from last year, the one with the hysterical wedding scene. Yep, one man's tragedy is another man's punch line. She looks at the picture on the back of the book, at me, at the picture, at me, raises the novel a bit, and I nod, pull my pen out, get ready to sign.

She says, "You look different on the back of your book. You changed your hair."

"Thanks. Surprised to see somebody in TGIF with a book. Want me to sign—"

"That wasn't a compliment. And no. You did Nicole a disservice by writing this . . . this . . . *this*."

This is her. Nicole's whatchamacallit. I stand there with a stupid for-the-fans smile frozen on my face.

She's a petite woman wearing a short leather coat over a slender black dress. A silver chain with a silver ankh on her swan neck. Silver bracelets are on her left wrist, just as many as Nicole wears. Subtle nose. Generous lips painted a deep brown. Something about her, her dark brow, the strong lines in her face that are more classical than beautiful, reminds me of the French actress Juliette Binoche.

Ayanna's bracelets jingle, sing an aggravating song when she stuffs her copy of my book inside her coat pocket. Pretty much bends the paperback to death getting it inside, as if it's not worth the price on the cover. Then she greets me eye-to-eye.

"My name is Ayanna."

I say, "Your name means blessed."

"In Native American culture, yes." The language in her eyes tells me that she's not impressed with my knowledge of things that would get me points playing Trivial Pursuit. Her stoic stare tells me that not much impresses her. Her voice is strong, articulate, wraps around me, seeps into my flesh; her tone is condescending. "It also means beautiful flower. I prefer the latter. Nicole prefers the latter as well."

I pause when she says Nicole's name. That catches me off guard.

"So," I exhale as I put my pen away. "Why does Nicole like beautiful flower better than blessed?"

"Aren't you a nosy little fucker? That's between Nicole and me."

I say, "Guess I made it here first."

"Nope. I was here before you. Saw you strut in from your fuckhaven across the way."

That catches me in my gut. I nod, stay polite to this woman, ask, "How long have you been here?"

"Long enough to watch you watch other women."

"Making accusations?"

"Just observations."

She shakes my hand, her flesh warm, and then she looks at her palm.

I ask, "What are you doing?"

"Counting my fingers."

"Maybe I should do the same."

"I'm not the thief."

"I've known her for seven years. So who's the thief?"

Her mouth opens like she's about to say something important, but she rests in her seat, sips her water, then speaks. "Don't irritate the alligator until after you cross the stream."

"My feelings exactly."

Ayanna sits across from me, our chairs next to the window. Sits like she's the perfect lady.

With an unimpressed tisk she says, "I see your books everywhere."

She said that like she's been trying to escape my face, pretend I don't exist, but can't.

"Black History Month," I say. "We be boss for twenty-eight days. Twenty-nine in a leap year. HNIC until March rolls around. Then we get downgraded to servants and returned to the master publisher, or tossed in the back forty."

With sarcasm she delivers, "Nicole says that you were almost a *New York Times* best-seller."

"Almost." I nod. "Next book maybe."

"Then NYT must mean Nigga You Tripping. That's the list you need to be on. Your writing is trite and commercial."

"So I've heard."

"You're no Baldwin."

I'm jarred. She said that as if she knew about my moment in Chicago, as if she made that comparison based on my past, as if she were there standing next to me. I breathe through my nose, feel the lines grow in my forehead as I respond with mild venom, "Never said I was."

Her teeth grind. "There are many writers right here in the Bay much better than you, people who write about something important, but you do better than them. I don't understand."

I shift. "You'll have to ask the people who buy the books."

"Maybe better to ask the pimps who are selling them."

Her eyes stay away from mine as mine avoid her. Not out of fear. But out of pretense to be in fear. At times it's better to pretend to be weak. To make your opponent over-confident. The breakdown of an opponent starts with the mind, disabling him or her mentally. Ayanna wasted no time with her attack.

In my periphery, I search for flaws in this creature that calls herself Ayanna. She has amber, catlike eyes, sensuous lips, an aerodynamic build. The brain is the sexiest part of any creature, so I don't know if a cerebral deficiency is her flaw. I find flaws in others. Recognize the flaws in me. Flaws remind me that there's a difference between what's real and what isn't.

Ice covers her voice. "Nicole tells me you have an eatapuss complex."

"Does she?"

"I guess it's a physical thing."

I refuse to wince. "She's never said anything about you. Guess she's not impressed with . . . whatever you do."

The music in the back room kicks up three levels. People are dancing, creating so much heat, and with the humidity that Ayanna has brought to the table, it begins to feel like July in Houston, and I'm inside a car at high noon, windows up, air conditioner off.

Ayanna says, "Every man's fantasy."

"What?"

"She's offering you every man's fantasy."

I've thought about that since Nicole has eased her carnal desires on my table. Once upon a time, that was my fantasy, to be able to give and receive pleasure with more than one, to create euphoria for two. In some parts of my brain, maybe the primitive part, maybe the part that holds fantasies that will forever be unfulfilled, it still rests in an easychair, sipping on lemonade made from fruit nurtured in the California sun. But that fantasy was never meant to be reality. And it didn't include someone I was involved with on a serious level, always a distant face on the cover of *Ebony*, or a *Jet* centerfold, maybe even a hood-rat–looking Miss Scoop with a Pa-DOW! body, but never Nicole. Experience has taught me that one woman is enough. One is drama; two is trouble. And I'm staring trouble between the eyes.

I tell her, "You've got a helluva mouth. Got your ass way up on your shoulders."

"I take that as a compliment. Never been good at make-believe."

She twists a napkin in her hand, chews her bottom lip, then turns her eyes away. My fingertips are tapping anything they can reach: my legs, arms, the table.

She leans in. "You don't understand what we represent, do you?"

"Maybe I don't."

"Figures. I'll skip the psychology and dumb it down for you. Without you, Nicole has no interest in me. And without me, she has no interest in you."

I laugh the kind of laugh that tells her she almost had my respect, almost had me by the throat. "So, you're telling me, in a Psych 101, *Fraiser* kind of way, that combined we make her complete."

"Just repeating what I've been told. That's the bullshit she's feeding me."

"Bullshit's out of season in this stable. I'm more important to her than you."

"Oh, really? Let me hear your argument."

"Adam and Eve, Ayanna. Adam and Eve."

"The greatest myth ever told."

"Truth is always powerful." I say that, and for a moment, I hear my old man's voice coming out of my body. "Truth is always powerful."

"Your weakness is that you think like a man. A dick will never be more powerful than a pussy."

Again I'm jarred by the contradiction of her feminine face, articulate words, intellectual eyes, and brutal lexicon. First my career, now my dick. She's trying to dismantle me.

I reply, "Now I know where she gets her new crassness from."

"Let's face it. Men are on this earth for two reasons: to kill each other and fuck over women."

"So do you piss standing or squatting?"

She nods and says, "Touché."

Then she stares out the window as if I'm unimportant, as if I'm a pebble destined for the curb and her heartbroken face will one day be engraved on Mt. Rushmore.

She says, "Look, I'm upset. Long day. When I'm pissed and tipsy my tongue gets pretty sharp."

I warn her: "And iron sharpens iron."

"Proverbs twenty-seventh chapter, verse seventeen."

"Biblical knowledge, too. I'm impressed."

"Don't be. Not my intention. But impressing someone like you is always easy."

"You don't take compliments too well, do you?"

"From those I admire, yes. You misused the scripture, which is typical. I see that you do as men do and bend the Word until it fits your own purpose."

I sip the last of my hot chocolate. The waitress stops by. She pretty much loses her mind: "Oh, my God. *It's you. It's you, it's you, it's you.*"

I raise my head, reach for my pen, but she's talking to Ayanna.

"You're the attorney who took that racist Christian school to court. Don't tell me, don't tell me. They kicked the kid out because he wore locks. The kid was a straight-A kid. His mom and dad were from the islands and that hairstyle was part of their culture and you—"

"And you know the whole case. Impressive. I didn't think anybody cared."

"You were awesome." The girl is so excited that she sits down at our table. The girl is lost in time, drowning in awe, as if she is facing an Amazon from the island of Themyscira. "Oh, my God. This is a trip. Seeing you on television, the way you handled the system and didn't back down, I mean, you went deep and pissed so many people off— Oh, my God. I'm having an intellectual conversation with you. We're like, talking to each other on the real. This is awesome. I wish my group could meet you."

When the girl slows her verbal rampage, Ayanna asks her what type of group she's in. The girl says that, outside of college, she's involved with a group of young people, male and female, who are working on an AIDS awareness campaign, trying to educate kids in an upward bound program.

That's when Ayanna puts on a soft smile. An intelligent smile that makes her look beautiful. And her voice, its tone has changed. Sounds beautiful, clings to the ears.

The girl tells Ayanna that her mom died from AIDS fifteen years ago. Blood transfusion after a car accident. Back in the days when nobody wanted to touch the body. Her mom had to be cremated, ashes scattered to the winds.

Ayanna offers, "Maybe I could come speak to your group one day."

"Would you? Oh, my God. You are way cool."

Ayanna says with a soft laugh, "Don't you have to work?"

She looks around, her eyes wide, as if she just woke up from a dream. "Hot wings. Have to get those people their hot wings."

She takes two steps, then hurries back to leave her phone number and shake Ayanna's hand. "Didn't mean to keep interrupting you and your man."

"He's not my man." Ayanna motions toward me. "This guy's a writer."

The waitress looks at me. "Oh. What do you write?"

"Fiction."

"I don't read fiction."

Victory rises in Ayanna's eyes.

The girl leaves, and Ayanna and I are face-to-face again.

"When you come to Oakland," Ayanna says as if she were never interrupted, "when Nicole tells me she's going to be gone a day, maybe two, I can't eat, lose sleep. I know she's kicking it with you, I know where she's going when she packs her little bag, and I put on a big-ass smile and tell her I can handle this situation, which is whacked to the nth degree, tell her it's cool by me, tell her to go see her friend, to be happy, to get what I can't give her, that I'm not insecure. But I can't close my eyes one damn second without seeing you and her. I stare at the ceiling, wondering what you two are doing."

"I think you know."

"Oh, I know. Your smell gets in her skin. She thinks she's washed it away, but I can smell you on her. I can taste you on her. I taste you. Just like when you're kissing her, you're tasting parts of me. Tasting this beautiful flower. How does that make you feel? Knowing that we're already so familiar?"

It fucks with me. Can't help it. I imagine Ayanna taking bubble baths with the woman I desire and smell in my dreams; hear their catlike whines in the middle of their adrenaline-laced rhythms. I know how Nicole likes to touch herself while we love then put her fingers in my mouth. I imagine them doing the same. My heart is in my throat, trying to climb out and run for its freedom. I sit face-to-face with my enemy, evil thoughts damaging my spirits, unable to breathe out my pain.

Our enthusiastic waitress brings our drinks back, says a few more words to her role model, then moves on, making her way through the crowded room.

I sip my steaming chocolate.

Ayanna sips her wine.

She says, "Little Miss Punctual is late."

Without warning I say, "So, you're taking your aggression out on me because you hate men."

Ayanna speaks swiftly, but her tone isn't rugged. "No, I'm not a man-hating woman. All of my experiences add to my life. They add to the essence of me. To answer your question, which is driven by stereo*typical* thinking, I love my brothers as much as I do my sisters."

"Just trying to see where you're coming from."

"Kind of figured you would be shallow enough to think that," she says. "My problem is that you're having relations with my woman."

"Geesh. We have the same problem. Who would've thunk?"

Her eyes tighten at my sarcasm.

"Yep, you're munching my woman," I say. "At least you are for now."

For a moment we trade our animosities for silence, well, as much silence as we can get in a crowded room filled with rumbles and music driven by a hard bass line. We share an occasional glance, evaluating and summing each other up. In the end our eyes meet and stay that way, both of us refusing to be the first to break the stare, both of us refusing to be weak, refusing to be run away.

She tells me, "You're not what I expected."

"What did you expect?"

"God."

"Oh, really."

"You're not as tall as I imagined. Not as big. Ordinary."

After she finishes dissecting me, I tell her, "You're not what I expected either."

"What did you expect?"

"Lucifer in a push-up bra."

"That's Nicole's mother."

We crack up. I don't want to laugh, she doesn't want to laugh, but we both know Nicole's mother.

I think she's done, but she keeps going. "And speaking of Beelzebub, why did you call Nicole's mother as soon as Nicole left your fuckhaven the other morning? Talk about a wuss."

"That's enough."

"What was that supposed to prove?"

"That's enough."

When my expression shows hostility, she backs down. That surprises the hell out of me.

I take a deep breath.

Ayanna knows too much. Knows all about me, about Nicole's family, knows all the soft spots to strike to deliver pain. She has the kind of knowledge you learn in stolen moments.

Again, my mind drags me naked across barbed wire, takes me where I don't want to go. I imagine them lying in the bed like cats, peach-scented candles burning, Sting playing low and easy, licking each other's genitals, singing each other love songs in response to what they feel. The think lines in Ayanna's forehead, the vein that keeps rising and falling in her neck, the stiffness in her jaw, the way her teeth grind off and on, tells me her imagination is working overtime too.

Ayanna stops tapping the table, checks her watch, looks at me again. "Please understand me. I don't have anything against you. Not yet. I don't know you; don't want to know you."

"Ibid."

"I hate what you represent."

"Ibid."

"What the hell does ibid mean?"

"Same as above. Feeling's mutual."

"Feeling's mutual." She mocks me, then chuckles, shakes her head, messes with her heart-colored mane. "You don't have a clue what I represent. Or how I feel. Or what I'm going through."

She shifts. I join in with her incessant tapping. Two instruments out of tune.

She tells me, "I love her better than you can imagine."

"How do you figure?"

"Because of what I'll do for her. Because you love with your dick. Let's face it, all men do."

"Do we?"

"A woman's libido is connected to her heart."

"And a man's dick?"

"To his nuts."

I say, "Lay off the crack pipe."

"I love from my heart." Ayanna speaks like I'm a child. "A relationship is built on trust. Not sex. I say this through experience. Love ain't sex and sex ain't love. Do you love her or are you just fucking her—"

"Fucking her?"

"Glad you're not hard of hearing. Do you like fucking her when it's convenient for you to pop up here for a couple of days and get your swerve on?"

I smile and lean so close she can feel my breath. "You know what—*fuck you.*"

"Not if I was out of batteries, cucumbers were extinct, and you were the last dick on this world."

That halts me. This time I say, "Touché."

She sips her wine. I lean back and sip my hot chocolate. Our words are harsh, but the tone is easy, at a lover's volume. No real frowns. Poker faces. Two players trying to win with the hand they've been dealt. People at the tables on either side of us can't tell our true relationship. The room's too noisy for our voices to carry.

I glance out the window, peep at the shops across the cobbled walkway.

My heart double-times.

Nicole is right there. A stone's throw away. Inside Jack's Bistro, in the bakery part, sitting on a barstool. Sipping coffee. Eyes trained on us. Watching, watching, watching.

Ayanna's eyes follow my interest, look to see what changed my expression. Her reflection jumps when she sees Nicole.

I ask Ayanna, "Did you know she was over there?"

"No. When did she . . . she's been right there?"

"Watching us like we're a damn science project."

For a moment we lean forward and whisper like players on the same team. For a moment.

Nicole has on jeans, gray sweater, brown leather coat, shoes the same tone as her jacket. Exposed, she comes out of Jack's and heads straight toward the window. She has an expressionless face, and then she crosses her eyes and sticks her tongue out. Makes that cute monkey face. A juxtaposition of moods.

We laugh at her silliness; she smiles.

Ayanna extends her left arm toward Nicole, the one with the bracelets, makes them jingle. Nicole hesitates, then does the same, extends her left arm, makes her bracelets sing back. Like a ritual.

Nicole heads through the crowd out front, a line that has grown at least forty yards since Ayanna came to my table, and Nicole struggles her way toward the front door.

The fire in my loins; my obsession.

In the moments that she's no longer visible, when we're no longer visible, we stop smiling.

I tell Ayanna, "Like I said, I've been with her for seven years."

It's taking a long while for Nicole to get inside, to make her way to the front door. The place is so packed, is becoming a borderline fire hazard, and security is working too hard, all the GED-looking rent-a-cops acting like they're in the Secret Service, keeping people from coming inside. Nicole smiles, and when the guard tries to assert some minimum wage authority, she frowns and points toward our table.

I repeat, "Seven years. You're just a bump in the road."

As Nicole approaches, Ayanna says, "I've known her for eight years."

Her tender words slam me headfirst into a brick wall.

"So, blind man, who is the thief?"

My mouth remains open like the capital letter "O."

She says, "Stop looking like you have lockjaw."

I close my mouth. "You're playing games."

"I don't play games. Not even bid whist on the Fourth of July."

I try to hide the fact that she's cutting into my skull with a knife. She's good. A worthy opponent.

When Nicole gets close, we both give her happy faces and wait to see which one of us she will hug first, on which side of the table she will sit.

Nicole stops shy of the table, smiles an ethereal smile, and with the sweetest voice tells us, "Let's go. This place is too crowded."

Ayanna asks, "You sure?"

Nicole tisks and shakes her head. "If assholes could fly this place would be an airport. Let's bounce outta here before my peaceful spirit leaves me acting stupid."

I leave enough money on the table to cover my drink; Ayanna does the same for hers. She leaves her business card and a healthy tip for her number-one fan.

12

We take the cobblestone walkway toward the Amtrak station, then turn around and come back, eye browsing all the specialty shops. We pass a few homeless women, another brother wearing a shirt that screams STOP THE EXECUTION OF MUMIA ABU-JAMAL!

Nicole says, "Ayanna's mother is a fascinating woman. She's German and Dutch, born in South Africa, and raised in San Antonio, Texas. Her dad is from Kalamazoo, Michigan. But she grew up in D-town, went to Pershing High School, graduated valedictorian, then moved out here to go to Berkeley on a full scholarship."

"So, genius," I say to Ayanna. "Your mother is German?"

"And Dutch. Problem with that? You're looking kinda yellow yourself. If we did a DNA test, bet we'd find some traces of Thomas Jefferson in your blood too."

"Just saying. You don't look it."

"How am I supposed to look?" she says with stern eyes. "You sound bigoted over there."

"My mom's Creole: French, Indian, black. I'm the Rainbow Coalition, so how bigoted can I be?"

Ayanna nods. She didn't know that. She knows a lot, but not all.

Nicole says, "Her dad met her mom when he was in the military. Beautiful couple. Beautiful."

Nicole seizes the opportunity to start a political conversation, one that I've seen on Montel Williams and Jenny Jones too many times to count. Talking about racism is futile and after listening to my old man preach about it all my life, tonight it numbs me, has gotten to the point where it doesn't move me.

But Nicole has a way of pointing the conversation in her chosen direction. It feels like this is a warming up exercise, something to reveal character and expose corners of our value systems. She's trying to paint a clear picture of Ayanna for me, also letting her lover know who I am, maybe even rationalizing why her lover should appreciate me as well. She's selling me Ayanna the same way she tries to sell me Oakland, feature by feature.

Nicole argues, "Personally I think people like status quo. Are afraid of evolution. I mean, let's be real: if Black people mix with Europeans, if Caucasians procreate with Asians, if Mexicans make babies with African-Americans, what's the worst case scenario?"

With mild sarcasm I say, "Me."

"Anyway, mankind will still be here," Nicole replies. She's nervous, choosing her words. "Narrow minds will become wider. But when change is in people's faces, everybody goes into panic mode, everybody freaks out and starts to worry about what they would lose, and not what they would gain."

She takes Ayanna's hand with her left, mine with her right, sending both of us a subtle message. Then she lets our hands go, adjusts her purse, and folds her arms across her chest.

With the magic of Nicole's momentary touch, Ayanna's sashay livens up. "Maybe all of those stupid -isms that have held so many people in psychological bondage will go the fuck away."

I ask, "Okay, people, is this an exercise in existentialism or what?"

We laugh, Ayanna too.

Nicole says, "People are always searching for new ways of being racist. Hair, complexion, religion, height, weight."

"Sexuality," I toss in.

"That's a given," Ayanna says.

Nicole's vibe is different tonight, shows me another side of her being. Shows me that she is developing into a whole new being; her words glow in hues of reds, yellows, and blues. New colors, new energy I've seen corners of, but never in full throttle. She's found a new center for herself.

I look toward the moon, look at the stars that have become diamonds resting on an endless black canvas, and I feel so small. That makes me wonder about the big picture. About other life, other things, other possibilities. Makes me wonder if this rotating rock has the oldest life.

"So, Ayanna," I ask as we cross Embarcadero, a very rugged street, trying to avoid the rises in the two sets of train tracks and the countless imperfections in the road, "are you an atheist?"

"I'm part of a society that accepts you as long as you don't ask certain questions."

"What do you mean?"

Ayanna says, "Being a preacher's daughter—"

"You're a preacher's kid?"

Nicole says, "Her dad has a small church."

"Like I was saying," Ayanna says stiffly, "When I was a kid, one Sunday at Sunday school they were telling us that God made everything."

I make an *uh huh* sound.

"Had to be about seven, maybe eight years old. Anyway, they assured me He makes the air I breathe, the food I eat, the clothes I wear. I asked Daddy if God made everything, then who made God?"

Nicole says to me, "That question has never been answered, not to my knowledge."

I say, "It can't be answered. That's the definition of faith."

"Maybe that was why my old man put his hands over his ears and told me to shut up." Pain is in her voice, but she steadies her tone and goes on, "And of course, me being me, I didn't shut up."

I say, "I'm not surprised."

Ayanna actually chuckles that time. She says. "I reminded him that he taught me to ask questions about things that I didn't understand, things like the letters to the Philippines and the letter to Bernadette. Guess that million-dollar question was different."

I ask, "What happened?"

"My pops turned red, slapped me so hard I saw Africa."

"Damn."

"Then had me on my knees praying so long my skin was raw and bleeding. Excommunicated me from the rest of the family and sent me to bed without dinner."

All I can say is, "Wow. Your old man beat you down."

"Yep."

"What did your mom do?"

"What all weak women do. Cried. Nothing really."

Nicole says, "Maybe we should change—"

"It's okay, Nicole," Ayanna maintains her cool pace. "My old man let me know where women stood in his house. He let me know what value my opinion had. I was to be seen and not be heard."

Nicole is squeezing Ayanna's hand, consoling her.

Ayanna says, "It's cool though. That's just what men do when their true weaknesses are exposed."

I say, "Sounds like you've had a few experiences."

"A few." She clears her throat before she goes on. "Enough to know that when men are proven intellectually impotent, when they realize they have no power, they turn Cro-Magnon and resort to violence."

Ayanna smiles at Nicole. Nicole returns that smile. They look like teacher and student.

Ayanna folds her arms tight as she walks.

I say, "So you are an atheist."

"And if I am?"

"You could end up on the express train to West Hell talking like that."

"Well, my fax machine is working, pager is on my hip, cell phone is turned on, and my home number is listed. I'm not hiding from anybody. If I'm doing wrong, all He has to do is call. Until then, I'm telling it like I see it."

"Yes or no, are you an atheist?"

"Is it any of your fucking business?"

Nicole butts in, "Hold up, hold up, hold up."

We stop. She takes a deep breath, faces us, and smiles.

"It's a little nippy." Nicole twists her lips. "I need to change the temperature around here."

She floats to me and kisses me. Holds me and kisses me as if I were the only one who matters. Ayanna is watching, her bottom teeth clamped down on her top lip.

Then Nicole goes to Ayanna. She kisses her. Holds her ass and kisses her. Ayanna's eyes ease shut, her shoulders relax, and she coos, melts under Nicole's touch.

My heart races. Thump-thumpity-thump-THUMP-thump.

When Nicole is done, she turns and looks at me, licking her lips, her eyes taking my temperature, checking out my reaction. My heart slows, downshifts, calms.

I tell myself that it's not so bad. That wasn't so bad. I can deal.

Nicole says, "I did it. I put it out there. Now it's real for both of you, for all of us. Let's not pretend. No more bullshitting."

She takes a deep breath.

I do the same.

Then Ayanna.

Nicole's voice is sweet, loving. "We're faking like we're hanging out to talk about racism, or sexism, the absence or presence of a supreme being, yada, yada, and tonight, well, you know what this is all about. Love. Both of you know what I want. No secret about that. No hidden agenda is my mantra. I love you both beyond reason."

She tells us how she is a soul divided, a love divided, and she speaks from her gut. Yes, she is divided. But so am I. And I assume so is Ayanna. Nicole is the knife that has split us so seamlessly; the knife that will cut away all that won't fit in this world of hers.

She says, "I want you both without condition. If

anybody can't deal, doesn't want to go into the night with me, doesn't want to experience something beautiful and new, to have our own corner of utopia, you can back away. No harm, no foul."

I swallow. Nicole jingles her bracelets at Ayanna; Ayanna shifts and pushes her full lips up into a smile. Then she jingles her bracelets back at Nicole.

"And we have rules," Nicole says, matching Ayanna's cool expression. "Rules. Not a free for all. The rules will keep this from being chaotic, we know what to expect, or not to expect, from each other."

Nicole touches Ayanna's hair, moves it from her face. Ayanna's hard, attorney eyes are gone.

I ask, "So this is more complicated than a ménage à trois?"

"I never told you, but I hate that term, what it implies," Nicole says. She grins as if she's pleased with my question. She goes on, "I love both of you because both of you are about the heart, and both of you have come in my life for a purpose, a positive purpose, and I want all of our souls to evolve through loving each other. Love is our journey. Not sex. But the wholeness we can get by being open and honest."

Nicole takes Ayanna's hand in her left hand, mine in her right.

She says, "Before we go on, I don't want to assume. I have to hear two yeses."

Ayanna's eyes come to mine, and mine go to hers. Two yeses float in air and meet halfway.

Nicole whispers, "Kiss. Seal it with a kiss."

Her words are simple, intense, wanting, so very hypnotic.

"For me. Kiss. For each other." She sounds like a spiritual advisor. "We have to tear down one wall at a time. Replace the old with the new. Then we create something wonderful."

In a daze, I stare at Ayanna, the streetlights brightening up half of her face, giving majesty to her heart-colored mane. She moves toward me, licks her lips over and over. She's nervous. So am I.

We meet halfway and she tiptoes, eyes open, her liberal fragrance easing to dance with my contemporary aroma, and we kiss like Bogey and Bacall in *The Maltese Falcon*, or Cary Grant and Ingrid Bergman in *Notorious*, stay eye-to-eye, soul-to-soul, as we press lip-to-lip, no tongue, just her breath mixing with mine, and that breath being blown away by the breeze. No hands touching faces, no groin pressing groin. Her skin is as cool as the night, lips are soft, and like mine, they could use a little moisture, but they are full and soft.

Nicole is beaming. "That was . . . sweet. Wow."

In minutes, she's taken us from being strangers swapping insults at a table to two people pressing lips. Ayanna had said that a dick wasn't more powerful than a pussy; she failed to mention whose pussy had the power.

Ayanna isn't so bad, not at all. I understand her mood. She wants the same thing I want, and no matter how many degrees she has, she can't intellectualize this situation to be in her favor. She has no power, just as I hold no keys to this prison we share. She wants me to leave, as I want her to leave. We both want to be the last man, or woman, standing.

Nicole jokes, "But don't even think about doing that on your own."

After that, hand-in-hand, Nicole becomes our centerpiece, our Dorothy on the first steps of this yellow brick road. We walk at a brisk pace into the breeze, skipping over the litter that is blowing in the street, move in sync without talking. Now everybody seems warm, as if they just had a Shiatsu massage at Glen Ivy. So warm our breath fogs in long streams as we exhale.

I know who Ayanna is. She's a thief. And a thief comes to steal and kill and destroy. She's my competition. Be it in the flesh or of the spirit, competition is about death. I want her spirit dead. If going through with tonight, if giving Nicole what she needs will kill Ayanna, then the ride will be worth the price of the ticket.

13

We don't rush right into it. Nicole still wants to keep it a nice date night.

I do too.

So we stop at an adult video over on Broadway. Xanadu has glittering neon lights that call us into that cul-de-sac of erotica, that's where we're led.

Nicole and Ayanna stop by the condom rack. I follow, pass by vibrators the size of a Louisville slugger, and stop near a magazine rack, skip over *Out*, not into k.d. lang, and pick up *Clikque* because it has twenty good-looking sisters on the cover. I flip through the pages until I get to an article about beautiful black women loving down in Atlanta, all naked and loving each other in a hot tub.

I close the magazine, put it back, and look at Nicole, then at Ayanna.

Nicole asks, "What's better, Rough Riders or Barebacks?"

Ayanna makes a face. "I never liked that brand. Those irritate me. The Rough Riders with the bumpy things on them feel pretty good."

Nicole shifts to one foot and raises a brow. "Oh really?"

"From what I remember."

No one asks me.

Nicole jokes that Lambskins stink, are too messy, then winks at me and proclaims that their lubrication isn't something a person would want to taste, no matter how intoxicated. Without lowering her voice, she announces that another brand steals all the feeling, is less real than a vibrator.

I've never seen this open side of Nicole.

Ayanna picks up a package of Midnight condoms. "What about these?"

Nicole chuckles. "I like it black, but not that damn black."

Ayanna says, "Obviously you like 'em high yellow."

Then in Ayanna's eyes I see her thinking, wrestling with a monstrous, difficult thought. She keeps moving, goes from the section with battery-operated vaginas, to the love creams, the butt plugs, to the XXX CD-ROMS. No matter which way she turns in this den of high-tech fuckology, a small room stocked with a thousand tools for everyone from the novice to the professional fuckologist, she can't escape the carnality.

Then she goes to Nicole. I'm right there, standing next to Nicole, holding her hand.

"What brand do you use with—" Ayanna stops on a dime, then clears her throat in retreat, but it's too late to retract, so she moves forward with her words, "What brand did—do you two use?"

I tell her, "We don't."

"Oh."

Nicole says, "It's okay, sweetie. We've been together too long."

"You live here, and he lives elsewhere, travels a lot. Have—never mind."

"Do we need a quick sidebar?" Nicole asks.

"Nah. Court is in recess."

Ayanna blows Nicole a kiss, throws her a wink. Nicole smiles.

Ayanna proclaims, "I want to dance."

Nicole blinks a few times. That caught her off-guard. "Where?"

"Anywhere in San Francisco that serves a decent cosmopolitan."

"If we go over the bridge, let's take him to the Crazy Horse."

"What's that?" I ask.

"Like your favorite hangout in Atlanta," Nicole answers.

"Medu Bookstore?" I ask.

"Nope. Magic City."

Ayanna cuts in, "Let's take him down Telegraph to the White Horse instead. That'll blow his mind."

Nicole laughs. "He's not ready for that. Crazy Horse. He likes strip shows."

I ask, "Okay, what's up with the White Horse?"

Nicole says, "This . . . it's a . . . a secret world. Not many can handle it."

I swallow and wonder what kind of sensual life Nicole has here without me. I'm experienced, but I feel like a babe in these woods. I want to know more about Nicole's life here in Oakland, try to get a grip on her unrestrained appetite, her new forms of entertainment that surpass anything I've ever done. Try to understand the person she is when she's with Ayanna.

Nicole said that when her body is with Ayanna, her thoughts are on me. I wonder if Nicole cries in the shower, if Ayanna holds her shivering body when her emotions overload like they did yesterday morning.

Nicole glances at her watch. "You're acting a little stressed."

"Rough trial today. And I picked up another case."

"Like you're not busy enough. What's the deal on the new case?"

"Stupid-ass elementary teacher went wacko and made a kid lick the blackboard with her tongue."

"You're joking."

"Who is certifying these morons?" Ayanna says. "Just hearing the parents talk about it had me so stressed that I wanted to run to Market Street."

I interrupt. "Market Street?"

Nicole pushes her lips up into a shallow smile, the way she does when she feels exposed. "Downtown San Fran. Weed city. Blunts haven. Indo-ville."

Ayanna bumps Nicole, says, "And I'm running low on my indo. I want to go to Hoe Stroll and pick up a little package from my connection."

"We're not going to Fillmore, Ayanna. We're not getting arrested supporting your medicinal habit."

Ayanna retorts, "Oh, now it's just my habit. Guess you haven't told him you dibble and dabble."

"Not like it's a secret. I've smoked a few trees with him."

I say, "Years ago. Thought you said you had kicked the habit."

Nicole laughs a bit, glances at me with guilty eyes, then bumps her hip into Ayanna. "Maybe we should chill out. Get to know each other better."

"I wanna dance." Ayanna shakes her ass in a hot and humid Luke Skywalker from Two Live Crew kind of rhythm, one that surprises me and gathers my attention, sends heat to my gut like a shot of rum, a shimmy that says she's loosening up, but anxiety still blankets her timbre. She laughs then puts on a playful face and pouts. "And I gots to have me an apple martini. Let me have at least one decent apple martini."

Nicole says, "Thought you wanted a cosmopolitan?"

Ayanna laughs.

I say, "Cosmo. Weed. Martini. Sounds like you want it all."

Ayanna says, "We all want it all."

She shakes her ass.

14

Nicole drives us across the bridge and we go to a club in downtown San Francisco on Sixth. A multi-leveled, warehouse-sized hangout. Dark place. Oldies bumping in one room. Hip-hop upstairs. House music on the main level. Cages on the bottom floor like go-go girls used to dance inside on *Laugh In*. Or in those *Austin Powers* movies.

The combined beats rock the building like an earthquake in the making. Crowded with people whose sweat reeks of the fermentation of imported beer, clothes from hip-hop to Wall Street to garage band grunge, hair in everything from earth tones to shades of orange and purple. All types of people are staggering back and forth, chasing the vibrations of a song they can't catch.

Ayanna sips her second lime-colored, bourgeois brew and watches me and Nicole dance. Ayanna licks her sultry lips as we sweat and laugh. She's taken her coat off, put on a sultry face. Her black dress displays an extreme arch in her back, a curve that forces her toned butt to stand out as if it has a mind of its own.

Nicole says, "Isn't she wonderful? Isn't she beautiful?"

"Beauty is all mathematics. You inherit the right nose, right shape of face, right this, right that, then, as long as you don't have an industrial accident, you look good."

"Admit it. Her body is off the chains."

"Her clothes are cool. Haven't seen her body."

"Ha, ha. What do you think of her?"

"She has a big mouth. Needs to learn when to shut up."

"Whatever. But can't you feel her passion when she steps in a room?" Nicole runs her hand across my face. Her words soften: "Can we go kick it at your hotel room when we leave here?"

"Sure you wanna do that? We could drop her off and go spend some time alone."

She shakes her head. "If you're craving oatmeal cookies, apple sauce won't do."

"Is she okay over there?"

"She's fine. She always acts like that."

"Well, this is a new adventure. If somebody's nervous, they can't enjoy new things."

"I said she's fine," Nicole says with measurable force, then pulls back, downgrades her tone with a wink and a rising smile. "She's jittery because this is exciting. Just like I am."

My talk of nervousness is about me, not Ayanna. Nicole's focus is beyond this moment. She winks toward Ayanna, crosses her eyes and sticks out her tongue, makes a monkey face, an act of silliness that, for seven years, I thought was reserved for me. For us. Another illusion is withering. In response, Ayanna glows like a movie star.

Ayanna's love has risen to the surface, so thick an elephant can ice-skate on it.

"How long have you known Miss Esquire Atheist?"

Nicole smiles in my face, some guilt in her eyes, but doesn't answer. She knows I know.

I ask, "And what else haven't you told me yet?"

Nicole nibbles my ear, whispers, "I love you."

I want to steel myself and become cold, but those three words create instant warmth, at the same time sending a chill up my arm to my brain, setting my head on fire.

She says, "We've gone through so much together. The death of your grandparents. My daddy. Lost a couple of friends along the way."

"Parking tickets."

She frowns. "You had to bring those up."

We laugh.

She says, "And other things. Countless other things."

"Lots of other things."

"And Paris."

That is my tender spot. Nicole is a good warrior. Knows how to win with simple words.

A spiritual connection that has been nurtured over more than half a decade weakens me, and I say that yes, whatever craving you have that can't be denied, I'll see to it that it's quenched. I'll go into the bowels of hell to rescue the woman I love. I'll sacrifice my sanity to get you oatmeal cookies.

I'll fuck you three ways from Sunday if that drives Ayanna insane. I'll do that.

She runs her tongue around the outline of my lips, sucks my tongue, makes my nature rise as she once again reminds me, reminds me as she laughs, "This is your fault."

I taste her tongue as I hold the soft part of her ass,

the part where her flesh curves into her hamstrings, the part I grip when she's on top of me, or I'm on top of her trying to find that new room. I palm that part of her ass, pull her to me, and I press against her.

"I'm serious. This is your fault."

"Well, the way I see it, it's like this: it was there in your blood. Waiting to activate at the right moment. If it didn't happen in Paris, it would've happened somewhere else. Am I wrong?"

"If you throw a match in a house filled with gasoline, who gets blamed for the fire? The gasoline or the man who tossed the match?"

Ayanna watches our passionate conversation, one of accusations and denials and tender kisses. She folds one arm underneath her breasts, shifts her weight on her left leg, stands alone in the crowd and sips her apple martini.

Nicole sips on a mimosa, her backside rolling up against me, the spirits in her head and the rhythm of the boob-shaking, booty-bouncing song by George Clinton taking control.

With a feminine stroll that could stop a show, Ayanna sashays over to Nicole, overlooks me. "I need some attention."

"You always need attention."

"I hate being ignored. Taste this."

She lets my ladylove sip from her drink. Nicole leads Ayanna's glass to my lips, turns the part with the dark lipstick to my face. I sip from that part. Nicole gives Ayanna a sip of her mimosa, makes sure the lipstick part is where Ayanna drinks from, then does the same with me. Indirect kisses on glass.

Ayanna tells Nicole, "Dance with me."

Nicole giggles and tells Ayanna, "Dance with us."

Ayanna finishes the drink, brings her rhythm to the floor, moving with a cha-cha-cha Latin syncopation, on one side of me, rubbing her heat against me, bumping her breasts into me, then her hips into me, again her breasts, turning and vibrating and pushing me with her backside, turning again and pushing with her thighs, making me a sandwich, doing that over and over, showing me that she has more fire, that she's the better dancer.

Nicole rides the rhythm, floats closer to Ayanna, does her dance of enticement, puts her tender and firm body next to her other lover with enough coyness to tantalize, hips moving with naked abandon.

Ayanna smiles and blushes like an innocent girl excited by eroticism, but I can see that she's an experienced woman who loves to dance. Once again, she runs her hands over her locks, bounces her shoulders, spins, shakes, gets lost deep inside the rhythm. The moment Nicole touches her, Ayanna's eyes light up and, despite my ill, maybe not ill, just awkward feelings for her, Ayanna glows and becomes attractive in her own way.

Nicole eases away, puts her hand on Ayanna's ass, touching Ayanna the same way I had just caressed her, creating a look of ecstasy and acceptance on Ayanna's face. Nicole pushes her toward me and says, "Ayanna, I want you two to dance."

"Why can't I dance with you?"

"Get your groove on and chit-chat. I'll be back in a sec."

Ayanna asks, "Where are—"

"To the bathroom."

"I'll go—"

"I can handle it." Nicole's voice sings, as enchanting

as a flute, as seductive as a saxophone. "If I need help I'll scream. Dance. Talk."

We hold our smiles as if we're waiting for a camera to flash.

Ayanna stands in front of me like she's been left naked in the snake house at the zoo. I do the same. Her scent attracts my senses, floods me with the smells of alcohol, patchouli, fear, and indecision. If I close my eyes, I can fool my heart into thinking she's the woman I desire. Her fingers are longer, hands smaller. Imagination fails.

She asks me, "What do you want from her?"

"To get married."

"I see."

"Then travel."

"Uh huh."

"Make love in different countries, as many as we can."

She sings, "Okay."

"Then when we're ready, have kids. Pack up the SUV and take her to brunches on Mother's Day and have them do the same for me on Father's Day."

"Why, that's very *Leave it to Beaver* of you."

"I know. It's a *Nick at Nite* fantasy, but hey, corny ain't always bad."

"Damn shame. Slavery was outlawed years ago, but marriage is still legal."

I chuckle at her humor, start to understand, almost appreciate her sarcasm. "So cynical."

"So, your ultimate goal is procreation. To send your sperm on an Easter egg hunt and enslave her with snotty-nosed children as her shackles."

"Sounds good to me."

"Don't make me puke. Be real. People get married,

have kids, then realize they were better off and much happier being single. I've been counsel at enough divorces to know that for a fact. I've seen too many love relationships become love-hate relationships, then just hate relationships."

"Which are you in now?"

She runs her tongue over her gums. "Which are you in?"

"No hate in my house. Just a struggle to understand."

"Why do you have to struggle to understand what's in your face, what's clear?"

I run my tongue over my gums as well. I tell her, "I'm into family. My dad has seventeen brothers and sisters, all but four by the same mother."

"Talk about overkill. Did your grandmother ever stand up long enough to get a glass of Kool-Aid?"

"They did go all out back in the day."

"Thank God for birth control and *Roe versus Wade*."

I laugh a little.

She tisks. "What you want is a major conflict. You want to serve your ego."

"C'mon. And you're not serving yours?"

She chuckles. "Typical, typical, typical. So self-absorbed that you can't see beyond your own desires."

Her hand smoothes her hair. Her locks have a wonderful aroma, sensual and fruity. And they are irresistible. I want to touch them, feel their texture. But I don't give in to that urge.

I ask her, "What do you want?"

She sighs. "Love perpetually. Resolution eternally."

"You're working those adverbs."

"And Chinese food twice a week. Have to have my orange chicken."

A moment of us dancing, holding each other rocking, and just dancing. She feels warm, relaxed.

"The Chinese food part is easy." Ayanna sighs again. "Love can be the best thing that happens to a person, and can be the worst thing at the same time. That's not fair."

"We're on the same page."

"Writer Boy, we're not even in the same book."

Nicole rushes back through the crowd, eyes those of an excited child, a wild and naughty smile on her golden-brown skin.

She grabs our hands and tells us, "Quick, follow me."

Ayanna asks, "What's wrong?"

"Somebody's tripping on ecstasy."

We run through the crowd and race upstairs. Inside the tiny coed bathroom, alcohol, urine, and perfume permeate the air. Women are in the mirrors, giggling, doing makeup. Men and women are crowded inside one stall, either tiptoeing or standing on the edge of the toilet, cheering as they look over the metal wall into the other stall. We push our way into the powder room, move into the cheers, ease a few of the stumbling drunks aside, and look over into the other stall. Two girls are in the booth. Away from the rest of the world, living in their own little box. Face-to-face. Pretty much bottomless. One straddling. Kissing. Hips rolling against each other. Making love for the crowd that they are too intoxicated to care about. Too deep inside their sin to notice a hundred eyes hovering over their heads. One gets too excited. Moves too fast. Their vibrator drops. Rolls to my feet. I kick it back. The one on top grabs it. Without looking up, they say a well-mannered thank you and keep on loving. On our tiptoes, we blend with the crowd and keep on watching.

I tell Nicole, "Ecstasy. I heard that if you take that shit you can see dead relatives."

"Now you know where they got the plot for *The Sixth Sense* from."

"Truth or truth: ever try it?"

"Once. That crap gave me a depressive hangover. Had a serious Terrible Tuesday."

I nod and wonder who she was with, where she was when she took the drug. "I read that men can't get erections when on it, but when it fades, it's like being IV'd to Viagra and Yohimbe."

"Yep. It has that Spanish Fly effect. You'll feel so wild that you'll do anything."

"Speaking from experience?"

She gives me a curt smile. "I can get you one."

"Where?"

"Look at these weirdos. All I have to do is ask anybody here."

"Serious? Wow. How much?"

"About forty a pill."

"Forty ducats for one pill?" I shake my head. "This is wild."

"You haven't seen wild yet."

Then this sound, like a cat whining in the distance, a purr that grows and grows with their kisses and grinds, and not to forget the humming of that love handle supplied by Black and Decker.

"Look at her come." Nicole says that, her words blending with all the *ooo*s and *ahhh*s. "She's on a magic carpet ride soaring at thirty thousand feet. She looks so beautiful."

Ayanna has been watching the whole time. Listening to us talk, holding Nicole's hand, and watching the performance.

When the show is over, hands are pumping in the air, and there is scattered applause.

We go back to the dance floor. We all dance. And we stay close to each other, with Ayanna dancing closer to Nicole than she does to me. Watching the live porno has changed everyone's mood, has heightened our senses, accelerated the sensuality. Now people are watching us as they dance, as they pass. Ayanna's eyes glow when Nicole touches her, say yes, whatever you need, I'll make sure you get.

A guy peacocks over and intrudes on our flow. He has short brown hair, a six-footer, inches taller than I am. A weightlifter's build under baggy clothes. At first, based on his smile and gaze, I think he knows Nicole, or Ayanna, maybe both, but it becomes apparent, by Nicole's reaction, that he doesn't.

He gets too close to Nicole and asks, "Wanna dance?"

Nicole cringes; her grip tightens around my waist. "No thanks. Have a nice night."

The room is filled with women, coochie central for the coochie deprived, some beautiful, some cosmetically challenged, yet he persists, eyes always on Nicole, eyes fucking her over and over.

He licks his lips, doesn't back away. "One little dance?"

"Back off," I snap.

His cold green eyes meet my stiff gaze. My steel gray eyes become blacker than the political climate of the sixties and twice as volatile. I'll protect Nicole from all enemies both foreign and domestic, do what I have to do. He chuckles in his inebriation and winks at Nicole, reaches to touch her locks but she moves her head. He persists, "I know he can't handle both of you.

I can do more for you than watching some freaks get busy in a bathroom."

Ayanna has become quiet. She moves closer to Nicole.

He reaches for Ayanna, she moves away. Nicole moves to protect her.

The guy's eyes fill with surprise, then he smiles. "I get it."

Nicole snaps, "Brother, please don't disres—"

I pull Nicole away and repeat, "Back off."

"Fuck you and them dykes, faggot."

I push him and he stumbles three steps, drops his drink. The glass shatters. He teeter-totters and gazes down at the floor, watches his liquid foolishness soak into his trendy hip-hop boots.

I'm strong with men, strong with women too, except for my mother, who I love more than the air I breathe, and Nicole, whom I love in ways even I can't fathom.

We stare each other down for a moment, and the prelude to violence scents the air. He creates two fists, so do I, fists that feel like hammers, and the longer I stare the more his face looks like a nail.

Nicole is behind me, gripping my hand, pulling me, leaving me vulnerable, the worst thing a woman can do when a smack-down, no-holds-barred, foot-up-the-ass fight is about to happen, because now she's in the way. Her pulling me is leaving me vulnerable to the first strike in an impending war.

"Sweetie—"

My hand comes free when I pull. I become Sean Penn going after the paparazzi, a pissed-off Jack Nicholson with a golf club in traffic, ready to become the next American Psycho, bump by people and try to get within striking distance.

Nicole catches me, tugs me, gets in front of me, says

my name a thousand times, holding both my arms, again leaving me open to being attacked. I pull, try to jerk free. She will not let me go.

Then he laughs and backs away, his eyes the size of manhole covers, glancing over the part of the crowd who were watching us in a combination of fear, excitement, and boredom. He's not rushing, but as he staggers he glances back three times in ten steps, in caution, because the kick-ass-ask-questions-later look in my eye tells him that I have a dark side, one that will leave him bloody and bruised.

Or dead.

Or leave me dead, leaving this plane of existence with my dignity intact.

Nicole calls my name, her tone extreme, very firm.

I don't answer. My eyes are still on the prize that is fleeing.

Ayanna claps her hands twice, says, "Looks like the cowardly lion was run away by Toto."

Again Nicole calls my name, this time much sweeter.

We face each other.

She smirks. "It's okay, sweetie, it's okay. He's just another asshole."

Nicole touches me and anger fades; winter becomes spring, then when her lips press mine spring becomes summer. Under psychedelic lights her tongue eases to slow dance with mine and I see angels. Thousands of angels smiling with open arms.

Nicole smiles. "Oatmeal cookies?"

I nod. "Oatmeal cookies."

"Your hotel?"

Then I surprise her with my firmness. "No. Your home."

Then Nicole is jarred. "Where did that come from?"

"Your home. Let's shake the spot and go to your crib."

"Well," she elongates that word, "I'd rather go to your room."

I shake my head.

She says, *"S'il vous plaît?"*

Once again she has given me Paris. Once again she's trying to get her way.

I tell her, "Your crib or it's not happening. I wanna see your sugar shack."

"Maybe tomorrow then, after your book signing at Alexander—"

"No. Tonight is the night."

We go back and forth on that for a moment, my position never changing. I remind her that she wants us all to get along, to share, to move toward communal lives at some point. Then she should have nothing to hide. No reason to not want this to happen in her space, in her nest.

"Your hotel. Please?"

I want to ask why she doesn't want us to go to her home and create her fantasy. I know the answer. The same reason I won't take this party back to my room. Only a stupid bird shits in its own nest.

Without shaking my head, without a word, with direct eye contact, I stay firm.

She chews her lip and whispers, "Okay."

Ayanna is behind her, her ears tuned to our conversation. Nicole tells her the new game plan. Ayanna turns and heads for the door, shaking her head. It doesn't take me but a second to catch on. I think Ayanna agreed to give Nicole her fantasy, but didn't want it to happen at her home.

Nicole calls, "Ayanna. Wait."

Ayanna stops on a dime, touches her hair, toys with a long reddish lock, but she doesn't turn around. Nicole goes to Ayanna, caresses her, and I watch Ayanna's expression change. Her anger melts like a snowball at the equator. Ayanna's eyes soften, she licks her lips, licks their ripeness in a way that tells Nicole that she wants a kiss. That she needs a kiss. Nicole gives her a smile, runs the tip of her fingers across Ayanna's mouth. Ayanna's tongue licks what she can get as those fingers pass.

I take one last glance through the crowd. Search for the enemy before I turn my back.

Again Nicole comes over and touches my face, her embrace asking me to let it go.

She asks, "Would you have kicked his booty for me?"

"Would've kicked his ass back up into his mother's womb."

She smiles like I've just slain the almighty dragon. But I haven't. The true dragon is standing nearby with heart-colored hair, the hue of a raging fire, wearing a dress as black as our intentions.

One way or the other, I will slay her. Have to slay her before she slays me.

All for Nicole.

In this age of foolishness, in my quest for wisdom, during these best of times, in the midst of these worst of times, she is my Lolita. With a smile she can get me to do whatever she pleases, give her what she needs.

15

Nicole drives us back over the bridge and heads into North Oakland, takes Broadway to Broadway Terrace, then rides up the winding streets. Hundreds of trees, plenty of leaves that need to be raked. We pass by apartments, small homes, a golf course, see a raccoon or possum dead in the road. Then the houses get larger, start looking like the pages of *Architectural Digest*. The type of area where the hardworking people who ride buses to this part of Oakland and clean these museum-sized homes will never make enough money to own one.

I say, "All the cribs look brand-new up here."

Nicole says, "This is the area where there was a huge fire back in ninety-two."

Ayanna corrects her, "Ninety-one."

Nicole goes on, "Broadway Terrace above the Caldecott Tunnel, this burned down back in ninety-one. Those wood shaker roofs were a hazard."

I say, "Same thing that burned down a lot of Baldwin Hills."

"Yeah. Up here, it was ten times as wild. Flames jumped from house to house. Landscaping was too tall, that's what people tell me. Correct me if I'm wrong, Ayanna."

Ayanna says nothing. Nicole tells me that mountain lions, woodpeckers, deer, all kinds of wild animals live up here in the hills. And these are the hills she runs, why she is getting so much stronger. With every word, she's selling me Oakland again. Ayanna says nothing at all, but I hear her thoughts.

I look at the houses. No two the same. Some are an architect's dream.

"We can see the whole city from our home," Ayanna says, then turns and faces me. "You have a view at your place in Carson?"

"All I can see is the stucco house next door. Maybe a corner of Cal State Dominguez."

There is a smile. Her energy heats up the car. A victory for her.

While Nicole drives, Ayanna goes on, "Nicole tells me you live in a planned community."

"I do."

"Can you add on?"

"Nope."

"How many floor plans?"

"Six. Twelve if you count reversing."

"How many color choices?"

"Three."

She turns back around. "Not much."

"No," I say. "Not much."

Yep, only three bland colors, so the individuality, the freedom I'm witnessing here does not exist in my world. Mine is all about conformity and comfort. About seasons of predictability. This is about freedom to create and be. Once again, I'm living in awe. Once again jealousy rises.

Nicole says, "Everyone was devastated by the fire, clinging to the old, to what was comfortable, but now everyone sees that change is good. They let go of the old and everything came out better."

There is a pause, long enough for Nicole's meaningful words to sink in.

Nicole's fire started in Paris, the flames from a woman, a dancer who set her on fire for ten dollars. All that was old about her has been burned away, cleansed by fire. And now Ayanna is her new flame.

I wonder when Ayanna's fire started.

We pass by a huge house that has an American flag out front. The fifty stars are in place, but the red-and-white stripes, those patriotic symbols have been replaced with rainbow-hued stripes.

I ask, "What's up with all the flags?"

They look at each other.

Nicole shifts, clears her throat.

Ayanna speaks up. "That means the people inside are—"

Nicole cuts her off. "That means they have an alternative lifestyle."

Ayanna makes a sound, like maybe she's not down with the alternative lifestyle statement.

I say, "And they put flags out front?"

Ayanna says, "They're proud. Not ashamed."

For a moment there is tension swimming in the silence.

Then it is interrupted by a *beep-beep-beep*.

Nicole pulls out her I-pager, reads the message, tisks and frowns. "Bad thing about an I-pager is that your job can always find you. This is nothing but an electronic leash."

Ayanna asks, "South Africa?"

"Of course. I'll be so glad when this gets wrapped up."

"We'll celebrate that victory in Spain. We'll leave it behind."

My throat dries. Palms sweat when Ayanna says that.

We ride the rolling hills, pass by land that used to be the home of deer and skunk, ride until I'm lost. Nicole pulls her car up into a huge Spanish-style home. A palace made of mauve stucco and red Spanish tile. Hidden spotlights shine on five or six Mexican palms out front. While we wait for the garage door to whir open with a whisper, I squint and search for a colorful flag. I don't see one out there flapping in the night breeze.

The moment we come in from the garage, Ayanna uses a remote to turn off the house alarm.

Ayanna kicks off her shoes at the door, Nicole does the same, and I follow their ritual. Their unspoken rule. Ayanna walks ahead of us, taking off her leather coat, her stroll still as inviting as the girl from Ipanema. She hand-fluffs her locks, goes into the kitchen, dumps everything on a huge white-tiled island, pulls a bottle of E&J from the cabinet, a new unopened bottle that looks a bit dusty, then asks, "Anybody want a hit of over-the-counter panther piss?"

"I'm fine," I say, then motion toward a picture of Nicole, Ayanna, and the mayor of San Francisco. It stands high over the fireplace. Nicole and Ayanna are in white gowns. The mayor in a black suit. Looks like they're at a highbrow function. I say, "You know Mayor Willie Brown."

Nicole tosses her keys on the island; they hit the white tile hard. That steals my attention away from the picture.

Nicole says, "Haven't you had enough, Ayanna?"

"Just making a short one. Nothing serious."

"We running tomorrow?"

"I'll be fine."

"Drink plenty of water so you won't be dried out with a headache."

Virgin white walls are all over, reminds me of Paris. Candle scents and potpourri odors waft in, making the house as sweet as the inside of a Z Gallery. A sixty-inch television. African sculptures. Erotic limited editions by Gayle Coito. Italian-style furniture in the family room and dining area.

I head that way, toward the picture over the fireplace, but Nicole pulls me back for more kisses; this time more comfortable, more passionate than before.

Without pretense of what's about to happen, we head upstairs, walk over soft carpet that steals the sounds of all of our footsteps, move by a sitting area that has a floor-to-ceiling, built-in cherry bookcase, two oversize chairs, and a small table. Another wall filled with awards and pictures of Ayanna with the mayor of San Francisco, other politicians. Ayanna is in front. I'm behind Nicole.

I say, "Nice place."

I'm talking to Nicole, but Ayanna says, "Thanks."

I ask Ayanna, "How many square feet?"

Nicole answers, "Thirty-three hundred. You could be here and we wouldn't even notice you."

Nicole extends that invitation like she owns the house.

Ayanna asks me, "How many square feet does your house have?"

I answer, "Twenty-three hundred."

"Lot size?"

"Barely enough to hold the house."

"Look out back by the gazebo. That small building houses the Jacuzzi. We have lemon trees, orange trees, persimmon trees. This is a very large lot. Largest in the area."

I nod at her message. Lot size equates to dollars, or success, or ability to care for oneself, or the one you love. Yes, I nod at her message of superiority. She returns the favor.

Ayanna smiles at her minor victory, sips her panther piss, then she says, "I have to go potty."

While she handles her business, I stop in the sitting area, pulled there by my curiosity, look at plaques, certificates, laminated newspaper clippings from the *Oakland Tribune*, all about Ayanna. Photos taken at Soul Beat TV, then photos at Government Access TV. Pictures in Mexico, Spain, Italy, the most beautiful ones on an island in Greece, then peeps at other countries that I don't recognize. Nicole's with her on a few of the recent shots. Not a lot, just a few. Medals for a lot of 10ks, a few 5ks, quite a few marathons are on display along the opposite side, along with Ayanna's degrees.

And the books. All arranged by height. All methodical, like Nicole. Everything from Thoreau to Ayn Rand to Charles Darwin. Homer to Aesop to Plato. Then a shelf of the world's greatest religions: Buddhism's Dhammapada, Christianity's Gospels, Hinduism's Bhagavad Gita, Islam's Koran, Judaism's Torah, and Taoism's Tao Te Ching.

Below that is a shelf of books that deal with healing powers, archetypal hypnotherapy, reincarnational vedic astrology, transcendental meditation, reflexology, holistic massage, power stretching, exploring

masculine and feminine energy. Much more. More
than enough for one person to take in, then draw
their own conclusion and construct their own belief
system.

We go right through double-doors, into the master
bedroom. Room to room, I notice something about the
placement of the furniture, of the pictures, of this
whole subset of God's petri dish. Especially in the bedroom. Candles. Incense. The head of the sleigh bed, a
funky Circassian walnut-style bed that looks more like
art than furniture, is placed against the north wall.
Plants, the fountain that mists and fogs, everything is
arranged in a way that creates peace, positive energy,
the same way Nicole arranged and decorated my world
and told me that placement of everything affects your
spirit. Too much of this house reminds me of my own
setup at home.

Nicole turns on a small stereo, a flat Nakamichi system that's on the wall, tunes to soft, wordless music.
Then she holds my hand, traces her finger up and
down my palm and shows me around. The walk-in
closet has built-ins. One wall looks like ten pairs of
workout shoes and a thousand and one pairs of "I'm
a woman" shoe heaven. I recognize Nicole's wardrobe,
see how it's sectioned off into her workout clothes,
her I-feel-fat clothes, her PMS clothes, I-feel-thin
clothes, I-don't-give-a-fuck clothes, I'm-sexier-than-a-
mofo clothes; all that she had when she was living
and loving with me is here. And I see clothes, other
things I've bought her over the years. This is Nicole's
closet. The one she walks in every day. My walk-in
closet in the Southland is laid out the same way, so far
as organization. It's just as anal. I have many gifts
from her.

I say, "This bedroom is bigger than most apartments."

"Ayanna had a wall taken down. It's like a supersize suite now."

The sleigh bed faces the shower and tub area; no door separates those two rooms. I guess so one lover can lie in bed and watch the other perform a dance of cleansing. Plenty of colorful pillows. No television. Very aromatic and romantic. A sensual retreat. They have erotic art that celebrates the human body, celebrates nakedness, all limited editions by Kimberly Chavers.

By the time Ayanna comes out of the bathroom, Nicole is on the cordless phone, talking to the late-night workers at her job. I listen for a few, but all the techno-negotiation jargon flies over my head. By her tone, it sounds like it might take her a while to get whatever has gone awry resolved. She gets heated, raises her voice into a no-nonsense, hard-nosed manager tone and heads into another room with the cordless.

Ayanna opens the double doors and lets a chilling breeze in, steps out on the balcony, humming along with the radio, sipping her E&J, her eyes to the sky as she sways and sips, first gazing out toward the lemon and persimmon trees, then gazing up at heaven's vault.

I stand a few feet away from Ayanna. "You okay?"

She hands me her drink. That surprises me. I take a sip, hand it back. Maybe that surprises her.

She speaks with an unexpected tenderness, "I'm just looking at the light that has taken thousands of years to reach my itty-bitty eyes. Looking at the land and ocean that is the greatest story ever told."

I pause, my nose getting cold, let my eyes go to the sky. "Putting things in perspective?"

Her eyes wander across the vault of heaven. "Searching for the truth."

A moment passes. She sips her drink again, hands it off to me. I sip and give it back.

I tell her, "Your crib is impressive."

"I'm just a girl from the gutter who has done okay with her career and investments."

Nicole is still on the phone. She passes by, hands moving to emphasize whatever she's saying. Her voice fades when she walks away, moving with her nonstop words.

I ask Ayanna, "Why no flag?"

"Not everyone has a flag."

"You said that the people with flags are proud."

"I did."

"So that means that the people without flags aren't, right?"

She shifts in a defensive way that lets me know she hates to be the one in the hot seat. "Sounds like you're cross-examining. Dissecting my words, using them against me."

I smile at her controlled anger. "Just asking a simple question. Why don't you have one?"

"Nosy little fucker."

"All day long."

She picks her nails for a few seconds. "I did. Nicole wasn't comfortable with it."

I smile. Nicole isn't in her world, not all the way. She's not in mine, but she's not gone. In this moment, that is my minor victory. No size house can take away that feeling of hope.

Ayanna whispers, "Love makes no sense."

"True."

"It is an inextinguishable force that leaves when it's good and ready."

"That it is. Too bad you can't turn it off when you wanna."

"Well," she motions out toward Lady Oakland, out toward the darkness in the direction of San Francisco, "out there somewhere, the odds are someone else is doing the same thing we're doing."

We pause, listen for Nicole. She's still on the phone. Ayanna moves the conversation away from her, moves the focus back to me when she says, "What you did at the club was admirable, in a primitive way, but it was stupid as hell."

"Think so?"

"You pushed him. That was assault. Plain and simple. You could've been taken to jail. Or he could've had psycho friends and it could've become ugly."

I speak with ease and conviction, "And how would you protect Nicole from an asshole like that? By sipping on a drink and adjusting your tits?"

She nods a few times before she says, "Question?"

"Shoot."

"Did you get pissed-off because he called Nicole a dyke, or because he called you a faggot?"

I don't answer, just rub my hands together.

She says, "Just what I thought."

I back off, take a breath. I ask, "Is it always like that at that place?"

"Some nights it's a fuckfest," she says.

"But homeboy who was tripping, is it like that a lot?"

"Nah. That jerk had to be a tourist."

The lights of planes can be seen in the direction of Oakland Airport, each illumination creating the illusion of slow-moving shooting stars.

I release the thought that's been bugging me since it slipped from Ayanna's lips. "Eight years, huh?"

She sips the last of her drink, grins, puts the empty glass on the edge of the wooden rail. "Yep."

"Where did you meet her?"

"*San Francisco Chronicle* Marathon. Mile sixteen. Heading up the hill of all hills in the Haight-Ashbury district."

I chuckle. "I met her at the L.A. Marathon. Mile twenty."

"Lucky you."

"I don't believe in luck. I believe in blessings and divine intervention."

I believe that out of thirty thousand aching people, we ended up at Hollywood Boulevard and Western Avenue, running side-by-side at that moment, because it was meant to be. Mile twenty; where it hurts more to stop than to keep going. That day I looked to my right and saw Nicole in yellow shorts and a light green top, looking sunburned, dehydrated, skin ashen, her jet-black braids pulled back in a ponytail, so much pain in every breath. And I didn't look any better. I tried to use her as my rabbit, let her set the pace and block the wind, and at times she tried to use me as her rabbit, but on that day we were pretty even. We passed by so many people who had broken down and given up the race to go in search of Power Bars, Gatorade, and taxi rides home, but we stayed steady, moved through the agony, sipped water, bonded in our misery and determination, didn't even know each others' names until we finished those last six miles.

Ayanna intrudes on my thoughts with her whispered words, "Mork, calling Orson, come in, Orson."

I blink. "What?"

"Penny for those thoughts."

I own thousands of words, which in the right com-

bination and permutations are an endless means of ex-
pressing what I feel. But in this moment, language
fails.

Ayanna is staring at me, brain clicking and whirring,
trying to worm her way inside my head.

I try and push her in another mental direction, say,
"So, you know about Barebacks."

She laughs at the sky. "Once upon a time I was married. Married this guy I met at a club. Silk's over in
Emeryville. That place used to have at least four thousand people inside, and I was drawn to him."

"So, you're divorced."

"One better. Widowed."

"Sorry to hear."

"Don't be. I was devastated, but it freed me. Didn't
get my degree, didn't work this hard to sit at home
and fold socks. I'm no boy toy who wants to spend all
weekend separating whites from colors."

My tongue moves across my teeth.

She says, "My husband would come home with lotion on his back. That was how I knew. No way for a
man to put lotion all over his own back, not miss a single spot, not without help."

Her confession surprises me. I ask, "What did you
do?"

"Kept being a good wife, hoping he'd come home
the way he left, with an ashy back. Always hoping for
people to change into what I want them to be, but they
never do."

She nibbles her bottom lip.

I attempt to dig deeper. "Considering how you
come at me, how rugged your tongue is, that's pretty
passive."

"I've changed. You have to learn to ask the hard

questions, even when you know the answers. I used to be afraid to do that. Afraid of the truth."

"What changed you?"

"Law school brings out the rough part of everybody. A blessing and a curse. Plus, I'm older. Like to think the years have changed me for the better. Who I am now sure isn't who I was then. Life is so much better when a woman gives up chasing dick. So many prob-lems go away. Diseases too."

"If you say so."

"But I did love him." She sighs in a way that says she misses him as well. "My husband was Oakland PD. Stopped somebody for speeding. A no-brainer. And they shot him so they wouldn't get a ticket and have their car insurance go up."

I have no idea what to say. Her tenderness catches me off guard.

Ayanna asks me, "What's your best time at the L.A. Marathon?"

"Last March did it in four hours, seven minutes."

"Nine-minute miles. Hmm."

"What?"

"Thought you were faster," she replies with a smirk, then waits for me to ask her the obvious. When I don't fall into her game, she tells me anyway, "My best is three-fifty-two."

"Well, I ran four-oh-seven in a hard, cold rain with the wind in my face for the first fifteen miles. Had to skip over lakes, a wind shear pretty much came and went the rest of the time."

"San Francisco is tougher than L.A. More hills. Stay in L.A. It's flat and running flat is for wimps. You'd suck wind up here."

"Well, like I said, I ran in a storm."

I chew my bottom lip. There is competition.

I ask, "So, what are you?"

She chuckles, a brief noise that tells me she knows what I'm asking. Her tone becomes political as she says, "I know who I am. Nicole is walking a line. No matter how much you want to, you can't be both. It's like having a white parent and a black parent and trying to say you're both black and white. Society says you can't be both. Can only be one."

"Like praising two gods."

"That's extreme, but I guess you could say that."

"Tonight," I say before I pause, "in a way we're two gods."

"Two religions. Yep, we're two religions."

"Can't have two religions. No man can serve two masters."

She nods. "Once again I agree with you."

"But a master can have two slaves."

Her eyes widen, then she grins down at her fingernails as she shifts, clears the uneasiness from her throat. I've struck a nerve.

"That's the way society rules," she says. "Unwritten laws of shame and guilt that keep every culture in its own box. Society slides you a box and you crawl inside. Everybody lives in a box."

"Not everybody. I live in a wide-open field. No shame in my game."

In a tone I assume she uses in the courtroom, she stresses, "Everybody."

I pause, take a deep breath, then nod, let the tension ease before I ask, "What box do you belong in?"

"Whatever box Nicole is in. And there's only room for two."

Behind us the toilet flushes. I didn't hear Nicole pass

by and come back into the bedroom. From her reaction, neither did Ayanna. Nicole is still on the phone, but her voice is calmer, as if she's resolved whatever conflict had arisen. The shower comes on, steam walks into the bedroom from the open bathroom, creating a mist, like a spotlight before show time.

I ask, "We're on your home turf. Your castle. What's the next move?"

"I don't know about you, but I take a deep breath and practice kindness. I take the focus off my needs and accentuate the unmet needs of someone I love more than life itself. Something I've done too often. I've done it for my family, for my friends, for my lovers. One day maybe somebody will do it for me."

"Sweetness and self-sacrifice add up to nothing."

She sighs. "Tell me something new. Experience has taught me that. But I can't stop."

"If you allow her to violate your boundaries, it's on you."

"I could tell you the same."

"I was talking to myself."

"Excuse me for interrupting."

I say, "You can always tell her you don't want to."

"Talking to yourself?"

"No, to you."

She responds, "You could too."

"Then you must want to."

She smirks. "In some weird, perverted way, I want to see what makes you so special."

"Same here."

"I don't understand why she's so hooked on you."

"Same here."

"You offer her nothing that I can't give."

"Adam and Eve, Ayanna. You can't give her that."

She sips, hands the glass to me. I sip, hand it back.

She says, "I want to understand why you're so special. I tell myself that's why I'm here. I want to show you that you're not needed. Can you dig it?"

"Like a grave. But admit this too; I'm a good-looking motherfucker and you want to."

"Don't flatter yourself. Yellow men have never been my thang." She chuckles, then pats my hand with her cool, sweaty palm. With warmth she says, "Sex without love is a war fought with the genitals."

"I agree with you a hundred percent on that one, Counselor. I've had quite a few wars."

"Me too," she says. "Truth or truth?"

"Sure."

"You want this kind of battle, don't you? To be on this battlefield is every man's wish."

I shake my head. "Not every man."

"You're full of shit." Then she whispers, "Remember the rules."

It's cold outside. Very cold, some wind sings in the trees. But we stay in the night's chill.

I pat her hand. She holds my finger. Her lips move, and the expression on her face tells me that she's about to say something positive, something very human, but she doesn't give in. For a moment there is a spiritual connection. My energy mixes with her life force. Almost feels like love.

Her lips look soft, and I remember how they felt when they pressed against mine. Not like I thought they would be. Powerful, magnetic, sweet lips. She licks them. I lick mine. Nicole knows that for me, kissing is the ultimate seduction. I think it means the same for Ayanna. One kiss, we exchange energy, become part of each other for eternity, and no matter how hard

we wish to go back to ignorance, we can't, because
we're no longer strangers. One kiss, we're familiar forever. Again she licks her lips as she stares at my face.
Again I do the same.

Our names are called; we both jump a bit. We step
inside like children responding to a bell at the end of
recess. No, not recess. Like kids who were caught playing doctor in their parents' closet.

Nicole creeps through the dim candlelight, moves
with the ease of a cat, her boldness tuned to high, shoe-
less so she seems shorter, more vulnerable. Our topless
dancer waiting for us to sing her a song of approval,
her small brown breasts so round and womanlike. She
has a very ethereal expression, and her natural beauty
dulls my head, intoxicates me with the power of a shot
of heated rum. Nicole winks at Ayanna but comes to
me first, energetic with breathless excitement. She has
created this night.

Nicole kisses me, gives me little tastes, little bites,
we don't rush, nibbling lips, taking each other's breath
until every cell in my body catches fire. She's tipsy, her
breath sweet and sour, her flesh so eager. She pulls my
head to her right breast, the most sensitive one, my favorite appetizer, and gives her thick nipple to me and
I praise it with the warmth and wetness of my mouth,
fall into my own music, my own rhythm; the world
falls away.

Ayanna is watching us.

Trembles roll through Nicole's body. That excites
me.

"Ayanna," Nicole says. "Come here, kiss me, baby."

Ayanna eases into our space, her patchouli aroma
mixing with Nicole's herbal scent, and while I feed
and caress her wonderful breast, above me are the

sounds of tender whines and deep kisses. Their breaths create a warm breeze raking against my neck, flowing into my hair.

Ayanna is swallowing Nicole's throaty moans. She has one hand on Nicole's other breast, the other moving up and down the round of Nicole's butt. My fingers drift between Nicole's legs, fingers raking across her soft, damp, narrow hole, massaging that spot that swells, touching Ayanna's humid fingers at the same time, both of us trying to prove that we can please Nicole better than the other.

All the sounds that Nicole has made for me, all the noises that I wish were special for me, echo for Ayanna as well. Maybe even better, because this is her greatest fantasy, and she responds to the dual stimulation with more intensity.

Nicole inhales hard through her nose, releases air in spurts from her mouth, as if she were sprinting up a steep hill. Her right leg trembles, face furrows with pleasure as she shivers and moans, her words so hot and humid, "Shit, I'm not ready to come. Not yet. Let's take a shower."

Ayanna catches her breath, motions toward the sunken tub next to the shower, says, "I'd rather bathe."

I know what Ayanna's doing, trying to delay. The same reason she diverted us to San Francisco.

"Next time," Nicole says. "We'll eat fruit and bathe together next time."

And that is the end of that.

Nicole is always so very clean. Another thing I've always loved about her, always appreciated about her. Always smells fresh, never musty, never owns any after-pee taste down in the triangle. My Queen of Clean Hygiene doesn't treat us like slaves, but instead becomes our servant, the one who is aiming to please two. She undresses Ayanna, kisses Ayanna's breasts, her neck, her eyes, her fingers, touches her between her legs, does all of that as Ayanna blinks in and out of what she is feeling and watches me. I lick my lips. Somewhere between sweltering breaths, Ayanna does the same, blinks and licks and blinks and licks. My eyes stay on her body, which is slim, not much to behold. But she's toned, she's articulate, she's blunt, she's intelligent, she's feminine, she's athletic, she's arrogant, she's confident, she's aggressive, so I understand what's erotic and appealing about her. We're physical people who thrive on mental stimulation. Fools with educations and ambitions, and attracted to the same.

Ayanna's breasts remind me of sunrise in Maui, and her nipples are blacker than the long winter nights in Alaska. The most beautiful nipples I've ever seen. Full, erect, so thick. Blackberries screaming to be taken into a nice warm mouth. Moisture rises on her skin like morning dew. My eyes drift over her curves, over her lines, drift until they stop on her vagina, on her true ayanna, a beautiful flower with soft, curly black hair.

My adversary and me stare at each other, licking our lips, struggling to remember the rules of this war.

Seeing a woman naked for the first time is like visiting a new place. It forces you to take in the texture, inhale all the sweet smells, crave the tastes, admire a marvelous creation, encourages you to pack up your needs and journey into the unknown. To become immersed in that land, in its hills and valleys, to wet your mouth in the rivers, to be drawn into the undercurrents.

Nicole removes my pants, underwear, socks, shirt.

Folds my clothes and leaves some things on the brown leather chair, some things on the leather ottoman. My skin is cool but nervous sweat trickles down my back, finds its way into the crack of my rear.

Ayanna gazes at the lines that add up to me. No breathless excitement, just confidence and relaxed shoulders, then a long stare with piercing eyes that make me feel as if the skin is gone from my body.

At last, we're all naked in Nicole's garden.

16

We shower together. Lights off. Candles burning. Jazz on the radio.

Three shadows washing each other in the most personal places.

Nicole does most of the cleansing, again our servant, soaping us head to toe, rinsing us, then squatting and using a pumice stone to scrub the bottoms of our feet, making sure those erogenous zones are ready for the tasting. I leave them, stand outside the glass shower door on the tile floor, dripping water and drying off, listening to them, seeing their movements covered by the steam.

Even when the steam frosts the glass, the sounds from their lovemaking are so clear, like two instruments, Monk and Coltrane collaborating while Dizzy listens, and I can see their crisp notes floating in the air.

Ayanna comes out first, her heart-colored hair wet on the ends. Again our eyes meet. She chews her bottom lip. All of her insults, all of her harshness, all of that has evaporated like the steam that surrounds us.

Nicole is right behind her, her honey-blond locks looking a little wet.

Both of them are damp. Both have a glow that over-shadows the light from the four scented candles.

A wall-length mirror is over the sink, double mirrors are on the facing wall; we're surrounded by so many naked angles of us.

Ayanna goes to Nicole, top teeth on bottom lip, touching her face, claiming her as I watch.

Nicole says, "Isn't Ayanna beautiful? The perfect body."

Ayanna blushes.

Nicole says, "Look at her nipples. God, I wish mine were like that."

Ayanna and I stare at each other. Seeing her nipples makes my stomach growl.

Nicole comes to me, rubs my stomach. "Aren't these the best abs you've ever seen? He's so toned."

I smile, but I'm not sure if I mean it.

Nicole opens the cabinet and pulls out patchouli-scented massage oil. Then she lays a blanket on the floor, near the foot of the bed. And to the soft music we massage each other, exchange more energy, move toward Kama Sutra.

I suck Nicole's pretty little toes.

"Oh, that drives me wild."

I kiss her legs up to her inner thighs, moving to her breasts, and her breath thickens.

She tells me to love both breasts, never leave one breast jealous of the other. And while I do that, she does the same to Ayanna, loves her breasts. Kissing flesh, fingers grazing, heat rising. All the while Nicole talks to us, coaches us, tells us how beautiful we are to-gether, how this new world, this shared love is better than she ever imagined, because she can get so much more, that she is rising to a new level.

Ayanna asks, "Toys?"

"Not tonight," Nicole says. "Let's stay at this level. Have to get used to each other."

Nicole calls out for me; Ayanna moves away, so hot and restless. Her eyes tighten in envy as Nicole holds my penis and leads me to their bed. She pulls back the rust duvet, the top sheets, tosses extra pillows aside, climbs aboard the firm mattress, her legs open so wide. Underneath a still ceiling fan, I give Nicole my tongue, hands, and when she reaches for it, my penis.

It's awkward with Ayanna watching me; makes this almost a Viagra moment.

Nicole coaxes me, "It's okay baby, you're doing fine. Close your eyes if you have to. Pretend that it's just us. Pretend we're in your Jeep."

She kisses my neck, tells me there is no pressure, just love, just love.

I adjust, block out Ayanna's eyes, feel firm enough to make the transition into a flow only a man can give a woman. During this performance, and it is a performance, I'm moving with care, easing in, easing out to the tip, teasing her spot, listening to Nicole's body, feeling her nails dig into my flesh as she tells me what she needs. I love easy, but I'm still more intense than Al Pacino and Robert De Niro combined. Ayanna watches her, watches me.

Ayanna asks, "Is . . . is . . . is he hurting you?"

"No, sweetie, I like this." She jerks. *"Awwwww, yeah right there sweetie, right there."*

Nicole turns her head away, looks in the candlelight for Ayanna, jerks when I hit a spot, then closes her eyes and reaches in the direction of Ayanna's voice, pleads for Ayanna's hand, and when Ayanna takes it, Nicole puts her hand, her fingers in Ayanna's face. Ayanna sucks Nicole's fingers, savors them. Nicole sings like a sparrow, and moves like I've never felt her move before, like someone I've never met before. I touch Nicole's face, bring her eyes to mine, bring her hands back to me, ask Nicole to say my name and she does, closes her eyes, holds me and sings it in more octaves than Mariah Carey, makes more faces than Jim Carrey, but all are angelic.

I say, "Describe what you feel."

Her mouth becomes a letter O, then she moans, "In . . . de . . . scrib . . . able."

Tension sets Ayanna's face on fire, tension that treads in her inebriation. For a moment, she looks like a puppy that wants to curl up and howl its pain away. Ayanna pulls away a little more, stares at Nicole, her thoughts impenetrable. Then she makes a determined face, leans in and kisses Nicole once, twice, three times, and three times my heart pumps an erratic beat.

Nicole's face glows in psychedelic shades of red. She's in a zone, gone to a place far away. Her body goes into nonstop spasms, endless twitches. In her face I witness a lustful struggle, heaven and hell intertwining. She's gone, out of her body and out of this room, chants to God and Jesus in one nonstop moan, one that is both painful and beautiful.

Nicole is gone to a wonderful place, and I watch her in joy and envy. She's gone to a place I can never reach. A place no man will ever reach. And I hope I'm the only one capable of taking her there.

Ayanna waits until the rolling movement in Nicole's hips begins to slow before she runs her hand through Nicole's hair, says her name over and over. Nicole moves Ayanna's hand away and laughs a little as she spasms.

In the softest voice, Ayanna whispers, "I need you."

"I'm . . . too sensitive. Give me a minute . . ."

"Nic," Ayanna says, "I need you in the worst way."

"Give me a minute."

Nicole moves away with urgency.

Rejection appears in Ayanna's eyes. She looks so young, so immature. In this environment her degrees don't exist. Nicole slides and wiggles from beneath me, uses her elbows to drag herself to the far side of the bed, her body still jerking, her eyes closed tight, as blind to this world as I am to understanding what I must do to bring her back to me.

On hands and knees, Ayanna moves beyond me, her eyes scream that she is determined, so very determined to outshine me, and she runs her fingers through Nicole's locks again, untangles the tangled ones, watches over her the way a mother watches a child, making sure she's okay. Then Nicole reaches up, touches Ayanna's locks the same way, moves the red mane away from her heated face.

I go to the sliding glass doors, my giver of new life pointing in the direction of L.A. My thoughts slip away like mercury as I stare at an oceanside city that rests under a dark blanket filled with cold, salty air. In that flash, I think about my old man.

I have a flashback to when I was twelve years old, a junior usher in his church. Think about how people told me that I was going to be a preacher and follow in my old man's footsteps, that I'd be out there righting wrongs, a public servant until I lay six feet under.

Today I don't recognize who I am.

In the window's reflection, I'm but a shadow. A silhouette of man.

Behind my shadow, Ayanna and Nicole are together, their reflection looking surreal, almost as solid as a thought, caressing each other with palms, tips of fingers tracing each other's body, every carnal exchange so tender and gentle. So much familiarity in every touch.

Like me, Ayanna takes her time, tells Nicole she loves the aroma she makes, the smell of her skin, the taste of her flesh, asks her how this feels, is that too much. The same thing, but so very different from what Nicole and I have ever done.

Nicole calls me back, her face so emotional, begs for my kisses, needs both of us, now, right now.

I kiss her with my eyes open, feel her spirits wrestling, suck in her moans, let her bite my tongue, my ears, my neck. Do that and watch Ayanna touch the woman I love, watch how she curves her finger to reach that spot that swells, see how well she knows Nicole's body, knows it as well as she does her own.

When Nicole wants Ayanna, I move away. Inhale raw sex and move away.

Ayanna's bracelets jingle a serious song as her fingers massage Nicole's vagina, as she kisses her, as she fondles her breasts with expertise. While she does that, while that arch rises in Nicole's back, while Nicole cries out and claws at the bed, pulling the spread up to her face, Ayanna's eyes come to my reflection. The sweat on her knitted brows tells me she's better. That her love is the greatest. Tells me that she is here to prove a point. That no matter how much she played at cooperating this evening, she's at her own mile twenty and will go the distance to prove that I'm not needed. Anything Nicole needs, she can give her. Anything I offer, she offers more. She wants me to know that, wants me to see she too would crawl through hell to win Nicole. That her beautiful flower is more powerful than my dick.

Ayanna shows me her tongue, makes it snake, worm in and out of her own mouth, taunts me with the pinkness of that spongy flesh, licks her lips, cuts her eyes at me, kisses Nicole's thighs, the silver hoop in her belly, teases, kisses, teases, licks, teases, moves away, comes back, then when Nicole damn near screams that she can't stand it anymore, Ayanna puts her butterscotch face to Nicole's golden-brown triangle, gets lost in Bermuda with her mouth and hands.

"Good Lord, Ayanna, you have never . . . never . . . never been this intense. So intense. Oh God."

Again Nicole orgasms, stronger than what I'd offered her minutes ago. So severe that she flips and almost falls from the bed. Her lioness mane swings like a whip as she growls out hallelujahs and praises to God almighty and His son who died for our sins.

I realize that what I've given her in bed all these years isn't as special as I thought. It's like watching seven levels of ecstasy. Maybe there is more to this woman-to-woman thing than I imagined. This isn't like the movies I've seen; no posing for camera angles, zero roughness, no bogus fuck-faces. It's tender and emotional. Some things I can see Ayanna do, and what I can't see I witness the effects of it on Nicole's face, and when I can't see Nicole's expression, I hear coos and wetness mixing with the jazz, hear all the wetness combining with wetness, all the sounds they create is an opus.

Then Nicole works magic with her tongue, something I was curious about, but didn't want to see.

I swallow. Close my eyes. Open them. Face what's
real for me now.

I remember seven years back, when Nicole was shy
about being naked in front of me, when she fumbled
with sex. Back then she would only make love in the
dark, under the covers, with me on top. That was all
she needed. Back then she was curious about oral sex,
but wasn't into it. And when I loved her that way, no
matter how much she hooped and hollered, she
wouldn't kiss me afterwards. She was still afraid.
Everything new was too taboo.

And while I watch her make love to another woman
without shame, I remember Paris.

It's all connected. All of our actions are connected,
like it or not.

Nicole masters Ayanna's body with one finger, two
fingers, three fingers, four, her hand moving, cupping,
holding, entering, more passionate than Ayanna was
for her. She fucks her without mercy and with tenderness at the same time, watching and listening. I inhale
Ayanna's musk. Ayanna is on her back, first her nails
are clawing the sheets, then her fists pound the mattress. Her head turns side-to-side, squirming, buttocks
pushing up into Nicole's hand, sometimes clenching,
eyes rolling and showing the whites. She catches her
breath and sees me. Remembers that they are not
alone. Sees me with my mouth wide open. My naked
body. My eyes learning her nakedness. Witnessing her
most personal moment. Her silent scream says that she
wants to stop, but she can't stop. She can't turn back
because now she is crazy, the carnal insanity creating
almost a U-shaped arch in her back. The muscles rise

and fall in her legs, making her look so powerful, so strong. Each breath, thick and stuttering. Each breath taking her closer to madness and ecstasy.

She is there.

"Oh God Oh God oh God Nicole."

"Talk to me sweetheart, Ayanna, baby, tell me if you like this—"

"Yes, yes, yes."

I blink and see me making love to Nicole. I watch them, and for a moment, that's the illusion I see. Nicole does to Ayanna the same things I've done to her, saying the same things I've said to her hundreds of times. She's taken what I've given her, all I've taught her, and given it to someone else.

"What about this, Ayanna? Like this too?"

"I like that *oooo* damn I like that."

Nicole smiles down on Ayanna. "How much?"

"That's a ten. Dammit, baby. A ten baby, that's a ten."

"Come for me come for me."

Ayanna glows with sweat, makes the ugly coming face, the face that's atrocious and lovely at the same time, yanks the sheets and stuffs them between her teeth. Muffling the sounds of heaven entwining with hell, not as intense as Nicole, but a melody that, under more favorable circumstances, would be pleasure to my ears. She stares at me, a harsh deep glare, closes her eyes, squints like she's fighting off the inevitable, trembles, opens her mouth so wide, shrills out a series of sweet noises, a smoldering sound that makes my heart leap.

Then, except for the jazz music that had been drowned out, there are no words. Soft music eases through the incense and sex smell that permeates the room.

Ayanna's wide-eyed, staring at the ceiling, riding out the last of her twitches. She jerks and jerks and jerks, reminding me of old women in church, women who have caught the spirit. She's at that special place that women can reach, feeling things that only women have been blessed to feel.

Then all is calm.

Ayanna folds her arms, mumbles, "Did it. Actually did it. I actually did it."

This is the moment of the moment after. It arrives as expected. Reality falls like a feather but lands with the weight of an anvil.

Nicole's bracelets jingle as she reaches for Ayanna, and the second Nicole's hand grazes Ayanna's damp flesh, Ayanna's bracelets jangle as she scurries away.

Nicole's eyes open wide, her head turns toward Ayanna. She asks, "Sweetie, what's up with that?"

Ayanna sits at the foot of the bed on the floor. Nicole reaches for her again. Ayanna moves away. Nicole makes a sound of irritation, maybe disappointment, then stretches out across the bed, snatches part of the duvet over her legs, hands hanging toward the carpet, short fingers tugging at the thick pile.

I wait.

Ayanna stands for a second, her head down, legs trembling like she is still weak and shuddering from having the big O. She finds her balance, wipes her mouth, her heart-colored locks covering her face, a face that seems so small right now, hiding her from the world.

It's hard for me to breathe. The air has become super-charged with electricity. Humid and thick, the way air gets heavy before a storm.

Ayanna keeps her arms across her chest, hiding her breasts, turns off the jazz with a rugged slap on the stereo, and leaves the bedroom running, turns left, and storms away from the stairway.

I want to know, "She okay?"

"She's fine," Nicole responds.

Ayanna's coughing, gagging her way down the hall.

Then silence follows silence follows silence. Flames dance. Wax melts.

I walk out of the bedroom.

Nicole's voice rises and follows. "Let her be. She's okay."

In the hallway, I listen for jingles. There are none.

I look inside one room, and it's a large office. Lots of law books. File cabinets.

No Ayanna.

Behind another closed door is the other bedroom. Much smaller. Just a day bed and more art.

No Ayanna.

A third bedroom is empty too.

I tap on the other bathroom door and there is no answer. In my mind, wrists are cut and a river of blood is running from the walls. I open the door and see a sink. There is no sign of Ayanna. It's as if she has disappeared. Except I catch the faint smell of frankincense and patchouli. Then I see that there is another door inside to the right. I open it and peep in the darkness and see a toilet, a tub with a shower. The smell of sex, the scent of Ayanna gets stronger.

I pull the opaque shower curtain back, the silver hooks singing as they rake across the metal bar.

Ayanna is in the bathtub, in the dark, her butterscotch skin resting in a pool of cold, white porcelain, legs pulled up so her chin rests on her knees, arms around her shins, her fire-colored mane helping to hide all that defines her as woman. The same embryotic position Nicole had a moment ago, a child back inside of its mother's womb.

She starts rocking. Lips opening and closing. No words appear.

I extend my hand to Ayanna.

She shakes her head at my good sportsmanship.

She coughs. "You'd suck wind up here."

"I'd beat you like a runaway slave."

"Two slaves, one master, right?"

Then silence visits us again.

Nicole calls our names. I wait for Ayanna to answer, but she doesn't. She glances up at me, expecting me to do the same. To give in to Nicole's voice, to lose. No one answers. Nicole has been in control since the beginning, has taken this from incubation to this solemn moment we exist in now, and now we're trying to recapture some of that power.

Nicole repeats our names louder, the way a mother summons a child, then demands, "What are you doing together?"

Again our names are called.

I ask, "Do you trust her?"

"Don't know if I should."

I tell her, "If you don't trust her, then you don't love her."

"Her pussy has made you delusional."

I say, "You're butt naked in a dry bathtub and I'm delusional?"

"To trust somebody you have to know what's going on inside their minds, not what they tell you. I'm talking about their psyche, and there is no way you can know that."

Nicole appears at the door; anger is the mask she wears.

"The rules, Ayanna," Nicole snaps. Her petite breasts thrust with the power of mountains. Her eyes come to me and she stresses, "The rules."

"Your rules," Ayanna says, then gets to her feet and leaves the bathroom, moves away with clarity that speak volumes. Tells Nicole that she can't run away, but she hates herself and doesn't want to exist in the same room with her at this moment. "This is my house. I make up my own rules."

"Our house." Nicole follows. "Don't start tripping."

By candlelight, Ayanna dresses the best she can. Nicole stands and watches.

Ayanna coughs, then laughs over and over. "I actually did this shit and went behind him."

She takes slow, methodical steps laced with an inebriated rhythm. Her laughter grows; it's not quite hysterical, but it's not controlled either. "Are you happy, Nicole? Are you happy now? Clap your hands. Go ahead. You're happy and you know it."

Nicole stands near the door, blocking her way, asking her not to leave.

Nicole asks, "Can I hug you?"

"Don't touch me."

"Why not?"

Ayanna responds, "Because you always let go first."

"I don't."

"You ever notice that? I've been hugging you for eight years, you always let go first."

Nicole studies Ayanna's face before she says, "So, you're reading me my faults?"

"And you pray with your eyes open. Never trust anyone who prays with their eyes open."

"You never pray."

"That means I never pretend."

Nicole shifts. "Anything else?"

"The list is too long, so I'll keep it simple." Ayanna's voice catches in the middle, fractures like a straw that has been bent too far. "Your strengths I can complement. Your weaknesses I can compensate for. I do all I can to make your life better. But you don't do the same for me."

"You don't have any weaknesses, Ayanna."

"I'm facing my weakness right now," Ayanna responds by giving Nicole direct eye contact, her tone so strong, so lawyerlike, so much like a closing argument. "You are my only fucking weakness."

Ayanna's words chill me, stab me a hundred times a hundred, because my weakness is her weakness. Ayanna is my mirror. She's making me see my weakness.

Ayanna says, "You need to make up your mind which way you're going to swing."

"My mind is made up. We went over this a thousand times. You said you under—fuck it."

Nicole crosses her arms tight over her breasts. So many times over our years she has done that to me. Body language that screamed out her annoyance, froze me where I stood. It's fascinating seeing her do the same with her other.

Ayanna glowers at our headstrong lover like she's Tituba, the black witch of Salem. They stare without blinking, eyes radiating more therms than the sun. Neither backs down. Two panthers, waiting.

Ayanna takes her silver bracelets off, shakes them as she faces Nicole. Holds them tight, her hand turns into a fist. Makes me think she's got brass knuckles.

Nicole says, "Stop it. Put those back on."

Ayanna shakes her head, does that over and over as she speaks, "Once a fire gets started, if the wind shifts, it changes into a firestorm. It's unstoppable."

I watch. Hold my breath and watch. Don't know what to do, if I should grab Nicole, jump in between, or wait and see which way these winds are about to blow. I wait.

Just when my lungs are about to burst, Nicole blinks, lowers her head, moves to the side with her unhappy attitude on display. Ayanna picks up her purse, stuffs her bracelets inside, grabs her keys, marches down the stairs. The door sensor does a *beep-beep-beep* when it opens. Then closes. The garage door whirrs. An engine starts. Backs out with a disturbing calmness. The garage door whirrs back down. Ayanna zooms away, leaving us with nothing but the sound of each other's breathing.

Nicole sits on the edge of the bed, her eyes watching her palms as if she were reading tea leaves.

A moment passes. Nicole's voice becomes a moan, "Shit, she had four martinis."

"Didn't look tore back to me. She made it down all those stairs without cracking her face."

"She's fucking with me, doing this shit on purpose. Hurry and put your clothes on."

I do. Nicole throws on blue-and-gold CAL sweats, tennis shoes.

Then I'm following Nicole's fast pace down the stairs, grabbing my shoes as soon as we step on the tile, then running through the garage. We stop long enough to see a puddle of vomit near where Ayanna's ride used to be. Nicole double-times, damn near leaps into her car, and before I can buckle up, we're speeding up her street, down hills toward the middle-class, then the working-class areas, looking left and right. Nicole never stops talking, never stops worrying.

"She leaves like she's Miss Billy Bad Ass, but it's crazy out there." Her voice drops and she continues to shake her head and ramble, "Car-jackers are out there pretending they're cops, hell, three women just got jacked in Orinda. Don't do this to me, Ayanna."

"She seems too smart to do something this stupid. Slow down, Nicole, damn."

"Get real. This is an emotional thing, has nothing to do with being smart."

"That's why you need to slow—"

"Mayors do the same stupid thing. Police officers. Priests. So-called smart people get DUI's all the freaking time, so give me a break," she says, every harsh word defending Ayanna. Then she grips the steering wheel, clenches her teeth, and growls, "Don't do this to me, Ayanna. Don't do this."

She pulls out her c-phone, pages Ayanna, puts in 9-1-1.

I look down dark streets I've never seen before, ask, "Why did you freak out in the bathroom?"

"The rules. I can't . . . don't want to see you with someone else."

"Is it that you don't want to see me get with Ayanna, or see Ayanna make love to me?"

"Don't do this, okay."

"Was Ayanna supposed to deal with it any better than you—"

She raises her voice. "Not now, please, not now."

"Why not, Nicole? Slow down. Nicole, slow this bullet down."

"It's different. Seeing you fuck somebody is different."

"How?"

"I'm in love with you. I can't turn this off." She slaps the steering wheel. "I don't know why but it's different. I wouldn't be able to stand watching you fuck somebody else."

"Hypocritical. Since you ran the last two, you might want to stop at the next red light."

"You call me hypocritical." She shrugs. "So be it. I learned from the best."

"Selfish and hypocritical."

She curses me, snaps as she drives by stores, a few houses, looks for Ayanna's car. All the while we banter to and fro.

"Please," she huffs. "And your wanting me to yourself, at your convenience, having me do things that I was uncomfortable with when that was what you wanted, none of that was selfish?"

"But you torture me with your sexcapades."

"And you tortured me with K-Y jelly."

"Don't start with that shit again. That's old, Nicole. Very old."

"Well, pat yourself on your back, sweetie. You made me this way."

I snap, "I didn't. Will you knock that crap off?"

She retorts, "Was I like this before all of those X-rated videos, before you pushed me into your fucking fantasies? Was I? Hell no. Shoving all of those books by Anäis Nin and Henry Miller in my face. Making me read those scenes a million times."

She's driving too fast, searching, finding nothing. Nicole has been drinking too, has had enough to worry the world. In the back of my mind, once again, I remember us in Paris, not at the strip club, but driving through tunnel *du pont de l'alma*, the passageway where Princess Diana died in the thick of the night. This pace is so fast; if we had wings we'd be airborne. I'm wondering if tonight is the night I die. If she's leading me to the ultimate accident.

I say, "Those scenes were well-written, beautiful. That's what I was sharing."

"They were contagious. You pushed pictures by Rondu on me, put those pictures on every wall—"

"That is art, Nicole. Art. Did you forget the erotica plastered all over your walls?"

"Don't cut me off, dammit. You made me look at that art day in and day out, made me wonder about things I'd never wondered about."

"Those pictures are nothing compared to the videos on BET."

"We didn't have cable, dammit." She makes a few quick turns, ends up on the freeway. "But you brought Heather Hayes and Taylor Harris into my life in black plastic bags."

"Slow down. Will you please slow down, Nicole?"

"You were the one trying to act like he was going to be the next Mr. Marcus. Don't you get it? This isn't who I was in Memphis."

"Slow the hell down, Nicole. Slow down and shut up for ten seconds."

"This is what you turned me into."

I snap, "If your fucking faults are because of me, then who in the hell can I blame my faults on? Who can I use as a scapegoat for my shortcomings?"

She screams, "I'm talking about me. You ever notice that all you give a damn about is you?"

I go off, "And who do you give a damn about? Besides you. Who?"

I've never understood blaming others for things internal, never been one to point fingers and place blame. Something I picked up from my old man's way of thinking. A man takes responsibility for his actions.

Then, we're going at it again, cursing each other. The dark side of this relationship has risen to the surface. Words stop when we see flashing lights up ahead, traffic slowing, backing up, on this side. Looks like a pretty bad accident. A fresh accident with warm blood staining the pavement.

We both get quiet. As quiet as death on Sunday morning.

Nicole moans, "Oh, God. Please."

I reach over and touch her hand.

Traffic is thicker, more stop than go. Everyone is being diverted to the far right lane. Hundreds of headlights are behind us, changing lanes and getting nowhere. It's a while before we move single file into the bright lights of the fire trucks, into the flashing lights of the Highway Patrol, ease toward a vehicle that has overturned and caught on fire.

Paramedics. A body bag. Death is out on the concrete, dancing the cabbage patch.

For a moment, I hope that dead body is Ayanna. In my mind I see myself standing next to Nicole, holding her hand while she howls over a fresh grave on a rainy day. Then I have another fear, a fear that there will be another Ayanna, another beautiful flower in Nicole's life, someone who steps in to pacify a desire that Nicole has, one that I can't control. Wonder if there will be Ayanna after Ayanna.

Then I feel ashamed of what I just felt, of that selfishness. Then I'm afraid of myself.

Nicole grips my left hand with her right, holds the

steering wheel just as tight with her left. I grip her hand just as tight. All traces of alcohol have gone away. I'm feeling sober. Nicole has been in sober mode ever since we started this chase.

A black Mercedes has overturned. A single car accident. I can't remember what Ayanna drives.

Nicole whispers, "She owns an SUV. A black SUV."

"Not her?"

"Not her. Not her."

A moment passes.

She says, "Thanks."

"For what?"

"I wasn't talking to you."

"Okay."

"But thank you too."

"For what?"

"For holding my hand. For caring. For putting up with me once again."

I hold her hand again. She holds mine. Seven years of history. Seven quality years.

We leave the freeway. Get caught at a red light. She pulls out her c-phone, pages Ayanna.

She puts her hand on mine. "Do you see what I'm doing?"

"What?"

"What you did to me. What you taught me. Encouraging her to another level."

"You're pushing her and you need to stop it."

"Too late. And why would you want me to stop? I've become what you wanted me to be."

"Look in your rearview mirror; that's me way behind you, waving. You've passed me up."

"Yeah, I guess I have. Hold my hand, let me take you with me."

I nod, swallow, run my hands over my hair, yank on a single twist. "I said that to you one night."

"When you seduced me inside your Jeep."

I almost snap again, but I sit back and rub my temples, decide not to beat that dead horse. She always says she was seduced. That evening I'd cooked her dinner, made salmon, saffron rice, salad with strawberry and wine dressing, ate that as we sipped white zinfandel. And we kissed while we did the dishes. Kissed until our lips were raw, pressed up against each other and did a slow grind for hours. When we got in my Jeep so I could take her home, we didn't plan it, but we started kissing, and I pulled her to me, touched her here, kissed her there, and we went all the way. After that we ended up in my tub, her back to me, while we sipped more wine. If that's seduction, then so be it.

I don't snap, but I do say, "It always goes back to the Jeep. Light's green."

She pulls away. "Now I want you to work with me on this, let me show you new things."

"So," I say with a thin smile, "the student becomes the teacher."

"Yes, you could say that. I'm studying my sexuality, trying to find the boundaries of my own desires. I'm not ashamed. Love me for who I am, not who you want me to be."

"What are your boundaries?"

"Don't know. Really don't know." She runs her hand over her locks, sighs her way back to the land of the calm. "Afraid because I don't know. Excited because I don't know. Because I feel so free. All my life I've been taught that sex is taboo, that my body is dirty, now I'm questioning it all."

"Do you move from watching the girls inside a bathroom stall to becoming one of them?"

"Are you insane? Hell, no. I'd never do anything like that."

"But you tried an ecstasy. You popped a forty-dollar pill."

"Didn't you used to get high? You never tried anything a couple of times?"

Again she pages Ayanna. Then I let her talk, let her calm for a while, don't want to be accused of not being attentive.

Finally I ask, "Why are you with Ayanna?"

"The same reason you're with me."

"Because?"

"She loves me too much to leave."

"But you left me."

"Then I invited you to see some of my world. And you came."

"Yeah, I came running. That makes me stupid."

"No, it shows how much you care for me."

She hits the outskirts of downtown Oaktown, goes over to 11th, cruises the side street in front of the Bench and Bar, a multiethnic bar where a hundred average-looking men in all shapes and sizes are out front hugging other men the same way I hug Nicole. A couple walks out of the club, both looking like hip-hop Beach Boys, laughing, smiling, sweat on their faces, sharing a cigarette.

I say, "You're not going in that fucking place, are you?"

"Don't worry."

"I've heard about places like this. Damn. Never knew they were real."

"That's because you tune out everything that fucks with your manhood."

I choose not to comment on that. I could, should, but I don't. Too tired to fight right now. And her driving is already bad enough. If we make it through the night, I'll debate her charge on solid ground.

She slows down long enough to check the cars, passes by two men flirting, another in the parking lot creating his own steam by taking a hot leak on cold pavement. Nicole doesn't see anyone she knows. She drives through downtown and zooms over to Telegraph, heads into what looks like Tupacville, drives around the block to a dim and dark club that reminds me of a bodega in New York. The club has closed, but when we follow the jovial hip-hop crowd, we see at least one hundred people are in the back parking lot, mostly men, all black. Looks like a FUBU and Tommy Hilfiger convention. I expect to see a crop of Little Richards and Liberaces at a place like this, but they look like rappers, most are hardcore and hip-hop to the bone. An LL Cool J–looking brother in ripped shorts and a long leather coat is exchanging saliva and rubbing testicles with a brother who is larger than Suge Knight.

A grossed-out sound comes out of me so fast it scares me.

Nicole jerks, as if she's just realizing I'm still in the car, swallows, takes a hard breath, says an uncomfortable, "You okay?"

"This looks like prom night at Folsom State Prison."

"Too close for comfort?"

"Too."

She pulls over, stops right in the thick of things, takes out her c-phone and dials Ayanna's c-phone, gets no answer, then she pages Ayanna again. While we sit with the streetlight brightening our faces, the crowd shifts, the way a private culture does when they sense an outsider. Eyes come to the car. A woman in a long red dress passes by and looks down at our faces without shame.

Nicole rolls down the passenger side window, asks, "Have you seen Ayanna down here?"

"Not tonight."

The woman in red smiles. The alcohol on her breath is sweet, mixes with the heat and tropical aroma inside this car. She looks at me and asks, "Tops, bottoms, or are you versatile?"

I respond, "What?"

" 'Cause I can go with the flow. Know what I mean?"

Nicole jumps in, "Not your type, Perri. He's mine."

"What's up with you and Ayanna? Heard y'all went up to the Russian River and had—"

"Just back off."

"Well, excuse me." The woman in red stares me down. "He sure looks familiar."

Her Adam's apple is larger than mine. She laughs, shakes her moneymaker as she goes back to the crowd, hugs up with a brother who looks like a steroid factory with reddish cornrows.

Nicole says, "Why does this bother you and watching women doesn't?"

"This isn't part of my world, not my reality."

Nicole says, "This is the real world. Not a subset. It's part of the whole she-bang."

I ask, "You and Ayanna hang out here?"

She doesn't answer. She knows that wasn't a question.

"There are a couple more spots down in Berkeley—"

"Hell, no. Take me to my room."

She nods, sighs. "Sweetie, no, that is not one of my hangouts. I'd rather go hiking than clubbing, you know that. And regardless of what you think, I'm tolerant, but I still don't care for certain clicks."

"What do you mean you don't care for certain clits?"

"Clicks. C-l-i-c-k-s. Not clits; clicks."

"Yeah, whatever. Take me to my room."

I'm silent as she drives up Telegraph to Broadway, then through downtown, the edges of Chinatown, back toward the Waterfront. She wants me to go with her, to go deeper into her secret world, but I can't. It's best for me to go back to my own nest tonight.

A thousand police are out, patrolling the crowd of people who are leaving Oak Tree, a club across the street. A lot of women are together, some are with men, some not, and vice versa, and now I'm questioning every relationship I see. Nicole drives the cobblestone road at Jack London Square and parks in front of the hotel.

I reach for the handle to get out, but she asks me to wait. Her voice struggles, as if Ayanna's leaving on a sour note and my leaving on a similar tune will wreck her to the core.

I see her brain working, hear it clicking and whirring, her logical side busy trying to solve problems.

Nicole says, "When I'm with you I think about babies. I still want to have a daughter and give her all the love that I didn't get as a child. I want to be a better mother than the one I have."

"Well, without a trip to the jerk-off bank, you can't have that with another woman."

"You're the only man I want. The only one I've ever wanted."

"Why can't I be the only one you want, dammit?"

"I'm attracted to you and her. I feel that both of you are my soul mates."

"Adam and Eve."

"Well, it's not like Eve had a helluva lotta choices."

She looks at me, crosses her eyes, sticks out her tongue.

I don't see shit funny. On her hands, I smell Ayanna's dried nectar.

Nicole is watching me, her lips pulled in tight, trying to read my mind; she has to go find Ayanna, her fidgeting tells me that, but she's reaching, trying to not lose me. She stalls some more.

She says, "This morning, when I started crying, you want to know why?"

"I already know. Emotional overflow. Because of Ayanna."

"I knew you thought that. I didn't want to say it then because, it seemed perverted or something. Us naked, in the shower, you all up inside of me, and I start thinking about somebody else."

I repeat, "Somebody else."

"Your gray eyes are turning green." She wipes her eyes, maybe anticipating tears, but there are no tears. "My daddy. I think his spirit ran through me or something. One minute I was feeling as good as a woman can feel, then the next second I was thinking about that 4 a.m. call I got, when momma told me that daddy was gone. Don't know why I thought about him then, of all times, but that was why I started boo-hooing like a baby."

That hurt slows me down.

I speak just above a whisper. "You miss him."

"Always. He understood me. He'd love me no matter what. We were so close. Pops knew he looked good in that blue suit. I knew he was gone before I picked up the phone. Felt it. We had that connection. His asthma had been acting up and the night before when I talked to him and he said he was okay, I didn't believe him, no matter how much he laughed. I was crying before I answered the phone."

"I know. I was in the bed next to you."

"I'm glad you were. So glad you were."

"Held you for hours."

"That 4 a.m. phone call that everybody gets. It's inevitable. Sometimes I wonder who's gonna make that call for me. You know, all of us are gonna have someone calling for us, telling everybody who cares that we're no longer available for breakfast, lunch, or dinner. I wonder who is gonna call for me. Who will cry? I know my mother won't."

"She'll cry the hardest."

Nicole disagrees. "She'll sell tickets so people can spit on my grave."

I pause to let that moment go away before I say, "Let's live forever."

"Are you nucking futs? Can you imagine how bad my skin will look after a hundred years? I'll look like Cicely Tyson did in that Jane Pittman movie."

We both laugh.

She makes an ugly face and twists her lips to one side, "Varicose veins and skin that sags like ... like your balls do when you get out of the shower. Talk about a scary sight."

"Oh, you got jokes."

"I got jokes." She hums out the sweetest sound. "You know what I miss the most about my dad?"

"What?"

"When we used to go hunt rabbit. I was a straight-

up tomboy. He took me down to Olive Branch, Mississippi, sometimes over to Pine Bluff, Arkansas, taught
me how to use a gun, let me skin Bugs Bunny, let me
be Elmer Fudd and cook rabbit too. He did everything
for me. I was his baby. Momma and I never had that
kind of bond. He let me be me, never told me I had to
be who he wanted me to be. Never told me I had to be
a doctor or an engineer, that was momma. Always so
concerned about image. Always concerned about what
her friends think. What her sorority members think.
What the people at her church think."

"I know."

"Not like my daddy was. Daddy said if they don't
like it, screw 'em. He was so funny."

"I know."

"You remind me of him. All the good things I found
in him, I see in you too."

"I know. Who does Ayanna remind you of?"

"Me, when I was first with you. Of the mother I
never had. Of the best friend I always longed for. Of
the sister I always wanted. Of the kind of person I
wish I was most of the time. Of you at times."

I watch Nicole. She's a nervous wreck, trying to act
cool. Her mind whirring and clicking and clacking,
trying to come up with a solution. Afraid to leave me,
wanting to go.

I say, "Go look for her."

She stalls me again, says, "I do love her, you know."

"Yeah. I know. I could tell when we were coming up
on that accident."

"And I do want all of us to be able to coexist."

I'm listening to Nicole and thinking about Ayanna.
Remembering that moment when Ayanna was bare in
front of me, staring at me, a thing of beauty and vul-

nerability, licking her full lips, then her sweet expression as she burned and wiggled, letting out her whines and moans and shudders.

I glance at Nicole and see her in a different light. No more illusions. No more masks. So much familiarity between them, the knowing when and how to touch to create those kinds of moments.

I say, "Ayanna told me that she's known you eight years."

"I met her before you, but nothing happened."

"When did you first sleep with her?"

"It wasn't eight years ago, if that's what you think. Nothing happened."

"Something happened. Couldn't end up where you are now if nothing happened."

"She was married when I met her."

"And?"

"And I was there for her when she lost her husband. As a friend."

"Like I said, something happened. Couldn't end up where you are now if nothing happened."

Nicole takes out her c-phone. Pages Ayanna four times. Nicole's phone doesn't ring back.

I ask, "Coming back?"

"Not tonight."

"I'm only here a couple of days."

"I know."

"Seems like she takes precedence."

"Don't say that. This is not a damn competition."

"But eight years is more than seven, right?"

She leans over and hugs me. Hugs me and I notice that she lets go first.

She notices that too. She notices and shakes her head, like she's reading my thoughts.

She says, "I got that from you."

"Got what?"

"The letting go first. You always did that. Did that like you wanted to make sure you were in control. Like you were afraid to hold on the longest, like that would make you weak or something."

"I didn't."

"You don't now, not since things have changed. Not since the wedding. But you did. I'd want to hold you forever and you'd let me go. Trust me on that one. Not chastising you, just an observation."

I try to remember if it was like that. There are a lot of things I haven't noticed.

She traces her fingers down my face to my lips, and as I close my eyes and suck on her slender extremity, she whispers, "I love you. I need you. Please be patient a little while longer."

She kisses me; I taste Ayanna stirring on her tongue. I kiss her harder.

Nicole's hand eases into my lap, massages my penis. Under the lights of the Waterfront Hotel, people are walking back and forth, leaving TGIF, entering the hotel, and touring the specialty shops.

Nicole unzips my pants, takes my penis out, moves it back and forth. I grow.

She whispers, "You didn't, did you?"

"Nope. Didn't."

"Let me."

"No, that's okay."

"Let me. I want you to be able to sleep."

I take my penis from her, put it back inside my pants. She held my penis longer than she hugged me.

I wonder if that's how she sees me, as the owner of this dick, not as a whole man. If she thinks, after all these years, that sex is all I need, that an orgasm is all I'm about, when in the end, I want the totality of life, the totality of her.

I tell her, "Go find Ayanna."

I get out of her car, close the door, and wave as I walk backward to the lobby. Not sure what I'm feeling, or what I want anymore. I turn around and stare at Nicole as she pulls away, dialing on her c-phone. Ayanna is on my mind too. A minute ago, when Nicole was touching me, I was imagining that was Ayanna's hand. I shake that sensation away, give it to the night's breeze.

I put a smile on my face and speak to the beautiful Ethiopian women in the lobby, admire them as I always do, and for a moment I wish they would kidnap me away from this life and love me forever.

One stops me, "You signed Tseday's book yesterday."

I pause. Blink. Think. Remember. "Yeah. I did."

"That's all she's talking about. She has the biggest crush on you."

I don't want to be rude, or abrupt, so I say a few more words, then yawn when the timing is right.

I tell them, "G'night. Don't work too hard."

As I jog up the stairs, I remember what Ayanna said, about holding Nicole for eight years. Not since Nicole has been here in Oakland, but for eight years. Before me. Before me and Nicole met up at mile twenty. And I remember Nicole claiming that nothing had happened between them.

I can't explain why I'm so attracted to Nicole. No one can really explain why they are attracted to anyone, not when you get beyond the physical to the spiritual, to those hidden parts that make you cling to another with all of your life.

It's 3 a.m. when she leaves me alone with insomnia. I have miles to go before I sleep.

I go to my room, take out my cassette recorder, think about putting my thoughts on a brand-new tape, but push it to the side, change my mind and pull out pen and paper. No computer. Pen and paper make me think, get closer to my heart, closer to the truth.

I write. Write about domination and subordination. Women and madness. Men and obsession. Freedom and acceptance. Spiritual peace. What's right. What's wrong.

What's perceived as right, and what is considered wrong.

Write about three people. Drowning in pools of their own emotions. Two are in love with one woman, unable to break their illogical obsession for her, a woman who claims to love them both. I write about a beautiful woman who says that she is trapped, says she needs both to love, both to survive.

I write to understand what I don't understand.

I don't have the answers, not yet, but I do know this is certain; loving, running, and writing have one thing in common. The one who wins at any of those is the one who does it on the days he doesn't feel like doing it. The one who does it when it's hard. The one who sweats through the difficult times and endures the pain. Those are the people who succeed.

In between thoughts, I read bits and pieces of *Lolita*. No matter how many times I read it, he is still a fool. The only way this book will have a favorable ending is if I read it backwards, from end to start, then it looks like he moves from insanity to sanity.

I leave the book alone and write.

Two hours later, when I've written as much as I can

stand, after I've stared out the windows at the stars and endured the silence as long as I can, I pick up the phone and page Nicole. Want to know if everything is okay with Ayanna.

Nicole doesn't call back.

Night dwindles into dawn.

17

At 6 a.m., while seagulls are competing with sparrows for scraps of food, while the streetwalkers are pulling up their bloomers and getting ready to turn in for the day, while oversize trucks are outside my window unloading their heavy contents in front of Jack's Bistro, there is a hard knock at my door. A nonstop hard knock. I spy through the peephole.

I open the door.

She stares.

It's Ayanna. She's alone. Wearing a black business suit, black pumps, thigh-length black leather coat, holding a red-and-white gym bag in her left hand, her black purse and attaché in the other.

I thought that I'd destroyed her last night, thought that I'd won the battle. Maybe I did win that battle. But this morning the look in her eyes, her hostile sneer, that tells me that she's bringing me the war.

She marches in, shoulders stiff, back straight, moves with dignity and grace, with determination.

I pass by her, go back over to the bed and sit down. Her pager beeps a musical melody that is nothing but irritation at this hour. Ayanna reads her digital display then mumbles, "Forty-nine."

She goes to my closet. Opens the door. Rifles through the subset of my life I've brought to this room. Takes out my running shoes. Hurls them at my feet.

My toes grip the carpet hard enough to raise the top from the padding. I nod.

Friends close. Enemies closer. That's what I'm thinking. Keep enemies damn close.

Where she stands, she strips naked. Her skin glistens with oil. Her frankincense and patchouli aroma smells fresh. She squats to open her gym bag, allowing me to see the outline of her private parts. In that stirring position I see the definition of her legs, the tightness of her calves and thighs, the subtle definition in her back that speaks of lifting light weights, all of that strength comes to life.

First she pulls out worn running shoes with dried dirt on the edges, shoes that speak of many miles on pavement and asphalt hills and mountain trails. She lays them on the floor. Then she unfolds a yellow sports bra, black running tights, both faded.

Ayanna stares at me. Her eyes are dark, bleak, despairing, downright cruel. She's simmering.

I strip naked. Open a drawer. Start dressing.

She dresses too.

I move to the area with the sofa, my joints popping and aching as I do overhand reaches. Twists and turn. Heel holds. Wall leans. Squats.

Like a boxer, she remains in the opposite corner and uses the wall to flex her calves, then sits and works her inner thighs, her hamstrings, goes into a full split, does a Chinese split as well.

Her pager sings again. She reads the display and says, "Fifty."

She wants me to ask. Wants me to ask so bad.

Once more she digs in her bag, taking out Vaseline. She rubs a healthy amount of the gel on her nipples, rubs more between her legs. She softball pitches me the jar and I do the same, using more than enough gel on my nipples and thighs and groin to prevent friction burns.

She stands and moves near the door.

I say, "Wait a minute, Counselor."

My bladder needs to be emptied. So do my bowels. I take care of that business while she stands outside the bathroom door.

Her pager sings again.

Through the door I hear her say, "Fifty-one."

We take the long route, down the winding hallway to the lobby, take a swift pace out of the Waterfront and head across the cobblestone walkway toward the railroad tracks, the flags overhead flapping and snapping in the frigid air, sounding like a slave owner's whip. I have on a dark sweater. Long black runner's tights. Brown gloves. All she has on is a sports bra and her black tights. From skin to bone, I'm freezing like Frosty the Snowman. This chill is stiffening my joints.

Still, the weather is warmer than her attitude.

An Amtrak blows three times. We wait for the commuters to pass then jog to the steps in front of Jack London Cinema before we stop.

She makes an angry motion toward downtown. "Here to Twentieth, to Lake Merritt, around once, back to here. To this very spot we're standing on."

She uses her right foot to mark an imaginary **X**.

I nod. It's a 10K; a little over six miles. Right now, the way I feel, with the heaviness in my body, there's not much difference between six miles and six thousand.

With clenched teeth she says, "I win, you do what-

ever I ask. No questions asked. If I say get out of Oakland and never bring your no-writing, yellow-ass back
and never call her and never return her calls, not even
a single e-mail, you do that."

"No way."

"Chicken or just low on testosterone?"

I grit my teeth. We stare each other down like rival
gangs in the yard at Tahatchapie prison.

I say, "And if I win?"

"I do whatever you ask."

For clarity I ask, "Anything?"

"Absolutely anything."

We stare, eye-to-eye, boxers right before the start of
the first round.

I ask, "What are the limits?"

"No limits. Agreed?"

"Yes. Agreed."

We shake hands. The contract is sealed.

She adds, "And Writer Boy, no shortcuts on the
grass trying to catch up."

Ayanna holds up her stopwatch. It beeps when she
resets the timer.

I do the same.

Without warning, she breaks away running at race
pace, leaving only her scent behind. It's damn cold for
a man with L.A. blood and I'm a slow starter.

I chase her to the wild and crazy traffic competing to
get on the Tube. She darts through the cars zooming
toward Alameda, makes the leader slam on his brakes,
moves in an arrogant way that dares those impatient
people to even think about hitting her, and I slow
down, lose time and rhythm when I give them eye
contact to make sure they're not going to run me into
the cold, black ground.

A slight incline exists for the first mile leading into the heart of downtown, just enough slope to challenge my lungs, for me to realize that this isn't my pace, and even though I've run this way before, this isn't familiar terrain. I watch the way she slants her head, holds her arms at a comfortable level, how her feet land with an elegant heel-toe roll, all the signs of a refined runner.

A mile later we reach the crowded sidewalks on the outskirts of Chinatown. At last, my body starts feeling warm. The buildings of downtown are waiting for us, standing tall over us like uneven teeth.

Ayanna is half a block ahead, her yellow and black making her look like a bumblebee, and I feel as if I'm approaching maximum heart rate. Her arms are relaxed, her hands below her heart, a smooth rhythm, the same magnificent form Nicole owns when her feet pound the pavement.

Ayanna glances back over her left shoulder as she crosses an intersection, almost trips as she avoids pedestrians huddled at the bus stop in front of Walgreen's, sees that I'm in striking distance. She tries to leave me. I pick up the pace. At 20th, she steals another peek as she cuts right toward the lake. I can smell her fading scent, can hear her jingles echoing like laughter.

I'm getting closer, five seconds behind when we cross Webster Street. I'm hurting like hell, ready to slow down to an easy jog.

We run by the smokers outside Lake Merritt Plaza and by the time we take the contest toward the lake, my body adjusts to the agony. Adrenaline numbs my torment as if it were morphine. Then my pain outweighs nature's drug, becomes too great.

A quarter mile around the lake, I catch her, begin

stepping on her shadow, a shadow that comes and goes with the diffused light overhead. Oxygen flows to my muscles. I'm hurting. My mind is not ready for battle. I'm about ready to give this shit up. Ayanna runs like she has a high lactic acid threshold, can perform harder and longer at this level; a smooth runner who consumes very little oxygen, very little metabolic and cardiorespiratory stress, at least none that I can see.

My pace picks up, bluffs that I'm holding back and can perform better, with every stride I inhale through my nose and exhale through my mouth, using my technique to hide my pain, to keep me going.

But she's good. So natural. So well-trained.

Strong heart. Strong mind. Strong legs.

People are pausing long enough to stare at us.

Halfway around the lake, sweat rolls from my forehead to my right eye. I wipe it away without a thought. My pace is good and I'm floating. I catch her and ride her tailwind. Right before we get to the Veteran's Memorial Building, she realizes what I'm doing and steps aside. I move up and match her pace. Run at her side at a warrior's stride.

She makes orgasmic faces as she huffs, "You run like a bitch."

"Wow . . . Counselor . . . such—"

"Hard time talking?"

"—intelligent vocabulary . . . from a woman—"

"Not getting tired are you?"

"—with so many . . . degrees."

"I'm dumbing it down so you can understand. See ya."

She speeds up, pulls away with ease, baits my male ego. It's not until then that I see her strategy. She has pissed me off, made me run out of my comfort zone, and on top of that she's made me talk with the wind slapping me in my face. In that angry moment, the cold air attacks my lungs, causes them to contract, making it twice as hard to keep my pace.

Then we're back downtown, the Sears building behind us, Wells Fargo bank building in front of us, once again ducking and dashing by innocent bystanders. We're rude and in our own zone, sometimes stepping in the streets, running as many red lights as we can.

She's ahead of me again. Seven, maybe ten seconds. Looking strong. Running with arrogance.

I run facing traffic, stay on the outside of the parked cars. I do that because I notice that when she looks back, she always looks over her left shoulder, never her right.

In every war, there must be a plan. Must be a strategy. You watch your opponent, look for their weaknesses, see where they screw up, and you have to use it to your advantage.

With less than a mile to go, she glances back over that favorite shoulder and doesn't see me. I'm there. Hurting, but I'm there. Ten seconds behind her. With her steady pace, with the burning in my muscles, the pain in my hamstring, that is forever. My skin is being ripped away, the exposed wound soaked in Tabasco. I'm ready to slow, ready to concede, but her step falters, her arms come up higher. Losing form. She missteps, then recovers within six strides. Form slips again. Arms too high. Favoring her right leg. She's tense. She's tired. She's afraid to lose. She's becoming weak.

So am I.

She's ten seconds ahead of me when she goes under the 980 overpass. The people zooming into the Tube almost run her down, break her stride, but she recovers, looks back, doesn't see me. It's downhill all the way. I stay in the street, on the outside of the huge, circular support columns for the overpass, and once again she glances back over her left shoulder. Nope, she can't see me, not at all.

She doesn't slow down, like I'd hoped she'd do by the time she passed the Oakland Police Department, maybe by the time she crossed the Probation Department, but she doesn't speed up either.

I struggle to overcome my lack of natural ability with heart and dedication. My foot strike is right behind the ball of my foot, and I push off with my toes, my arms in rhythm with my legs, knees up, stride getting longer, longer, longer, knees up, breathe, breathe, maintain my pace, try not to waste energy by overstriding, stay steady, stay smooth.

I refuse to be beat.

Five seconds behind.

I refuse to be beat by her.

Her shadow is within reach.

I refuse to lose Nicole.

Knees high and changing to sprint mode, legs burning and chest aching, lungs on fire as I pass Ayanna two blocks before Jack London Cinema. She thought me wounded and dead, was ready to celebrate by feasting on my rotting flesh. I feel her surprise, hear her even breaths become a rugged jerk when I come from nowhere, feel her try and shift gears by lengthening her stride.

Her feet slap the streets, her huffing and puffing, the jingle of the bracelets on her arm rings like a warning, letting me know where the enemy resides. I never look back. Those desperate jingles fall behind.

I reach the designated spot in front of Jack London Cinema in thirty-seven minutes and twelve seconds. The jingles catch up five seconds later.

She stops beyond me, as if to prove a point, then walks in a circle. Sweat flows from her skin, sits in the hollows of her collarbone, giving her an early-morning glow. Drops of that salty moisture have collected in her crotch, are rolling down the trim definition of her back, being dried by the harsh breeze.

With her hands on her slender hips, she pants and kicks the pavement with the ball of her foot.

I say, "Next time bring your A-game."

"Where was your A-game on your wedding day?"

I frown. I'm two breaths from committing a felony.

She rants at me, "I don't see what she sees in you anyway. If you were a nice-looking, dark-skinned brother, I might understand, but—"

I snarl, "Pack your shit, get out of Oakland, never come back, never call her, never return her calls."

She scowls and wipes her face, at first I think it's sweat, but it's the beginning of tears. She coughs, sneezes, gags, starts to throw up.

I jog toward the lobby of the hotel, leave her tossing her cookies on the pavement as an Amtrak passes. A hundred passengers witness her misery.

18

Ayanna catches up with me before I make it back to Jack London Square. She follows me into the Waterfront, up the stairs, then down the hallway. Her body is in such misery that it's a struggle for her to keep up.

Ayanna speaks in both fear and the syncopation of love. "I don't want her stolen from me. I love her so much that if she had cancer, I'd want cancer too, just so she wouldn't have to suffer alone. Can you say your love is that strong? Are you capable of loving like that?"

My response is, "Geesh. And you said her pussy had made me delusional."

That breaks her pace.

Ayanna bumps by me when I open my door. The moment I close it, I take off my dank sweatshirt and T-shirt and remind her, "You said anything. No limits."

I take in her frame, the lines and curves that look more apparent in this moment, the swell of her breasts, the erection of each nipple as they stand chilled underneath her damp sports bra. My eyes roving from head to toe, my face frowning at the parts that differentiate her sex from mine.

Fragile lines appear on her face. That's the damage losing has added. I also see that her belligerence has doubled. Smoke portends fire.

Ayanna stares at the wall, runs her fingers through her lioness mane, her lips looking full, reminding me of the pouty and angry demeanor of Sandra Bernhard. "Selfish bastard. Is your love that damn strong? Would you sacrifice everything? Are you capable of loving Nicole like that? Or do you just love with your dick? All you are to her is another orgasm donor anyway."

"I did sacrifice everything. I sacrificed and you lost."

"Well, she dumped your ass and followed me here, so who really lost? She lives with me, so who has lost? All you get are a few stolen moments. One weekend a month, if that, like a damn army reserve. And when you leave here, she'll be with me."

That digs too deep.

"Like I said, bring your A-game next time."

"And like I said," she woofs back at me, "where was your A-game on your wedding day?"

I stare at her, heart racing, mouth dry, my fingers becoming fists.

She swallows, allows her fingers to pop and roll into fists.

She's desperate. Never attack a desperate enemy.

I back off, but I still say, "So you're reneging."

Her lips twist. She refuses to be banished from her own kingdom, forever living in solitude with a broken heart. From where I stand, in the section with the sofa and love seat, I can see that her heart is beating so fast it creates an abbreviated rise and fall of her damp chest.

Ayanna raises my blood pressure and brings out the worst in me. What I hate even more is that she has brought out the best in me. I've never run that distance that fast—something she doesn't need to know.

We continue to stare. If only she were a man, I'd kick her ass.

She moves by me and opens my closet, begins pulling out my luggage, going through my things.

I demand to know, "What do you think you're doing?"

"Why would she buy me coffee every day, and on weekends she always brings me my favorite M&Ms, never plain, always the ones with peanuts, but she still runs to you the moment you get here. What makes you so fucking special?"

She digs through my brown leather messenger bag, pulls out my journal and my pictures. Pictures of me and Nicole in Maui, Jamaica, Cancun. Skiing in Canada at Whistler. At the Louvre in Paris. Enough pictures to remind Ayanna that I've been more than just a dick to Nicole, more than a wretched orgasm donor.

Ayanna stops in her tracks. "These are the wedding pictures."

I turn on the shower, leave her sitting on the floor, investigating my life, being tormented by those indelible images, looking for answers to things no one but Nicole can answer.

I hear her bracelets jingle as I shower, that irritating song she makes irking me down to my bones as I scrub and deliberate why she's here. It's simple to ask her to go away, but I want Ayanna here. The reason is simple. Nobody can be in two places at the same time. If she's here tormenting me, she can't be with Nicole. That gives me solace. Gives me faux control. Faux because I know that Ayanna is here to monitor the same insecurities.

Water runs down my back. I close my eyes. And I see those pictures. Always see those pictures. The videotape of that day runs through my mind like the Mississippi runs south. I swim upstream against those memories.

Most of those pictures were taken an hour before the wedding that almost happened. Me and my grooms-men getting dressed, helping me put on my Kente bowtie and matching cummerbund, posing for the photographer, laughing and having fun to cover my nerves. Nicole with her entourage outfitted in white gowns, traditional gowns that her mother picked out, all trimmed in pink. All the women smiling and hoping to be the one to catch the bouquet, so they could pressure their mates across the broom, getting their hair curled or straightened, nail polish touched up, helping my love put on her silk and chiffon gown. Nicole, dressed in white, looking like an angel.

Nicole's mother was there with the rest of her family and friends; they'd all flown out to L.A. My father was doing the ceremony, and we were at his church. The AME church I grew up in. The church on Crenshaw where I ushered for many years. My old man's friends were there, people who flew in from his alma mater at Morehouse, friends of Littles and Kings, doctors and lawyers who marched the roads of Birmingham with him during the uncivilized days of the civil rights movement, people who had done the same in the north. People who believed in God and family.

A saxophonist played and Tammy Barrett sang as Nicole came down that red carpet. She moved so ethe-really across the roses that had been sprinkled on her trail, so many *ooos* and *ahhhs*, so many clicks and whirs from all the cameras flashing, floating with the grace of a princess, escorted by her stepfather, short nervous steps that looked so smooth, smiling at a few people as tears welled up in her eyes.

With all those eyes on us, in that temple, surrounded by warm smiles and teardrops waiting to fall, my father did his thing. He spoke of responsibility and trust, touched on all the things it takes to make a marriage work, with the emphasis being on work, of a man's role, of the woman's role, letting us know that no matter whether the sun was shining or if dark clouds were looming, and dark clouds would indeed loom, we'd be husband and wife, bonded through God, and we were to work it out.

Tears welled in Nicole's eyes too. So many tears ready to fall.

When my father asked Nicole if she would take me to be her husband, she opened her mouth, nodded, smiled, then this other look washed over her face.

She stood there forever, which in reality was no more than thirty seconds, then turned and looked over the congregation, over all of our friends and families, then told the church that we had to talk before we went any further.

A different tone of *ooos* and *ahhs* filled the sanctuary.

She walked away, hands holding the sides of her dress so she wouldn't misstep and fall on her face, her train separating us by almost ten feet.

I followed her into a side room, and before I could close and lock the door, she was crying, talking with her hands, rambling incomplete sentences, words coming out as fast as her tears were falling.

My voice trembled when I told her, "You're just scared. The jitters have you confused."

"No. I'm clear."

"Let's . . . all the people here . . . your sorors . . . the presents . . ."

"Damn the presents," she snapped. Now she was angry. "You never listen to me, do you?"

I backed off, tried to compose myself. "I'm listening, I'm listening."

Sweat gathered under my collar, in my armpits.

I pinched my nostrils, adjusted my bow tie, waited for her to pull herself together and vocalize her burdens.

"I love you," she said, her voice spent. "I want to be your wife. I want to have your babies. Just not today. I need to work things out."

"All you have to say are two words: I do."

"I can't."

By then, people were yelling and tapping on the door. We ignored them.

I lowered my head, ran my fingers through my short hair, wished that it was long enough to grip and yank out at the roots.

Outside, the pianist was playing an instrumental version of "Amazing Grace," no doubt doing that because he had no idea what to do in a moment like that, because an Anita Baker or a Luther Vandross song just didn't fit the bill.

Nicole rocked and hummed the old-time spiritual, closed her eyes, joined in on, "How sweet the sound, that saved a wretch like me . . ."

Her eyes opened, came to mine. She smiled.

"Okay," I said. "I can deal with whatever you're going through."

"I can't. That's the problem. I can't deal with this"—with that she gestured at herself, at her heart, at the church itself, then toward heaven, before she motioned toward me and said—"and you."

She slid the engagement ring from her finger, laid it on the table. A 2.5 carat emerald solitaire cut in platinum. Out there, resting in my best man's pocket, was a pinpoint diamond eternity band.

She said, "There are things I want to do, things I think I have to experience to be sure, and being married and doing them won't be right. Being married and not being able to experience them won't be right either."

Nicole leaned forward and kissed me. Held me for a few minutes. Held me until people began knocking on the door, asking if we were okay.

She pulled her lips inward, messed up her lipstick, smeared it all over her white teeth, said, "So this is what happens when Sleeping Beauty wakes up."

It took her over an hour to apologize to her bridesmaids, women who had taken sabbaticals, used up vacation time, a couple who were more concerned with who was going to reimburse them for all the money they had spent on plane fare and the useless dresses they had bought.

In the midst of all the turmoil, Nicole blew her nose, pulled her hair back into a ponytail and changed from silk and chiffon to ripped jeans and a Memphis in May T-shirt.

She had to have a word with her mother, a stern woman who gave me harsh eyes and extreme silence, posture that accused me of manly wrongdoings. So stereotypical. Nicole was forthright with her mom. Right there in church, she spoke her piece. Her mother's blood pressure went up so high she had to be taken to the hospital, prayer on her tongue and a Bible clutched to her chest. I do believe that was the last day they had words. Nicole left us all at the altar.

She tells me that with ten American dollars and a two-minute dance, I eased her to the edge and she woke up on the other side. A side of her that she needed to explore.

19

When I'm done showering, it's quiet. Too damn quiet.
I wonder if the enemy has gone to lick her wounds.
With reluctance, I call her name. No answer. No
sounds. As I dry off, I open the bathroom door; steam
wafts out into the cooler air and evaporates like hope
does for those whose faith is weak.

Ayanna sits naked in the middle of the bed, the
darkness on her breasts creating two midnight bull's-
eyes. Her body faces east, eyes closed, palms to the
heavens, either meditating or drying her nails.

My pictures of Nicole are spread around her in a
perfect circle. A shrine for her black Madonna.

I go to the table. To my laptop. Try to think and type.

Ayanna comes to life and hurries to the bathroom.
She takes a short shower, then comes back in the room
with a white towel around her body, sits on the bed
and rubs lotion on her flesh.

She whispers, "I want to know what she feels with
you. I need to feel what she feels so I can understand
what's going on inside her head."

I stop typing for a moment, breathing halts, my soul
both jarred and stimulated by her words. Heat flour-
ishes in my stomach, right between my navel and my
groin, in that dangerous area.

She asks, "Don't you want to know what it is about my tongue that made her leave you and move in with me?"

Finally, I breathe.

Ayanna speaks in a soft voice. "She told me that the first time she kissed me, she felt like a virgin all over again. And when I touched her, when she touched me, we both exploded. All the other sex I had ever experienced just fell away. No other love compares."

I type more words, use this computer as I always use it, to escape from the real world, to create my world where I control everything that everyone does, every word they say, every motion they make, a place where women do what I say, give me what I want without reservation.

"So much about her I admire. Haven't you noticed? I do my hair like hers. Looks better on her, though, don't you think? My bracelets, Mexican silver, just like hers. We bought them for each other when were in Puerto Vallarta. We went to the jazz festival down there, you know that?"

I inhale a smell that mimics Nicole's fragrance as well. The sounds. The aroma. Even certain inflections of Ayanna's voice ring of Nicole.

"The first time we made love, she laughed and told me it was like honeymoon sex."

That stuns me. Honeymoon sex has always been our phrase. Our pillow talk. My anger rises.

Ayanna goes on, "I'd never felt anything like that before in my life. She was my first too. That night I felt like a virgin all over again. All the other times I'd made love, they didn't compare, couldn't even be remembered. Every other lover became faceless. Went away in a poof. Just ceased to exist."

This is disturbing.

She whispers, "Ask me when that was. Ask me. Scared? Ask me?"

My breath catches in my throat.

She whispers, "Ask me if I was at your wedding. Ask me to give you the details. Ask me to tell you how pitiful you looked when you came back in and had to tell everybody that there was no wedding."

I imagine taking piano wire to her neck.

Ayanna is so persistent. So unrelenting.

"I want to be Nicole. Does that make sense?"

Hair the color of broken hearts and a new fire. Fascinating.

"If I have to be her to understand her, yes. If I have to feel you inside me to understand her, yes, I'm willing to go that far."

We stare.

In perfect French she mimics Nicole, *"Baise moi."*

I'm startled and she knows it.

Ayanna pulls the towel from her body, again showing her flesh, but this time her tight eyes tell me there is a difference. She's serious.

"Show me what makes you special," she says. "I'll show you the same."

For a moment, she has the glow of a thousand angels in her catlike eyes, in her sensuous lips. Her smugness remains, and that too has its own brand of attractiveness. I stare at her body. With every breath I inhale her scent. I feel vibrations from her brain working in so many directions, clicking and clacking and clacking and clicking, whirring and searching for deficiencies in me, trying to rip me apart.

"Baise moi," she repeats over and over. *"Mange moi,* if you want to."

She refuses to lose, even when she has lost. This war will never end.

She touches her breasts, pinching the darkest parts. Once again I stare at the most beautiful nipples I've ever seen. Blackberries that stand high, calling out for my tongue, for my hands, for my warm mouth.

I get on my knees, crawl toward the foot of the bed, creep toward her wine country.

She scoots back on the bed until her back touches the pillows, skin moist with oil, moves her legs apart, again showing me how limber she is, turning her body into a capital letter Y, testing my reaction, offering me a full view of her own ayanna, her beautiful flower that sends me the sweet scent of a wanting rose.

She touches herself, opens her beautiful flower for me to see.

I get up on the bed, move toward her.

The phone rings.

I back away, let the phone stop ringing. In French, Ayanna invites me to her mystery again.

She watches me watch her. I watch her watch me.

Then there's a knock at the door. I jump. A very soft, feminine knock. Nicole's cadence and rhythm. Before I can get to the door, it opens. An Asian housekeeper is startled when she sees me naked, more startled when she sees Ayanna on the bed naked, and closes the door real quick. The way Ayanna didn't move or cover herself let me know that she was hoping it was Nicole.

I sit at the foot of the bed, close to Ayanna. I want to fuck her hard, sex her into submission. It's a man thing. It comes with the testosterone.

She says, "Scared?"

"Let's . . . let's talk a minute or two."

I ask Ayanna about her first meeting Nicole, when they were at mile sixteen.

I ask, "What did you say to her?"

"Told her she had beautiful lips. I love lips. Then I asked her which way did she swing."

"And?"

"She laughed and we kept on running and talking, looking at each other, admiring each other."

My breathing gets ragged for a moment. I say, "So it went down like a man and a woman."

"Yep."

"Who was the man, who was the woman?"

She laughs at me like my words are banal, typical.

I ask, "Your family back in Kalamazoo, or Detroit, or wherever you're from, know about you and Nicole?"

"What is this, an interview with a lesbian?"

"Just trying to understand what I don't understand."

"Don't you get it? It's a secret world. You're not supposed to understand."

Her eyes go back to the pictures in her shrine. Another Amtrak whistles outside.

I ask, "This situation between me, you, and Nicole—"

"It's normal." She clears her throat. "That's what you were going to ask, right?"

"Yeah."

"There's always one who doesn't know if she's coming out of the closet or going back in." She shifts like she's disturbed. "A true lesbian wouldn't go behind a man. That's humiliation. An outright violation. A lesbian wouldn't let her woman go somewhere else."

"But you did."

"I did."

"By your definition, you've got one foot in, and one foot out, doing a hokey-pokey yourself."

She pushes her lips up into a phony smile. Throws in a thin chuckle to make it seem real. When she's done, her eyes settle on the pictures again.

I ask, "What's it like when I leave from up here?"

"When she comes back to our beautiful home and you go back to your shack in Carson?"

"Yep."

"She says I get in PMS mode. I won't touch her. She's either distant or too polite. We're both uncomfortable because I know where she's been."

"Fights?"

"Nope. She throws herself into her job, works late, and I pretty much do the same. She's wondering who's making love to her old lady while she's out making love."

"You creepy-creep-creep to see somebody else while she's with me?"

"Would you blame me?"

I say, "You avoid answering the tough questions."

"Nope, when she crawls from your fuckhaven to our heaven, she knows that she has to scrub your fingerprints off her skin and clean your smell off her flesh."

Then she looks down at a photo of me and Nicole at the Book Expo in Chicago, us standing and smiling with other writers and their loved ones. Man, woman, man, woman, Adam, Eve, Adam, Eve.

Ayanna says, "Let me cross-examine you for a change. What are you doing when you know she's with me night after night? I doubt if you're getting a good night's sleep."

I stop and think. Remember one-night stands with women who, from the first handshake, either sounded like, smelled like, had something about them that took me back to Nicole. They had to remind me of Nicole. A time or two I thought I could replace Nicole with a doppelgänger. No matter how brilliant or how beautiful, sunlight always made them have a different look in the morning. We all look different in the morning.

Ayanna doesn't wait for my answer, maybe she reads my mind, or already knows, before she turns on her side, pulls a pillow in front of her body. "The first time I was with a woman I was so scared."

"Why?"

"I was married, for one. In love with my hubby for two. Thought people would find out and start throwing stones. Thought I was gonna be shoveling coal in hell. It's nerve-racking. Thinking about doing it is stressful enough. You hem, you haw, you struggle, you lead her on, you back away, do this emotional cha-cha over and over, drive yourself crazy, then you decide you're going for it."

She laughs a little.

I laugh too. I ask, "Sounds like what a man goes through getting a woman to give up her virginity."

"Yep. Same struggle, same fear, because in that way you are a virgin. But this is much deeper. Causes confusion. When I got up the nerve to go there, I was liking it, but was thinking about all kinds of stuff when I was having an orgasm."

"Stuff like what?"

"Heaven. Hell. My husband. My parents. Looked down at her and wondered why she liked doing that so much and she was a woman. Shouldn't her tongue be swollen by now. If she's gonna go run and tell everybody. If she's gonna get attached and go psycho. My mind was all over the place."

I rub my hands together. "Was that first time eight years ago with Nicole?"

"You're trying to lay out a chronological map."

"I guess. Yeah."

She gives me half a smile. "Can you handle the truth?"

I nod. "I've been pretty good at it so far."

"I met Nicole first. But she wasn't in this zone yet. Curious, but scared." She laughs and hand-combs her hair. She does that a lot. "But my first time was with a Latina I met on-line."

"Wait a minute. Thought you said Nicole was—"

"Nicole was the first that *I* made love to. The only one. I let others *make love to me*. Get it?"

It takes me a moment, a few blinks, but in the end I say, "Got it."

"Good. The short yellow bus is catching up."

I repeat, "Latina?"

"Pretty exotic woman. Ten years older. Professor at Berkeley. She was married."

"Your own south-of-the-border Mrs. Robinson."

"With two children. Don't let a wedding ring and a baby carriage fool you."

"You're lying."

"I can go on-line right now and show you things at www.gayblackfemale.com that'll blow you away. I can pull up a zillion personal ads out at YAHOO! by married women. All ages. All races."

"No thanks. This is . . . wild. I'm . . . learning. Why didn't you get with a sister? You crossed over."

"In more ways than one." She laughs a little. "This is how it goes; lots of 'curious' women get their carnal knowledge on with a woman of another race. Especially my sisters. Black people and sexuality. Sex is so taboo with us, that's why half us are walking around with fucked-up heads."

I listen to the hum coming from near the window facing Jack London Square.

She talks on, "When we were done, she left the Hyatt, went back to her crib in Berkeley and fed her kids oatmeal and turkey bacon; I went back to folding socks in East Oaktown."

"With lotion on your back."

"With lotion on my back."

I ask, "Why the game?"

"I was scared. Curious, scared. In the end, it works out better that way. That way your secret doesn't have to come back home with you. You don't get embarrassed. You try it, see if it's your thing. You don't get judged. You don't get the stares. It's almost like interracial dating."

"Don't get it."

"You know how some sisters go out with white guys, or brothers hang out with white girls, but you never see them because they go kick it in European places, hang out where they won't get busted? Same thing. You're ashamed to be different, so you don't bring the drama to your space, you invade theirs."

"I see. I think."

"She spoiled me rotten. She taught me a lot of things. Things I've taught Nicole."

Ayanna talks and talks, each word sweeter than the last; she drags her fingernails down my back, arouses me from the inside out, gets my full attention, then she touches her breasts in a hypnotic way, her fingers circling the dark parts. My mouth waters. Without speaking, she offers them to me. I swallow and know that I have the eyes of a starving man. I tingle. Nature makes me tingle for her.

Ayanna puts her face close to mine, whispers, *"Mange moi?* A real man would jump to it."

I ignore her street-level psychology, whisper, "Tell me about your marriage first."

"My marriage? What's up with that?"

"I want to understand you. Might want to find out what makes you so special."

"I know you do. I saw the way you looked at me last night."

She sits in a pool of pictures, tells me about her tumultuous marriage. In a soft, matter-of-fact tone, she tells me about arguments that she can't remember. But that's the way relationships go. And when she told him about her curiosity, he flipped out. Slapped her and she ran to some friend's house.

I say, "Why didn't you call the police?"

"Call the police on the police? Get real. OPD takes care of their own."

She tells me that she made sure he was at work before she went back home, and when she got there all of her clothes and shoes and law school books were piled in the bathtub and soaked in bleach.

She says, "That night was when he was shot."

I don't say anything for a moment. Then I ask, "You didn't have any kids?"

I ask because, well just because I haven't seen any, doesn't mean she didn't have any and ship them back to Detroit. She doesn't have stretch marks, but that doesn't mean anything.

She lets out a sad chuckle. "Heck no. Glad we didn't have any kids. That would've been horrible. I know women who have had their kids turn against them. Lose respect. Call them names. Kids shouldn't be involved. It's complicated and draining. Regular divorces are ugly. When you're dealing with a woman leaving her husband for another woman, male ego is shattered, manhood is ruptured, somebody's little feelings get hurt and it turns mega-ugly. Much better when no kids are involved."

"Sounds like you have strong emotions. The kids thing, I mean."

"I've represented a few. Everybody loses when you have rug rats. That's a fact."

I rub my palms together, think so many thoughts, each a firecracker going off inside my skull.

Ayanna says, "I hate Nicole. God, I hate that one-foot-in-the-closet, one-foot-out-of-the-closet bitch. Nicole lives inside her own little cunt. That's her world."

I pull my lips in. I would say something, but at times I've felt the same way.

"She's acting like a fucking sociopath. Has no conscience. No feeling about how she uses people to get what she wants."

My mouth opens, but I keep my reaction to myself.

"I hate her lack of acknowledgment. She barely holds my hand when others are around."

I say, "She's been holding your hand."

"That's because you're around. She keeps all of us huddled up together, stays next to you so people don't know what to think. Makes you look like a pimp. Dances with me a hot second, then rubs up on you half the night."

"I thought it was the other way around. Thought she was more comfortable with you."

She sighs. I look at the clock.

Then Ayanna speaks, sounds sweet sixteen, sounds hopeful and damaged, "I always wanted to be intoxicated with the feeling of love; I just never thought about the hangover."

I remind myself that she's the enemy. That this is a war. And in war the objective is to win.

Her pager goes off again. I look at it, then at her. My phone rings. She knows it's Nicole looking for both of us. Ayanna knows that and she smiles, moves the pillow away, gives the bed her back. Her legs apart again, so limber and beautiful. *"Baise moi. Mange moi."*

She's done talking. It shows in her face.

She puts her hands under her breasts, raises them until the nipples point at me.

Her nipples, so erect.

My penis rises.

She spreads her legs, shows me her wonderful ayanna.

I move toward her.

CLICK.

She jerks, pulls her legs together, sits up and looks across the room. "What was that noise?"

She looks toward the dining room, sees my computer. Then on that same table she sees my black tape recorder. I walk to the table, push rewind, let it whir back in time; then I push play. She hears her voice. My recorder has been on for the last hour. I've captured all of her taunting, all of her vulgarity, all of her confessions, every word.

She jumps to her feet, comes toward me with slow steps, fear and hostility in her eyes. I hold the tape away from her. We stare each other down.

"Give me the tape."

"I'll just play it for Nicole."

I expect her to scream, shout, to double-up her fists and get ready to rumble, but she doesn't. She gives me another look of touché. A nod that says she admires the simplicity.

She says, "That was very Machiavellian of you."

She deliberates, looks like her mind is flipping through the pages of *The Art of War*, hunting for age-old wisdom on this kind of conflict, searching for how to succeed.

"I know people," she says with extreme calmness. "I've represented criminals and a lot of them are still my friends. You don't give me that tape, I make one phone call, and you're fucked for life."

We're back in our own little Tahatchapie, two prisoners staring each other down in the yard.

I don't respond.

She pulls her lips in and nods. I imagine her standing before the judge doing the same thing, the tip of her finger on the edge of her full lower lip, barely touching as she thinks of a new strategy.

She says, "You know what I was going to do? I was going to go to Nicole smelling like you."

I say nothing. She doesn't sound mad.

"I thought you were weak." She chuckles, shakes her head, does that hand to hair thing again. "I underestimated you big-time. Maybe you're stronger than I thought."

I go to the bathroom, floss, brush my teeth. She's right there hounding me.

I spit.

She leans against the doorframe, lets her hair fall free. "Let's be real. She's crossed over. She's never coming back."

She makes it sound like Nicole has gone through Hell Week, has survived mind games, has been abused and beaten and branded and accepted into an elite organization whose flag is made up of rainbow colors. That once you're in that sorority, you can never give up your membership.

My lips tingle, so many vulgar words right there, but I say nothing.

I go back to the bedroom, take clothes out. She stays close to my right hand, close to the tape.

"She's not coming back to you."

I look at the clock. More time has gone by than I imagined.

I start getting dressed.

She asks, "Where are you going?"

Ayanna rushes and does the same. She's slipping into panic mode.

She says, "Are you going to Nicole?"

When I leave, she follows me. Follows the tape.

20

Ayanna is a small woman who drives a monster-size SUV. I see her in my rearview mirror, stalking me from Waterfront to the freeway, reminding me of that creature in *Trilogy of Terror* as she rides my bumper. I head toward the bridge that leads into San Francisco. Ayanna stays no more than two vehicles behind me, sometimes right on my bumper, forcing me to speed up and change lanes.

She gets too close. I tap my brakes. She blinks her high beams in my rearview mirror, then leaves them on. I change lanes and flip her off. She changes lanes and returns the favor.

I push the Memorex deep inside the car's tape player.

Ayanna's voice comes on.

When I stop to pay my two dollars at the tollbooth, I think that moment might give me enough time to speed away from Ayanna, but she pays and catches up before we get close to the Treasure Island exit.

She pulls up next to me. I let my window down, turn the tape up so she can hear her own voice. I crank up the volume and play the part where she asked me to let her be Nicole, when she asked me to lay with her and allow her to feel what Nicole feels to help her understand what makes me special, to show me what makes her so special.

Then I speed away.

A man can go mad if he sees his woman fucking somebody else. The same goes for a woman.

We're both insane.

Ayanna follows me when I exit at Harrison, rides my ass through construction zones and ragged one-way streets that mark Mayor Willie Brown's territory. The tape is off, but I hear her voice inside my head, every rise, every fall.

My c-phone rings. I answer, expect to hear Ayanna's voice. It's Nicole.

She says, "Your father called me."

"You're joking."

"Then I got a call from my sister. What the hell have you done?"

I ask her which sister and she tells me. It's a younger one who she hasn't talked to since her revelation. Since her outing; since she kicked the hinges off her closet. A sibling Nicole doesn't feel comfortable talking to because she asks too many hard questions about her life in Oakland.

She asks, "Where are you?"

I tell her that I'm bouncing over potholes and heading to a hot spot on Second Street.

There's a pause, a very emotional pause from Nicole. I'm crossing Turk, trying to lose Ayanna.

Nicole says, "I can't find Ayanna."

"No shit?"

"I called the hospitals, even called the damn morgue, then I called the police station, even drove to her law office on Piedmont Avenue at the crack of dawn, thought she might've gone there, then walked up and down Piedmont, went to Pete's Coffee and Tea. She always goes there first thing in the morning to think and people-watch, but she wasn't there either. Stopped in Piedmont grocery, asked around in Don't Eat the Furniture, none of her friends have seen her."

She said *her* friends, not *our* friends. The lines are getting thicker.

She says, "Look, I'm at work. Running on fumes. Working overtime on the South Africa compromise, waiting for the database updates, stressing in more ways than you could ever imagine."

Someone comes in her office and her tone changes, becomes professional, devoid of all personal feelings, and she tells me to have a good signing.

We disconnect.

I cross an intersection on a stale yellow light. Ayanna is two cars behind. The car in front of her stops on the red. That forces her to stop. In the rearview, I see her livid expression. See her nakedness in my mind, her scent so damn erotic and inviting, hear her moan her way to heaven.

All the lots are either full or want damn near thirty dollars for a few minutes, so I end up parking a little over a mile away from the bookstore, and that will still cost at least fifteen dollars for around three hours. It's always colder in San Francisco than it is in Oakland, much colder, above freezing, but with the wind, it's hard to tell the difference.

At every intersection I look behind me, to the left, to the right.

No sign of Ayanna. One more victory.

I pass by super-size billboards of men in CK under-

wear, all sporting abdominal six-packs, not a love handle in sight. Not all the pressure to diet and look like a
superstar is on women, not like they think. Men have
to worry about the same physical things, get in groove
and get that 24-Hour Fitness look or lose her to a man
with better gluts.

But then again, this is San Francisco. And after last
night, with my new perspective on the world, that bill-
board might be a soft-porn offering for other men.
Never know.

I check out my reflection in the window at Ming's
coffee shop, and then look at the display with my picture front and center, again using the reflection to
make sure I look okay and nothing's in my nose before
I move through the pack of people getting off the bus
and heading inside Alexander Book Company.

As soon as I make my way through a nice-size
crowd, I see quite a few holding steaming drinks in
green-and-white Starbucks cups, then a few people
start whispering.

André is here. I see him as soon as I walk in. Can tell
that he's waiting for me. He has on black leather pants,
a green turtleneck, black leather coat.

Toyomi is right next to him, dressed in jeans, boots,
and a colorful coat. They're holding hands. My fraternity brother is grinning like a six-year-old and she
looks like a woman satisfied.

André says, "Just called your room a little while
ago."

Toyomi is so excited that it almost scares me. "I just
had to meet you. Again. I had no idea that was you. I
just bought all of your books again. I'll give my old
ones to my friends."

I thank her and give her a hug. She beams.

André says, "Now hook her up with some signatures so she don't have to get in line."

She says, "I can drop you off at the airport and come back—"

"He don't mind. That's my dawg."

"No problem," I tell her. Then ask André, "You heading out?"

"For real this time. She's gotta drop me off at the airport right now, then go back to her seminar. Sign 'dem damn books so I don't miss my flight."

I step to the side and start signing. Toyomi's talking to me, telling me she has a great story, something about some dude she used to go out with. Crazy shit she thinks I should write about.

People are watching, first looking at the picture on the back of the book, one with my hair much shorter, then at me, still not sure, but easing my way.

When I'm done, Toyomi thanks me, hugs me long and strong.

André and Toyomi head for the door. He's carrying her books and holding her hand. She's smiling wide. He's doing the same. They look like two high school kids.

The owner greets me with a hug and a smile, then leads me to the metal staircase in the back of the room. We vanish before people start trying to get their books signed too soon.

The owner says, "At least eighty people are already here. About twenty of them are men."

"Cool." I cover my mouth and yawn.

"You look tired."

"Long night. Long morning."

The owner laughs. "I'll get you some tea."

"Herbal."

"Always."

"Thanks."

The green room is downstairs, through rows of books, non-fiction and fiction, rows of wisdom and knowledge. I salute Ralph Ellison's masterpiece as I pass, do the same for Morrison, Mosley, and McMillan. I catch a view of part of the crowd, people in business suits, BART uniforms, jeans, all of the seats filled, the latecomers standing in the back, some crowding the other stairwell.

As I pull off my jacket, the owner says, "A guy called. Said he was your father."

I ask if the caller left a name. It's my father's name.

"What did he say?"

"No message. Just identified himself as your father, very polite man, then asked what time the event ended, and I told him it depends on the size of the crowd, no more than two hours."

I pause, and since my c-phone has bad reception in the basement, I think about heading back upstairs to a phone right then, but look at my watch and see that it's close to showtime.

I say. "I'll call him when I'm done."

"I didn't know you were the son of an activist."

"Yep. I'm the son of a preacher man."

"Eight books and you've never said? You should put that in your bio."

I smile and shake my head. "Nah. I wouldn't pimp my peeps' good name to sell my books."

"Shit, everybody else does."

I say, "Looks like a hundred people will be here before we get started."

My tone says that I'm more than ready to move on to another topic.

The owner goes on, "Tell your father that he should do a book. That would be so important."

I leave that at that. Once again, that petty feeling rises, but I let it be. All these people are here to see me, listen to me, shake my hand, hug me, so what I do has reverence.

When the event starts, they all applaud and I walk through the crowd, a big smile on my face, a copy of my latest book in my right hand, and with every step I think of my old man. He never calls me at book signings. Never. I didn't even know that he knew where I had a signing. I hope that everything's okay with my mother, hope nothing has happened to one of my brothers.

My eyes go to the crowd, gain focus, and I almost slow my stroll, some of my smile withers.

Ayanna is on the front row, center stage, no more than six feet away from the podium. Her leather coat folded across her lap. Legs crossed. Ladylike and feminine.

I start to talk, clear a corner of nervousness from my pallet, get my rhythm by doing a stock joke here, get a laugh there, then we're rolling. My hands move when I talk, my words are improvised, but feel orchestrated, not by intent, but by habit. I am my father's child.

It's a wonderful crowd. I talk about writing, dreaming characters to life, activism versus propaganda. Then a few ask questions about copyrights, advances, and then the determined want to talk about the struggles and rewards of self-publishing.

Ayanna stares up at me the entire time.

I say to the crowd, the microphone making my voice seem so large, making me sound so huge, "Let's see. I can either read a character set-up, or something juicy—"

A tall sister in a BART uniform speaks up. "The Jeep scene. You have to read that. I read the sex in the Jeep scene last night. That scene was so good I damn near ran out and bought a Wrangler. My husband sends his thanks."

More laughter.

I read a five-page section that has bits and pieces of erotica. Those words and phrases make a few blush, a few squirm and grin. Even more make mental plans for later.

And when I'm done, Ayanna raises her hand to ask a question. She's so close, her bracelets jingling, so she is impossible to ignore. I grit my teeth and select her.

She identifies herself before she speaks.

Everyone applauds.

When the thunder dies, Ayanna looks up and asks, "How do you make your sex scenes so vivid? For example, the ones in Paris are so detailed. Almost like soft porn. They sound real. What do you do for research?"

I wink. "I light candles, put on Victoria's Secret, and read your journals."

More laughter.

"One more question, and maybe you'll actually answer this one," she says. "There was a rumor. Didn't you get stood up at the altar? Isn't that what your wedding scene was based on? Someone said that your female character is based on the woman you were engaged to. Is that true?"

The room is first consumed by silence, then rumbles and mumbles echo.

She says, "I'm trying to figure out how reliable the narrator is, what parts of the book, if any, are actually fiction."

She has me cornered. I want to howl in her face, but I have to hold it all in.

One of the brothers in the back, a man with sixteen-inch arms, yells out, "Hell, reliable or not, that's over my head. All I know is that Jeep scene is off da heezy, and I'm driving a Jeep. So I'm about to shake the speezy, so if any of you sisters live in the direction of Dublin and need a ride home, just let me know. We'll get some wine and take the scenic route through San Diego. Ah'ight? I be out."

Everyone laughs.

Then with perfect timing, the owner speaks up, "We'll take one more question. Since there are so many of you here, we need to move on to the signing."

Ayanna nods her head, folds her arms, bounces her leg, sends me a smirk that says she's not done.

I look to my right, search for a hand to be the final question, but when I see the huge man who is standing in the shadows, a man in black slacks and a gray sweater, a long leather coat, his NBA-size hands large enough to palm a basketball, his dark brown eyes looking right at me, I almost freeze.

I look at that big man, a man with graying hair that's always cut a quarter-inch high, has been cut that way forever, and all of my thoughts are derailed for a moment. He moves his weight from one leg to the other, does that out of habit, not out of nerves. That old fellow is a handsome man with a few of the same uncomplicated features I have. His is in a darker shade. Like me, he's sort of bow-legged. One leg is longer than the other, not by much, just like mine, just enough to give his left leg a curve to compensate for that deficiency.

He nods at me. I nod back.

I motion toward him. "I see another one of my old-school fraternity brothers is here."

I ask him to come up front. Then I introduce him.

The moment I say his name, the room applauds louder for him than they did for me. As we stand together people *ooh* and *ahhh* and cameras flash like lightning.

That tall man with the big hands is my father.

Ayanna sits there with her mouth wide open, her butterscotch skin turning red. She pulls herself together, gathers her things, moves to the back of the room, watches us from the stairwell.

My old man stays to the side, chitchats with people in line as I sign books. People talk to him, take more pictures. He's patient with them all, but I worry about people wearing him down with questions and snapping photo after photo. He makes a simple hand motion that tells me not to rush, that he is fine, to do what I came here to do.

After I sign a few books, I look up. Ayanna's gone.

21

My father says, "Nicole's mother is coming to Oakland."

"You're joking."

My old man tells me that as we bundle up and walk through the brisk breeze. He had walked in the bookstore just as André was walking out. He stopped and talked to André and Toyomi; she was just as excited to meet my old man. More brownie points for André. Anyway, that delay was how I missed my daddy coming in the store. He didn't want to draw any attention, so he lingered in the back.

We step into the Starbucks that's on the other side of Pacific National Bank. We take it slow, because ever since a police dog bit my old man at a protest some forty years ago, cold weather has made his leg stiffen up. He has his good days and bad days. This is a bad one.

He tells me, "Nicole knows. I got her number from your mother and called this morning."

"How was she?"

"To be honest, I'm not sure. She said she was willing to see her mother, but I'm not sure."

"Was she willing right off the bat?"

"She's difficult, but not as difficult as her mother."

We get hot chocolates, sit at a bistro table facing the nonstop foot traffic on Second Street. For a second, when he sets the cup in front of me, I'm a child again. Then that feeling fades and I'm back to being a man. No matter how old I get, the same number of years will always separate us, and I will always be a child in his presence. Will always feel comfort under the canopy of his words.

A tabloid has been left on our table. It's one of the freebies that can be picked up on every corner, this one advertising S&M and bondage, has a picture of a European woman on the cover, a woman with a girl-next-door face, her body strapped in leather. And of course, she lists her two-dollar-a-minute number. I reach to take it away from the table, but my old man stops me, reads the cover, flips through the pages, grunts. His expression says it all as he folds then lays the tabloid on the next table.

I repeat, "Nicole's mother is coming to Oakland?"

He nods in the same rhythm that I always do, a rhythm I inherited from him. He says, "I couldn't catch up with you last night, wanted you to be the one to tell Little Nikki. I didn't know what your schedule was like after your signing, so I figured I should come up here and at least see her off the plane."

My daddy is smarter and wiser than I will ever live to be, a doer and a user of words. A master communicator. He knows the power of his own voice, recognizes how words can move, how the right tone can inspire, motivate, heal, make angry people smile, give hope in a time of sorrow, become light in someone's darkest hour.

Yesterday when I called my old man and told him what Nicole's mother had said, all I wanted was to lay the groundwork on getting them to have a civil conversation somewhere down the line.

But my daddy is a man who is always in motion. He knows that his task is monumental and his time on top of this soil is limited. Maybe that's why he never rests long enough to let dust settle on his shoes. Maybe that's why he attacks every problem with a sense of urgency, with immediacy. As long as the world keeps turning and things keep burning, he'll keep running to put out the fires that others have created; he'll keep helping. He's a walking angel, taking care of the world, helping strangers, putting his big arms around the people he loves.

I've seen a few things in my life and times, have seen my old man do a lot. This is the first time I'm sure he's created a miracle. This is almost like seeing him moonwalk on water.

He tells me, "She decided that she wants to meet with her child."

"Okay."

"But under her own terms. She'll give it one hour."

"She'll come two thousand miles for one hour? You gotta be joking."

"Sixty minutes. No more, no less."

I chuckle. "She has rules."

My old man grunts. "Yes."

"Like mother, like daughter."

"A very structured woman," he says with a chuckle of disbelief. "I have her flight information. Her plane will land soon."

Daddy came up from L.A. on Southwest this morning; they have shuttle flights every hour on the hour.

He can be up here, and then back home in less time than it takes to watch a Kevin Costner movie.

He said, "I tried reaching you at your hotel room last night, then on your cellular phone."

"You should've I-paged me. I was out late."

"With Nikki?"

"Yeah. I was with Nicole."

He pulls his lips in. That's his not happy face.

I say, "I didn't get a message."

"You know how I am about leaving messages. Either a person is there or they are not."

"You need to step into the new millennium."

"Well, some things are better left old-fashioned. Not all change is good change."

And for the first time, I don't believe him. He wanted to see what my events were like, what kind of people came to read the books I write. I think he was surprised that they are respectable people who could sit in the front row at his church.

I ask, "Is Nicole's stepdad, any of her sisters, any of her brothers coming?"

My daddy tells me, "Her mother is coming by herself."

"Why did—what did you say to make her hop on a plane and fly to Oakland?"

My old man shrugs and grunts at the same time. "It wasn't me."

"What do you mean it wasn't you?"

"We prayed together. Prayed long and hard. That took more out of me than doing three services on Easter Sunday. Then when we hung up, she was still unchanged. She said she had to go because a movie with Denzel Washington was coming on, then after that she was going to watch her favorite movie because it was on television too. *Imitation of Life.*"

"Uh huh. Nice to know that Nicole is less valuable than a rerun."

He chuckles, sips his brew. "Few hours later she called me back, sounding upset."

"Upset? Was the movie that bad?"

"Surprised me too. Said that she had to go to Oakland."

"Just like that."

"Just like that. I tried talking to her, telling her to start with a phone call to our little sheep and establish, more like reestablish communication, because it has been a while."

"What happened between the time you hung up and when she called you back?"

"She didn't say."

"How would watching a movie about a black woman passing for white—"

"Son, I have no idea. Maybe it was the Denzel movie."

"Denzel does have that effect on women."

He laughs a bit. "Maybe it wasn't any of that. That woman marches to her own beat. Has her own view of the way the world turns."

Silence.

A man leaves his *San Francisco Chronicle* on the next table. My old man reaches over and gets it before it gets bussed to the garbage. He puts his round glasses on, flips from an article on a new herpes vaccine for women, to another regarding nine gay tolerance bills waiting for the governor's John Hancock, and settles on an article that reads, "S.F. mayor's Open Door attracts 'diverse' crowd."

I stare out the window. A woman with pink hair, pink leather coat, pink boots, blue eyes, bright tattoos, and silver earrings in her eyebrow and bottom lip passes by smoking a rolled-up cigarette.

This world is so wild.

"At some school out in Greenville, South Carolina, can't remember the name," Daddy says, "female students have to wear knee-length skirts, young men have to wear dress pants and ties, like we did when I was coming up, and all dating must have a chaperone, even holding hands is prohibited."

And they will all grow up to be perverts. I think that, but I say, "Then there's San Francisco."

Daddy nods, puts the paper down, grunts again before he says, "Still, when all is said and done, Willie has been good at cutting through the bureaucracy. He works from his gut."

"Just like you."

"Not many of us left. You do what you feel is right."

He takes his glasses off, slips them in his pocket, sips his cocoa, the green-and-white paper cup getting lost in his huge dark hands.

I say, "I hope that, you know, my book, the parts I read, the questions—"

"It's fine, son. I already knew what to expect. I was at one of your events before."

"When? I didn't see you."

"You didn't see anybody. It was on the computer, in *Black Voices*, I think. Your mother and me logged on and we sat there, watched the questions people ask. I went into another one of those chat rooms. It's amazing what people talk about when nobody can see them. I guess everything that has been created for the sake of good is being used for illicit purposes, so why not the Internet."

"You don't leave messages but you use the Internet."

"The church has a web page. We have classes, Internet training, have to teach our people that technology is nothing to be afraid of."

Silence.

He asks, "Is Nicole at peace with herself?"

I shrug.

He grunts.

I say, "I met her friend."

He grunts again.

I say, "That was her on the front row, asking questions. The one with the red hair."

He says, "I was born at night, but not last night. Looks like she had it in for you."

Then I grunt.

I wait for him to ask about Ayanna, but he doesn't.

He says, "You be careful, son. Be careful. You're dealing in complicated matters. Affairs of the heart are always complicated. People do things that have no rhyme or reason."

We stare out the window at the crowd. People-watch. Two men pass by laughing. One has his hand deep in the other's back pocket; the other has his arm around his boyfriend's waist.

My old man shakes his head. He says, "The world has changed. No matter how hard you try to steer society in one direction, it goes in its own. Some for the good, some for the bad."

He says *society*, but I hear the word *children*.

He puts his chin in the web of his hand.

I ask, "You ever want to give up?"

"Time to time."

"But you don't."

"No. But black people don't seem to care like they used to. We have hundreds at rallies, where we used to have thousands. We have thousands when we used to have tens of thousands."

I sip my chocolate.

He smiles. "Seems like it's always easier to help strangers than the people right next to you."

Silence. I hold on to that silence like it's a bastard child who needs love. I'm thinking that it seems like it's easier to get praise from a stranger than from the person across the table.

He asks, "Why are you so determined with Nicole?"

I think about telling him about the mile twenty analogy, about how it hurts more to stop than to keep going, how if I win, if I endure, this could be the greatest love story ever told, but I don't think he'd get it. It's not internal for him, he's on the outside looking at a situation that owns no rhyme or reason, and he's not connected to Nicole on the same emotional level that I am, so I just shrug.

He says, "I'm not doing this to condone Nicole's lifestyle."

"Don't expect you to."

"I love her, have loved her as a daughter, as part of our extended family ever since you brought her into our lives, and I have prayed for her since she left Los Angeles in despair, the same way I have prayed for you to overcome your suffering—"

"I'm not—"

"Hear me out. I have prayed for each of you to receive understanding this past year. I'm not condoning her. Not condemning her either. I want that understood."

"I understand."

"My job is to help and to heal. I'm not the one who has to judge anyone for his or her actions, getting older has made me realize that. Her father was a good man. We fought a lot of battles together."

"No doubt."

"No doubt?"

"Uh," I say. "That means I agree."

He nods. "No doubt."

I sip my hot cocoa.

My father goes on, "He wouldn't want to see Nikki torn apart from her family like this."

"Well, her mom doesn't make it easier."

"You say it's her mother, and it is, but in reality it's both of them. From what I hear, Nikki doesn't call her siblings, hardly returns their calls since she came up here. I'm trying to rectify that. That's all. The rest of it, I leave that between her and her Lord."

I nod.

He goes on, "Just like you haven't been in touch with all of your people, your brothers, your aunts, your uncles. You've been busy since this came about."

"I've been working."

"Everyone works, son. That's no excuse."

"They have my number."

He tells me, "Just don't build a wall around yourself."

He glances out the window, watches a parade of people for a few.

A man passes by holding up a sign that announces his T-cell count in tall, bold letters. That sight is more than enough to derail our conversation.

Daddy grunts. I do the same.

We walk. My father wants to move a bit so his leg won't get too stiff. He collects refrigerator magnets, so we stop in a few shops and I buy him a few. Momma likes music boxes, so we get one of those. We look at charm bracelets that aren't charming, miniature cable cars, check out a few small Golden Gate bridges that aren't gold, but some funky rust color, just like the real one.

And when his leg needs rest, we stop, I grab tofu, brown rice, and an oat-filled California Suncake. He grabs a muffin. We sit inside another Starbucks, get fresh hot chocolates, and we talk like two friends who haven't seen each other in a while. A father and son sit shoulder to shoulder, and talk. We talk about Momma. About my three brothers. About my old man's fourteen living siblings. No talk about protests or my career. This time we just talk about family. With hearts as open as the sky, we talk and we talk. Not many sons are blessed with that kind of relationship.

Then my c-phone rings. It's Nicole. She's upset.

She says, "Somebody else called me."

"I already know about your mother."

"Not about that. They called and told me Ayanna was at your signing."

"Yep. She left before it was over."

"What the fuck is going on? Why didn't you call me and tell me?"

"I'm with my daddy right now. We're talk—"

"Your daddy's here?"

"Yep. Came to meet with your mother."

"Is this a conspiracy?" Her breathing thickens; I imagine her massaging the bridge of her nose. "First South Africa, then Ayanna, now this crap. Okay, fine. Where is this meeting to take place?"

"Your house?"

"No. Never. I'm not welcome in her home and she's not welcome in mine."

I pause. "We'll figure something out."

"Tell your daddy I said hello. Kiss, kiss."

We hang up. My father's eyes are on me, listening to my every inflection, reading my body language the way he reads the Word. Now our conversation changes, goes back to Nicole. To me. To putting up the foundation before the walls, to living in a house with no floor.

I ask, "You believe in soul mates?"

"I believe in people being equally yoked."

"Is that enough?"

"Even then you have to work at it, you create your own soul mate."

I nod. He does the same.

He says, "I wasn't born an old man. Wasn't born in wisdom. I haven't lived without trials and tribulations. Your mother and me have had our own tests over time."

I know what he's talking about. He's a man of power, a tall, decent-looking man, and in some ways he's a spiritual celebrity. Like with every other leader, my father has had his weaknesses, his moments, and there has been talk of other women over the years. Just whispers, no shouts, no scandals.

In that reflective voice, he tells me, "Every man has years where he is a lost sheep."

"Women too."

"But the thing about most lost sheep is that as long as they are with other lost sheep, they don't know they're lost. A fool amongst fools is a happy camper."

"You're preaching."

"And you'd better be listening."

I'm nodding, not knowing how to stop rubbing my thumbs together before they burst into flames.

He grunts. "I flipped through a couple of your books."

"It's fiction."

He says, "You say you're not in denial, not suffering."

"I'm not. It's fiction."

"Well, some of that fiction makes your mother cry. The parts that make everyone laugh, makes her cry. People, who are in our church, people who were there, they all know, son. And Nikki's mother, people tell her what you have written, tell her that it's Nikki. That hurts her, son."

"If I am writing the truth, then it's part of my experience, and that's my right."

"And you have to be sensitive to others."

"Writing is about being bold and honest."

"Without empathy, writing is nothing."

My head moves in a motion just like his, nodding over and over while I keep rubbing my thumbs. At some point I sigh, focus on my breathing, on my life force.

I say, "It's my therapy. It's been rough on me."

"I know, son. I know."

"And it's all I have. All I can do right now."

Her reaches over, lays hands on my left hand. My father. My healer.

I struggle to take control. I calm down, rest my chin in the web of my right hand.

He goes on, "The main reason I'm doing this is for you, son. Not for Nikki. Not for her mother. Not for her family. I knew what you were asking me to do."

I nod.

He says, "You're the flesh of my flesh. Blood of my blood. You're my son."

We finish our chocolates and leave. Father and son. Saint and sinner.

22

Compared to LAX, Oakland has a small, easy-in, easy-out airport.

Her expensive L'eau D'issey scent gets off the plane three minutes before I see her, pulling her small designer luggage-on-wheels through the gate. She's been wearing the same brand of perfume since I've known her. Consistency is one of her well-known qualities.

My nose twitches.

My father says, "A southern storm has arrived."

From a distance, she looks like an older version of Nicole.

She's a short, breasty woman, wears an ankle-length, brushed-gold rabbit coat over her red pantsuit, a pantsuit that looks like a fiery sunset on the coastline of Mexico's Ixtapa, a cream-colored silk blouse and colorful scarf, and carries a King James Version of the Bible in her right hand. Walks as if she's Lena Horne en route to an exorcism.

Her red shoes match the candy-apple shade of her purse to the T. If she were in L.A., with all that red, people would think that she was queen of the gang bangin' Bloods, but here people think that she must own this city. The one thing missing is the red carpet.

Her outfit upstages the world. The same golden skin as Nicole, flesh that reminds me of the beauty of Cancun, only with a few itty-bitty moles that come with age sprinkled over her cheeks, like the fine jet-black sands on a beautiful beach. It doesn't show as much in Nicole, not with the influence of her father's genes, but her mother's features do have some Spanish architecture: it shows in her thin lips and narrow nose. She wears her salt and pepper hair hot-combed and parted down the center. And when she opens her mouth to speak to me, I see the gold trim on her front, right tooth. A queen of the old South.

We meet and greet without hugs or handshakes. I smile. She eyes me up and down, unforgiving. It's been a while since I've seen her, a very long while.

My father asks, "How was the flight?"

"I had a middle seat between two fat people who snored like hogs calling hogs."

"Sorry to hear" is my father's response.

She lets it be known that she's surprised to see my father, and doesn't waste time telling him that he is not needed, tells him to go ahead and go back to L.A., and when all is done, she will call him. My father is reluctant, asks me to let him have a few words with the Queen, and I step to the side. Move near the windows and watch the red, white, and blue planes descend from gray skies.

When my father calls my name, before I make it back to them, I can tell that whatever she said has convinced him that trying to reason with her is useless. In a voice heavy with concern, he asks me if I can handle it. With a smile and a pat on his back I say yes, even though I'm anxious, palms are getting damper by the second, and I don't know what the hell I'm supposed to handle. The Diva of the South dismisses him. We hug, do our good old secret fraternity handshake, kiss cheeks, say kind words, and he heads toward Southwest Airlines.

With sadness, I watch my father leave, watch him have a rough moment with that leg of his, then he gets the pain out, and walks like a champ. I don't like seeing my daddy getting old. Not at all.

Then I'm alone with Nicole's mother. The first thing she tells me is, "Have me back in four hours."

I say, "Four hours?"

"Not a minute later. That's one hour before my flight back to Memphis leaves."

"After that long flight, you're not spending the night?"

She wrinkles her nose. "In San Francisco?"

"Oakland."

"Same difference. Have me back in four hours."

I nod. She heads through the crowd before I do, but she stops and waits because she has no idea which way to go. She doesn't rush, frowns at people who scurry by. She moves with grace, like she is being escorted into the Cotton Club, glances at the people, evaluating, dissecting.

Locks, twists, braids, short Afros, long wavy Afros, baldheads, we pass by them all. A beautiful woman, who looks like Rah Digga with a reddish Afro, smiles at me, her eyes telling me she loves my hair, gives a flirty grin that speaks of power, positivity, and solidarity. We pass each other.

She says, "Women out here don't comb their hair."

"It's the style."

"Used to be a time when you couldn't get a job with all these nappy African styles."

"Used to be a time when we couldn't get a job, period."

"When I was in the Mississippi Freedom Democratic Party, we always made sure we looked presentable. No matter how hot, how cold, how dusty, we were always presentable. That was back when we had pride, back when I met my first husband."

"Uh huh."

"Now black people go to work looking any kind of way. Black women don't wear makeup. Earrings all over their bodies. Stomachs all out. Rears all out. Tattoos everywhere. Walk around looking like pirates and acting like men. On television, proud to be having babies and not be married."

She goes on and on. I stay out of her rambles and wonder if this meeting is a good idea.

While we do a slow stroll, she quits chastising and stares at things and people as if she's from Tasmania, a place isolated from the rest of the world.

She says, "Did your father explain to you my terms?"

"Yes. One hour. You'll be in the room with her for one hour."

"Follow my terms to the letter."

"No doubt."

"What?"

"I will. That means I will."

"Did you explain them to . . ." Her words trail off and she makes a flimsy hand motion.

"I did. She said that she was familiar with your ritual. That you used to do the same thing when you were at odds with her daddy. Or the time her brother went out with a white girl."

"And?"

"Nicole says she knows the routine."

"Her spirit is gone. My daughter is dead. I have no daughter here."

"Then why did you come?"

She shifts.

Again I ask, "Why did you decide to come all of a sudden?"

"Why?" Her voice almost strains, as if I hit a spot by asking that question, a spot that was her kryptonite, and she sounds so very human, so very hurt, and so very afraid. With each breath her words change from being compassionate to being stiff and defensive as she says, "You kept calling, throwing this in my face. Your father calls and runs my blood pressure to the sky. I'm here and you're asking why? I was happy at home watching *Family Feud* and *America's Most Wanted*. I spent over a thousand dollars to come here. Is that so important? Is that your business? The point is I'm here. This goes against the grain of what I believe in. But I'm here."

I clear my throat. "Your suitcase feels loaded."

"I brought what I need. I have my own food. My own water. Other things."

"Thought I smelled chicken. You could've ordered room service."

"I hear they put something in the food out here. That's why all the people act funny."

"I never heard that."

"That's because it's a secret. You know how they do it?"

"No ma'am. How?"

"The chicken. They put it in the fried chicken because they know all black people eat fried chicken. That's why the Colonel won't tell anybody his secret recipe. That's how we get diabetes, sickle cell, and all those other ailments that plague black people and kill us off. That's how they make us confused. They put it in the chicken."

A moment passes. I say, "Coke has a secret recipe too."

She huffs at my misplaced humor.

Inside the car I attempt small talk, ask her how she likes being the principal at Carver High, ask her if she misses being in the classroom. The conversation goes nowhere.

I turn the radio on. Listen to the traffic report. West-bound 80 to MacArthur maze traffic slow. The 101 past the 380 is looking smooth. East 80 at San Pablo, an accident. Richmond, Walnut Creek, Oakland, they give the weather for those areas. All between forty-eight and fifty-four degrees, all looking at the possibility of showers between tonight and early morning.

Then there is talk about the number of people who have flooded the Alameda County Recorder's office down on 11th Street and Madison for a Valentine's Day marriage-fest in previous years, and they anticipate the same rush of last-minute "I do's" this year.

She asks, "Are they talking about men and women getting married?"

"I think so. Yes, ma'am."

"The front of the *USA Today* showed two women getting married in Vermont."

I say nothing. Pretend I'm too busy driving to carry on a conversation.

"Another woman cain't do nothing for me but bake me a cake," she says. "And I don't eat other folks' cooking."

I wish my father were still here. He's much better at this. Much better at dealing with her.

The news people ramble on about Oakland teachers being underpaid, then about quite a number of senior citizens being evicted by the Oakland Housing Authority because their grandchildren were caught selling rock cocaine. She tisks, shakes her head, and asks me to turn the radio off.

I do.

She sits there, her expensive perfume filling my lungs like smoke, rocking and humming "What a friend we have in Jesus; all our sins and griefs to bear." Her humming is worse than Nicole's singing.

She says, "You went and changed your hair."

"A while ago. Decided to try something different. You like it?"

"No."

"Didn't think so."

"Reminds me of those Rastafarians. Did you change religions?"

I say, "No, ma'am."

"Drugs?"

"No, ma'am."

"Muslim?"

"No, ma'am."

She pulls her lips in, rocks a bit. She asks, "Is she still funny?"

I have to pause and think about what she means by funny, have to go through my mental Rolodex and flip through the juba-to-jive section, before I answer, "She's . . . nothing has changed."

"You funny?"

"No, ma'am."

She relaxes some, not much.

She continues her questioning. "When was the last time you attended church?"

I try to remember the last time I've set foot in a gospel café and dined on spiritual soul food. That good old place that's filled with sinners. What some people call a hospital for the spiritually sick.

I answer, "Been a while."

"What's a while?"

"Couple of months. I've been on the road."

"They have churches on the road. I hear that churches are in almost every city."

She starts back humming.

I say, "I pray every day."

"Three times a day?"

"No, ma'am."

She shifts, starts back humming.

23

The Amtrak train is blowing its warning into the darkness of an overcast sky. A sky filled with clouds and promising a winter rain. That means snow in Tahoe, Mammoth, and Mountain High.

We're back in my room at the Waterfront Plaza. I'm sitting on a footstool at the foot of the bed. Dr. Laura is on the television in the living room/dining area of my suite. Nicole's mother sits on the sofa, looks at her watch a few times before she goes to the window and stares out at Jack London Square, then her head moves and she gazes at the Bay waters behind Scott's Seafood, cranes her head and glances toward a ferry that is heading out toward San Francisco.

She asks, "How much this room cost?"

"Four hundred."

"A day?"

"Yes, ma'am."

"Lord, Lord, Lord."

The phone rings. I answer on the first ring. It's Nicole. She's downstairs.

Nicole asks, "I called Memphis and they said it was no joke. I'm still hoping this is some prank. A very unfunny prank. Is my mother really up there?"

"She's here."

She falls silent. "I'm not afraid of her. I can do this."

She hangs up.

"Was that her?"

"Yes, ma'am." I rub left palm over right palm. "She's on the way up."

"My terms," she says. "Remember my terms."

I turn the lights off. Turn the television off. Close my laptop so the screen saver doesn't give any unwanted illumination. Close the shutters. She sits on the sofa, puts her back to me and faces the waters; this time she sees nothing but shadows and multicolored curtains.

We wait.

There is a soft knock on the door. I look through the peephole, then open the door.

Nicole comes inside, each step so slow, as if she is thinking about turning around, or waiting to be told to turn around. Her eyes go to me, then across the room. She knows that her mother is on the other side of those closed shutters.

Nicole rushes back to the door, hurries out into the hallway.

I race out behind her.

Looks like she's about to run away, but she leans against the wall, forehead first, her left hand on her chest, trying to control her breathing.

"I feel her energy. Her perfume is in the hallway, on the elevator, right here. I should've wrapped my hair." Nicole says all that, then chuckles as she shakes her head. "At home, Momma used to put curtains up between her and whoever. So childish."

"Where did she get that from?"

"Big Momma. Her momma. Something passed

down from generation to generation. Satan has to be at her back at all times."

I take her hands. "Be yourself. Stand up to her."

Nicole closes her eyes. She's a child being sent to the principal's office.

But we are not children. We don't have to go to the office.

"You up for this? I've got your back either way. It's your call."

"I have to. She's still my mother."

She gets herself together and we go back inside. The moment the door closes, as if she senses her daughter's life force the same way Nicole senses hers, she asks me, "She has arrived?"

I answer, "Yes, ma'am."

"Tell her to be seated. Give this to her."

I hurry to our southern-fried diva and she opens her luggage, hands me a big black Bible, one that is tattered, dog-eared, has seen better days and better nights. She tells me to give it to Nicole.

When I do, Nicole says, "This was my father's Bible. The one he preached from."

Her mother says, "Tell her to keep her hands on the Word. To keep her hand close to her father. To keep her hand with the Father."

Nicole nods.

"Ask my child if she believes in God."

Nicole holds the timeworn Bible in her right hand for a moment. Stares at it. Then pulls it to her chest, holds it close to her heart. Her left hand comes up to her locks, drags across her face to her temples, her eyes squeezed shut.

I want to hold her, but I stay where I am.

Nicole sits at the foot of my rented bed, here in my

den of sin, here in my fuckville, with her back to her mother as her mother's back is to her, and she answers, "You know I believe in a supreme being."

I sit in a red-cushioned chair in the bedroom area, between them, but closer to Nicole.

With clenched teeth her mother retorts, "Ask her."

I ask Nicole, "Do you believe in God?"

Nicole sighs, rocks herself like a little old lady. Her answer is "Yes."

I tell her mother, "Yes."

Her mother tells me, "Ask her if she believes in sin."

I do. Nicole's answer is yes, she believes in sin. And when that question passes through me, I feel pain. My own personal pain starts to bloom, it swells like skin branded with iron.

Her mother hums. "Ask her if she thinks that what she is doing is a sin."

Nicole's answer is sometimes yes, sometimes no.

"Tell her that she is either with God, or divorced from God. There is no sometimes. In between yes and no is only confusion."

Nicole's irritation rises. "Why is it so important that we have to think the same things, feel the same way? Can't we just be allowed to be individuals, and in the middle of that, still find a way to be mother and daughter?"

"Listen to her, Lord, listen. My daughter has lost her soul. Her soul is waiting for her body."

"Don't say it, please don't say it again, Momma, please—"

"Nicole is dead."

"I am not dead. I'm right here. You hear me. I know you hear me. Then I am not dead."

"My daughter is—"

"I am not dead!" Nicole pretty much shouts. She stands, moves by me, and breaks the rules.

When she sees her mother, she slows, maybe taken aback by the new age that rests in her mother's flesh, the aging that tells Nicole that her mother is getting closer to the ground every day.

Nicole kneels. "I am right here. You can hear me, you can smell me, look Momma, that's my hand on your hand, I know you can feel me, and if you open your eyes, if you please open your eyes, you can see me. I am not dead, Momma. I am right here."

"I will open my eyes."

"Please."

"I will open my eyes." She speaks with difficulty, like an old woman. "If when I open my eyes you can show me in your father's Bible, show me where it is written that what you're doing is alright with my Lord and Savior."

"You know I can't do that."

"If you can show me that, I will open my eyes. If you cain't, you are dead."

"Momma, please. Don't be silly."

Her mother addresses me. "Tell her to get behind me."

With a mixture of intrigue and anger, I play this stupid game and I tell Nicole. Have to remind myself that my role is about observation, not confrontation.

I say, "Nicole. Come back over here."

With reluctance, Nicole stands, eyes watering, touching my hand with love as she passes me, then moves back to the bed, puts her back to her mother once again.

"Aren't you the least bit shamed?" her mother asks, not filtering the question through me, as if she's forgotten her own rules. "You grew up in a Christian home, you weren't abused in any way, shape, form, or fashion. We sent you to the best schools, surrounded you with the best people. How do you decide to be the way you are?"

"This is who I am."

"So, you've turned your back on all we taught you?"

"No. I'll always embrace what you and Daddy gave me. I have spiritual practices."

"So do devil-worshippers."

"I'm not a devil-worshipper."

Her mother huffs. "You come over here, get up under me smelling like voodoo-oil—"

"It's herbal."

"As in marijuana?"

"Not herbs, herbal. Natural. Of this earth."

"Voodoo," she says, shaking her head. "Nothing but voodoo. Where is your belief?"

"My beliefs are strong. I believe in good, in tolerance, in empathy, in love, in—"

"In foolishness. You cannot shape God to fit your own image, you cain't modify what is written to fit your life. You have to go to God. He does not have to come to you."

"What's the point of you coming here? To torture me? To make me feel bad?"

Her mother doesn't answer, just makes a rugged sound.

I get back to the rules, repeat Nicole's question: "Nicole wants to know why you came here."

Her mother takes a deep breath. She whispers, "Everything happens in threes. Good or bad, it all comes in threes. Momma always told me to look out for threes. Those were signs from the Father, the Son, and the Holy Spirit. That's how He taps you on your shoulder, three times."

She hums a while. We wait.

When she's ready, she says, "There were three signs."

She says that my father calling out of the blue was the first sign. Then Denzel's movie was on. *Philadelphia*. The story about a gay man who had a big disease with a little name. Watching Tom Hanks die, feeling herself being pulled into what she considers to be a homosexual movie, was her second sign. The moment that drama went off HBO, *Imitation of Life* came on TNT.

She leaves that right there. Nicole asks me to ask her how was *Imitation of Life* the third sign.

Her mother says, "The funeral. When the daughter was crying over her mother's coffin. That was my third sign."

Nicole lets out a low moan.

I don't really understand, but that doesn't stop her mother's thought process from chilling me. Every word puts a bag of ice in my stomach. I'm not superstitious, not afraid of black cats, or ladders or broken mirrors, not afraid to go to the thirteenth floor of any building, but the way she says it, the way she believes it, that frightens me, damn near makes me accept the power of threes.

Nicole says, "And you believe that what you interpreted as three signs is holy and righteous?"

"He works in mysterious ways."

Silence.

With unexpected calmness Nicole says, "I can't be who you want me to be. Accept me."

"If I accept you as you are, then I accept homosexuality. If I accept homosexuality, I go against my God. If I go against God, then I am with the devil. You have to come to me. I cain't go to you."

More silence. I rub my hands back and forth until my flesh is dry.

Nicole speaks in a low tone. "Are you done?"

No response.

I repeat Nicole's question. "Are you done?"

Her mother responds, "No."

I'm pissed, but at the same time I admire Nicole's mother. She's wounded, a parent who expected something different for her Little Nikki, but she stays so firm in her faith.

I thought Nicole would crumble when confronted, but even with her head down, even with teary eyes, even with a strained voice, she is not running away from her mother. She seems stronger, more sure of who she is, of how the rest of the world operates. I'm proud of her.

And at the same time, I want her mother to win. Her victory will be my victory. Her victory will drag us all from this place that has no exit.

But when I glance at Nicole, I don't want her to lose. Because what I admire about Nicole is the same thing I admire about her mother. Her strength, her conviction. Her refusal to compromise.

"Will you please tell my momma I'm an individual. I'm not her. Will never be her. That she has to accept me as I am. Just as I am. She has to look at me for who I am and not who she wants me to be."

I tell her. It's the same thing Nicole has been telling me and Ayanna.

Then her mother gets her second wind, her strength doubles like Popeye after a can of spinach, and the questions come nonstop, they come hard and strong, a hurricane confined to this room.

"Maybe you just ain't found the right man," her mother says.

Felt like she stabbed me in my chest.

"Just gotta find the right man." She rocks, hums. "That girl left Ellen Degenerate and went back to a man, now she's back in her right mind. I want to know if this is a phase. I read that this is another one of those trends for your generation."

I repeat that the best I can.

Nicole says, "Tell her I love both a man and a woman. One man. One woman."

"You either this way or that way," her mother responds. "Like your grandmomma used to say, either you is or you ain't."

"Well, I'm in love with a man and a woman."

"Hear my words: no such thing. One or the other."

"I was with both of my lovers yesterday, and for a while, even if it was only for a few moments, I was where I wanted to be."

"All of you were together?"

"Yes."

"All three of you together. Lord, Lord, Lord."

I swallow. My own saliva goes down like castor oil mixed with Buckleys.

Nicole says, "If you want the truth, I will give you just that. But don't ask any questions that you don't want answered, Momma, because I will answer them all."

"You should be ashamed. Animals in the zoo don't behave like that."

"I'm not an animal."

"You're below animals."

"Well, don't ask anything that you can't handle."

It's takes me a moment, but I find enough air to breathe again.

Nicole's mother never stops shaking her head as she opens her bag, pulls out a white tissue, dabs her eyes, blows her nose. Across the room Nicole does the same thing, the same motions, same movements and rhythms that are inherited, the idiosyncrasies that are passed down from generation to generation.

Nicole says, "Can you see this from my perspective for one moment?"

"You need to get a rubber room at Poplar and Dunlap," her mother snaps. "You need to be psychologically evaluated."

"Free thinking never is rational to the narrow-minded."

Her mother retorts, "It's free because it ain't worth a dime."

There is a pause, and silence returns to visit us, touches us with power and force, the way silence touches people in those moments my father pauses in one of his sermons.

Nicole talks for a moment, tries to explain. Tries to relate diverse thinking to someone whose rules are engraved in the Ten Commandments. She's talking to her mother, but at times I know she's talking to me.

Nicole asks for understanding, never for forgiveness because of who she loves, who she is, no apology for that, and in the end says, "You think I'd want this if this isn't going to make my life easier? My own sister, I love her too, but she acts like I'm a child molester in the making; my used-to-be best friend doesn't want me around her kids. I was their godparent, the one she trusted them with if anything happened to her. I send her e-mails, and she deletes them without reading them, so I guess she has de-godmothered me."

"What did you expect? A parade?"

"I'm just saying. I'm not mad at them. But I have to deal with all of that. The people who love me are still here. It's a struggle for them, and I love them more for accepting me the best they can. I just wish that you were one of them."

"If I accept you, then I go against God. If I divorce myself from my Savior, then I will never be reunited with my people in heaven. I will not burn in Bee-luther-hatchee for you, for any of my children."

My eyes are misty, my cheeks as warm as an oven on Thanksgiving. My throat, tight. I want this to be over. Want this to be over because I realize why Nicole's mother wants me here. I was slow, thought I was here as a mediator, but I know. She's trying to work on both of us at the same time. Like she has a two-for-one coupon or something. I feel her. She's trying to pull me away from Nicole. Trying to make me think the way she does. My insides are aching. I want this over.

"White people," her mother says. "You've been around too many white people. Started when you went to Memphis State. Should've sent you to Spelman."

"What do white people have to do with this?"

"White people," her mother rambles on. "And San Francisco."

"How can you love God and dislike white people? What, white people aren't God's children? To be a Christian, to be holding a Bible in your hands, isn't that hypocritical? Don't you think that kind of bigotry can keep you out of heaven?"

Her mother doesn't answer.

Nicole says, "The Bible, the one you're holding right now, that came from white people. This isn't the religion we would have if white people didn't use that same Bible to justify slavery, to persecute everybody who didn't see things their way, to force them into their religion, into their belief system. Africa is where we're from. And where in the Bible, which I do honor and respect regardless of what you may think, is there anything written by black people for black people?"

"Lord, Lord, Lord."

Then all is silent.

"I have to deal with a lot." Nicole's mother sniffles. Tears are falling over her makeup, but she doesn't wipe them away. "People talk, whisper, come up to me and ask if it's true, some ask if you're dying from that gay cancer. Every church I go to, people run in my face and ask me how you're doing. And I know what they're really asking. If you're still sinning with a woman. And I know they blame me. Want to ask what I did to you, or your daddy did to you, to make you this way."

"Did you listen to anything I said?"

"Did you find the justification for your lifestyle in the New Testament? In the Old Testament?"

"Momma, I can't deal with being across the room from you. I can't deal with you turning your back to me. Can I come over there? Can I hug you?"

"I cain't touch you, child, I cain't. Listen to your momma. I didn't get to be this age by being a fool. If you stay here, you become like the people here. If you go away, if you get away from here, away from this smog and people who act that funny way, your head will clear; you'll go back to thinking right."

"Momma, don't fool yourself. There are plenty of women back home that feel the same way I do."

Her mother says, "Why are you doing this? To punish me? What did I do wrong as a mother?"

Nicole puts her hands to her temples and massages.

Her mother says, "Come back to Memphis with your momma, baby. We can fix this. Prayer changes things. We can get you away from here, maybe take you out to the ranch in Millington for a while, get you some fresh air, some good cooking, get you away from these people, and we can fix this."

"You don't want me back there. I embarrass you."

"I want you back." She reaches into her purse, pulls out her wallet; waves an American Express platinum card in the air. "We can buy you a ticket to go back to Memphis. Leave all that has been tainted with this world here."

"I can't."

Again, silence. Everybody is shaking heads and thinking.

Her mother speaks first, "Cain't give up my God. Cain't give up my God for no one. Not for my mother, and not for my child."

Nicole says, "God knows my heart. I've reconciled a lot within myself. With God."

"Not with my God. My God does not compromise."

"We're human. Can we compromise?"

"No parent has to compromise with a child."

Silence.

Nicole says, "Momma—"

"If you cain't do as I ask, then stand behind me, Satan."

Tears fall.

"Momma, can I hug you? Please?"

"Stay behind me, Satan. Satan must always stay behind me."

Our Queen, our Diva from the South straightens her red pantsuit, the colorful scarf around her neck, caresses her golden Bible.

Her words are back to me. "I don't know her, don't know her at all. She came from my womb. Do you know what it's like to loathe something that you gave birth to? To be humiliated, sickened, embarrassed, betrayed, to feel nauseated every time someone speaks your child's name?"

Nicole sniffles, her words thick. "You don't listen. Why don't you ever listen when I tell you what's going on inside of me?"

"She is too far gone," her mother says as she gathers her coat, her luggage on wheels, as she heads for the door. "There is an echo where she used to be."

Nicole rubs her father's Bible, speaks with that childlike quality, "I don't like feeling like an orphan, Momma. Don't do this."

"I hear that echo every time I breathe, and it pains me. I tried to save her. Yes, Lord, I tried and I tried and tried. And it hurts me. Hurts me so bad. Pains me that I can't bring her back. But ain't but one man ever raised the dead, and shame on me for ever thinking I could do the same."

Nicole cries. Not loud. Soft and gentle.

Her mother says, "Tell her that the next time we see each other, that it will be in Memphis, down off Elvis Presley Boulevard, and one of us will be holding flowers, and the other will be getting lowered into this earth."

"Don't say that, Momma, don't—"

"And I hope I have the flowers, because I don't ever want to lay eyes on her again."

"Momma. I love you."

"I loved my Little Nicole. My sweet child. I loved her so much."

"I'm right here, Momma. Don't start talking like I'm not here. Don't make me invisible again."

"Her soul has been sucked from her body. Poisoned with all kinds of strange thoughts. She is dead. When this is over, we will both go to two separate places. Yes, Lord. I will be with you, at your side, with the king of kings. And my child, your will be done."

"Stop it, Momma, stop it."

"I saw the signs, saw the three signs sent to me by the Father, the Son, and the Holy Spirit, and I came. And I tried. I stepped into the lion's den and fought my best fight. And I have failed you. Please forgive me, your humble servant. Please forgive me, Father."

Nicole rocks, moans through clenched teeth, holds back the tears, fights with those tears so long her face turns red, like a furnace on the verge of exploding.

I say, "Nicole—"

She makes a hand motion asking me not to touch her, to leave her alone.

Nicole's mother tightens her golden coat around her red outfit, looking like sun and fire, sunrise and sunset, and with her Lena Horne stroll and her breasts leading the way. And when she passes her daughter, she wobbles a bit, leans toward me. I use my left hand to steady her.

Her eyes go to the sky and she says, "Forgive me."

She gazes back at Nicole's teary face. Nicole looks up at her mother's tears.

They stare. They cry.

An ice storm rages through me.

Nicole says, "I'm a good person. My character is still the same. I'm still the same."

She wants to go to Nicole. I feel her muscles twitching, I feel her inner struggle. But she moves by me, leaves me with her luggage-on-wheels as she moves toward the door.

"I pity that child."

Nicole responds, "I pity you, Momma. You have no courage."

"Her father is turning over in his grave. Turning over in his grave."

Nicole sobs. Turns her face from us, falls across the bed, and sobs.

When our Diva wipes her own eyes and opens the door, we are both taken aback. Ayanna is out there. My favorite stalker is right in front of the door, wearing the same black she had on earlier, leather coat open, scarf loose around her neck, purse on her right shoulder, keys and gloves in hand. Her eyes are the color of a old tomato, tears roller-coasting down her face, leaving a puddle at her feet. She's been crying for a while. She's been listening for a long while.

The door clicks closed, separating Nicole from us. Again, three people in a small space.

Nicole's mother looks Ayanna up and down, then down and up, before her eyes come to rest on Ayanna's hair. Her eyes widen and she mumbles, "Oh, God. I got the sign all wrong. I saw red and gold in my vision, and I thought that was your way of telling me what to wear into this place. My colors of victory. It's her hair. The red and gold, it's the color of her hair. You warned me of the devil."

Ayanna wipes her eyes.

Nicole's mother's voice now sounds strained, coarse. "You look like an ugly, black Raggedy Ann."

Ayanna yields a hostile, defiant stare.

Nicole's mother spits in Ayanna's face. That liquid anger splatters right below Ayanna's right eye.

I shout out my surprise, jump in between them, but Ayanna still doesn't move. No fear in her face.

They both stand strong.

Nicole's mother walks toward the elevator, marches away from a smoldering battlefield, leaving Ayanna right there, a butterscotch statue with liquid anger dripping from her cheek, being absorbed into the softness of the carpet without a sound.

24

Rain falls like bullets while we wait for the valet to bring the car around at the Waterfront. With the dark skies and the downpour, it looks more like London than California. In the lobby, people are huddled around the fireplace, laughing, having drinks, eating fruit, reading newspapers. Oblivious to what is going on in my world. I hear my name and turn to speak to those beautiful Ethiopian women behind the counter, absorb their warm smiles. I need smiles right now. As many as I can get.

One laughs and says, "Hey, famous author. When are you going to bring the rest of us books?"

I manage a soft chuckle, a wide smile. "I'll hook all of you up before I leave."

Nicole's mother looks at those women. I can only see the back of our Diva's head, but the Ethiopians stop laughing.

I head for the door, would rather stand in the freezing rain.

Nicole's mother follows me, dragging her chicken on wheels behind her.

I'm fidgety, worrying about Nicole because I hate to leave her like that, but I want to get her mother away from here as fast as I can. She can sense that. She's no southern-fried fool from the old school.

I confront her, "Why did you spit on her?"

She responds without hesitation, "You have a good imagination."

"From time to time. Yes, ma'am."

"Imagine having a son. Imagine him telling you he was sinning with another man. Try to sleep imagining them like that. Tell me how you would react. Let me know how nice you would be."

Inside the car, she shifts and hums while I drive up Broadway toward the Tube. I turn the radio on. I turn the radio back off. Fingers tap the steering wheel. Eyes cut toward her. She's still shaking her head. Her hands tight, like little hammers.

She says, "When that child was in the third grade, I caught her in my closet kissing a boy. Little nappy-headed Clark boy from down on Blair Hunt Drive. I whooped her hind parts good. Thought that would be my biggest problem. Trying to get her to not be fast. Never expected this. Never."

I drive.

She shifts, rocks, mumbles, "Used to take her to get Big Macs, candy. She used to watch *Fat Albert*. Loved her some chocolate milk. Couldn't make her stop playing Pac Man. Her and her brother and sisters would have pillow fights. She would put a dishtowel around her neck and pretend she was a superhero. Would yell about zephyr winds blowing and say 'O Mighty Isis,' and turn in circles for half an hour. And that girl would hold her arms out and run and run until she got out of breath."

I open the glove box, hand her a tissue to wipe her eyes, and I drive.

Drive back in time and think about me playing on the fields at Hamilton High, going to Quik N' Split for a meal, drinking Kool-Aid and making my tongue turn red, climbing trees because they were there, watching girls play hopscotch, and huddling with my brothers so we could watch the *Bugs Bunny Roadrunner Hour*. No way I could've predicted being where I am now. No Ouija board or palm reader gave me a hint. I look at my hand, the one holding the steering wheel, and see the flesh of a man. A man who will get older with every passing second. That child is gone to wherever children go. Wish I could go back, but there is no road to yesterday. I can only drive forward.

So I drive.

Nicole's mother asks me, "You love her more than you do the Lord?"

She jars me back to her world. I swallow, lick my dry lips.

Love. Lust. Infatuation. All of that comes to mind when she asks me that simple question. The simplest questions always seem to be the most complicated.

When I'm near Nicole, when I'm away from Nicole, I crave her. Crave to please her and be pleased by her. That testosterone level in my body runs high when she's near. And those good old neurotransmitters, dopamine and norepinephrine, make Nicole glow in my eyes. Makes me want to dance and romance her until the sun rises and falls and rises again. Gives me euphoria, makes me giddy as a sixteen-year-old, makes it hard to think about anything but her. She lives in me. Makes me want to hunt and gather and lay all of my victories at her feet.

It's too complicated to explain. I'm a writer, but it's not always that easy for me to articulate real emotions, not with getting them down on paper. That's my downfall.

So I answer, "Sometimes yes, sometimes no."

Then silence. And in silence, there is always judgment.

I say, "We're all being pulled in a lot of directions at the same time."

"Not all of us. Just the weak. Only the trees with weak roots fall in a storm."

I drive. Windshield wipers struggle to slap water away.

She goes on with the last of her mini-sermon, "That girl, that devil took Nicole from you. Took your wife from you. In front of your family, your fraternity brothers, your friends."

My hands become fists.

"People say you're weak for allowing this. Say you have no courage. That you don't think clear anymore. A real man would not allow this."

"If being a real man means turning hurt into anger, and anger into gasoline and matches, then no, I'm not the type of man you consider a real man. In most states, that kind of a man is called a felon."

"What do you think you are? Tell me?"

"I have hope."

"Hope has trapped many a fool."

Then we're at Oakland International. I park and walk to her gate. She checks in.

For a moment our eyes meet, and she no longer looks like Lena Horne, but more like Billie Holiday in her drugged out days. Tired. Worn. Weary. A woman who tries to do what's right.

"Tell her to keep her daddy's Bible," she says. "May it become her lamp back to the Lord."

We're on time, an hour before her winged chariot is due to depart and take her back on the other side of the great Continental Divide. I offer to sit and wait with her, but she dismisses me.

She tells me, "Don't stay out here too long. You'll lose what's left of your soul."

Without a good-bye, I turn to leave. Her awful humming follows me, blending with other conversations, with intercom pages, with the sound of luggage on squeaky wheels. I hurry through a crowd of anxious people rushing to get flights to points all round the world. People who are rushing to get away from Oakland before their souls end up MIA.

Nicole. My mind is on Nicole. How she had broken down.

I begin to jog on these aching muscles. My jog turns into a light run. I run faster. With each stride that expensive perfume and homemade chicken aroma fades.

I run to get away from that woman, but I can't get away from myself.

25

Nicole's car is still at the Waterfront. Ayanna's super-size SUV is gone.

My hotel room is empty. No sign. No note.

I remember the route, take Broadway to Broadway Terrace, ride the winding roads above Caldecott Tunnel up toward the sky, in the land of museum-size homes and mini-mansions. A right on Proctor. Pass by a couple of houses with rainbow-colored flags. The few, the proud, the alternatives.

I park across the street from Ayanna's house, from the house that shelters Nicole every night. I rub my temples as I sit out front. Nicole's mother's voice is stuck inside my head. Won't go away.

I ring the doorbell. A long moment passes. The porch light comes on. Goes off. The sensor beeps three times when the door opens.

It's Ayanna. She's barefoot. Has on blue-and-gold CAL sweats.

She says, "I was hoping that was you."

"Were you?"

"Please, let's not. Not now. She needs us."

"How is she?"

"How would you be after something like that?"

"She shuts down when things get too hard."

"I know."

She takes my coat, hangs it in the closet by the front door.

Ayanna says, "She needs your energy right now."

I look down the long hallway toward the kitchen and the living room area. Light is glowing. Soft peaceful, ethereal music that reminds me of Enya.

The stunning art. The Italian furniture. Once again I take it all in. Once again I'm in awe.

I follow Ayanna. Her feminine sway so easy.

The fireplace is burning. Candles are in the kitchen, on the white tile counter, more on the tile island. Orange and vanilla. Smells like a cleansing ritual is going on. Nicole has on blue-and-gray sweats, University of Memphis, and a black sports bra, thick socks on her feet. Her hair is hidden, wrapped up in a black and white handkerchief. She's in front of the fireplace, sitting with her legs spread out, staring into the flames.

Nicole doesn't turn her head. "Where is Momma?"

"Dropped her off."

She comes over and hugs me. "You're freezing."

"Pretty cold out. Pneumonia weather."

"Was worried 'bout cha, boo."

"Sorry I had to leave you."

"Sorry I put you through that madness. You looked pretty tore up when you were leaving."

"You didn't look like a homecoming queen yourself."

"I never have looked like a homecoming queen. I'm a cute gerbil on my best day."

Ayanna is in the kitchen, sitting on the island, her right hand going back and forth over the candle, playing with the flames, never stopping long enough to burn. Watching us interact. Listening to us. Learning us. Our relationship. The depth of our caring. I ask Ayanna if she is okay.

Ayanna pulls her knees to her chest. "Nothing like a little phlegm to wake an ugly, Raggedy Ann sister up."

Nicole goes to Ayanna. Ayanna jumps off the counter. They hug.

Nicole says, "I'm sorry—"

"Shh," Ayanna says and she rubs Nicole's back. "Not your fault."

I watch the depth of their relationship. See how they react in the worst of times.

Outside the rain starts coming down again. It slaps the roof of the house like light rocks. Can hear the streets flooding, water running downhill. Oakland is being cleansed.

Nicole wanders back over to the fireplace, stares into the flames, falls away from us. Ayanna looks at me, chews her bottom lip, her expression asking me if I know what to do to make Nicole feel better. How to heal her.

Then Nicole shouts, "Would you believe she brought chicken on a damn plane?"

There's a pause, then we all break out laughing.

Nicole cackles. "Good thing she didn't cook chitterlings. She would've funked up the Waterfront. Jack London Square. North, South, East, and West Oakland."

We double over and laugh hard enough to sweat. Nicole falls to the floor, kicks her legs in the air and laughs the hardest.

When the cackling is done, our sides are aching, we're exhausted, and we're all smiles.

Ayanna goes upstairs, comes right back with blankets and a purple bottle of oil, its jojoba aroma lighting up the air around us. She lays the blanket out in front of the fireplace, asks Nicole to take her clothes off. She does.

Ayanna tells me, "Come here. I need help."

She asks me to pour oil in her palms, then she rubs her palms until the oil is warm, and gives Nicole a deep massage. I watch her work her magic. She's good.

Nicole moans. Tenses. Relaxes. Moans. Moans.

Ayanna says, "You familiar with reflexology?"

I shake my head. "Heard about it."

"It's an art of healing. I'll show you."

She moves her hands from Nicole's feet, to her body, to her hands. Ayanna talks about the five koshas, the different layers of the body. About emotional wholeness.

Nicole groans as light and easy as the music that's playing in the background. It sounds as if all that's bad is leaving her body with each breath, leaving in whispers and sighs. Ayanna touches my hands with her hands, her eyes on mine as she guides my hands, tries to teach me, shows me how to do the same.

Ayanna says, "If you knew how to do this, you could help her out when she's cramping."

I say, "Never knew."

"What do you usually do when she's got the cramps real bad?"

"Toss her a bottle of Midol, a pound of raw meat, and a box of chocolates."

We chuckle. Ayanna has a beautiful laugh. Her skin glows.

Ayanna says, "We do this for each other. It strengthens our bond."

Nicole's breathing deepens. She's asleep. Her face again that of a woman-child. Ayanna covers her with another blanket, fluffs part of it up like a pillow, eases that under Nicole's head.

Ayanna says, "Come over here and chill out. Let her rest."

We move to the kitchen. Ayanna boils water in a teapot and makes us large cups of orange spice tea. I sit at a barstool and add honey to mine. Ayanna gets on top of the island, folds her legs, both hands wrapped around her oversize cup.

Ayanna speaks softly. "We both love her."

I match her pleasant tone. "Yep. Beyond reason."

"Maybe, if we really try, this could work."

I ask her, "Why the change? Why are you so down with her program now?"

"Thought about it. Have to be real. I knew how she was long before you came along. No one can be everything to anyone. So, I decided to lay my burdens down. Try and make it equal. Be optimistic."

"Why the change?"

"I heard her and her mother. Me and my mother went through the same drama. She thinks that since I was married to a man before, at some point I'll go back to a man again."

"Really?"

"Mothers have this image of what their daughters should be. When you don't fit that mold, they can't handle it. They take the shit so personally."

"Daddies are the same way."

I stare at Nicole. Sleeping near the fireplace. Her hand is near her face, looking like a child who wants to suck her thumb.

Ayanna says, "She did better than I would have.

Nicole stood up to her mother and told her how much she loves both of us."

"Did it with her hand on her father's Bible."

"Yep. That took courage and conviction. And like it or not, that should count for something."

In the dancing candlelight, Ayanna and I watch each other for a while.

Ayanna says, "When she hurts, I hurt. If she had cancer, I would want it instead. If she needs you in her life, then I will accept that. Can you accept me? Do you love her that much?"

A moment passes.

"You're still loving with your dick. And that will never be more powerful than what I give her."

I say, "Remember who lost the race."

"Eight years. Our relationship is deeper than you thought."

We stare. Ayanna kisses her fingers, touches my lips with those fingers. I taste her fingers, kiss her fingers, suck her fingers over and over. She moans. Her eyes have that erotic look. I give her my hand and she does the same.

"What's your game, Ayanna?"

"I don't play games. Not even bid whist on the Fourth of July."

She kisses my fingers, tongues my palm. My breathing gets ragged.

Nicole shifts. Her bracelets sing a restless song as she turns over.

We stop. Stop and stare, first at her, then at each other.

Ayanna goes over to Nicole, touches her hair. Lies down next to her. I go over, lie down on the other side of Nicole. Ayanna and I stare at each other, hardly blinking.

Ayanna closes her eyes first. I close mine, listen to their breathing. Ayanna's inhales and exhales fall into rhythm with Nicole's. Sounds like one person breathing. My breathing matches their cadence. Sounds like one person is in this room, on this floor. Sounds like peace.

Warmth covers my body. I fall asleep.

When I wake up again, the rain has stopped. The room is a little darker. I'm on the carpet, lying next to Ayanna.

Nicole has blown out three of the candles, is standing in the patio window, looking out over the lemon and persimmon trees. Her socks are off her feet. She walks from the dining area to the window, to the living room, back, does that over and over. Moves like a woman wandering in the desert. She's holding her father's Bible to her chest. Humming. She stops at the window, staring out, into the skies, as if she were looking for her mother's plane. She rocks, wipes her eyes with the back of her left hand.

Ayanna moves. Bracelets jingle. Nicole turns around, comes toward us.

She sees me watching her. She smiles.

I sit up.

Nicole puts the Bible down and sits on the floor between her two lovers. She leans and kisses me the way a mother does a child. Then she kisses Ayanna the same way. Wakes her up.

Ayanna asks her if she slept much.

Nicole says, "Dreams woke me up."

"What you dream?"

"Dreamt I was driving on I-240 trying to get to the 55 South."

I ask, "Where the hell is that?"

"Memphis. Saw Elvis Presley on the side of the road trying to thumb a ride."

"Negative energy. Anytime a sister dreams about Elvis Presley, it's nothing but negative energy."

We laugh.

Ayanna says, "Should've showered before I massaged you."

Nicole jokes, "Now you've rubbed all of that yucky stuff into my karma."

Ayanna takes Nicole's hand and they go upstairs, Ayanna leading the way. Seems like the energy switches between them, moves back and forth. Makes everything seem so equal.

I sit on the sofa, in front of the big screen. The water comes on. Then there is the sound of footsteps coming down the carpeted stairway at a very happy pace.

Ayanna sticks her head around the corner and asks, "Coming?"

We stare.

Ayanna says, "We can at least try. One honest try. Is that too much?"

Her bracelets jingle as she reaches her hand out for me.

I take her hand, let her warm flesh hold onto mine, and follow her.

We turn the lights off and bathe by candlelight. The bathtub is huge, but a tight fit for all three of us. We twist and turn and laugh until we all get in. This time it's different. Ayanna and I wash Nicole with soapsuds the size of Mr. Bubble. Nicole shows how flexible she is and she raises her leg, does that so Ayanna can shave Nicole's legs while I scrub Nicole top to bottom.

And we talk, splash water on each other, tell jokes

about chicken and white people and San Francisco, and we give Nicole kisses to resurrect her soul.

Nicole says, "I can't wait to get to Italy."

"I feel ya," Ayanna says, then smiles at me. "Too bad you can't go with us."

Nicole is beaming, sucking up the attention, giving us laughs and kisses.

We run through the shower, knock all the suds off our bodies.

By the time we oil our skin with sweet patchouli and dry off, Ayanna has gone downstairs and come back with a plate of fruit: mangos, kiwis, other exotic treats. All cut up and ready to eat.

We sit on the floor, wrapped in towels and bathrobes, and I feed Nicole a grape. Ayanna feeds her a strawberry. Nicole feeds us melon, then she kisses the juices away. Uses her tongue. We touch. Feed. Kiss. Over and over. And one of those kisses between Nicole and me, it goes on and on, gets pretty torrid. I rise. She touches me as I rise. She strokes me and I rise.

And in response I touch Nicole between her thighs, run my fingers over her sliver of hair, move to her hollow, touch the outside, slip inside, do a slow massage until she shudders.

I tell Nicole, "Kiss Ayanna."

She does. I take Ayanna's hand, put it where mine was. Nicole is touching Ayanna in the same spot, her other hand touching me, moving me up and down. Coos and moans rise like clouds.

I say, "You're wet enough to seal a thousand envelopes."

"Sweetie, I'm wet enough to seal a million envelopes."

Ayanna leaves for a sec; comes back with a black-and-green can of Kama Sutra Honey Dust.

Three smiles dance.

We play with each other, use the feather that comes with the dust, a light feather that awakens all the nerves, use that feather to paint and tickle and tease each other head to toe with that sweet dust, then under the influence of jazz and candles, we unpaint each other with our tongues.

It's different tonight. Unplanned. Very erotic.

Ayanna loves Nicole while I kiss her, steal her breath, swallow her every sound. I get high when she spasms; the sound of her orgasm feeds into my mouth.

Nicole sits on me, coos, bites her bottom lip, her eyes roll as if she's about to drown in pleasure as I slide into her den of sin. She finds her breath and moves over me like a ballerina. Rises and sits and rises while Ayanna kisses and touches her and massages her. Then Nicole clamps her mouth down on my neck, and that is my number one spot. Another tongue touches my knees, traces and licks my kneecaps.

Ayanna asks, "What can I do to help?"

Nicole whispers, "His feet, Ayanna. He's so sensitive on his feet."

Ayanna's tongue moves down my legs, makes love to my toes.

"That's right Ayanna. God, look at his face."

"You should see your face. You're floating. How does it feel?"

"Shit yeah. This is a ten baby . . . this is a ten."

That much stimulation is new to me; I go crazy. Overwhelmed. Can't breathe. Feel like I'm a sixteen-year-old kid having my first orgasm, excited and terrified at the same time.

They're talking, laughing, and I'm too busy pulling sheets.

Toes curl. I fight to hold it back.

"Listen to him moan."

"Hush, Ayanna."

"Talk about an ugly face. Looks like a pit bull with cramps."

Nicole laughs.

Eyes roll into the back of my head.

The world vanishes, changes into shades of bright red and brilliant yellows.

Water seeps through the dam. Can't hold the floods back any longer. I damn near sit up when I release myself into the start of my orgasm; I let go, give in to my own jerking, but I don't let go too fast. I wrestle with the heat until it burns. Then I stop and let them do all the work. They have me. I'm a slave. So much heat. Let it build, let it torture. I lose that battle, numb with pleasure.

I jerk, pant, wail like a banshee.

26

We all lie in the bed touching each other. My eyes are closed. I think I passed out because we're all in a new position. I'm fogged in the aftermath of brilliant love-making. I crack my eyes and the world is as fuzzy as my grandmother's favorite slippers. I see that Ayanna is on her belly, hand across Nicole's belly, looking so devoted. Nicole is staring at the ceiling, as warm and fogged over as I am. A smirk, a smile, something joyful is on her face. I close my eyes. Try to recuperate while Lady Godiva and Joan of Arc talk in ladylike whispers.

Ayanna says, "How long will he be in the Bay?"

"Not sure. I know he goes to the east coast in a few days."

"He lives on the road."

"Pretty much. Just like his father. Always gone, never home."

Ayanna chuckles.

Nicole asks, "Wanna share?"

"Just remembering how much you used to tell me that his being gone used to bother you."

"It did. He'd be gone all summer. We'd miss all the jazz festivals. He's on the road on my birthday. Then he'd be flying around all of Black History Month. A lot of weekends in between. And when he was home, he was writing."

"An absentee boyfriend."

"Yup. Travels just as much as his dad does, if not more."

Trapped in an epiphany, I don't move. I have never thought of it that way.

Ayanna says, "Let's have a home-cooked dinner before he leaves the Bay. I can make tuna taki, or defrost the duck. I've been wanting to cook that duck for two weeks."

Nicole pauses. "Knowing him, I'm sure he wants to get to writing."

"Is that what he calls it?"

"Don't like it, don't read it."

"I just don't think he should be making a living off of your misery."

"Well, I don't mind. Some sisters don't get letters, some don't even get postcards. I get books written about me. I get books dedicated to me. You know how many women would love that?"

Ayanna doesn't answer. Inside, I'm glowing. Love hearing Nicole defend me.

Ayanna says, "Was thinking."

" 'Bout what?"

Ayanna pauses again. "We should complete the circle."

"What do you mean?"

"We should all experience each other."

Nicole gets quiet.

Ayanna asks, "You scared? It's okay if you are, because I am too."

Nicole responds, "I'm not scared . . . just surprised you would want that."

"You looked so warm when he went inside you. I'd think you'd want me to experience the same nirvana."

"So, then you want to be penetrated by him."

"Penetrated? Why so clinical all of a sudden?"

"You know what I mean."

Bracelets jingle.

Ayanna presses on, "That's the next logical step, don't you think?"

"What are you saying, Ayanna?"

"Maybe we should just go for it. Explore and see what we all like together, as a team."

"No, that creates chaos. We have to have boundaries. So no one gets hurt."

Ayanna huffs. "No one, or just you?"

Nicole sighs.

I want to say something, but I don't. My curiosity is strong, but I will not kill the cat. Not yet.

Ayanna says, "I've bent for you. I've put up with all kinds of shit. Your mother has assaulted me. He's bent for you. Was ready to beat some fool down in a club for you last night. Catch my drift?"

A long pause. Ayanna hums.

Nicole says, "Both of you have bonded through me. I'm the focal point. There's no connection between the two of you. No real connection."

"Is that how you feel the most secure? With no connection between us?"

A moment passes. Nicole asks, "Why are you pushing this?"

"I'm dealing with reality. If we're going to do this, then let's not half-ass do it. Let's do it. I'm giving you everything you want."

Ayanna gets up and leaves the bedroom. Sounds like she goes downstairs.

Nicole says my name. Shakes me.

She asks, "We going out tonight?"

I toss out a fake yawn. "Sure. Ayanna hanging out with us or what?"

Nicole says, "She has to work. Just us. I want to get out and get some air."

"Ask Ayanna—"

"Just me and you, sweetie."

We shower and dress, then walk downstairs.

By then Ayanna has heated up leftovers. She makes salads, fixes plates of vegetarian spaghetti. We sit at the counter, pig out, keep our glasses filled with sparkling Pellegrino. Then she serves us tiramisu.

Ayanna jokes, "We were like that tiramisu. All three of us. Italian cream cheese and Marsala custard and espresso. A perfect blend."

I say, "Corny, corny, corny."

We laugh.

I ask, "Who does most of the cooking?"

Ayanna smiles. "I do. I'm the Wolfgang Puck in this domain."

After that Nicole loads the dishwasher.

Ayanna makes herself a cup of vanilla coffee. Says she has work to do on her case against the school system. She sees that Nicole has packed an overnight bag. Ayanna kisses me, holds me a while and smiles at Nicole. Then she kisses and hugs Nicole a long while.

Ayanna tells Nicole, "Give it some thought. Could be as sweet as tiramisu."

Nicole nods.

"We running in the morning?" Ayanna asks as we head for the door. "We have to keep our training on track for the marathon."

Nicole hesitates.

"Meet us at the hotel," I tell Ayanna. "We'll run a course up into Piedmont."

At the door, Ayanna raises her left arm, shakes her bracelets at Nicole. Nicole does the same.

Inside the car, Nicole asks me if we can go by my hotel first.

I ask, "For what?"

"You have the engagement ring?"

"You're asking questions when you know the answer."

"Wasn't a question. I want to wear it tonight. Want to be your fiancée tonight."

"Are you my fiancée?"

"Wish I were your wife."

27

Nicole and I end up across the bridge, on Market and Taylor. With the freaks that come out at night, the home of the 49ers looks as seedy as Times Square before it was Disneyfied.

We make our way through a crowd of people coming out the Warfield Theater, worm our way to the bright lights at the Crazy Horse. From the outside, it doesn't look like much. Nicole pays twenty-five bucks for me, fifteen ducats for her, parts with that poor man's fortune and we walk into a packed theater-style room. At least three hundred men are in a narrow room that has very few empty seats.

I hold Nicole's hand, the one with the ring.

Hard-core music is bumping as a naked woman in clear six-inch stilettos crawls across a T-shaped stage, a lioness trekking a dollar-lined Serengeti. Women in thongs are all over the place, flirting, getting eye-fucked sixty-nine ways, all putting on Hollywood smiles and trying to get men to buy private dances. The woman on stage picks a guy out of the crowd, pulls his face between her legs, smothers him.

I ask, "Think she knows him or is that a random act of kindness?"

"Think he cares?"

The headliner, Siren, comes out next. Decked in dark shades, leather tam, black leather and six-inch stilettos. Music, pantomiming, guns, she has an over-the-top, Hollywood-style act. She's exotic.

Nicole says, "This is the girl I wanted you to see."

Siren picks a Pee-Wee Herman–looking horny toad from the crowd and starts doing a masturbation–oral sex number. At the right moment, when we think they are in nirvana, the dildo shoots colorful confetti twenty feet in the air, confetti that flies over the applauding crowd like a rocket on New Year's.

I sit there with my mouth wide open.

Nicole applauds. Then she stops all of a sudden. Stops with her hands up, as if someone took the batteries out. She looks around at the people and her smile goes away. She looks nauseated.

I ask her if she's okay.

She asks me if I want to stay for the second half. I shake my head, enough of this thong-in-cheek freak festival.

"Me neither."

I want to ask if her mother's visit has done a number on her. I think she wants to ask the same. She doesn't ask. Neither do I.

We leave there and drive back to Oakland, land on the outskirts of Lake Merritt at the Jahva House on Lake Shore. A shotgun-style hangout that reminds me of the original 5th Street Dicks in Los Angeles's Leimert Park. Jeans. T-shirts. Turtlenecks. People are drinking Heinekens and talking about the revolution. Where the sisters aren't trying to look Caucasian, Japanese, or Asian. With the dreads, twisties, braids, a few who haven't let go of the perm, all the women are as beautiful as the African photography on the wall. Mostly African-American, African, and Jamaican with some non-black Berkeley-ites who appreciate the culture in the place.

I'm comfortable here.

While Bob Marley sings that he doesn't want to wait in vain, we grab coffees and head upstairs, sit on a soft peach velour love seat underneath a picture of Ramses. Everything here is friendly, including the furniture. The way the brothers are watching the sisters up in here, and the way the sisters are sipping their brew and peeping at the men over the rims of their cups, the place looks hetero. But in this world, sexuality is smoke and mirrors. I'm learning that. There are so many appetites in this world. So many different versions of God.

Nicole asks, "You record your book signing?"

"What?"

She repeats the question. I tell her I didn't record.

She asks, "What kind of questions did Ayanna ask?"

"Ask her to give you a repeat performance."

"I heard she was slaughtering you. Sure you didn't record?"

"Positive. Now let's move on."

We talk about other things. Allow our soft words to blend in with other meaningless mumbles.

Nicole asks, "How you like this place?"

"Off the chains."

"They keep it real here. I don't get to hang out in this environment too much. Not like this."

"What do you mean?"

"Couples. Like this. I miss going to Atlas Bar and Grill, kicking it at the Sky Bar with you."

"Where do you hang out up here?"

"Ayanna likes the gay joints. If it's the first Friday, she has to go to Backstreet. That's all she ever wants to do."

"Power struggle?"

"Always."

She cuddles up against me like we were at home in front of the big screen. She moves the conversation in a new direction, tells me that Dwayne Wiggins from Tony Toni Tone owns this place, and Greg Burgess from KPFA hosts a spoken word show here on Wednesday. Talks about poets Paradise, J Crow, and Roxanne, claims they are the best from the political to the erotic. I tell her that I doubt if they can touch the poets out of World Stage in Leimert Park. Those poets are deep.

She says, "Is everything a competition with you? Can't it just be about the art?"

We laugh.

She tells me about other places I might like, places like the Blue Candle and Mambo Mambo. She talks, flirts, kisses, each word sounds like she's back to selling me Oakland, but I know Nicole. She's trying to ease the conversation somewhere else, trying not to be abrupt.

Nicole asks, "Do you think I'm an animal?"

"Nicole, baby, don't go there. Let's have fun."

Nicole says, "I keep thinking about my life. The damage I've created. Momma, never saw her look like that. She brought it all to me. I've hurt my family. Disappointed my friends. Even got you to pull away from your family. Got your daddy running up here. Momma flying out here. Made Ayanna compromise her mind and sexuality to please me. Driven you crazy. I'm one powerful bitch."

I let it go for a moment. She sniffs.

I ask, "You crying?"

"Nope," she says. "When Ayanna suggested that we complete the circle, why did you pretend you were asleep?"

"How did you know I was pretending?"

"I didn't. Not until now."

"You're a regular Perry Mason."

"What did you think about what she was saying?"

"Everything's been so hedonistic. Dunno. Not sure how to answer that."

The waitress comes by, checks on us, tells Nicole she's wearing a very nice engagement ring, checks it out without shame, then leaves with a friendly wink. I sit and people-watch, something I can do all night long.

Nicole says, "You think that this thing with us and Ayanna could work?"

She says *Us and Ayanna*. Like Ayanna's the odd one out now.

I say, "Given the right compromises."

She chuckles. "Damn. Both of you have done a one-eighty."

I rub her hand.

We sip our java. Listen, rock, and sway to the reggae. Reminds me of us years ago, when we first held hands, before the first kiss. Before the Jeep. Long before Paris.

I'm trying to remember who I was then. But I can't. I'm the same, but at the same time I've changed in so many ways. Seven years ago there was no way I would've considered woman-sharing as an option to curing a broken heart. At least I don't think I would have.

"Ayanna was at our wedding," I say.

That catches her off guard. She sighs, puts her drink down, sits up, steeples her hands, straightens her back the way a person does when they are ready to face the truth head-on.

I ask, "Why didn't I know about Ayanna?"

"She used to call me at work. We usually chitchatted between nine and five. Think she called me at home once or twice over the years and you answered. You never asked who she was."

So true. If I was at Nicole's and answered the phone, and I heard a professional female voice on the other end, I would have no reason to question who she was laughing with.

I ask, "When did you two hook up?"

Nicole tells me that Ayanna would fly down to L.A. early in the morning, they would hang out, run together, shop together, go to the Body Clinic and get massages and facials, or go to the Herb King in Santa Monica and get acupuncture, maybe drive to Malibu and eat at Gladstone's, do whatever they wanted to do on those honeymoon days, and Ayanna would be back home in Oakland that same evening, in time to cook her husband chicken and waffles. Nicole would do the same and get back in time to be with me.

She asks, "You're angry?"

I say, "Keep talking. Tell me about these rendezvous."

Sometimes Ayanna stayed overnight in L.A. and they'd meet at Peanuts, a soft-legged alternative joint in Hollywood, and somewhere down the line they went to Palm Springs, two hours outside of Los Angeles, miles away from anyone Nicole might know, shopped at the mega outlet out that way off the 10, then checked into a private women's resort at Casitas Laquita.

She emphasizes, "But it was not sexual."

"You went to a lesbian compound and it wasn't sexual?"

"It's not a . . . I wasn't sexual. Sensual, not sexual. Just running with the wolves. Investigating. Not like I was doing that every week. Just a handful of times. Curious. I was curious. Having fun."

I nod, bite my top lip. Remember how Ayanna said her husband went off on her, beat her down. I'm feeling that right now. I rub my palms until the sweat dries, until my heart calms.

She says, "She was in school, working full-time, changing careers. I was doing the same. Ain't like we had a lot of extra time. Mostly we kept in touch by e-mail."

"I see."

"Lots of people build relationships on-line."

"Yep."

A girl across from us gets happy, shouts and almost breaks out with a Holy Ghost dance when she hears Marley's "Redemption Song" on the system. Everyone laughs and smiles at her enthusiasm.

I clear my throat, rub thumb over thumb until they start to burn. I ask Nicole, "Where was I when you finally crossed that river with Ayanna?"

"On tour. I doubt if you paid any attention."

I do have that type of job. Gone for weeks at a time. Just like my father. I sell stories. He sells hope.

She tells me, "But I was through with Ayanna. Through experimenting."

"Were you?"

"I was dealing with my issues, but I was off that page, out of that book, completely yours."

"What happened?"

"Paris."

I see something that I didn't see before. It comes back to me in a rush now. It's surreal, I'm here, but I'm also back in Paris, in bed with Nicole, looking down on her tortured face as she says, *"I close my eyes and I can't stop seeing her . . . smell her perfume all over my skin . . . can't stop tingling . . . feel her breasts on me . . . so wet . . . her nipples . . . little-bitty penises . . . wanted them in my mouth . . . on my skin . . . never felt like this before."*

Wrong. That day, I think I'd seen it all wrong, heard it all wrong.

I think of Ayanna, of that first moment I saw her naked, when she stood in Nicole's garden facing me, her nipples, those ripe blackberries looking so full, so erect. Like little penises.

I ask Nicole, if that day in France, if she was talking about the French girl, if that was whose touch was haunting her then. Or if she was talking about Ayanna.

She smiles a nervous smile. "It was Ayanna."

"Not the French girl."

"The French girl touched me and . . . I guess . . . guess she only made me think about Ayanna."

Nicole says more, tells me that when the French girl danced, in Nicole's eyes, she saw Ayanna. Nicole can't remember the French girl, not the way I do; she can't remember the color of her hair, the freckles. Only the feeling.

I could let go, but there are things I have to know.

"How many times did you get with Ayanna?"

"Three times."

"First time?"

"After Paris."

"Where?"

"Palm Springs. Queen of Hearts."

"Another resort."

She says, "Well, I wasn't gonna go to a Motel 6."

"Second time?"

"Not too long after that."

"Third time?"

"Weekend before the wedding."

"Geesh, Nicole."

"The last time just sort of happened. Was not planned at all. I had avoided her after that first time."

"Why do it and avoid her?"

"Women do it with men and avoid them. Same difference."

"Don't get off on a tangent."

"Guess I wasn't too happy about it. About me going there. I liked it, loved it, loved her, but it's not the kind of thing a sister wants to put on her resume."

"Back to the third time. When? Where?"

Nicole fidgets. Sighs again. "Weekend before the wedding, Ayanna brought me a gift. I went to Santa Monica, met her there, just went to tell her good-bye. We met for lunch on the promenade."

"How did you get from the promenade to being butt-naked?"

"When you care, when you love, when two people meet to say good-bye forever, well, it got to be a bit emotional, on both of our parts."

I rock and nod. I'm about ready to shoot the sheriff and the deputy.

Two songs, "Rebel Music" and "No Woman, No Cry" come and go.

Nicole says, "I feel better. Since you know I feel better."

"Not sure how I feel."

She leans against me, snuggles up to me, softens me with her touch. "I love you both."

"But?"

"But right now, I don't think I can stay with Ayanna anymore."

"Where did that come from?"

No answer. Not right away.

She says, "I want to be able to go back home and see my nieces and nephews, maybe take them to the Rendezvous to eat ribs, or Memphis in May, or walk through the Civil Rights Museum. Want to be able to do that and not feel like I'm being whispered at, don't want to be looked at like I'm a child abuser or some kind of freak. I hear them whispering now. I always hear them whispering."

She leans back into me again and I rub my fingers on her hand.

She asks, "Ever wonder where we would be if we were married?"

"Every day."

"Hmm. Wonder what people would say, how they would act if we eloped."

I want to tell her that people whispered yesterday, whisper today, will whisper tomorrow. And I know they say things about me. The fool who pursues the woman who left him at the altar.

She goes on, "Like Momma said, it's not like anybody threw a parade, right?"

I let that settle.

She asks, "What if I had married you and kept this to myself?"

"Had your thing on the side?"

"Could have. Seems like everyone does."

I remember all that Ayanna told me about her and

her Latin lover, how they did their thing and fooled two husbands, and I hate to admit it, but in my heart I know she's telling the truth.

Nicole says, "I was fine yesterday, now I'm afraid."

"What's there to be afraid of?"

"Being alone."

"After tonight, why would you feel like that?"

She sighs. "Ayanna wants to complete the circle. What if you do it with Ayanna and like what she gives you better than what I give you? Or the same with her? What if neither of you need me anymore because all you need is each other?"

I say, "I don't love Ayanna."

"What if she flipped the script and went . . . and went . . ."

"Straight?"

"Yeah. What if you stop desiring me?"

"And what if you went insane trying to win me back?"

"Yeah."

I pause a moment, let all of that seep into our pores, then I say, "Thought this wasn't about competition?"

She runs her tongue over her lips. "Hard to not be jealous when it comes to you."

"You haven't given me much of a choice when it comes to you."

Nicole's I-pager vibrates. She checks the message. It's Ayanna. She's home working, about to crash, and wants to know what time we're going to run in the AM, if she should defrost duck for dinner tomorrow. Nicole types a message back to Ayanna, tells her that we're running at seven, rain or shine, and to meet us at the Waterfront.

When she puts her I-pager away, she says, "Truth or truth?"

"Shoot."

Nicole has a serious, what I would call a very literary face. "You want to fuck her?"

I say, "Fair exchange is no robbery."

"Pussy is pussy, right?"

I retort, "You should know. You get more pussy than I do."

"That wasn't nice."

"Don't dish it out if you can't take it."

Nicole loses her intellectuality, sounds like Ayanna when she's frustrated and feeling powerless, and takes me to the pussy level. What I need is higher than that, much higher: physical, emotional, mental, spiritual, a combination of many things.

I tell Nicole, "It's never ever been just about the sex. Not even when we were in the Jeep. Not in Paris. Not last night. Not this evening. My loving you makes me want to love you all the time."

"Really."

The reggae, the chatter, the sound of a cell phone ringing, a glass breaking, fills in the space.

Nicole hums awhile. A couple of brothers sporting back-length dreadlocks come up into this private den. They come over and hand her flyers for a lot of hip-hop shows going down in the area. Kelly Price, Case, and Tamia at the Henry J. Kaiser Arena; another about The Justice League; one promoting the East Oakland Voices at the El Haaj Malik El Shabazz Community Center.

Nicole stuffs them in her purse, says positive things, wishes the brothers eternal peace, and they leave, both smiling like they are in love.

Nicole leans, melts into me. Our thoughts as deep as a Toni Morrison novel.

Slow song comes on. Bob Marley's "Three Little Birds." We stand up in front of the love seat, and in the intimate space we dance in the chatter. No one else dances. We don't care. She holds me and I think of how Ayanna says Nicole won't hold her in public. When the dance is done, we sit back down.

My body is aching. Reminding me that I'm not as young as I used to be. Not old, but not that young anymore. It takes nothing to get old. All I have to do is wait, be idle or be busy, and age finds me. I tell Nicole that thought, let her know that even if we do this circle thing, I won't be there forever. That I know for sure.

She says, "At some point, I'm still going to have to choose."

"Or I'll have to choose. Or Ayanna will have to. At some point."

I love Nicole; there is no doubt in my mind or my heart about that. But today I'm still like that man in *Lolita*. My feet are still in concrete. At times it feels like it's loosening, but maybe, like worn shoes, that sign of loosening is not a sign of freedom, just comfort.

We talk for a while. Share laughs at our own expense.

Nicole puts on her serious face, says, "What if we had a baby?"

I ask, "How would Ayanna fit into that picture?"

"She wouldn't."

"What are you saying?"

"I just said it. I want to have a baby. Want my child to play with my nieces and nephews."

"You want your mother to accept you."

"Don't analyze me."

"Tell me I'm lying and I'll drop it."

"Do you hear what I want? I want you. Nobody but."

Pause. More heavy thoughts. If this were a week ago, I'd be turning cartwheels and flips, calling my father and my brothers and her mother and planning welcome back parties all over the country.

Today I'm uneasy. Have some strange feelings for Ayanna. A moment ago when she I-paged Nicole, I smiled. I was just as happy to hear from her. She's part of my five senses, so her face, voice, aroma, taste, touch, all of that trickled over my skin when her message came through. Made me almost wish she was here talking, playing devil's advocate like she always does.

Ayanna has been with us for a long time. Even when I didn't know her name, wasn't cognizant of her existence, she was there. And now with the knowing of this eight-year thing, I know Ayanna has been here since day one. There has always been three of us in our bed. Always.

Nicole sees the lines in my face, those railroad tracks that come when I'm thinking. She rubs her hand over my forehead, smoothes out those tracks.

She says, "You don't believe me, do you?"

"You love Ayanna. It's in your eyes, see it when you touch her. Don't fake the funk."

"Of course I love her. I can't imagine her not being in my life. That's why it hurts me."

"What hurts you?"

"What I'm going to have to do."

"What?"

"Pack my bags. Break her heart. Divorce myself from her."

My insides become hollow.

I shake that empathy away.

Ayanna is the enemy, my antagonist, the one who keeps me from achieving my goal. She has invaded my love the way the Moors invaded Spain.

I touch Nicole's honey-blond hair; she reaches her hand back and touches my light brown twisties, runs her hand across my chin, along my stubble, her bracelets jingling when her arm raises.

We sink into the love seat, do that in a room filled with chit-chatty strangers, hold each other until we can't hear the music, or the people in the other peach chairs laughing on their cell phones, or pagers going off, or see the people who are walking by on the green carpet and damn near stepping on our feet, or smell the coffee, or smell the beer, can't hear see smell feel touch taste anything but us.

The world falls away. We're in our own garden.

She doesn't let go first.

When my arm goes numb and I try to let go, she holds on tighter, holds on the longest.

28

Back at the Waterfront, Nicole gets on the phone. Working on contracts and compromises at the midnight hour. Leaving messages for clients at Honeywell, Motorola, and Ford.

I'm thinking about all the stuff we talked about. All of her honesty, all of the revelations.

She was with Ayanna three times before the wedding. That hurts.

Part of me wants to hurt Ayanna back.

Then I tell myself to let it go, that Nicole is mine.

Then I remind myself that nothing is guaranteed. That I have to give her that extra push, have to make sure she doesn't renege on her promise the way Ayanna reneged on hers when she lost the race.

Again I tell myself to let it go.

I look down at that statue of Jack London, then across the mall at the colorful flags that are always flapping in these frigid bay winds. So many colorful flags in this city. So many realities in this world.

She gets off the phone, says, "I'm about to hop in the shower. Coming?"

"Go ahead." I smile at her. She's still wearing the engagement ring. "I'm going to wind down."

Nicole always showers a long time.

I pick up *Lolita*; think about reading a few pages but I know I'm not in a reading mood.

I take the cassette out of my jacket. I've had it with me all day. I place it on the dining room table, right next to my recorder. Then I change my mind, grab the tape, think about ripping it to shreds and dropping it into the trash can, but I don't. This is a weapon. A powerful weapon.

I put the tape back down. Go back to the window.

Nicole comes out of the bathroom, one towel around her body, another around her hair, dancing like she's been injected with the spirit of Bob Marley. Nicole says, "God, you have the nicest ass."

I smile. "Booty or ass?"

She laughs.

I head for the shower. Leave Nicole towel drying her hair and watching the news on Channel 4. The shower is loud, the door closed, so I can't hear anything but the echo of water bouncing off the wall of this chamber. When the shower goes off, I hear voices.

"I hate Nicole."

Ayanna's voice is so strong.

"God, I hate that one-foot-in-the-closet, one-foot-out-the-closet bitch."

So intense.

"I want to be Nicole. Does that make sense? If I have to be her to understand her, yes."

Water is dripping from my body when I open the door.

"—fucking sociopath. Has no conscience."

I run into that voice.

"No feeling about how she uses people to get what she wants."

Click. Whirr.

"If I have to feel you inside me to understand her, yes, I'm willing to go that far."

Nicole is sitting at the dining table, both towels have fallen from her, one from her head, the other from her body, and they lay at her feet, soaked, like two lovers intertwined after a night of passion.

My chest feels tight. I stand behind her.

Nicole releases a rugged breath.

I say her name.

She doesn't turn around. Over and over, the recorder clicks, whirrs, stops.

"Nicole lives inside her own little cunt."

She pushes rewind. Click. Whirr. Stop.

". . . her own little cunt."

Click. Whirr. Stop.

"Mange moi."

Click. Whirr. Stop.

". . . lives inside her own little cunt."

"Baise moi."

Click. Whirr. Stop.

"Nicole lives inside her own little cunt."

I turn the tape off. She doesn't stop me. Then I wait for words.

Finally she asks, "Did you fuck her?"

I shake my head.

Nicole gets in the bed, pulls the covers up to her neck, turns her back to me.

She says, "Saw the tape. In plain view. It wasn't there when we came in."

I don't say anything.

"Thought you had recorded your book signing. Just wanted to know what kind of questions Ayanna asked. Like I said, I heard she was giving you a hard time."

I dry off. Get in the bed.

She says, "You left that tape out on purpose."

"Yes."

"Why? I told you I was yours."

"You've told me that before."

"Was that necessary?"

"Yes."

"Why?"

At first I don't know why. Then I do. So many deceptions have passed before my eyes. In the beginning Ayanna had the upper hand. That was how she could steal my woman from me.

Now I want to achieve order, restore balance in my life. The first step to doing that is by introducing more chaos, a new calamity.

Or maybe I'm just plain old scared. We stood at the altar before, and she walked away. I need to do what I have to do.

It pains me, but I have to strike while confusion rises. Strike when it hurts me to do so. This is about my own sanity, my own survival. About reestablishing calmness in my realm. And to do that I have to show Nicole Ayanna's deception, make sure Nicole doesn't renege on her promise.

And all this time, I thought it was Paris. But it started long before. I carried that guilt for so long.

I could struggle to articulate all of that, but I don't.

I whisper these words to her, "Seven years. I've loved you for twenty-eight seasons. We've sat underneath almost a hundred full moons together."

"Because you have to win."

"Because I refuse to lose."

The bottom line is that I'm beyond my mile twenty. Way too far beyond. Hurts too much to stop.

Her foot bounces.

I think of Ayanna. Smell her. Feel her kisses on my face. Grit my teeth and remind myself that she is the enemy.

Nicole sniffles. She's mumbling, talking to herself, maybe praying.

"Sweetie."

I say, "Uh huh."

Silence. Then the bracelets jingle. Jingle as she takes them off and drops them on the dresser.

She whispers, "You win."

PART THREE

Butterflies

29

Amtrak blows three times as Ayanna walks from a well-lit hallway into my room, her bracelets jingling as she struggles to carry all of her gear. Ayanna carries a folded Runners World in one hand, her huge black-and-red gym bag, one with many compartments, over the same shoulder, a half-eaten Power Bar in the other.

"Good morning," Ayanna says with a short yawn and a long smile.

"G' morning," I reply. "You're loaded down."

"Brought fresh clothes," she says. "I have to leave here and meet with a client."

She dumps her bag near the foot of the bed.

She kisses my lips. "Nicole up?"

"Bathroom."

Ayanna's bracelets jingle when she taps the bathroom door. "Morning, sweetie."

Nicole eases out of the bathroom, busy tying a purple scarf around her locks.

Ayanna says, "It's supposed to rain again. We better get rolling."

They make eye contact. Good morning smiles on both faces.

Ayanna has mischievous eyes. "I'm making Peking

duck tonight. So, if we can all get together for dinner in front of the fireplace, that would be a nice way to end the evening."

Nicole opens her mouth, her eyes come to me for a moment, then she closes her mouth and busies herself putting on her running shoes. Ayanna moves to the dining area, stands in front of the window, looking out at Jack London Square as she does heel holds. Wall leans. Overhead reaches.

We all have on black tights, all of us in gray sweatshirts. Coincidence.

I lead the way as we head out of the hotel. Nicole stays close to me, damn near on me, leaving Ayanna behind us. Nicole glances at me, gives me a brief look that tells me that all will change, that everything will be different by the time we return to this fuckhaven by the sea.

It's cold and foggy outside. Colder than it was when I ran with Nicole two days ago.

Once again we take off, pass by Yoshi's, do a slow jog up the incline, go by Urban Blend Café, move toward the police station and the people gathering out in front of the Probation Department.

Nicole is quiet. She speeds up, gets in front of us by three, maybe four steps. The pavement on this strip is wide, at least twelve feet, plenty of room for three people to run shoulder to shoulder, but she leaves us. No matter what Ayanna says, Nicole is not responding.

Ayanna is planning for the future, her future, our future.

Nicole is doing the same.

Part of me wants it to stay the way it is. With Ayanna in our lives. But there's that other part.

Ayanna is chattering about doing tempo runs and

hill training, saying that we need to train like the Kenyans. She talks cross-training, doing fartleks, and 1000-meter repeats with one-minute recoveries.

My eyes are on Nicole, on her body language, on her silence, as I feed Ayanna's conversation. "One-minute recoveries. That'll hardly give you enough time to take a deep breath."

Ayanna shrugs, palms to the sky. "That's what you have to do if you're serious."

"How many repeats?"

"Four or five, no more than seven. Ten would be nice, but too much for me."

"Sounds good."

Nicole is still silent. She's a few steps ahead.

Ayanna tells me, "Build that into your running schedule. Raise your threshold. You'll knock ten minutes off your marathon over the next year. Might even be able to keep up with me."

We make it to the 980 just as the subtle *coo-coo, coo-coo, coo-coo* lets us know we have the light going north and south.

I say, "We should take Broadway to Twentieth. Around the lake. Then over to Oakland Avenue."

The first mile is a low seven, once again faster than I start. My adrenaline is high and I push on.

We're coming up on Telegraph when Ayanna says, "Nicole, we need to talk about Spain. I need to make sure you can—"

Nicole cuts her off, "I'm not going to Spain."

Ayanna is jarred, it shows in the way her arms lower, in the way her neck curves all of a sudden, shows in the way her running rhythm slips, her breathing changes.

It's here. That moment is here.

Ayanna loses her brilliance. She responds, "Not going?"

"Not going."

"Tickets are non-refundable."

"So what? I'll eat the loss."

"What, are negotiations with South Africa falling apart?"

"Nope."

"You can't get off work?"

"Why would you want to be in Spain with a one-foot-in-the-closet, one-foot-out-of-the-closet sociopath who lives inside her own little cunt."

The running halts.

"I heard the tape, Ayanna. Heard every damn word."

At that moment, I hate myself for what I've done.

Bus after bus passes by, spits carbon monoxide into our dampening faces, and all three of us standing as rigid as that statue of Jack London that guards the square named in his honor.

Ayanna's eyes go from Nicole to me, then back to Nicole.

Her eyes tighten as she shakes her head at me. Her grimace asks how could I do that to her.

Nicole sounds hoarse when she says, "How could you disrespect me like that?"

Ayanna inhales, the rising sorrow and fury in her eyes darkens her butterscotch complexion. I expect her to deny it all, but she doesn't play games, not even bid whist on the Fourth of July.

"Tell me how you could say those things then smile in my fucking face and claim to love me in the next breath? I've never—"

Ayanna says, "Nicole—"

"—no matter what, I've never said anything like that—"

"I said that to get at him."

"You called me a sociopath. A cunt. Know why? Because that's how you really feel about me."

We stand there. In the cold.

I want to say something, but I'm torn. Yes, I want Ayanna out of my life. No, I don't want her to leave. But I can't change our path. We can only drive forward from here.

Winter's rain starts seeping down from those darkening skies.

Nicole raises her arm. Pulls her sleeve back. She shakes her arm. There is no jingle.

Ayanna loses her breath. "Oh, God. You're not wearing your bracelets."

Nicole doesn't answer. Tension swells.

Ayanna asks, "So, now what?"

Nicole says, "Go to Spain."

"We have to resolve this before I go."

"It's resolved."

"What are you going to do?"

"When you get back, I'll have my own place."

"You're leaving me?"

"Yes."

Nicole pulls the glove off her left hand. She's wearing our engagement ring.

Ayanna groans out a death sound.

There is nothing for me to say. The polls are in my favor. No need for a recount.

Once a fire gets started, if the wind shifts, it changes into a firestorm. It's unstoppable.

Ayanna is still. So still. All except for her right hand. It starts to tremble like she has some neurological damage, as if Parkinson's disease is setting up camp in her body.

Her voice trembles as well. "Tell him."

Nicole stares at her, defiant.

Ayanna raises her voice. "Tell him."

Water falls on my face. I blink. Try to slow my breathing so I can comprehend.

Ayanna sees my confusion, says, "We've had a ceremony. We're married."

I look toward Nicole. Her eyes don't come to mine.

Ayanna goes on, "You looked right at the picture in the house. Willie Brown was at our reception. The one we had after we had our ceremony in Guernville."

"A commitment ceremony?"

"A wedding. We had a ceremony at the Russian River. Three months ago."

I stand, stunned. Head aches.

Ayanna raises her arms, shakes it. She says, "We gave each other bracelets. Eight bracelets. One for each year that we've been together. How long it took for us to get to where we are. Our eight wedding rings."

Once again I'm slammed into a brick wall. Slammed so hard all air leaves my body.

Nicole runs off; Ayanna follows her.

My body becomes anger. The kind of anger that makes a man want to kill and destroy. I sprint and catch up. Demand that Nicole tell me Ayanna has lost the war and lost her mind.

She doesn't deny what Ayanna said.

Ayanna says, "Leave her alone. Nicole, don't let him—"

"Back off, Ayanna," I snap.

I move in between them, block her from touching

Nicole. I hold Nicole's arm, stop her. Grab her hard and make her face me.

I snap, "Did you have a commitment ceremony?"

She snaps back at me, "It's no biggie. Ceremonies aren't legal."

"Talk to me, Nicole."

"Stop. Cars are slowing down. People across the street are looking at us. Let's not make a scene."

I say, "Listen—"

Ayanna shouts, "Let her go."

"—to me. Back away, Ayanna."

I push Ayanna. Push her and her bracelets jingle-jangle with her stumble. I'm ready to kill and destroy. My winds have shifted; my firestorm is unstoppable. She doesn't challenge me. Her eyes widen, double in size. She sees my anger.

Ayanna backs away and says, "That's assault. I'm going to have your ass arrested."

Ayanna steps into the street, looks like she's trying to flag down Oakland P.D.

Nicole takes off the engagement ring, forces it into my palm.

Firecrackers ignite inside my brain. I ask, "What are you saying?"

Nicole takes off running. Heads back toward the hotel. Is running at top speed.

Ayanna calls her, races after her. At first I palm the ring, tell myself fuck it, let Nicole go.

But resting under two tons of anger, my love for her is still there.

I charge after both of them.

In this direction, the wind meets us head on. The rain falls harder.

Nicole does not slow down.

The pace is impossible, frantic. My adrenaline is high, but I'm worn from running three days in a row: two long runs, then that early-morning race with Ayanna yesterday. Nicole rested yesterday. She's fresh. She's flying, running red lights, putting as much distance between us as she can, bumping into people on the sidewalks, dodging black men in bow ties who are selling fresh bean pies, goes by Walgreen's so fast it looks like she covers that block with one giant step.

Ayanna gets winded. So do I. Both of us slow down.

Then Nicole's going downhill, racing into the darkness of the overpass at Sixth.

Nicole runs like a river that has broken through a dam. She moves relentlessly toward the Tube, comes up on a big yellow sign that reads YIELD TO PEDESTRIANS, gets caught by the light, too many cars zipping by to jaywalk, so she backs off, frowns back at us. Sees us storming toward her with grimaces on our faces. Nicole jitters back a few steps, jerks like she's thinking about running east and west, going wherever she has to go to get away, but she stands trapped...

Nicole frowns at the ground, hands on her hips.

Where she is, under that bridge, behind that huge support column, in that darkness, she is invisible to traffic. I imagine that she is crying, a mixture of tears and sweat leaving her vision as dark as the sky.

Then there is the *coo-coo, coo-coo, coo-coo*.

Nicole hears freedom calling and takes off. Moves like a jaguar.

So does traffic. Impatient. Arrogant.

Nicole darts from behind the column.

The driver of an SUV does the same. Tires spin a little, not much, making that moist, sticky sound as they roll over the wet asphalt; the driver rushes to make that left turn to get on the Tube.

Ayanna sees the oversize monster too. Sees that elephant on its early morning rampage.

We both scream Nicole's name. But she doesn't think it's a warning. She thinks it's anger.

Nicole. My Nicole.

Nicole does the same thing I did two mornings ago, when death went by me in a whisper.

Nicole is in the entrance to the Tube. The SUV slams on its brakes. On most days, maybe that would've been enough. Today, streets are wet. Maybe the oil that has risen to the top is clinging to that spot. The weight of that carriage is too much, no way to stop a charging elephant on a dime.

The SUV hydroplanes, rides that thin layer of water and grease like it weighs nothing.

Already there is a long continuous wail. At first I think it's a siren and the paramedics are zooming to get here. But it's not. That nonstop shrill is coming from Ayanna.

Horns blow like Gabriel's trumpet trying to wake a sleeping world. Nicole freezes. She's afraid. I know she's frightened because I was terrified. I remember how my heart tried to break out of my chest when I was almost run down on that very spot, remember how my body became a prayer.

My scream tears my throat and blends with Ayanna's when the SUV runs Nicole down, when she thuds and bounces off the hood, when she flies like a beautiful bird, an angel without wings, and lands on the wet pavement like a broken doll.

30

Things happen fast and slow at the same time. Can't remember moving. Panic fogs memory.

I get to Nicole first. Ayanna is right there, on my heels.

I expect to see Nicole's head wide open, or half of her face caved-in, or parts of her body here, other parts there. Her clothes are twisted, she has scrapes here and there, but she's not really bruised up, not from what I can see, not from the outside. More like she's taking a break. She's Sleeping Beauty, on her back, resting on dark asphalt, the rain beating down on her golden skin, relaxing with a twisted left leg. A broken leg that looks like a prosthetic turned at a bad angle.

Ayanna falls to her knees hard enough to rip her running tights and bloody her knees, reaches for Nicole, but I grab Ayanna's shoulder and snap, "Don't touch her."

And just like that Ayanna knows. It's not about jealousy or possession or whom Nicole belongs to. It shows in her eyes, the fear from thinking that she almost did the wrong thing.

My voice vibrates, doesn't sound like me at all.

"Could've caused more damage. Get someone to call an amb—"

Ayanna yells, "Nine-one-one dial nine-one-one."

But at least a thousand cell phones are already out, all dialing. A few early risers pass by with could-careless eyes. They just want to get from point A to point B on time, and this woman who is unconscious on the asphalt is blocking their way.

Then the rain pounds, pounds, pounds down on us. As if someone has taken a surgical knife to the belly of the cloud over us.

Ayanna crouches beside me, trembles, "Is she . . . is she . . . ?"

Her voice fades in the noise. People are stopping, gathering around; I don't see them, but I feel them. All asking what happened. Voices buzzing like pesky bees.

I'm trembling too, talking to Nicole, asking her to answer. Her purple scarf has flown off her mane, is feet away, and now her head is bare, hair mangled, resting on oil-stained pavement.

"I seent the whole damn thing man, I seent the whole thing." Some brother sporting fatigues and a shoulder-length Jheri-Kurl appoints himself as the designated spokesperson, talks with no punctuation, "I was walking down the skreet minding my own biddness right 'cause I was trying to get the probation on time cause 'dem damn probation officers be tripping and I'd just stepped off the 58 bus and I heard this loud noise and I said myself oh shit what was that loud noise and I saw this lady fly up in dah air like she was Wonder Woman and land on the ground said BOOM—"

Behind me another shrill voice rises. A cry of distress comes from the driver of that death carriage. She's telling people that she tried to stop, that Nicole came out of nowhere, setting up her story, placing blame on Nicole, the one others only know as the woman on the pavement.

The man in the fatigues talks on, "—said damn dat lady flew up in the air I said oh shit den this udder lady was screaming *ahhhhhh* 'den other people start screaming *ahhhhhh* and everybody people started screaming *ahhhhhh* like dey had a screaming disease and—"

I yell, *"Shut up shut up please shut your ass up."*

A jolt of electricity pours through me. I yank off my gloves, throw them away, move Nicole's honey-blond hair, try to remember how to check a pulse, put two fingers on her neck, feel nothing, no rise, no fall, then put my face close to hers.

Ayanna asks, "What are—"

"She's not breathing."

"Oh God oh God oh God."

I snap, "Don't, Ayanna. Don't lose it. I need your help."

"Okay, okay."

"You know CPR?"

"Yes, yeah, CPR, of course."

"Help me."

Water beads off Ayanna's chin. She fidgets, reaches for Nicole, wipes water from her face, trying to contain her own agony.

"—yelling her please help her I mean 'cause she was up in the air like a bird a plane like she was damn Superman so I just sat my ass down and waited 'cause I knew dey was gonna need somebody to tell 'em what happened 'cause 'dem people was too damn hysterical."

Ayanna moves to Nicole's mouth. I stay at her chest, my hand on her heart.

Five compressions.

One breath.

I'm Nicole's heart. Ayanna is Nicole's lungs.

Then we change.

Ayanna becomes the heart; I become the lungs.

Rain runs through my hair, dampens the gel, rinses a bitter taste into my mouth.

Five compressions.

One breath.

Seems like we do that forever before a siren makes its way through the rubbernecking traffic, seems like years go by before flashing lights brighten up the Tube like rainbows. EMT comes through the crowd. Oakland Police Department gets here too.

The man in the fatigues hurries to OPD. "Seent the whole damn thing she went BOOM and flew like she was a superhero she ain't gonna make it that woman ain't gonna make it she went BOOM too damn hard to make it somebody got a cigarette 'cause I sho' been traumatized and being traumatized makes me wanna smoke don't tell me ain't none of y'all got a smoke hell it's my damn lungs."

I move back and stand at the edge of the overpass, rain beating down on me.

Ayanna is close to me. Her bracelets jingle as she trembles.

My child is dead.

I try to shake Nicole's mother's voice out of my head, but it won't go.

Ayanna whispers, "Don't let our girl go on the concrete. At least let her get to the hospital where she can be warm and dry. Not in the rain, not on nasty-ass

Broadway, not in front of a fucking Probation Department in front of all of these people. Not in front of strangers. Please, please, please."

EMT does their checks. Things I don't understand, but I watch with critical eyes.

Ayanna watches too. Watches and moans and prays.

I'm speechless. Own no words, not a single coherent thought runs through my mind.

A police officer puts blankets around us as the EMT does a complete physical assessment. Complete physical assessment. That's the term I hear them use. The EMTs, they become our gods, the ones we defer to, the ones with all the power, our only hope for a miracle.

My insides are folding, tightening, waiting for them to cover Nicole's face.

I don't feel the cold anymore. Don't feel the rain anymore. No wind. Only the numbness.

I want to make a deal with God. Want to tell him to let her stay and take me.

Ayanna holds my hand. Something is going wrong with me and she feels it. She puts both of her arms around me.

Head injuries, punctured lungs, a lot of things could be wrong. With every thought my insides are folding, never unfolding. I'm in agony.

Ayanna holds me tighter.

I'm overwhelmed by images; I see bits and pieces of our past. Seven years that have been mostly good. These last few days have been too intense, too confusing.

All of that plays over and over, plays until I can't take it anymore.

Like a wounded dog I pull at my hair and stagger in circles, howl to the heavens and ask for mercy, ask for our overseer to take me, to leave Nicole be. Ayanna cuts me off, slows my roll, pulls me underneath the overpass, out of the rain, puts her arms around me, and holds me tight. Pulls my head to her chest. Shushes me like I'm her child. Tells me that everything will be okay.

The winds sing, but no voice comes from above. No deals are being made today.

They put a neck collar on Nicole. A leg splint. EMTs call the emergency room.

Ayanna asks them, "Where are you taking her?"

"Alameda County."

"No, do not take her to County—look, if we can by-pass Alameda and Kaiser—"

"Have to take her to the closest."

But that doesn't stop Ayanna from putting on her lawyer's voice. "Alameda is the ghetto and Kaiser's an HMO, which is worse. If she's stable, you have to take her to UCSF."

"Have to take her to the closest."

"She has medical insurance."

"Ayanna," I snap, raising my voice, "let him do his job. Let him do his job."

She doesn't back down. "She has insurance. Any-where but County."

This time I become strong, put my arms around Ayanna. A stranger walks over with a box of tissues. I thank him. Or her. It's all a blur. I give some tissues to Ayanna before I blow my own nose. I hold her. Let her tears fall on my damp sweatshirt.

Someone gives us his or her umbrella. We thank that person as well.

The paramedics come to us, come to get us.

Seems like forever has gone by, but ten minutes ago we were all running.

Soaking wet, we ride in the ambulance with Nicole. Siren on. Lights flashing.

Watch her life signs, watch them work on her, watch each other.

I ask, "Is she . . . she going to make it?"

The paramedic can't say. Maybe doesn't want to say.

Ayanna dabs her eyes and mumbles, "Didn't mean it. Was mad, that's all. Don't leave me. Please don't. Anything but this. Anything."

My own guilt has me by the neck, won't let me go.

At the hospital we wait.

Time becomes ice. I'm a glacier floating at sea.

We sit in a room filled with people who are waiting for news, wet, refusing to leave, and we wait.

At some point, when so many tears have fallen, when she's paced as much as she can pace, Ayanna comes to me and pants out her words, "My husband. He died on the street. On the pavement. In the rain."

I put my hand on hers. She holds my hand. Holds it tight.

She says, "Don't know if I can handle this twice in one lifetime."

And we hold each other.

I say, "Don't know if I can handle it once."

Finally there is news. The kind of news that brings no smiles; dries no tears.

Nicole is in a coma.

Not here.

Not there.

Somewhere in between.

31

With the exception of the humming of machines, the room is quiet. A catheter drains the fluid from Nicole's bladder. IV in her bruised arm. Blood being taken. Neurological tests being done. So much poking and probing, so much has been done to her damaged body.

Nicole's not on a respirator. She's breathing on her own. Breathing as if she refuses to let a machine do the work for her. Still stubborn, even when she's drifting in the twilight zone.

Outside of her leg, outside of a few bruises, considering the circumstances, everything is in order. Not good, but not as bad as it could be. The main thing is that there isn't any internal bleeding.

She's on oxygen. In a private room. Away from others. Ayanna has all the information about Nicole's insurance, all the things it takes to make a place like this give you real service, makes sure they know she's a lawyer. I make sure they know that I'm the son of a very powerful man.

Ayanna and I are the hospital's nightmare; we ask too many questions. We want details. Want to know what is going on, what to expect, what not to expect.

There are a lot of questions, but the answers are few. Hard to get answers for what they do not know.

Time holds all the cards.

I leave long enough to catch a taxi to my hotel, change, grab Ayanna's bag and come back.

My cell phone keeps ringing. So does Ayanna's. Everybody is calling everybody.

My father calls. My mother is on the other line. The phone beeps and on the other end are people who have known Nicole over the last seven years. People who still consider her family. The calls pour in non-stop, just like the rain.

André calls. The word has spread to him, and he's just waking up in L.A.

"Need me to come back up there?"

"Nothing you can do. I'll let you know."

"Talked to her peeps in Memphis?"

"Not yet."

"Call 'em. When you get your head together, call 'em."

The same madness is on Ayanna's phone. Friends. Relatives. And her mother. She ignores all other calls when her mother calls. They talk a while. A long while. They talk like mother and daughter.

I call Nicole's mother. Leave a message. Then I call her sisters, two of her brothers.

32

The nurse tries to explain to us that Nicole's hooked up to a telemetry machine, a heart monitor that keeps its eye on t-waves, s-waves, makes sure that a heart attack isn't in the horizon. My eyes go over the EKG machine, the TPN coming in through an IV, two liters of oxygen, a nasal cannula in her nose.

The nurse says, "Looks like she's in pretty good physical condition."

I tell the nurse, "She's a runner. Runs marathons in four hours."

"Her heart rate is low. Has a very strong heart."

I keep going on and on, rambling to the nurse about Nicole, telling her how wonderful she is. That urge to say something may come from guilt, but most of it comes from fear.

I have to watch Nicole being given medication to keep fluids from building up. People coming in and probing her as if she's just another patient, bringing syringes to take away blood so they can check potassium and sodium levels.

"Yep. Good thing she was in excellent physical condition," the nurse says to me.

They show us how to turn Nicole every two hours,

how to keep her from getting bedsores. How to clean her when her bowels move. It reminds me of something my old man used to say: Once a man, twice a child. And now she is a child again. We are the parents.

The nurse asks, "Who administered CPR?"

At the same moment Ayanna and I say, "We did."

I ask, "Did that hurt her?"

The nurse shakes her head. "That saved her. Kept the oxygen flowing to her brain."

I ask, "What else can we do from this point?"

She explains to us that the last sense to go is the hearing. That what she hears gets to her mind, and the body is the servant of the mind. If we give her fear and hopelessness, that's what she'll respond to. We have to realize that she hears every word, and our verbal diets will be what feed her.

She says, "Keep that sense alive. She can hear you. Let her hear you."

Before those words can settle, the EKG machine starts beeping; Nicole moves. Starts jerking. Twitching. Eyes roll. Her bowels move. The nurse runs to the displays.

Ayanna and I have to hold each other as we leave the room, stand in the hallway and watch people rush in from all directions.

Ayanna drags her fingers through her heart-colored mane and moans, "No, no, no."

We stand. We wait. Then after we wait, we wait some more.

They bring Nicole out and wheel her away from us, take her down for another CAT scan. Check for respiratory distress, for heart rate, to see if she's about ready to stop running in this race.

An hour passes before the doctor comes to have that

talk. To bring us that reality. I get a chill. Feels as if we're trying to save the Titanic by dumping water with a teacup.

We're told that she's stabilized, but this can still go one way or the other. We set up camp in Nicole's hospital room. I bring flowers. Pictures. Ayanna does the same.

We abandon our sadness at the door and talk to her in upbeat voices, talk to each other and include her in the conversation.

Ayanna brings music: Kravitz, Pru, Macy Gray, Marley, Prince, Santana, Kina, Pink, Sting.

Ayanna says, "Put on Prince. My girl has to have Prince."

"She's a Prince-aholic. That was all she played when we met."

"Who you telling? We went to his concert at the San Jose Arena in December. She played Prince for days." She laughs at the memory. "Prince, Prince, Prince. Drove me mad."

I laugh with her. Laughter sounds better when it has a friend. And music.

I say, "Time to turn her."

We do.

We watch Nicole like she's a premature child, hold her hand, touch her, talk to her.

Sometime during the night, when insomnia is my friend, and that same insomnia is Ayanna's companion, I look around the room at all the flowers that have come so fast. From Siebel Systems. From Motorola. From GE. A lot of people have called. I realize what a full life Nicole and Ayanna have here in the Bay.

I say, "You let her see me. Why?"

"How could I stop her from seeing you? How could you stop her from seeing me?"

Ayanna stares out at the darkness for a while, her eyes walking across heaven's vault, before she turns around and stares at Nicole. She looks so sad. Then she gives me a strange smile.

Ayanna says, "Your hair is a mess."

"Is it bad?"

"Looks like half a 'fro."

I chuckle. "What does the other half look like?"

"Hell if I know. Never seen anything like that in my life."

"Guess I'll have to see Ana again."

"Let me."

"Another hidden talent?"

"Who do you think does Nicole's hair?"

I understand what she's doing. We're in the same book, on the same page. She wants to be alone with Nicole awhile. To say whatever she needs to say while Nicole can still hear. Before that sense fades like a candle at the end of its burn.

I just hope I get my turn too.

At dawn I go back toward the Waterfront, my pager at my side. I pull over at the Tube. Stare at the spot where the accident happened. It's clear. As if nothing wrong ever occurred on that spot.

Inside my hotel room, I gather a few things. Then I stare at Nicole's silver bracelets. Her toiletries. Her clothes. Walk around and touch all the things she left behind in this room. We all are collectors of things, and in the end, we leave all those things behind.

I sit there for a while, trying to think, to breathe.

Lolita is staring at me. That book is next to my laptop, pages bent from days of reading. I pick the book up. A story about a man and his obsession. I walk to the balcony, stand in the chilling air, and I let *Lolita* fall. Let that book twist and turn and land on the cobblestones five floors below.

I take the back way out; avoid the friendly people who work the lobby.

Then I drive around, drive until I find an open store, get a rat's-tooth comb, some gel.

All of that seems trivial, is very trivial, but I have to keep moving.

When I get back, Ayanna is drying her eyes. Her words have been said.

She says, "Time to turn her."

After that, I sit between Ayanna's legs, surround myself with her warmth while she does my hair.

Nicole's chest rises and falls.

My cell phone rings, cuts off our conversation. It's my father. I tell him what's going on; talk to him a good twenty minutes.

Two beats after we hang up, Ayanna says, "Your father, he's a great man."

"Why didn't you hang around to meet him at the bookstore?"

"I saw him and felt like an idiot for the things I was saying, and he was right there. One of our leaders was right there witnessing me act like a fool. And the way everybody applauded and wanted to touch him, it was amazing, so I guess I just ran back to my ride as fast as I could."

"He's just my daddy."

"Don't take that for granted."

I chuckle.

She asks, "What was it like growing up with him?"

I tell her about my old man. About my hero. Tell her

that for the last forty years, since before my time on this earth, my old man has been a church-aholic workaholic, either on the road or in the pulpit, so in my eyes, he's been pretty much absent, even when he was at home.

She says, "I've always wondered what the kids felt like."

"What you mean?"

"Kids of our leaders. With their fathers being gone off on a quest for righteousness, soldiers in our war, always putting themselves in danger at the drop of a hat, in front of a camera all the time."

"Yep," I say. "It's a war out there. He's a gladiator. Always in battle."

Nicole's breath gets choppy for a second. Then it smoothes out.

We both tense, then sigh out our worry.

I check on Nicole. Look at the machines. Look at the lines that add up to life. No change. Ayanna follows. She whispers, "Didn't mean those things, boo. You know how I gets from time to time."

We go back and sit. She gets back to my hair.

Ayanna asks, "Did his being gone so much leave your momma lonely?"

That catches me off guard. In a good way. "Momma was busy taking care of her four little boys. She was proud of her husband."

"He's done a lot for his people."

I say, "But everything has a price."

"Elaborate."

"Long story."

"Does it look like I'm going anywhere?"

That warmth, her sensitivity gets me to talking. Right now I need to talk. Think I'd tell the world the truth about anything. So, I tell Ayanna about my momma. About all the nights I woke up and saw her walking the floors of our home by herself, her Salem 100 burning in her right hand while she held herself with her left, her short nails running up and down her Creole skin. Talk about her restlessness, her loneliness, heard the covers rustle as she tossed and turned, as she slept alone with her smokes by her side, hoping our phone didn't jingle at 3 a.m. with bad news.

I say, "And when my old man came home, his suit-case never had a chance to get cold."

"That bothers you?"

"Well, when it's time for my family, I wanna be there. Want my wife to be able to sleep at night. Want to see my kids when they wake up in the morning. At least I hope I will."

"His being gone all the time still bothers you."

"What bothers me is how much he gives and gives to a world that doesn't seem to care."

Then I chuckle.

She asks, "Wanna share?"

"Thinking about when you said your old man slapped you for asking who made God."

"I'm not laughing up here. That's a sensitive issue for me."

I tell her about when I was a teenager and I wanted to let my hair grow long, wanted to fit in with the crowd, with my peers, have it in a shag, or get a curl, and my old man refused to have his sons walking around looking like that.

I tell her, "I stood in his face and said, 'Jesus had long hair.' "

Ayanna laughs, because she knows.

I say, "He slapped the shit out of me."

"His hands are huge."

"Knocked my ass into the middle of next week."

We laugh a lot. Talk a lot. Look toward Nicole a lot. Wish this laughter and openness was in trio.

Ayanna tells me about growing up. Good Fridays and wrapping the maypole and holy water and penance and years of Latin and giving up things for Lent and corporal works of mercy and contests to see who could keep the ashes on the longest.

And excommunication.

I say, "I'm confused. Thought your daddy was Baptist or something?"

"He is. Momma's Catholic. And once a Catholic always a Catholic."

"So you're Catholic."

"I'm a lot of things. We all are."

"What are you now?"

"Right now I'm struggling. I believe in hell, just not so sure about heaven. Not the kind of materialistic, gold-lined place that people in the pulpit promise on Sunday mornings."

We talk some more on that. The struggling. I guess I'm struggling too.

When she's done with my hair, after it dries, we clean Nicole, then turn Nicole again.

Ayanna tells me, "You're different."

"How's that?"

"I thought you were weak, but you have depth."

I say, "Things are never what they seem."

At some point I fall asleep.

When I wake up, Ayanna is sitting next to Nicole, one hand on her, reading one of my books.

I watch her read. She smiles when she sees me. Then goes back to reading.

Ayanna leaves around noon.

While she's gone, I have my moments with Nicole. Hand-holding moments as the sun fills the brilliant blue skies with hope. Ayanna comes back an hour or so later, comes back in clean, colorful, oversize sweats, looking comfortable and ready to wait for eternity, and she has a huge bag from Tropix. It's filled with Jamaican food.

And three cups of overpriced hard-to-pronounce java from good old Starbucks. That reminds me of when I stood in my hotel window, watching Nicole struggle to be at two places at once, a divided soul wanting to please two lovers.

While we eat and sip, Ayanna taps my books and says, "I'm sorry . . . sorry for all the evil things I said to you."

"Ibid."

She smiles.

We both sound like we're in some sort of AA program, because I guess we are both addicted, now going through the twelve steps, this step being where we apologize to all we have done wrong.

If my love for Nicole was fire, and Ayanna's love for Nicole was gas, we could blow up the universe. We hug. Hug and see who will hold on the longest. Our spirits dance a long dance.

After we eat, Ayanna gathers all the trash and takes it away. When she comes back she says, "This could go on for weeks. Months. That's what the doctor said."

"I know."

"How long will you stay?"

"I'm not leaving. I've never left her."

She smiles. "Check out of the Waterfront. Stay at our house."

I smile. Match her generosity with appreciation.

I say, "You sure about that?"

"I can't do this alone. You can't do this alone."

I nod. And that simple gesture seals that deal.

Days slip by.

I'm in the hallway stretching my legs when I see a nurse hugging a man. He has long-stemmed roses and a box of candy.

I go back to the room and say, "Ayanna."

"Yeah, sweetie?"

"It's Valentine's Day."

She blinks and blinks. "Already?"

Time has escaped us. They would be in Spain now, and I'd be on the east coast selling books from city to city. Spain, books, none of that is important anymore.

Ayanna dresses up like she's on a date. I do the same.

Flowers, candy, heart-shaped balloons, we decorate the room with it all. Have our own little party.

And in the middle of all that celebration, the EKG alarms again.

Then come the jerks, the spasms; worse than the first time. Her bowels scent the air. Eyes rolling, peeping at the backside of her brain. The emergency crew comes. Take her. MRI. CAT scan. Hours pass before they bring her back. Let us know that the ship is sinking deeper into the murky abyss.

Joe Black walks these halls. It's Valentine's Day, but he never takes a day off. They have a special room down in the basement for the people he shakes hands with. Treats newborn babies the same as adults, men the same as women, black the same as white. An equal opportunist who whistles while he works.

I call Nicole's mother again. This time she answers.

While I tell her what has happened since my last message, she listens.

In the end, when I'm done, she calmly says, "That was God."

I say, "It was a truck."

"It was God."

"When did God start wearing high heels and get a California driver's license?"

"It was God."

And she hangs up.

I try to call back, but the machine has been turned on. Nicole's siblings call. Other members of her family call and want to know if they should come right now. The phone never stops ringing. The phone rings and rings and rings. Not a jingle, not another word from Nicole's mother.

The spasms come again.

And again.

Nicole sinks deeper. Moves farther away from us with every breath.

Five times a day, Ayanna faces the east, palms to the sky, and prays.

Three times a day, I go down to the chapel. Face the altar and say my words.

33

When you're underwater holding your breath, two hundred eighty-eight hours is forever. Twelve days. That's how much time goes by. Four in the morning. That dreaded four in the morning. The time when the world makes those calls to let someone's friends, someone's family know that they are no longer available for breakfast, no longer available for lunch, will never make it to another dinner.

I'm sitting next to Nicole, lights on low. Sleeping. I jerk awake. I glance over at her and she's watching me. Not blinking. The eyes of the dead.

Once again my insides fold; I inhale so deeply it hurts my ribs.

Then Nicole's lips move. Her chest rises and falls. She blinks. Eyes move around.

I say, "Nicole?"

Ayanna is on a cot near the window, locks wrapped in a bright yellow scarf, moonlight falling on her butterscotch face, sleeping in jeans and a WHARF TO WHARF RACE sweater that swallows her frame.

I jump, push the button for the nurse, call Ayanna's name, lean over and shake her. She jumps out of her REM sleep. Eyes looking worn, heavy under the bottoms, as if years have gone by in days.

I keep talking, "Nicole? Stay with us. We're here."

Ayanna talks too. "Sweetie. I'm right here. Can you hear me?"

Nicole's eyes are moving around, out of focus. Searching.

Nicole frowns. Frowns like waves of pain are waking up her body.

We smile at her agony. Only the dead feel nothing.

Ayanna holds her left arm close to Nicole's ear, jingles her bracelets.

Nicole struggles, sounds like she says, "Itch. Ing."

We laugh light and low. Ayanna's trembling, rocking, leaning forward in sprinter's position.

Nicole keeps trying; "Itch. Ing."

The nurse comes. The rest of that team comes too. Nicole's doctor's not here, has to be called back to the hospital, but another comes in her place. They rush into a room of nervous laughter.

The doctor asks her if she knows who she is.

"Nah. Cole." She fights, says that in two syllables. "Nah. Nah. Cole."

They ask her more questions. She knows who she is. She knows me and Ayanna.

Other things are not clear.

At some point, when I'm sure she's back, when the doctor and his helpers need a little more elbow room, I leave the room. Ayanna stays. They ask her to leave, but she stays.

I go down the hallway. My lips turn to the sky and once again I cry a bit. Relief. Happy she's back on this side. A moment later it looks like an entire medical team is heading into Nicole's room. They're not rushing out of fear, just rushing to witness a miracle.

I open and close my hands, can actually feel my own stiffness. Taste the inside of my mouth telling me that

I need to floss and rinse and brush away a stale smell. Can hear the sounds of other machines and the moans of strangers, especially the groans from an old man a few rooms down and the squeaks from nurses' shoes as they trek the hallway. I'm defrosting. Melting back into this world. Shaking off my numbness. The numbness that has blanketed me since Nicole left me at the altar. Everything I feel, good or bad, all of it reminds me that I'm alive. That I'm still here.

And I can smell. I inhale and I smell everything.

Yes, my senses come back. Either that or I'm delirious. I smell an expensive perfume. And I smell chicken. Fried chicken. I look up in time to see someone leaving. Someone pulling her luggage-on-wheels, someone wearing red and gold. She looks back long enough to see me.

I nod.

She nods to me in return.

Then she hums as she goes through the double doors. Gets on the elevator. And she is gone.

Maybe she was there. Maybe she wasn't. One man's hope is another's denial.

Ayanna comes out of the room, jars me from my trance.

We stand next to each other and stare out at the dark clouds smothering Lady Oakland.

Ayanna beams. "Sun's gonna shine bright today."

"Sure is," I say with equal enthusiasm. "Sure is."

We both do some stretches. Nothing extreme. Just enough to realize how stiff we are.

She says, "Maybe we can sneak in a short run before the day's done."

"Maybe."

Later on we'll find out that Nicole's memory isn't

there. Not all of it. But it will come back in bits and pieces. Will move in slowly. Roll in like the fog in the bay. And her speech, she'll talk, but it won't be much, and it will be slow and easy, like a nice run through the hills. Soon it will be time for physical therapists, speech therapists.

Once again they take her out, and this time the wait isn't bad. Not at all.

While we walk the hallway I say, "I'd like to stay a while longer. Until I know she's out of the woods."

"What are you saying?"

My answer is inside my silence.

The sounds of pages and white shoes squeaking over tile floors fills in the silence.

Ayanna's eyes water up, this time for me. But I don't need any tears.

I tell her, "Not yet. I'm not leaving yet."

One step at a time. That's how you move away. That's how you move on.

She says, "She'll miss you."

"I'll miss her too."

"I'll miss you."

"I'll miss you too, Ayanna. Might even miss you the most."

We stand there awhile. Watching the city.

I ask Ayanna, "You smell chicken?"

"Yeah."

34

Winter changes to spring. Our season of cold is behind us. And as a great writer who calls herself Sister Souljah says, that was our coldest winter. Things are changing; things are in bloom. Things are always changing. So many wonderful colors are alive. People are walking, running, jogging, lounging around Lake Merritt, sitting outside at Good Nature, Jahva Coffeehouse, and all the other sidewalk eateries.

I ask Nicole, "Where were you?"

She's a beautiful woman in red sweats, walking with a cane, her locks in a ponytail.

"With my daddy," she tells me with smiling lips. "I think and I think, and all I can remember is being at Riverside Park. Out at Lakeland. Fishing for crawfish. Think I heard you talking to me. Felt you kissing me. When I was with Daddy, I'm pretty sure I heard you talking to me. Heard you crying. That's why I came back."

"What did I say?"

"You said that you were sorry. That you still loved me, that you had my back, no matter what."

That's what Nicole always tells me when I ask her what she remembers the most. I always ask to see if some new memory has come to the surface. We do our slow walk around part of Lake Merritt. Walk with a loaf of bread in our hands, feed the ducks along the way. I do that with her twice a week.

Nicole says, "God, look at her run."

We slow and watch a nice-looking woman fly by us with wings on her feet.

I say, "Was that her?"

"Regina Jacobs. I think that was her. She went by so fast. God, look at her form."

"Nice booty."

Nicole laughs. "You need to quit."

"She's gonna get a speeding ticket. Catch her."

"You got jokes up the yin-yang today."

We walk at her pace. She's a miracle woman. Determined to do six months of rehab in half the time. Wants to get back to work. Wants to do a lot of things.

When she gets tired, we rest on a bench facing the waters and petting zoo at Fairy Land.

With a gentle breath, I say, "It's time."

I say that and there is a long pause. One of those knowing pauses where we stop like they do in the movies, stop and look at each other face-to-face, like we're hitting our marks and posing for over the shoulder shots.

We both know. It's been coming for a while.

Nicole asks, "What are you saying?"

I take a short breath. Hold her hand.

I say, "Going back home for a while. New book, you know."

"Don't make excuses, sweetie. You could do that all from here."

I shake my head. "Have to move on."

"Why?"

I could say that we're not old, but we're not young. I have a better understanding of the realities of this world. And soon a gray hair or two will show its head in ungodly places. I'm still six years older than she is, will always be six years in front of her, and she is still pretty young, will always be young and beautiful in my eyes. But time flies. Nicole may not care that she's at that borderline age where a woman needs to make those maternal decisions, but I do.

So, my answer to her is, "Because butterflies never become caterpillars."

She understands. Her smile tells me that.

Her voice catches when she asks, "How soon?"

"Not too soon. Never too soon. Just wanted you to know."

"You can go. I can make it, you know."

"I'm not ready. Just getting ready."

Her eyes water as we stroll. "This love I have for you, what do I do with it?"

"Same thing I do with mine. Give yours to Ayanna."

"And you? Who you gonna give yours to?"

I shrug. "Dunno. I'm outnumbered nine-to-one."

And we walk around that lake, stopping every now and then to toss crumbs to the ducks.

That night we made love, slow and easy. I slipped inside her like a whisper, once again an oyster clamped around a pearl, and while her tears fell like rain, we moved like thunder. I touched all of her, tried to steal it all to memory.

Oakland is a beautiful woman. It's always hard to leave a thing so beautiful.

I stayed in Oakland that whole season, until spring came along. Until things started to bloom. Long enough for Nicole to get out of the hospital. Long enough to help load her up in the SUV and help Ayanna take her back and forth to rehab. Long enough for Ayanna to get everything situated at their home. Long enough to take long runs through the hills with Ayanna at my side, those beautiful red-and-gold locks bouncing as I chased her up the hills.

Long enough for me to finish that book about three lovers.

Before I say my good-byes, I do go back by the Waterfront. For a while I eat apples and talk with the beautiful Ethiopian women who work the front desk. Give them books and smiles and conversation.

Tseday is happy to see me. She's always happy to see me.

She beams, can't wait to tell me, "I have a great idea."

"Oh, boy. I'm listening."

"You should put an Ethiopian in your next book."

"Oh really?"

"As a good guy. I mean girl. She has to be good."

I laugh. "Everybody wants to be in a book, but nobody ever wants to be the bad guy."

She laughs along with me and shrugs. Her eyes sparkle when she smiles at me, looks into my eyes.

I invite her to lunch at TGIF. She says yes with a hesitant smile.

I say, "It's for research."

"Okay. For your research."

Over hot wings, salads, and fries she tells me about the trouble in her country.

I say, "You're political."

"You sound surprised."

"Yep. I am."

"My family is very political. My brother was a POW in Eritrea. He was released a few weeks ago."

At some point it gets lighter, more personal. She tells me that she grew up in Addis Ababa. Went to an all-girls school, the Nazareth School, from kindergarten to twelfth grade. A Roman Orthodox.

I say, "Is that Christian with an attitude?"

She laughs.

I ask, "Whassup with the attitude?"

"We were never colonized."

"So you have bragging rights."

"You better believe it. We kicked the white man's butt. And we're beautiful."

She tells me that she came to the states to go to college. But got married and that slowed down her ambitions, and now she's divorced, no kids, older, wiser, enrolled at Berkeley, and back on track.

I ask, "What's your major?"

"Epidemiology and bio-statistics."

"That's a serious double major."

"Yep."

We share smiles.

After lunch, we shake hands and she sashays back to the Waterfront.

I watch her walk away. Watch her look back and wave. I wave. And when I raise my right arm, seven silver bracelets sing and reflect in the sunlight.

I say her name loud enough for only me to hear.

Whisper her name and look at the bracelets on my arm.

If only I were ready.

I chose to stay on the road, chose to keep moving. Books had to be written. And my old man needed me by his side from time to time. A lot of injustice still goes on, and somebody has to show up to complain for the people who don't have the time to protest. Between writing and bitching about a system that changes too slowly, there are too many marks on my day planner to slow down. Moving and distance did me some good.

My I-pager lives on my hip and vibrates with sweet words from her. We'll send e-mails for a while. I'll send books. Christmas cards. Cards for Kwanzaa. She'll send thank-you notes dipped in sweet patchouli or frankincense. I send her flowers when they spotlight that miracle woman in *Essence*. Not every woman takes a punch from an SUV and comes out of a coma ready to laugh about it.

From time to time, Nicole would show up at my book signings in the Bay area. I'd see her walk into the crowded room, lingering in the back. As beautiful as the sun is warm. Those honey-blond locks now a shade of auburn, several cowry shells in the end of her mane. Afrocentric from head to toe. A queen amongst queens. My locks touching my shoulders by then. And I'd be wearing a goatee. Some gray coming into my light-brown mane. Not much, just a strand or two to let me know a change was on the way. And I'd see corners of gray struggling to come out around her temples. My one true sin would stay in the back, near the door, leaning on a cane, barely leaning, and smile at me like she was so proud. She whispered that she still loved me. Always will.

She'd blow me a soft kiss, then wave her right arm at me, the arm with the silver bracelets singing to me, telling me that I'm always welcome, always wanted in her life.

I'd salute her with a kiss as well, then wave my right arm at her, my silver bracelets jingling right back at her. Seven silver bracelets she gave me after that day we walked around the lake, when I told her I was leaving. One bracelet for every year we had together.

And while I signed books, she always vanished.

And I knew where to find her.

Once when I was done, I followed her heart, let it lead me up Broadway into North Oakland. Beyond the golf courses and the mini-mansions onto Broadway Terrace. To Proctor. And I parked across from that house with the huge palm trees, the city lights dancing behind me.

A beautiful flag, one with the brightest rainbow was in front of Nicole and Ayanna's home.

No more running.

We did complete the circle. Not at that house. We completed that circle on a cold February morning, under dark skies, in the rain, with Ayanna being Nicole's lungs and me being Nicole's heart, then me being Nicole's lungs, and Ayanna being Nicole's heart.

We loved Nicole back to life. And in the days after her eyes opened, we brought her healing. Healed us as well. We completed that circle. So, I guess we're forever bonded.

That's why when, for the hundredth time, when Ayanna reminded me that I had won that race around that lake, I told her what I wanted as payment.

She asked, "What's your fee?"

I told her that I wanted her to be kind to Nicole. Forever kind.

I stayed long enough to learn about a different kind of love. Learned from Ayanna. Fell in love with two women, in different ways, for two different rea-

•

sons. Two beautiful women. And I had to leave them both.

Now it was time to move on and find someone new to give all that love to. Time to build a new foundation. Time for new walls. A new roof. My own house with a floor.

I had to become my own butterfly.

I think I was right about Nicole a long time ago. I was the thing that kept her from her truth, from her freedom. And now I'm gone. And now she's free. No longer living between yes and no.

So, after I sat out in front of Nicole and Ayanna's house for a while, I drove away, but not too fast, at my own pace, never once putting my eyes in the rearview mirror. Headed down that asphalt mountain for the last time, got to the 580, cruised that stretch of freeway to the Hegenberger exit and found my way back to the airport.

And if you listen, you can hear the jingle from my seven bracelets. The ones on my right wrist. But listen while you can. At the airport, I take one silver bracelet off. I'll remove one every six months until my arm is bare. Then that wrist will be free. And I will be ready to try again.

Don't get me wrong. I'll miss Nicole. Will miss that slice of Memphis. That is not a sin. I won't stick my chest out and front about that. No lies from this mouth of mine. I'll miss her. When I become an old man, I hope that what I feel for that wonderful creature will ebb away, but from time to time she'll cross my mind, and I'll miss her still. When I turn to dirt, I just might miss her even then. And if I come back, I'll miss her. And I'll look for her. See who she is then.

But for now, if I don't hear from Nicole, from Little

Nikki, from my sweetie for days, for weeks, for months, if I don't get an e-mail, if she doesn't return my e-mail, firecrackers no longer pop inside my head. I don't go crazy when I imagine that her love is moving away from me. Because mine is racing in a new direction. I'm no longer a stone that is trapped under ancient walls.

I'm at peace with myself.

I won my freedom. She won her truth. Ayanna no longer has to compromise.

There were no losers.

Somewhere down the line, I read about Ayanna's victories in the *Tribune*, then that mega-ass whooping she put on the Oakland school district was in every black magazine I picked up. Seemed like every airport I walked in, the first thing I saw was some magazine with her photo on the front, looking like she was about to become the female version of JC. Not Jesus Christ, Johnny Cochran. She's one OJ away from real fame.

In due time, I found my way back to my father's church. Went back down Crenshaw and parked outside that mega-church that blocked parts of the city's skyline. Did that gradually, at my own pace. Not as often as I should, but I went back to that part of my life, hung out with those sinners in search of salvation.

And one Sunday, while he sat in the pulpit with my three brothers at his side, he surprised me, motioned toward me, asked me to stand, then introduced me to the ever-growing congregation. He had me stand in a church that served close to twelve thousand of his faithful. Told them all that I was his next to the youngest son. Told them all that I was the son he was so proud of, the writer.

And he said that with so much pride that all of his sheep applauded like thunder.

And I cried. Right there, waving at my old man, and him waving back at me, I cried and blew him kisses. That last suppressed emotion volcanoed its way to the top.

Yep, I tried to not give in to the tears, not in front of a crowd, but I did.

Not because of the hand praises, but because my father called me a writer.

And I am his son. His problem child. His prodigal son.

And I was home. I was back home in more ways than one.

He'd always been there, through my measles and mumps and chicken pox and broken legs and broken heart. Stayed within arms' reach through both my hope and denial. And acceptance. Not many men can claim that about their own fathers. I don't know where that praise came from, what was on his mind, his heart, or why he did it at that moment. Maybe it's that thing that comes with age. With recognizing your own mortality. Because from time to time, he does lose his place, does have to find his way back to his own memory. The same thing I did when I was lost in Nicole. Had lost my place. Had to find my way back. Only his is different. And we're getting worried. For now he's okay. For now.

In the meantime, life waits for no one. Age finds us all.

I write. I love. And I run.

Life is nothing without those three.

Tears dry. Life goes on. New smiles replace those old tears.

I travel and like a river I flow to places a lot of people will never be blessed to see. I have to see the world. Have to witness as many spectacular sunsets as I can.

Every six months, no matter where I am, a bracelet comes off. That is how I lighten my load. That is how I stop being the Bag Man, that masculine version of Badu's Bag Lady.

Every March I look forward to the L.A. Marathon. Rain or heat, I'm there.

Whenever I get to mile twenty, I slow at that marker hanging high over Hollywood Boulevard, and look around.

Look through that crowd of thirty thousand determined people for those locks, for that style that originated in Kenya as a sign of resistance, hungry to see what color those ropes of ethnic pride are now, how long, listen for the sound of her bracelets, maybe hope to catch a whiff of patchouli sweetening the air, that earthy and spiritual aroma that will always remind me of her.

Sometimes I see Nicole; she's so clear. Running toward me. Sometimes I think she's there.

But she's never there.

Mile twenty. Where it hurts too much to stop, but it also hurts too much to go back.

While I put my hand to my forehead to block out the sun, my wife, my friend, the beautiful Ethiopian named Tseday, asks me in that intellectual British accent, "You looking for somebody?"

"No," I say. "Not at all."

She asks, "You okay?"

I say, "Hurting. You?"

"Never hurt this bad in my life."

"Wanna stop?"

"Never." She manages a determined smile. "Pain is just weakness leaving your body."

I return the same strong smile. That's what it says on my T-shirt.

I say, "You got jokes."

"I got jokes."

And we keep running. We're moving at a decent pace. We're trying to finish this race together.

ACKNOWLEDGMENTS

As always, thanks to my magnificent editor, Audrey LaFehr. To Lisa Johnson and Kathleen Schmidt in publicity, thanks for all the hard work you do behind the scenes. And to my agent, Sara Camilli, thanks for the wonderful encouragement and feedback. Pamela Walker-Williams, thanks for the wonderful job on the Web page! *www.ericjeromedickey.com* is smoking!

Ana at Head to Toe in Oaktown, thanks for keeping my hair looking smooth. Thanks for allowing me to call ya in the middle of your workdays and ask Q after Q.

Jennifer McDaniel, thanks for wanting to read this as it came off the printer. Tell Kennedy to read it in about fifteen years.

Stacey Turnage at Pages Book Club, thanks for glancing over the manuscript. I loved the way you claimed these characters like they were your own children. Do you ever run out of opinions?

Lolita Files, o ye transplant from Florida, you's my twin for life! Thanks for the chicken soup on dem sick days. Your encouragement from word one has meant so mucho.

And Yvette Hayward, my dawgette, much love to

my NYC gal. Thanks for letting me e-mail ya bits and pieces of this one. And the last one. And the next one.

Special thanks to Sylvia E. Wiggins up in Oakland for giving me six hours of scandalous chit-chat. That interview was the bomb.

Katherine "Kat" Barnes, thanks for helping me find what I needed on-line at the twelfth hour. Trust me, that one piece of data about the marathon will make a big difference. You's my girl!

Shannon Allen at S-Systems in Emeryville, thanks for the 4-1-1 on the j-o-b. Tell the family I said Whassup!

Foxyrose out there in cyberspace, whoever u r, thanks for the e-mails and telling a bro about the dark side of Lady Oakland. See ya at Marcus Books.

Susan Kyles in Memphis-Town—here is your name, chile!

Dana Lynn Wimberly, thanks for hooking me up with Sharon Crowder in ATL. Sharon, o ye queen of nurses, thanks for letting me call you at work and allowing a bro to ask a zillion and one "what if" medical questions. You saved somebody's life!

Four Seasons West, thanks for letting me kick it with you peeps at Mammoth!

And finally, thanks to all my loyal readers. I hope you enjoyed this one as much as I enjoyed creating it.

03/26/2001
Virginia Jerry's grandson
Eric Jerome Dickey

New York Times bestselling author
Eric Jerome Dickey is back with a sexy,
gritty, powerful novel about making ends
meet on the wrong side of the law. . . .

Turn the page for a special early preview of

THIEVES' PARADISE

A Dutton hardcover available in May 2002

Momma shrieked.

The walls echoed her cries for Daddy to get his hands off her, brought her pleas up the stairs to my room. I jumped and my algebra book dropped from my chestnut desk onto the floor.

My father cursed.

By the time I made it to the railing and looked down into the living room, Momma was in front of my father, begging for forgiveness. Her petite frame was balled up on our Aztec-patterned sofa. She was holding her lip to keep the blood from flowing onto the fabric. I watched her rub away the pain on her cinnamon skin, then run her fingers through her wavy coal-black hair.

My old man looked up at me and grimaced. "Go back to your room, boy."

I was fifteen and a half. Less than half of my old man's age.

He stomped toward Momma.

She screamed and moved away from him like she was trying to run away from the madness that lived here every day.

My chest heaved as I stumbled past the grandfather clock and rushed down the stairs. My heart was pounding. I tightened my hands and hurried to my momma's side.

"Momma," I moaned as I kneeled next to her. "You okay?"

"I'm all right, baby. It's nothing. Nothing."

I looked at my liquored-up old man. He bobbed his head and pointed back at the kitchen. "I work hard all day and come home to no dinner?"

He was slurring and sneering down on us.

I said, "Nobody knew you were coming home tonight."

Momma tried to get up. "I overslept. My pills made me—"

"*Carmen*," he shouted. "Get up off that sofa and cook. *Now*. *Planet of the Apes* comes on in an hour and I want my food on the table by the time Charlton Heston—"

"Don't ever touch Momma again."

"What you say?"

"He didn't say anything." Momma touched my arm. "I'm okay, baby. Go back and finish studying for your test."

Daddy's back straightened, his bushy mustache crooked as his lips curved down, his eyes widened. "What you say to me, nigger?"

"I'm not a nigger. My name is Dante."

"So the nigger speaking up for himself."

"You heard me the first time. And I ain't a nigger."

"You challenging me? What, you think because you got a little hair over your dick you're a grown man now? Ain't but one man in this house."

Momma spoke carefully to Daddy. "Don't get upset."

I frowned at the shiny badge on the chest of his tan uniform, then at the gun in his leather holster.

He sucked his teeth, nodded and jerked the badge off. He threw the gun holster on the love seat. He stepped away from the glass coffee table, opened his arms and snapped out, "You want to be a man? Come on. I'll give you the first shot. Nigger, I'll knock your black ass into the middle of next week."

Momma gripped my arm tight enough for her nails to break my skin. I glanced at the golden cross she had on her chest, the one she had got from her mother just a few weeks before Grandmamma died. I looked into my momma's light brown eyes, which looked like mine. "Let me go, Momma."

"No." She put her nose on mine and whispered, "Momma's okay. It's just a little scratch."

My knees shook when I stood and faced my old man. When his eyes met mine, his anger held so much power that I forgot how to breathe. Heart went into overdrive. He balled up his right fist, slammed it into the palm of his left hand; it echoed like thunder. "What are you gonna do, nigger?"

I trembled, backed away and said, "Nothing."

"Nothing, what?"

"Nothing, sir."

I kicked my bare feet into the rust carpet, then slumped my shoulders, wiped my sweaty hands on my jean shorts and turned around to go back to my room.

Then that motherfucker chuckled.

A simple laugh that stoked up the rage inside of me. I charged at him as fast and as hard as I could.

Momma screamed.

Daddy's eyes widened with surprise.

Pain. Anger. Fear.

Three screams from three people.

From the backseat of the police car, I stared through the wire cage at the colorful rotating lights that were brightening Scottsdale's earth-tone stucco houses. I was hostage under a calm sky. The spinning glow from twelve squad cars looked like rainbows chasing rainbows. Colors raced over all the sweet gum trees and windmill palms, moved like a strobe light over the vanhoutte spirea in the front of the three-car garage.

The reek of cordite was on my flesh. Couldn't really smell it over the stench of my stress sweating. I concentrated on the colors to make the pain from the tight handcuffs go away. Watched the rainbows come and go.

The door opened. A dry May breeze mixed with the sweltering car air. A police officer stuck his sweaty head inside. His face was hard, his voice angry and anxious. "Your mother wants to say something to you before we lock your ass up. We shouldn't let her say a damn word to you after what you did. Do you mind?"

I stared straight ahead. "No."

He raised his voice. "No what?"

"No," I repeated in a way that let him know I thought that all of them were assholes for making me out to be the bad guy. "I don't mind."

He gripped the back of my neck. "You're pretty belligerent."

I was a knob-kneed reed of a boy. Hadn't lifted anything heavier than an algebra book and could barely run a mile in P.E. without passing out. That was before I started pumping weights, before squats, before doing two hundred push-ups in the morning to start my day, doing sprints, before the hooks and jabs and side kicks and roundhouse kicks and spinning back kicks became my trademark.

I said, "Fuck you."

With his other hand he grabbed the front of my throat and squeezed, made me gag and look into his blue eyes. He growled, "Say, 'No, sir. I don't mind, sir,' you insolent bastard."

He let me go when another officer passed by. I gagged and caught my breath while perspiration tingled down my forehead into my eyes. I tilted my head and looked at him.

He smirked. "Now what you have to say?"

I spat in his face.

His cheeks turned crimson. He stared at me while my saliva rolled down his scarred face into his ill-trimmed wheat-colored mustache.

"That's your ass, boy."

Veins popped up in his neck while he stood there, clenching his teeth and wiping my juices from his eye, handkerchief in hand. He kept watching me, wanted me to break down and show my fear. It was there, but I refused to let it be seen. Another officer passed by and scarface told him what I'd done. It looked like they were about to double-team me, but the second officer said to report the assault and they both stormed away.

A second later the door opened again and my mother eased her bruised face inside.

She said, "Don't hate me."

"Love you, Momma." I smiled. "Get away from here."

She fondled her wedding ring. Tears formed in her eyes. She dropped the police blanket from her shoulders, took her cross off and put it around my neck.

She used her soft fingers to wipe the sweat from my eyes.

"Somebody'll come get you out. Maybe Uncle Ray. You might be able to go back to Philly and stay with him for a while."

"Uncle Ray don't like us. We're Catholic. Jehovah's Witnesses don't like nobody but Jehovah's Witnesses."

"Stop saying that."

"It's true."

"I'll call him anyway. I'll tell him you made honor roll so he'll know you're still doing good in school. Let him know you might get a scholarship. You could help him around his grocery store in the evenings."

I shook my head. "Don't worry about me. Get away before he hurts you. All he's gonna do is beat you up, then go out to Fort McDowell and spend the night with that Indian woman. He ain't been home in two days, then walks in complaining about some stupid dinner. Tomorrow he'll be mad about his shirts. The next day his shoes."

My old man was standing in a crowd of badges, guns and whispers. The ambulance crew had bandaged his head and he was back on his feet. I'd beat him with everything I could get my hands on.

He made a single-finger gesture for Momma to come.

My beautiful momma looked tired of the life she was living, and that made me sad. She wiped her eyes and kissed the side of my face. "You understand, don't you? You're a big boy now. Almost a man. You can take care of yourself. You understand."

I kissed the side of her face as my answer.

"Don't be angry." She twisted her lips. "Don't be like him."

"I won't." I smiled for her. "Go back inside before you get in trouble. Stop taking so much of that medication."

She rubbed her eyes, then dragged her fingers down across her lips. "It calms my nerves."

"Why you wanna sleep so much?"

"Sometimes"—she patted my legs with her thin fingers—"sometimes I have nice dreams."

She was distant, reciting and not living the words.

I said, "Dreams ain't real, Momma."

"Sometimes—" She stopped and kissed my forehead. Her voice became as melodic as the poetry she always read. "Sometimes they're better than what's real."

I fought the dryness in my throat that always came before my tears. I was scared. Fifteen and a half and living in fear.

She wandered away, wringing her hands and looking back at me with every other step. We blew each other dysfunctional kisses.

I'd be in juvenile hall, then a boys' home until I was old enough to register for the draft and vote.

Living with criminals would be like going to a different kind of school. Nigerians, Mexicans, Whites—no matter what nationality, they were all caught up in the same game. And didn't hesitate to lend to the schooling on everything from three-card monte to rocks in a box to pigeon drops, even broke down how to pass bad checks. A few were bold enough to run telephone scams from the inside.

That was different from the education I was after.

I had dreams of getting into Howard, to a frat life and a world filled with sorority girls. Always wanted to stomp in a Greek show. Make enough money to get a small place, get Momma to move in with me. I was working on our escape.

But that night, guess I had had all I could stand and couldn't stand no more. I wanted to be like a superhero and rescue my momma. That was my mission in life. What motivated me.

Hard to save anybody when you're locked up, when you're too busy trying to fight to save yourself. When you've made yourself a prisoner.

I did want to save her. That gave my life a lot of purpose.

But there would be no Howard. No sorority girl at my side. And the closest thing to a frat I would see would be a bunch of young hardheads lining up for roll call, all wearing prison blues, most with tattoos. Our Greek show was marching in sync to go get our meals.

Momma would find her own way to freedom.

My momma would take too many pills and become an angel.

My daddy would be found dead behind the wheel of his Thunderbird at Fort McDowell. Ambushed and shot outside of a married Indian woman's place.

On that night of changes, I sat in the back of that squad car, staring at the colorful lights dancing in the night to make my pain go away. Watched the rainbows chasing the rainbows.

NEW YORK TIMES BESTSELLING AUTHOR
OF *BETWEEN LOVERS*

ERIC JEROME
DICKEY

THIEVES'
PARADISE

A NOVEL

DUTTON